WIRE&BONE

Wire and Bone is the fourth novel by Colin King. His first three books are Detective Sergeant Rory James murder mysteries set in regional Victoria. Colin lives in Bendigo as well as spending time at the writing bolt hole he built in Grampians bushland. In pre-author life, he directed major government projects.

Detective Sergeant Rory James mysteries by Colin King

A VINTAGE DEATH
WETLAND
DEEP DOWN

Praise for Detective Sergeant Rory James mysteries

'It's a ripping yarn, full of greed, violent death, jealousy, and a smattering of sex. Oh, and lots of wine, of course.'
THE AUSTRALIAN

'It's extraordinary.'
'An amazing book based around the Grampians.'
THE ABC

'King understands perfectly Central Victoria's potential for a ripper read.'
'A suspenseful novel which is both surprising and satisfying.'
Reviewer for THE AGE

'The splendid first novel by Bendigo writer Colin King, A Vintage Death, cleverly uses Heathcote and Bendigo as a historical setting for his "full-bodied murder mystery".'

BENDIGO ADVERTISER

WIRE&BONE

COLIN KING

A Mallee Murder Mystery

Copyright © Colin King 2024

 ColinKingAuthor/
The moral right of the author has been asserted.

ISBN 978-0-6453131-4-7 (paperback)

Cover Design and layout by Jacqui Lynch, Preloaded Design

A catalogue record for this book is available from the National Library of Australia

Glove Box Publishing
PO Box 285 Strathdale Vic 3550 Australia
vintagestaff@hotmail.com

For Zel and George

Wire and bone appear in the drift
Lit up and sown threaded and stitched
A change from the west the dust turns to green
It's probably the best start I've ever seen
And near the best that there's ever been

From the song *Wire and Bone*
by Mallee band — The Lazy Farmer's Sons
Written by Andy Gosling © 2013

When Ella ran past him to take the lead again, André knew it was her grief talking.

A wilderness run was always on the cards during the bereavement-filled visit they expected to last a week or so — two weeks tops. Sombre reality prevented either of them from making the suggestion out loud, but each packed their gear in any case. For committed adventure runners, not slotting in a training session was never an option. In normal circumstances, they'd be gleefully animated at the prospect of having endless Mallee desert on their doorstep. That, and André's brand new ultra-light twin hammock tent — which of course meant their workout would be an overnighter.

What André hadn't counted on was the emotional distress driving Ella into the red zone. Her overexertion was threatening training efficacy, as well as doing bugger-all for her headspace. A two-person adventure-racing team relies on both runners sharing responsibilities as well as the hard slog, especially when crossing uncharted desert scrub. What they didn't need was a lopsided skill base because one of them hogged the all-encompassing lead runner's role — setting the pace, zig-zagging over sand dunes covered in a spikey understory of hakeas, spinifex rings and brittle fallen Mallee branches — all the while having to chart the least taxing route.

Ella had made the call on the day of the funeral; they would set off the following day. If André thought that was too soon, he kept it to himself. He was fearful of Ella's pain spiralling even further if she hung around Rosenfeld, the homestead where her mother had died suddenly of a heart attack.

Now, for the seventh time that day, and the fourth time in a row, Ella resumed the lead-runner role way ahead of the agreed changeover point. André let it pass … again. He continued to embrace it as a way for him to help. His attempt to make her hurt his own.

He settled in for a nonetheless welcome breather at the back of their two-person peloton. The pace rose a notch but he was no longer glancing at a compass, his watch, the map, or fixing on navigation attack points in the landscape. The change to concentration-free running quickly settled into autopilot rhythm. He stopped being aware of his physical body now that it connected to Ella via an invisible length of elastic. Best of all, his brain was free to ponder whatever question came into his head. *I reckon I'd do all right on Survivor. Did I pack my toothbrush? What else can I do to get Ella through this?*

He tried but couldn't stay focussed on her sadness — his own grief was not in the same ballpark. As much as he really liked and admired his prospective mother-in-law, Miriam had somehow kept familial closeness at bay with an air of affability. Now there was no knowing whether that barricade would have fallen if, or when, he solemnised the mantle of son-in-law. He fell back to the default focus of his internal running monologues: pain and pace.

Oh shit! That feels like a blister. I should have broken in these shoes for heaps longer. Are we going too fast? It feels like she's still leading way faster, but fuck it — I'll check it later — this is my respite, my no-thinking time.

For a brief while, that's exactly what happened. No conscious thoughts formed in his brain — not until the view ahead revived an old favourite.

It really is a great bum. It's perfect. I mean, in black Lycra it looks even better than in the flesh. Is that counter intuitive? Maybe I could google it. Maybe someone has done a PhD on the phenomenon.

It was the same view of Ella that greeted him the first time he laid eyes on her, three years earlier during a race on Queensland's Bribie Island. On that occasion, he was steadily making his way past a string of runners who'd gone too hard too early. He reeled them in, one by one, until only Ella lay ahead. Then, in that barely perceptible way, the gap between Ella and him began to widen. He panicked to retrieve lost ground and hang in at a sustainable viewing distance for the remaining eight kilometres of the race. The stimulus to remain in lockstep with her bum earned him his best time ever.

Post-race, he sought Ella out to thank her for unknowingly pacing him to his PB. Then boom! Adventure racing romance ignited into a thing before their flights back to Victoria. Thereafter, he liked telling their "how-did-you-guys-meet?" story, right up until the time Ella chimed in with, "Was it really me pacing you, or just you perving on my bum?" His stammered response told her the answer she already knew.

Nothing had changed since. The same view ahead and his same reverie was being transposed to the Mallee in a silent movie re-run.

It really is a perfect bum …

And then, everything did change. The bum blasted into orbit.

It played out before him like Ella was running hard within a mammoth see-through balloon and unsuspectingly slammed into its inside wall. The impact launched her rearward towards him in a flailing, upright frenzy of air-backstroke and air back-peddling.

'E-u-u-u-u-r-r-r-r-r-r-a-a-a-a-a-a-a-a-a-a-h-h-h!'

In André's trance, the upheaval played out in muffled slow-motion, shattered only when he burst back to life to avoid crashing into her. Noise rushed back in and he found himself clasping her shuddering, sleeveless shoulders from behind. She had landed, unfathomably, over two metres back from grinning, near-skeletal, human remains. The tread-print of Ella's shoe was imprinted across a half-buried tibia.

He peered over her shoulder expecting no less than a threatening sand goanna or the glossy armour of a deadly brown snake. The toothy corpse stared back instead, its head raised slightly, seeming to have burst from beneath the desert floor to gasp for breath. Tufts of detached blond hair appeared to grow from the sand that held it in place around the skull.

'Fuck me! How did that get here?'

'It's a woman, isn't it?' Ella murmured shakily through fingers held over her mouth. Her unblinking gaze remained fixed on the spectacle.

'Yeah. Probably. But how did it get *here*?'

Ella managed a small jerky shake of her head.

'Hey, come away. That's a trauma magnet.'

She shook his hands from her shoulders.

'What's left of a trauma magnet,' she clarified with regained composure.

Ella unclasped the waistband of her backpack and slid it

from her shoulders. Its ventilated harness had not prevented her blue singlet top darkening with sweat. She pulled her unyoked shoulders back in stretching motions.

'Are you all right then?' André asked.

She removed her cap to wipe her brow and looked around for shade in the Mallee scrub.

'Yeah. I'm okay. Skeletons in the drift aren't uncommon growing up on a Mallee farm. Never usually human though. It's the teeth that threw me … set in a sneer like that. Kinda cartoonish really. Like something in a ghost-train ride.'

'I suppose, but it's been here a while to be in that condition,' André observed thoughtfully.

Ella pulled her black pony tail back through the cap adjuster, donned it, and began studying the remains again with her hands holding her hips.

'If dead sheep are anything to go by, then she's been here about six months. And how did she get *here*? This is the dead centre of nowhere.'

The dead centre of nowhere was the middle of Wyperfeld National Park in the Mallee country of northern Victoria. Wergaia Country. One of those enormous patches of green on the map that looks large enough to be a small country — or several countries if you count the likes of Monaco, Malta, and Liechtenstein. Most of the park is the furthest you can be from human impact in Victoria, be it an actual human, a road, windmill, shack, burnt out Datsun, drink can, KitKat wrapper, iPad, or anything else that passes as civilisation. As obvious as that may appear on the ground or on a map, someone still found it necessary to formally designate big chunks of the park as *remote* or *wilderness*. In a similar statement of the obvious, the park lay within the much larger Big Desert, which the desert undoubtedly was, despite not cracking a mention on the list of Australia's ten biggest. Nor is it a treeless desert. The sea of endless dunes is cloaked in an astonishing diversity of flora, all ingeniously adapted to subsist in the brutal climate of infinitesimal rainfall and a pittance of soil nutrients. The peculiarly Mallee form of eucalypt barely grows as high as the kitchen ceiling. The closest gatherings of humans are in surrounding hamlets, like Hopetoun and Walpeup, which vie for the state's hottest temperature on the nightly-news weather reports.

André followed Ella in shedding his cap and backpack to enjoy the freedom of his quick-dry trekking tee-shirt. He too wore Lycra longs and knee-high Gore-Tex gaiters as a defence against the spinifex and snakes.

'She didn't walk here in those clothes and shoes,' he said, ruffling his black cap-hair free.

Windblown sand and leaf litter had not completely covered the body. It was late spring and tattered bits of skirt and blouse were weathered crisp by the extremes of a desert winter, and torn by eager eagles, crows, foxes or feral cats vying for flesh. All had long finished their banquet. The near complete collection of exposed bones was bleached white against clinging remnants of flesh, now dried hard, thin and black. The ants had also given up and moved on. A white sandal with a sharp heel hung around the skeletal left foot poking from the sand. Wire protruding from her bra had rusted, although her belt remained intact. Its large chrome buckle gleamed defiantly.

'"*Wire and bone appear in the drift*" indeed,' Ella observed. 'That's a lyric by a local songwriter.'

'Spot on … even prophetic,' André nodded.

'Maybe there's an unmapped track around here. Maybe she came in a four-wheel drive,' Ella speculated.

'I'll have a look, but we'll need to be careful. This is a crime scene. How will it look with my footprints all over the place?'

'Hey, no heading to the bat cave to start solving this, detective,' Ella said. 'You're on leave — compassionate leave — or at least I am.' she qualified.

It was a vain hope that Detective Sergeant André Marshall's day job would not kick in automatically. The homicide detective nonetheless struggled with the incongruity of randomly stumbling over a dead body and its confluence with his partner's still anguished loss.

'Sorry, El. This is so … '

He gestured with his arms at the arrangement of sand, bone, hair and clothing remnants before them. There was something of an artistic composition about it.

'This is no sheep El. This is someone, and, you know, after your mum died just down the road … you don't need something like this in your head right now. The whole thing is so friggin' freaky. What it is. Where it is. Me finding it. Us finding it. That's not supposed to be a thing.'

He put his arm back around her shoulder and they both looked thoughtfully at the remains.

'It's okay, "A". Really.' "A" was her pet name for André. 'You're a homicide cop. If anyone knows how to deal with this …'

'Yeah, but that's when someone *else* finds it. *They* phone it in and I come along and deal with it like any other case, however bizarre, they're all different. But finding the actual body is someone else's job. The same with reporters, you're not supposed to become part of the news either, are you?'

'What do you mean, part of the news?'

'Well, you're a witness now. You'll need to give a statement at some stage. *I'm* a witness.'

'But I can still write the story, can't I? Right now, we're the only two people on Earth who know about this. This is so newsworthy, not to mention an exclusive. This will be mega for me.'

'What?' André stood back from her to give a questioning look.

'What, "what?"' she responded.

'You just had a go at me for putting my cop hat on. Now you're a journalist writing an exclusive?'

'And you weren't the one who dubbed it a "crime scene"?'

Her glare floored him. Their impasse had arrived in a flash. He backed off.

'All right. I did slip into work mode … briefly. That was autopilot kicking in before I'd had time to think. But I thought work would be the last thing on *your* mind. The way you've been running with such vengeance is scary. I can see the raw pain still raging in your head … and you're keeping it all locked up. All I can do is just be here for you. Jesus, El. I'm sorry. Neither of us needs this right now.'

He had slowed to a stop, panicking when her lower lip began to quiver.

'That's all I meant,' he added nervously.

Crying took hold where she stood on the spot, invading her face, then taking over her body. A big ugly, bawling crying that eclipsed every hitherto bout — the initial phone call, the funeral, random moments. André stepped over and held her.

She couldn't return his embrace; every part of her was bereft of responding. He clasped her shaking frame and hanging arms nonetheless, not lessening his desperate grip, even when her gulps eased and stuttering sniffs crept in. She sensed his alarm and let her forehead fall to his shoulder. When she was ready, she stepped out of his embrace and managed a bashful grimace. She set about wiping her face every which way.

'I know how stupid and selfish it sounds but I'm just so angry at Mum. For dying when she did. Can you believe that? God, she was only sixty-six. I wasn't ready for that. I mean, we'd hardly spoken to each other all year, let alone seen each other. And nor should I be ready for that. It's not like I was avoiding her or anything. It was just how things fell as we both went about our lives. How was I supposed to know?'

André put his arm around her shoulder again and leant his forehead against hers with a pained look of empathy. She stepped away again, not ready to be consoled.

'And Lila, my own sister, being a no-show at the funeral, the same as at Dad's. You'd think there'd be a point when stuff like that can be put behind you. She's all the family I've got left and she still can't show her face. Not even when her own mother dies. Now. Look at me. Here. Thirty years old and alone in the middle of nowhere with no one. Sorry. I know you're here, "A" and I'm grateful, but as far as family goes, how more alone could I be? It just shits me. It really shits me.'

She wrung her arms in frustration.

'But I am here, El. We've got this. Us. That's not nothing as far as I'm concerned. And I'm not going anywhere.'

'I know, "A". But your life's connected. And I feel such a dick even thinking like this but I can't help it. You've still got a mum ... and a dad. And sisters and a brother. That's been shitting me too. How fucking fucked up, hey? I'm sorry. That's not your fault. What am I saying? It's not a wrong thing that's anyone's fault. That's exactly how the world's supposed to work, but I still let that shit me. How fucking fucked up indeed.'

She stepped away from him shaking her head and turned to look across the desert. André kept his gaze on the tiny pink heath-myrtle flowers at his feet. Their silence stretched.

Ella spoke first.

'It is beautiful here, isn't it? I always thought this was the best part of living in the Mallee.'

Andre looked up, and studied her back. He spoke calmly.

'You're not fucked up, El. You're grieving.' It was the first time he dared say the "G" word to her. 'It's what you're supposed to do, whether you want to or not. It takes time. It's going to take a lot of time. You know that.'

Ella turned to give him a sheepish smile. He continued.

'And you couldn't be less lonely, right here, right now — unless you're giving me the flick. If that's what this is about.'

Her smile turned wry.

'Yeah. As if.'

He waited. She moved her arms slightly forward to invite a hug. A true sweat on sweat hug.

'Hmm,' he said, mid-hug.

'Hmm yourself,' she replied.

They stepped apart and gazed at the skeleton.

'So, what are we going to do about Grinning Gretel?' she asked.

'Buggered if I know. We can't continue the trek now, and it's too late to go back. Let's just find somewhere to camp. It's not like she's gonna sneak off anywhere.'

'Okay. But maybe over the next dune, hey? That's another thing homicide cops aren't supposed to do.'

'What's that?'

'Sleep with the corpse.'

Marathon runners race a Herculean 41.195 kilometres. They joke that they do it because it's like hitting yourself on the head with a hammer — it feels so good when you stop! So, based on a pain per kilometre comparison, what greater form of self-brutalisation would adventure racers rejoice in stopping?

Sometimes, the length of their rugged courses only come to an end when they reach the sea and there's literally nowhere else to go. Like the 243-kilometre coast-to-coast race in New Zealand, so far tackled by over 20,000 competitors. Tasmania has its own coast-to-coast event covering a whopping 435 kilometres. On the mainland, the Coast to Kosci race stretches 240 kilometres from the port of Eden on the NSW south coast to Mount Kosciuszko, the highest peak they could find on the continent. It would have been a race from the very bottom to the very top, except that the centre of Australia dips sixteen metres below sea level. Teams navigate their way unsupported on these non-stop events, the only respite — if that's not the wrong word — being a change to equally backbreaking stages tackled by bike and kayak. And then there's expedition racing.

If adventure racers are from another planet, then expedition racers are from a quasar galaxy. These events extend the voluntary masochism to three to eight days on end, and for well beyond 500 kilometres. The more remote, the more rugged, the better, although many fail to finish.

A few rules have been introduced since the country's first non-supported expeditions headed into the wilderness — like that of Burke and Wills. For a start, it's now mandatory to carry a GPS tracker/emergency communications device — something that might have been handy in those nineteenth century saddlebags.

These days, Australia has clocked up over a decade of national championships, attracting as many as eighty teams at a time. Striking, high-resolution website galleries show fit thirty somethings like Ella and André can't get enough. Most remarkable is the absence of competitors looking as buggered as normal mortals would after a mere ten minutes of bulldozing themselves up a mountainside. Competitors in full flight typically look keenly intense, relaxed, smiling, sometimes even laughing — but rarely in pain. They show up at events beaming, obviously elated to finally be among their own kind and free from continually having to rationalise their obsession to others. Beyond the finishing line, the fervour is no less contagious. It remains un-extinguishable for days.

Ella and André had worked their way up to compete in half-course expedition events for which two-person teams are still eligible. Their upcoming challenge was a 180-kilometre event in the Flinders Ranges — on Andyamathanha Country. What better lead-up than a training run through Victoria's Mallee.

André, being an adventure racing gear junkie, had taken a punt with their camping setup. He packed the brand new two-person hammock tent he was dying to try out, but he did so without being certain the Mallee scrub could throw up a pair of suitably strong and suitably spaced trees to hang it between. Because Mallee eucalypts were too raggedy and fine to do the job, André had put all his money on finding a pair of native cypress pines that weren't too short. They grew far more sparsely than the eucalypts and, in some patches of scrub, not at all. The risk was, if they couldn't set up the hammock tent, they'd be spending a miserable night sleeping in the open on the ground.

The hammock tent on its own offered a weight and bulk advantage over carrying a ground tent and two sleeping mats. André argued they could use that extra capacity for the luxury of his micro espresso coffee pot.

'This is training, not competing. So why not shout ourselves the comfort of a real coffee?' he rationalised.

'Great. That'll be just what I need to keep me dry when it rains, keep the mosquitoes at bay and, stop the ground from being hard and cold.'

After voicing her view on the matter, Ella didn't have it in herself to do more than acquiesce. That left André feeling the heat until he did find two ideally spaced stout cypress pines in the sandy lee of the adjoining dune. It offered pleasing shade and a windbreak. And it was a good 150 metres from the dead body.

'I like this sand. It's like camping on the beach,' he said once the tent was hung and the first shot of coffee was safely brewing on the micro ultralight titanium gas camping hob — further proof that adventure racer camping setups are a NASA-like world of high-tech innovation and materials.

'It probably was a beach, about half a million years ago when the massive Murray Gulf penetrated this far inland. Wouldn't that be something? Sitting here looking out over the Southern Ocean,' Ella replied.

They both pondered the ocean that was no longer, listening to the small blue flame roar as coffee brewed. André sat on the side of the hammock, Ella on their tough lightweight cross-linked polyolefin groundsheet. Nothing less would do the job for adventure racers.

'So, what's the plan now, detective?'

André didn't need to ponder the question.

'I'm not gonna call it in until we get back to the car at Wonga camping ground. We'll have proper mobile reception there. I know I can send a short message on the inReach GPS now, but how many questions would that raise? And you know how painfully slow and tedious it is entering a reply message on the thing. Besides, the subscription we're on has a ten-message limit, plus a character limit like Twitter. Hardly ideal for a text conversation about a complex police investigation.

'I'd have a go if it was life threatening, but according to your expert opinion, Grinning Gretel has been lying there for six months. In any case, Glenevis is not going to believe what we came across, and how it happened … and where we are. I really do need to speak to the boss directly.'

The coffee spluttered through the espresso pot and André poured a small cup for each of them.

'How do you reckon she died?' Ella asked as he passed her a cup and joined her on the groundsheet.

'Too hard to tell in that state. It'll need a post mortem, and they won't have much to work with. I'm gonna have a better look around.'

Ella sipped and savoured the short black, a tad smugly, André noticed.

'I'm wondering if she fell from an aeroplane,' he mused.

'Are you serious?'

'Well, we're here because it's the most track-free part of the state. I haven't had a good look yet but there's no sign of any vehicle having bashed through the bush from wherever. And you'd be flat out getting here on foot without the specialist training and gear we have. How else could it happen?'

'But wouldn't people be looking for her if she did fall or jump out of a plane?'

'Not if she was pushed.'

'What? Murdered?'

'What better place to hide a body. You wouldn't get odds if they ran a book on which bit of Victoria people were least likely to ever set foot in — or allowed to set foot in if it comes to that. We've probably passed into the proclaimed wilderness area. It's possible we're the first Europeans to ever set foot right there.'

'Hmm,' Ella thought. 'Do you realise we wouldn't have seen her if we had passed ten metres either side?'

'Yeah. Maybe less than ten metres. That makes it all the more amazing. If it is a dumped body, the murderer is going to be more than a tad surprised by its discovery.'

'If finding the body at all is so improbable, then the odds of the finder being a homicide detective must be incalculable,' Ella said as they kept talking up the marvel of their find.

'Hmm,' she added, and stared harder at the landscape. 'It's such a speco story. You couldn't make it up. I mean really speco. You're gonna have to play for time so I can get some copy lodged.'

André looked hard at her.

'What?' she responded. 'Mum dying doesn't change any of this. The cop wheels are still turning in *your* head, and you're lapping it up. Nothing wrong with that. And I'm a journo with The Age. You think I should ignore a front page that's fallen into my lap? That I should just let them find out about it from your media unit and let one of my colleagues cobble together whatever they can? I'm here. Now. I'm living it. I own this as much as you do. Maybe more.' Then she resorted to her childhood clincher for sealing an argument. 'I saw her first!'

André's stare morphed to stunned, then to wry head shaking.

'And here's me worried you'd be in shock. Well apart from all the emotional stuff I've watched churning within, a working farm has landed in your lap. Have you thought about that? Because, buggered if I know where you'd even begin. And all your Mum's will and estate stuff. Those are no small matters facing you as soon as we get back from this training session. Are you really sure you want to run with this as a story? Are you sure you can with all that stuff hanging? I mean, I'll do what I can to help but do you really want to add to the load right now?'

Ella mulled his words as they sat side by side, staring vacantly at the wilderness. She slowly put her thoughts into words.

'I'm definitely not in shock. Maybe I should be but this is different. It's got nothing to do with Mum. This is something I can separate and deal with professionally.

'As for the farm, that's the last thing I need to spend time worrying about. I spoke to Trent Hofner at the funeral. He's happy to manage things for the next while. It's a step up from the off-and-on leading-hand work Mum's had him doing for years. He's been checking the house every day since she died.

He can't do enough.

'Trent also knows probate will take months and that will give him time to get his finances in order. He was too polite to say so, but I know he'd like to make an offer for part of the farm … if not all of it. He's young enough to take it on; after all, it does neighbour his own modest holding. For now, he'll be pretty eager to please … and Mum's accountant says the farm can afford it. So don't worry. I won't be jumping on the tractor anytime soon.'

She gave André a quick sideways glance and continued.

'As for the estate stuff, I've already got a meeting booked with Mum's lawyer. I'll see what that throws up and deal with it when I'm back at work. I've had my compassionate leave. Now it's time to get back to doing what I love. I can tell you, there's no way anyone else at The Age is going to write this story.'

She then turned to face André, having resolutely despatched the concerns that had popped into his head, and a few others besides. He dropped his head and examined the empty cup he was holding. Having reaffirmed that he had in fact drunk all his coffee, he looked up to say, 'You know, suddenly, a campfire sounds like a really good idea. I'll get some wood in, hey?'

André scrolled his mobile phone as he wandered back into their camp. The morning's sharp edge lingered and Ella sat close to the fire. She looked up from eating muesli out of a hard plastic bowl.

'You been taking pics too?' she asked him.

He stopped in his tracks to answer.

'I took a few. Mainly the spot where we might be able to get a helicopter in. I sacrificed my Snowy Mountain Classic tee-shirt to mark the spot — the orange one. I hung it in a tree. That only leaves me with the top I'm wearing. Things could get pongy.' Then his voice raised pitch with realisation. 'Did you take pics too?'

'Naturally.'

'Well, you won't be able to publish them you know. At least not the bones.'

'Oh yeah? It's a public place. I was out for a run and took a few snaps.' She paused to think of further argument. 'It's not like there's police tape strung up or anything. Anyway, it will be my editor's call. Nothing to do with me.'

'"Oh yeah" yourself. It may be public land, but that doesn't mean we're allowed to be in here. It's not like we told the park ranger about our plans. We both could have some explaining to do ourselves.'

'Maybe we could just not mention this to anyone. Leave her here. Pretend we didn't find her. Did you think of that possibility?'

He knew she wasn't serious. He ignored the question to pursue his thought.

'If someone does arc up about us being in here, we'll need to keep it under wraps — as far as publicity goes, I mean. We need to make sure none of this is about us. It's not like we committed the crime. If it wasn't for us … '

'Worry about that if it happens,' was media savvy Ella's dismissive advice. 'Did you discover anything else on your scout around this morning?'

'I did a wider sweep and I still can't see any signs of a vehicle bashing its way in. A trail bike or a quad bike could make it this far but its tracks would be less obvious — they'd probably disappear altogether in this sandy country. We can use the chopper ride in to have a better look. If we get a park ranger to accompany us back into the site, they might recognise any signs, if they exist.'

'Oh.'

'I still reckon falling from an aircraft is the most likely explanation,' André said.

'Can you tell by looking at the body?'

'It would have been beyond doubt if she'd landed in a tree or something. If she did fall from above, she managed to clear everything and come to earth in a patch of bare sand. It doesn't look like the wildlife has moved things around too much. Most of the body still seems to be in situ. I suppose the injuries her body sustained, bone fractures and stuff like that, would be the same as someone falling from a tall building. We'll need to get a forensic pathologist in with all their gear. Fuck knows how.'

Ella swallowed another mouthful of muesli and held the spoon pensively.

'Have you fixed the location on the inReach tracker yet? You wouldn't want to be entirely reliant on spotting a tee shirt in this kinda scrub.'

'Yeah, of course. Done all that. I also did that for a couple of potential helicopter landing sites. And I did the morning check-in message to Ashley. If he checked our on-line tracking, he's probably wondering why we stopped ahead of time yesterday.'

Ashley was the friend they entrusted to remotely keep tabs on them for safety's sake. A fellow adventure-racer who knew the drum.

André set about re-loading the coffee pot.

'There's at least enough gas left in this canister for another cup each this morning. What'd'y reckon?'

Ella nodded "Yes", then surprised with an added comment.

'I want to see her again before we head back,'

'You sure?' a mystified André asked.

'Certain. I've collected some of those tiny flowers to leave beside her. She's a person who died in a lonely place. I think she deserves a human touch after all this time.'

'I suppose, but it was probably the touch of a human that caused her to end up here in the first place.'

The remark elicited a glare from Ella before she declared, 'Sometimes I don't know if it's because you're a man or because you're a cop. Can't you spare a thought for the person?' She jammed the empty breakfast bowl into her backpack and began gathering up the rest of her stuff.

'Sorry. But I am a cop and it *is* a dead body.'

'Maybe you should have stopped at "sorry",' she retorted, then moved the conversation on.

'Will it be hard to find out who she is?'

'That should be the easy part. Missing persons are called missing persons because they are missed by someone. It'll be surprising if she's hasn't been reported and is not on our books already. Mind you, dental records might be all that's left to go on, perhaps some DNA. Most of that stuff is already collected on file from the families of missing people.'

'I don't reckon this would be a bad place to end up,' Ella said, as she stood back from the small posy of blooms she had placed beside the bony remains.

'It's beautiful out here and her white bones have become part of it. She would have had the place to herself forever if we hadn't come along. Better than being in the cold dark world of six feet underground.'

'Most people regard deserts as a hell, not heaven.'

'I know. But I'd be happy to be placed out here whenever I go. You know Gram Parson's friends stole his corpse from the funeral parlour and took him into the desert at Joshua Tree National Park in California?'

'Who?'

'Gram Parsons. The alt-country music genius of the seventies. He wrote Hickory Wind.'

'Uh-huh,' André nodded unconvincingly. He wasn't into music like Ella.

'Her shoes and belt?' he asked, 'They look expensive. Can you tell?'

'Yeah. You can still tell that she was well dressed. I don't think you'll find your victim was a battler. Nor from the country.'

'Hmm. Right to go then?'

André took the lead and the first navigating stint. The brisk pace, somewhere between trail running and trekking, was halted on dune ridges to take compass bearings and attempt to select distinguishing features to aim at in a homogenous landscape. Route choice was not simplified by hills or failsafe handrails like a river or a track. He oriented the map, checked the wrist altimeter — which was next-to-no help in the desert — and concentrated on pace-counting to keep track of their progress. Success would be known when they hit Meridian Track, hopefully by day's end.

It was Ella's turn to switch to automatic pilot, its inbuilt sensor now keeping *André's* bum several metres ahead. Her lost thought of distance running imagined naturalist Arthur Herbert Evelyn Mattingley recognising the un-obvious beauty of Wyperfeld when he ventured there in 1907. Travelling at pre-internal combustion engine pace, he too would have seen beyond the drab desolate Mallee panorama to the microcosm of flora revealing itself to Ella — dunes and hollows of heaths, tea-trees, banksias and other small plants somehow surviving among the omnipresent Mallee eucalypts. Tiny flowers, gaudy parrots and an endless list of other bird species added glimpses of brilliant colour, along with the melodious tinkling of a rare white-bellied whipbird.

Mattingley vigorously promoted what he regarded as the best birding site in Victoria and unique Mallee Fowl habitat. Through his advocacy, it became Victoria's second-ever national park after Wilsons Promontory.

The compass bearing brought André and Ella to the dry Round Lake. The shallow expanse resembled an oversized cricket ground overgrown with dry grass. Its eastern bank provided the first sign of human existence — a narrow sandy walking path. Thereafter, race-pace was uninterrupted until Black Flat Track. Its vehicle ruts allowed a side-by-side talking-pace stroll into the sparsely occupied Wonga camping ground. Ella checked for mobile phone signal as they passed faded fox bait poisoning signs nailed to black box trunks.

'Two bars,' she confirmed to André. 'Who are you going to call first?'

'I've been thinking about it all day. I'm gonna bypass the local guys and phone Glenevis. See if he'll let me run with the investigation straight off.'

'Your boss? Does it have anything to do with Homicide before you're certain you're dealing with a murder? Won't it be treading on the local coppers' toes if you get involved at this stage?' Questions kept popping into her head as she spoke. 'Are there politics or protocols involved?'

'All of that. But I'm already involved and it's unlikely not to be a murder. *And* I want to make sure I stay with this one. I feel attached to it.'

Realising what he had just said, he asked Ella, 'What about you? Is the story yours without question? Any protocols you have to worry about?'

'Whatever the case, it's all academic. I've already written it in my head. I just need to get back to my laptop at the farm.'

'Well, talk amongst yourself for a bit, I've got a call to make.'

Ella stopped to drink and replenish her water pack at the first water tank they reached in the camping ground. André wound up the first call he'd made.

'That wasn't Glenevis. I was just letting Ashley know we're back safely. He can't believe we found a dead body in the middle of the park, at least one that's not archaeological. He knows about that stuff. Apparently the ancient remains of Mungo Man and the Cohuna Skull were discovered within driving distance from here.'

'You told him about it?'

'I kinda had to. He's not stupid. He checked the tracker on-line and wondered why we went off script. It was easier to tell him. And I trust him. Ashley's the last person to spill his guts. It's totally cool. The next call's the tricky one.'

Inspector Rab Glenevis was fond of letting his colleagues know that before he emigrated, he was cutting his chops with Strathclyde Police in Glasgow, including in 2005. That was the year the World Health Organisation dubbed Glasgow, "the murder capital of Europe". His fellow Victorian cops would take the piss: "*The place had one good year and you never shut up about it*". His time in homicide at Glasgow nevertheless made him immune to whatever the next case threw up, especially when it came to the age-old dilemma of murderers — how to get rid of the body. Most attempts at burying were too shallow. Tell-tale variations on the surface usually give the game away, that's if the cadaver dogs haven't already sniffed it out. Just as incredibly, forensic traces sometimes survive house fires and being fed to pigs. Burying bodies under graves and in concrete pours have a better success rate, but even these methods are not beyond coming to light eventually.

André was more worried about how Glenevis would react to him being the finder of the body, however random the circumstances. He also had to interpret Glaswegian — the thickest accent in Scotland — without the clues you get being face-to-face. André brought up Glenevis's contact details on his mobile phone and braced himself.

The call connected and began to ring. In his head, André could hear the ringtone so familiar to him and his colleagues. The first crisp snare drum roll, drones kicking in for a second drum roll, and finally, the bagpipe classic, Cock o' the North bursting into full pipe band life. He pictured Glenevis tilt his head to enjoy a bar or two, as if it had been years since he'd had the pleasure of hearing his favourite bagpipe composition. A composition, not a melody. In André's mind that would be a stretch too far. Glenevis swiped.

'Hullo André, everythin' goin' a'right a' th' funeral. Is Ella okay? D'ya need more time aff?'

'Nah. It's not that. It all went like these things are supposed to. Something else came up, though.'

'Aye? What's up then?' His voice slowed with hesitancy.

André told him what was up.

'Nae shite. In th' middle a fookin' nowhere you find a stiff? This soonds like a right wind up. Like when you told me Ange Postecoglou was made coach of Celtic.'

'But he *was* made coach of Celtic.'

'Ah know tha'. Your problem were, he mighta once bin coach of Australia, but back then, none of ma countrymen had heard o' him, let alone knowed how to pronounce his fookin' name. What I'm tryin' ta tell you is, you're s'posed to leave findin' th' bodies ta dogwalkers André. It's never th' job o' th' polis.'

Although he saw it coming, Glenevis's warped logic and piqued tone bugged him.

'It's illegal to walk a dog here … and you're the one that taught me that bodies always show up,' he answered.

'Maybe, but th' local Crime Investigation Unit is nae gonna be pleased that a Melbourne homicide cop o' all people is doin' th' findin'.'

'I know,' André drew a deep breath before getting to the crux of his call. 'I haven't phoned them yet but I can already hear the CIU's chip-on-the-shoulder greeting. That's why I'm calling you first. I want us to run with this one from the get go.'

'Why's tha'? Even if it is a murdah, dinnae mean it'll stay in our bailiwick. Cood be the local farmer chuckin' his good wife's body out the back of a fookin' ute. Why nae see if they know what's goin' on first? I dinnae like the idea of gettin' people off side unnecessarily.'

'You'd have more chance of driving a ute to the middle of Port Phillip Bay. I don't reckon this is local. Ella is certain the dead woman is a city dresser. I reckon she'll already be on our books as missing.'

'Even so, why no' let 'em look at it first?' Glenevis said with more than Devil's advocate curiosity.

'Because I'm pretty sure the body was dropped from an aircraft and we'll need some clever forensic pathology to confirm that. There's not much more than a skeleton to go on after six months in the desert. It would also be nice to know if she was dead before she fell but there'll be bugger all for a pathologist to work with. They might be able to tell from how she landed.'

'Awayyego! You're talkin' aboot a fook'n' aeroplane are you no'? Is your bum nae out the window?'

André took the mobile phone away from his ear to look at it questioningly.

'I'm pretty sure it's been dropped from a plane — if that's what you mean. Yes.'

'C'mon André, the local guys are nae dumb. And won't you be

there in any case ta show 'em where th' body is?'

'I just want to make sure nothing clumsy happens.'

'Hold on. Hold on. Even if ah did think it were a good idea ta run with this, dinnae you have a conflict of interest? Ah'd probably end up havin' ta get one of your colleagues ta deal with this instead of you? Is tha' what you want?'

'What?' It wasn't something André saw coming. 'What conflict of interest? I've only got one interest in this and that's to investigate it and solve it. There is nothing whatsoever to conflict with. I've got no idea who the deceased is yet. When we do find out, I'll be the last person on earth with a connection to her.'

'Weel let me remind you. You do know the only witness you've got so far. Tha's if you dinnae count yourself in all this.'

'Ella? Come on, boss. Since when is a random person who discovers a body got anything to do with a case? Isn't this just arse-covering stuff that's sprung into your head?'

'Dinnae forget, tha's mah job. Ah'll be checkin' it with legal. Anyways, how can you be so precise aboot how long the body has bin there? Have you nae had an expert in already?'

'Kind of,' André said, relieved that Glenevis was moving the conversion along.

'Dinnae tell me. Is tha' Ella's giving her local farm lassie slant on things?' Glenevis guessed, *'And how is everyone gonna get in there?'*

'Well, that'll be another circus. I don't reckon there are any vehicle tracks within fifty ks … or even walking tracks for that matter. It'll also be touch-and-go to land a chopper without cutting down a bit of scrub. That's if Parks Victoria let us. They don't even like you walking through there like me and Ella did. We'll probably end up needing someone to talk to their head office to let us do anything. Someone like you with connections in the other echelons of government.'

'Let's nae get ahead of ourselves just yet. Won't they be shitty at ya for goin' in there in th' first place?'

'They might be, but at least we're environmentally aware and tread lightly. I'm hoping they'll be too distracted by the dead body and by the media to worry about me and Ella. They'll have their hands more than full when those cowboys start trying to land news choppers and drive four-wheel drives around their locked gates.'

André could hear Glenevis thinking.

'Ah s'pose Ella's writin' the story 'n' Ah'd be reading aboot it in The Age if you dinnae call me?'

'I asked her to hold off until I could call you. But the reality is, I can't stop her writing what she saw. Ella came across the body before I did.'

He listened to Glenevis think some more.

'How sure are you tha' this woman fell from a plane?' he eventually asked in a level tone.

Yes, André thought. *He's starting to think about it.*

'Ninety-five per cent' André estimated. 'She was dressed to shop or dine out, not for a sojourn in desert scrub … not even in an air-conditioned four-wheel drive. We'll need to take another look around with the ranger to make sure there are no vehicle tracks. A trail bike's a remote possibility but she certainly didn't walk in.'

'You know we had one o' these in Glasgow like. Someone chucked some jimmy out o' a helicopter, with nae parachute. It were a gang thing. They were getting' ambitious and wanted ta send a wee message ta their rivals. One good thing, though. He landed on the doorstep o' ma local, the Hobkirk Inn. It couldnae been more

handy. Turns out his mates were havin' a wee drop there when he landed. We think they got th' message.'

'That sounds like they wanted the body to be found. I don't think that's what we're dealing with here.'

'You may be right, but at least they had the courtesy of doin' it where there's some sign o' civilisation. So … tell me where this place is again?'

Civilisation? André sighed within.

'Wyperfeld National Park. South of Underbool.'

Silence.

'Ouyen? Murrayville?'

More questioning silence.

'West of Patchewollock, although the cop-shop at Patche has been closed for a good while.'

'Are you sure it's in Victoria? Where's th' nearest proper coffee?'

'You don't even drink coffee.'

'But Ah've lived in Melbourne long enough ta ken it's the yardstick of everythin' around here.'

'Fair enough. Probably at Horsham … an hour or so south. Although … if you want to play it safe, I'd recommend getting one at Ballarat.'

A non-coffee-drinker going on about coffee? André decided Glenevis had now decided. He let another pause finish the job.

'Okay then. You get onto th' local cop straight away. Ah'll telephone th' regional superintendent ta let him know we're treatin' it as one o' ours. Ah'll send Alex up, just in case anyone gets funny aboot you havin' a finger in th' pie … in which case you back right aff. An' dinnae thank me. Just make sure you're on top o' it 'n' there's nae demarcation brouhaha, otherwise we'll be re-openin' th' station at Patche-fookin'-whatever-it-is for your exclusive pleasure.'

'Okay, boss. Tell Alex to check into the Eureka at Rainbow.

That's a hotel and a town — in that order.'

'*Eegit. You just remember — Patche-whatever-th'-fook.*'

Ella idly flicked through the unmanned information centre visitors book while she waited for André to finish his phone calls. The hand written entries are what passed for reviews in the pre-internet age. Boredom set in by the third page with most obeying an unwritten tenet: stick to gushing clichés. The only entries to show any flair were those by bird observers. "Twitching the Night Away" began one entry about a very successful night-spotlighting excursion that revealed tawny frogmouths, a rufous night heron, spotted nightjars, barn owl and the southern boobook. *Baby Boomers*, Ella concluded from the Dire Straits tune word play.

"Grey nomad meets grey falcon … " began another entry, " … not to mention who might have met the whiskered tern, the hoary-headed grebe and the red-necked avocet." It went on. *This bloke had a whole routine worked out* Ella thought, now smiling. *I'll bet he was a riot around the campfire.*

Even the guided bird-tour clients had a bit of character, "More parrots than you can poke a stick at." *Obviously not an overseas tourist*, she decided.

'What are you smiling at?' asked André.

'What makes twitchers tick,' Ella answered cryptically. 'All done?' She asked, to wipe the quizzical look off his face.

'Yeah.' he said, snapping back to earth. 'And by the way, if you're looking for a birthday present idea, get me one of those apps that translate phone conversations between different language speakers in real time.'

'Scottish to English, right? You know there is an actual

English to Scottish text translator on-line.'

'Nae shite,' André said in his best Glaswegian.

'Hah ha. So, what *is* happening?'

'Nothing until morning. The local cop is coming out with the park ranger. The regional CIU investigators will be here a bit later.'

'What about you? Is Glenevis letting you run with it?'

'After some arm twisting, yeah. He's sending Alex up to help.'

It dawned on him that his mind was racing with logistics that did not include his and Ella's next movements. *Might she be pissed off?* Before he could realign his antenna, she surprised him.

'I want to take the car and head back to the farm now. I need to get on my laptop and file the story. I've spoken to Rita and she's giving me page three, maybe page one. You know how it works. The whole media will be on this now that it's in the police system. What's the use of being first at the scene, or being the scene for that matter, if I can't be first with the story?'

'You're gonna leave me here?'

'Well, where the hell were you going to leave me?'

'Touché. It's just that I wasn't expecting to spend the night out here by myself.'

'I know. You'd better get whatever you need out of the car. Give me a call when you know what's going on and when you want me to drive back to get you.'

Chapter 4

Would it have been better never to have found her? She had arrived at a version of paradise for her last resting place. The centre of a beautiful wilderness, set aside never to be intruded upon. A fate that surpassed having a pyramid built exclusively for one's after life. Its natural treasures of subtly rich flora and fauna would outlast those plundered from Egypt for the world's museums. Alas, I was as guilty as Howard Carter entering the tomb of Tutankhamun in 1922 when I transgressed Wyperfeld National Park's official wilderness zone. That's where I inadvertently discovered the last, but one, resting place of ...

Too high brow and florid? Ella wondered. When it came to murder, it wasn't that long ago that the serious daily she worked for had been guilty of the odd tabloid flourish. With Melbourne's gangland wars raging in the 2000s, the paper had not always been averse to depicting its blokey crime writers affecting pseudo mug shots beside their by-lines — all shades and hard expressions.

Stuff it, she thought, *I was there. It doesn't need melodrama or crime sensationalism. This is the scene as I found it. A discovery yet to divulge its full gamut of tragedy and suffering. Nothing wrong with a respectful approach is there?* Ella rationalised to herself.

The imagined arguments were allayed by Rita's return email of more than expected praise. Ella and Rita had not spoken about the paper's crime reporting style but she now suspected her sub-editor was of like mind.

Chapter 5

André sat leaning against the information centre veranda pole watching a pair of wedge-tailed eagles catch morning updrafts rising from the desert floor. In the adjacent camping ground, a grey-haired couple were dismantling the canvas annex of the sole caravan, looking to be on the road early. A handful of tents besides vehicles were scattered further afield.

No doubt Graeme and Elaine would see it unfold on the television news that evening. They would recognise their barely cold campsite and be astounded at what had erupted there since their calm and unknowing exit that morning. Perhaps they would also be resentful. André and Ella had chatted briefly to the grey nomads the previous evening as Ella was leaving. Politeness outweighed their curiosity about why André was staying behind. Ella had looked at the ground to avoid their quizzical gazes. She was embarrassed by the protocols that prevented André divulging what would soon be bursting onto everybody's news feed of choice.

Perhaps it was unfair not to have warned them, André was thinking when he noticed both eagles abandon their fixed-wing spiralling climbs to disappear into the tree tops with uncanny speed. Was it their celebrated eyesight, their vantage point, or even their acute hearing that alerted them to an approaching helicopter? It was several more minutes before the rotor's faint flutter reached André's ears. He knew before he saw the craft that it would be media. The wheels of justice would turn much more slowly.

The pilot set the helicopter down midway between Graeme and Elaine's caravan and the information centre. As the engine's pitch wound back, a male reporter and female camera operator scrambled clear and scanned their surroundings for a crime scene. They gestured and shrugged to each other until the rotors slowed to a droop. The jarring intrusion had caused bird chatter to cease — the ensuing silence now absolute. A pilot emerged to join the mime scene and pointed them in André's direction. They wandered over.

'I've been doing a bit of desert trekking,' André fudged and left it to a dumbfounded Graeme and Elaine to field the reporter's questions.

'We wondered if something was not quite right,' was the sum total of Graeme and Elaine's knowledge.

André's presence at the scene would be tricky enough without stealing the local CIU's media thunder. And at least Graeme and Elaine had not missed the excitement. It wasn't long before André noticed the annex being re-erected.

He looked at the now-empty sky and resumed work on the crime scene notes he was making on the back of information centre pamphlets.

His mobile rang. He swiped and greeted Ella calling from Rosenfeld.

'Hey, I'm down to seventeen percent. I forgot I'd have no

way to charge my phone. How are you?'

'*Guess who just showed up?*' Ella demanded to know.

André sensed that whoever it was, was as welcome as an outbreak of yellow leaf spot in Rosenfeld's wheat paddocks.

'I dunno. Who showed up? Are you all right?'

'*Fucking Lila.*'

'No-way. What's she like?'

'*What do you mean "what's she like?" She's like fucking Lila always is — only worse.*'

André had never met Ella's sister. Lila had been estranged from her parents since Ella was ten.

'It's been twenty years since you've seen her yourself. She won't look the same for a start.'

'*She's still the same fucking Lila to me. Turning up now — if there was a time for her to show her face again it was at the funeral. But now? This is her being a jackal. Just a heartless jackal. I've already told her it's not gonna happen. Mum made a will and I know what's in it — and I know what's not in it.*'

'Shit, El. Are you sure you're all right. Do you want me there?' He turned towards the road into the park and added, 'Oh fuck.'

'*What?*'

'The cavalry's arriving.'

'*You go. I've already dealt with this. I just wanted to let you know.*'

'No, El. Tell me what I can do. Are you going to be okay?'

'*You go. I've dealt with it. She's not coming in the house. I said she can stay in the shearers' hut for tonight. Then she can piss off. Trent's here doing farm stuff. Nothing's going to happen. Save your battery and do what you have to do. Love you.*'

He knew she wasn't okay with it. And he knew the long

disused shearers' quarters was packed to the hilt with herbicides and sheep dip.

'I can sort something out,' he said.

'I'm fine. Love you. Bye.'

'Love you,' he snapped, to get it in before she ended the connection.

One by one, the convoy of three branded, white four-wheel-drives pulled to a stop to find André still looking at his phone in dismay. The Police livery of blue and white check; the orange check equivalent of the State Emergency Services; and a single giant eucalypt leaf emblazoned across the Parks Victoria vehicle.

First to alight was Senior Constable Chloe Lane, the local cop stationed at Rainbow that André had phoned. She gave him a wave, then milled with her fellow uniformed drivers, taking in their surroundings. André wandered over. Up close, Chloe was tall and trim-ish, with short ruffled blond hair and a calming smile beneath a broad-brimmed police hat. *Well into her forties,* André estimated.

'Chloe,' she confirmed, holding out her hand.

'André,' he said as they shook. 'Detective Sergeant André Marshall. Homicide Squad,' he elaborated for the benefit of the other two arrivals.

'Ella Richie's boyfriend,' Chloe nodded knowingly. 'I heard she was seeing someone from the Homicide Squad. Pleased to meet you.'

André cocked his head with curiosity.

'I was born and bred here,' Chloe confessed. 'Apart from when I did my training — and my first stint on the job. That was mainly in Horsham. Tell Ella I was sorry to hear about

Miriam. She was a lovely lady.'

'Uh huh,' André managed.

A short lull descended before Chloe introduced the others.

'This is Blair Hope from Parks Victoria — and Anna Melnyk. As you can see, Anna's with the SES.'

Chloe continued as handshakes took place.

'Blair's acting ranger-in-charge. I believe he normally looks after parks down south. He's staying in town until Madeline comes back from her holiday in New Zealand. She went with her sister to do some walks.'

André twigged a country wont to over-elaborate.

'Mr Marshall,' Blair Hope clipped, still clasping André's hand with an overly firm grip. *Not André,* André noted. The words came with a penetrating stare that informed André: *we won't be doing this the easy way.*

Blair Hope was shorter than André, with hare-like build and fitness. Bare arms and legs of tanned leather intimated having more than his fair share of Mallee sun. *Over dedicated and over protective of the national park* André decided to himself — *and the recipient of a country-hospitality bypass.*

'Call me André. What a great workplace you have, Blair,' André tried.

'Yeah. Is that the latest fashion for a walk in the bush?'

His eyes disdainfully scanned André from feet to face. André's competition Lycra, hi-tech gaiters and Gortex shoes were light years away from the Steve Irwin shirt, shorts, socks, and boots of Hope's standard-issue uniform. Only the cloth Parks Victoria badge and dark buttons lifted it above drab.

'I could have dressed down if I knew you were coming,' André shot back. It took a perceptible pause for Blair Hope to recognise the slight. In his head, André awarded himself a touché point.

'You've got a dead body in your park.'

'So I hear. I'll get the map out and you can show me exactly where it is.'

Blair Hope went to his vehicle for the map. André turned to Chloe.

'You've made a call on the SES already?'

'Not officially, no. But the pic you sent me wasn't much to go on. From what I can gather, the body's half-way to the South Australian border.'

She swept her arm to indicate 180 degrees of their immediate surroundings, then lowered her voice to add, 'Which, by the way, I think is a restricted area.'

This came with an exaggerated I-wouldn't-want-to-be-in-your-shoes expression and a conspiratorial nod of her head in Blair Hope's direction.

'I mean, you're talking beyond any vehicle tracks known to man. Other than a helicopter, I've got no idea how I'm supposed to get to the crime scene and secure it, let alone retrieve a body. Will you need SES volunteers scouring for evidence? And most importantly, how do we keep from getting lost ourselves?'

She held her palms out in a help-me-out-here gesture. Before André could decide where to start, she began answering her own quandary.

'I know Anna from when I worked in Horsham and I know she's got a lot to offer whenever you have a problem go off track. Literally, I mean.'

André gave a cursory nod. He'd become distracted by Blair Hope spreading his map out on the vehicle bonnet, and by the male reporter and female photographer wandering over from their helicopter.

'Can you keep them back and tell them they'll have to wait until the local CIU gets here?' André asked Chloe.

'Sure.' She responded, pleased to escape the looming next round between André and Blair Hope.

Blair Hope spread a 1:100,000 scale map on the bonnet of his four-wheel drive and held it down in the slight breeze. He cocked his head, inviting André to look. The larger scale map was much more detailed than the one he and Ella used. It took a moment for him to become orientated and realise the extra features on offer were beyond the massive blank expanse of green they trekked into. All he could do was hone in on grid references along the map's margins and determine roughly where the co-ordinates, still fresh in his mind, intersected.

'About here,' he estimated, and placed his finger on the map to show Blair Hope. 'I've got the exact co-ordinates on my inReach.'

'What the fuck were you doing there?'

'Going for a wander.'

'And you walked from here?'

'Mostly we ran.'

Blair Hope gave a dubious-filled side-eye without lifting his head from the map.

'Where were you going?'

'Out and back. We did intend to go deeper but … we were distracted.'

'You know how easy it is to die out there if you don't know what you're doing. Become lost. Run out of water.'

'Yeah. Of course.'

'And you and your girlfriend know what you're doing?'

'I'm here, aren't I,' André gestured with both arms.

'And where's your girlfriend?'

'Ella went back last night. Not that that's got anything to do with this.'

'You know that's an official Remote and Natural Area where you're required to stick to the tracks.'

'"Advised" to keep to the tracks, according to the visitor guide I've just been reading at your information centre. Tracks which don't exist beyond the perimeter, by the way.'

'Then you would have noticed that you are "advised" to keep to the tracks to protect soil and vegetation. If I get out there and clock the merest sign of any damaged flora, I can do you for … '

'Calm down, you two. We're got a job to do here and we're supposed to be on the same side,' Chloe interrupted using her breaking-up-a-barney police voice.

'Sorry, Chloe,' André said, but turned to Blair Hope. 'Look. Let me get this out of the way. Ella and I do adventure racing, which I'm sure you know about in your world. The events go for days over hundreds of kilometres through all sorts of wildernesses. We were out here doing a two-day training run. We carry a GPS tracker that tracks our movements, which one of our friends was monitoring on-line. We respect the bush and tread lightly. When the wind blows our footprints away, you won't know we've been there.'

'Well, if I find so much as a Cherry Ripe wrapper —' Blair Hope began again.

'Well, someone has discarded something a bit more substantial than that, so tell me exactly how you deal with … ' André began to challenge back.

'All right, all right,' Blair Hope said, finally backing off, if not exactly down. 'What do you want me to do? You said yourself, there are no tracks into there.'

'How close *is* the nearest track?' asked André.

'What you see on the map is what you get. There's nothing beyond Meridian Track for nigh on twenty ks. But even half that's a long way to walk in this country. And you'd need to send the least number of people in.'

'You're joking. We need to get a full crime scene crew in with forensics, and all their gear. Without meeting any of them yet, I reckon you and I would be the only two up for that kind of walk. No offence, Chloe.'

'None taken.' Chloe chipped in. 'There's no way I would want to carry out a dead body for thirty ks through this country, even if I could.'

André turned back to Blair Hope.

'So, we're talking a helicopter, unless you want to bulldoze a new track. As far as landing a chopper goes, there's no convenient dry lake bed within cooee, but I photographed a couple of relatively flat sites that might do the job … if you're prepared to lop a bit of stuff.'

'Well, you're stuffed on both counts. Being a Remote Natural Area means you can't build any new tracks and specifically, you can't remove or lop vegetation,' Blair Hope informed him matter-of-factly.

'I've already told my boss we'd strike something like this. I know you're doing your job Blair, but this looks like a murder and I can guarantee we will be going in there. Can you honestly imagine it won't happen, or that everything will go on hold until they can re-write the regs, or change an act of parliament? Don't tell me you throw these sorts of obstacles up when there's a bush-fire. There's gotta be out clauses for the essential stuff.

'What we should be focusing on is doing it with minimum impact. And I'm not just referring to our team. Look at that media crew.'

André nodded in the direction of the parked helicopter.

'They were here before you were. When all their mates show up, they'll be driving into no-go areas around your locked gates and trying to land their choppers all over the place. Or they'll be sending drones in that will end up out of range and dropping from the skies to add some more litter to the joint. A small cleared area for a helicopter will be the least of your worries. Of course, we could help you manage all that if you want. Can you ask anyone higher up in the organisation, or do you want me to deal with it?'

Blair Hope cocked his head quizzically.

'Is this a deal?'

'We like to call it co-operation. Tell him, Chloe.'

He knew Chloe wouldn't let him down. She was a policewoman ahead of any other country town loyalties. And he was pretty sure none of Chloe's drinking buddies would be hard core greenies.

'Be all over in a couple of days, Blair. We could do a flight exclusion for the whole park. We can have a radar and breath testing set up on the road in — let 'em know in no uncertain terms how they need to behave.'

Flight exclusion zone? Where did she pluck that from? Can she actually do that? André thought.

'I'll get you to fly in with us,' André said. 'We need to exclude the possibility that a four-wheel drive or trail bike bashed its way in. Is that within your areas of expertise or will we need an indigenous tracker? Maybe get a bunch of environmentally unaware coppers and SES volunteers trampling the place. No offence, Anna.'

'We can be as environmentally aware as you like. But it's not my call.' Anna smiled, happy to keep out of the bunfight. They all turned to Blair Hope.

'You're a hundred and fifty years too late to find a black tracker in these parts. Looks like you're stuck with me,' he said.

Was it the threats or the flattery that seemed to be bringing Blair Hope around? he wondered.

'I'll take it up with the Regional Manager,' Blair Hope finally relented. 'He might even have to take it higher. If you do get the okay, you'll need a fire rappel crew and it'll cost you.'

'A what?'

'They're fire-fighters that abseil from a hovering chopper into remote areas. We can drop them in with mini chain saws to clear a landing site.'

'Can you get on to it and let me know how soon they can be here, please?'

Did I just say please to him? André reproached himself.

'It won't be today. I'm heading back into town now. Email me the pics and co-ordinates.'

He handed a card to André.

'It doesn't need to be today. The body's been there for months. It can wait until tomorrow,' André said as Blair Hope headed to his four-wheel drive. He backed up and buzzed down his window to offer André a departing comment.

'Nice work clocking the site by GPS.'

'High praise.' Chloe laughed into the vehicle's departing dust. 'Can I take you into town?' she asked André.

'Do you mind going a bit further to drop me at the farm? Ella's there with our car.'

'No problem.'

'Can you also get on to CIU and tell them to meet us at your station? My offsider, Alex Castellanos is coming up from

Melbourne too. He'll be staying at the Eureka.'

The anticipation of buzzing police on her patch brought a smile to Chloe's face.

'The CIU blokes are staying at the Eureka too,' she said, 'I'll organise the pub's dining room for a proper briefing.'

'Sounds good. Graeme and Elaine can handle the media in the meantime,' André declared as he waved to their perplexed faces from the departing police four-wheel drive.

Chapter 6

"Rosenfeld" homestead was antipodean to its European namesake in more ways than mere physical positioning on the globe. In weather terms, the German town nestled below the Black Forest had twice the rainfall and was only half as hot. If such a scale could be devised, it would also be officially ten times greener.

Rosenfeld was built more than a century earlier by Ella's newlywed great grandparents Conrad and Zelda Hass. Along with fellow countrymen and countrywomen, they moved from German settler enclaves around South Australia's Barossa Valley to take up new Mallee allotments being made available by the Victorian government. Although Conrad was the last of his family to bear the Hass surname, the farm's family-ownership lineage remained unbroken. It had passed to the new married surname of their daughter, and in turn, to the new-er married surname of their daughter's daughter — Ella's mother, Miriam Richie.

Miriam was in her forties when her husband Roy died — young enough for her to ramp up her own farming input and assume active control. It was an era when harvesters and tractors had morphed into towering airconditioned monsters. The size of Mallee farms also continued to grow as the more successful snapped up the land of neighbours chucking in the towel — sadly in some cases, as a result of suicides. Under Miriam's stewardship, Rosenfeld saw off the Millennium drought and kept pace. Success came not simply by doing more stints in the airconditioned cab, but with a deep dive into new-fangled farming. Things like digital agriculture using drones, mega sausage-bag grain storage, alternative crops, engaging agronomists and farm business consultants — a new form of wankery — as well as an old-fangled farm hand or two.

Now it was all Ella's. The third-generation female to hold Rosenfeld in her own right.

By the time they turned into the front gate to Rosenfeld, André was drowsing in late-morning sun streaming through the passenger window. Chloe's soliloquy about life in Rainbow only warranted an occasional uh-huh. It took a vehicle barrelling towards them with a dust cloud in tow to break his trance. An unfamiliar van had set off towards them, down the gravel driveway from Rosenfeld homestead perched on a hillock across the paddock.

'Can you stop so I can wave them down for a word?' he asked Chloe.

A woman driving a white HiAce van came to a halt where André stood beside the marked police car. The dust cloud on the other hand, kept coming. She waited for it to pass André before buzzing her window down. South Australian number plates and signage on the van came into focus as the dust moved on — "Neu Hass Estate".

'Is there a problem?' a replica of Ella asked.

'You're Lila,' André croaked with genuine surprise. He realised he'd never seen a photo of the sister Ella had so often maligned. The same alert almond eyes stared back at him in the same slightly rounded face. The same pleasing lips spoke to him. The same thick crown of near-black hair, although the cloned version was cut shorter to shoulder length.

'And you are?' she shot back.

Obviously, Ella had not mentioned him to Lila, which he found way less surprising. As far as he knew, she and Ella had never spoken in the few years he'd known her. The family resemblance was not slight but the difference in perceptible age was. André's brain was already taking in what Ella would look like seven years down the track, and he wasn't disappointed. *Lila is recognisably older — no question,* he concluded to himself. *If on the other hand, Lila had a less serious countenance tucked somewhere up her sleeve* — he had to stop himself to speak out loud.

'I'm her partner. André Marshall. Detective Sergeant, actually. I've been dealing with a police matter that came up.' He nodded to the police car. 'I'm pleased to meet you, Lila.'

He held his hand out for a physically awkward shake through the driver side window. She nodded in an "I-see" kind of way. Not approvingly, nor disapprovingly. He felt judged nonetheless. She offered a pursed lips smile, although not smiley enough to shake her serious demeanour.

'I'll bet Ella's not.'

'You've been mentioned once or twice,' he admitted.

'Really?'

There was a pause. It wasn't a conversation either expected to have.

'Are you going back,' Andre asked, not knowing where that would possibly be.

'No way. I'm just going into town for some supplies. I might see you later on.'

'Hmm.'

'Pop over to the shearers' quarters if you're allowed. I'll pour you a cup of tea — or a beer if you prefer.'

So, the stony face can be friendly. André looked even more mystified.

'Look, I know it's not your fight, but … ' Lila paused, thinking better of launching into a broadside of justification. She diverted her eyes to the windscreen, gave an exhausted sigh, then turned back and spoke in a deliberately benign tone.

'Sorry. Not here. Not like this. And definitely not with Ella in denial — it's too big a can of worms. But she'll have to face up to things sooner rather than later — and I'm not going anywhere until she does.'

'Uh huh.'

'That's right. Too much too soon for you to get your head around,' Lila interpreted from André's increasingly perplexed face.

'See you later,' she said as the driver's window rose from the car door.

The house / farmyard paddock was defined with a perimeter of scattered black box trees. André had Chloe eschew the formal drive to the front door, and instead, circling past the machinery sheds and silos to the lived-in rear quarter. The building's grand but atypical brick and limestone style reflected those built by Ella's South Australian forebears — a style driven by the dearth of available timber in that state. Some Federation detail and the oasis of an aged, non-native garden was a welcome incongruity amid the broad acres of baking Mallee wheatland.

Ella rose from the cane easy chair on the back veranda before the police car came to a halt. They had only been apart overnight but Ella was a vision to André. Now showered and barefoot in a strappy summer dress, her clean rippling black hair spilled over bare shoulders. André had the sensation of being too grubby to be touched after three days of exertion in the desert.

She was oblivious and ran to him, newspaper in hand, face beaming.

'Page one,' she blurted as she threw her arms around him and crushed her lips onto his. It wasn't a real kiss yet, just an exclamation of excitement.

'So, it's officially news then? And you've been into town to get the paper already?'

'Of course. Page one!'

'What about the tabloid opposition?'

'They missed their print edition all together. So far, all they have on-line is *"Breaking news: Body found in national park. More to follow"*. But I got to write the real story. Page one. Not the lead story, and some of it spilling onto page eight, but still page one with a by-line. Do you want to see it?'

'Yeah … and I believe you know Chloe Lane.'

That slowed Ella. She'd been oblivious to Chloe stepping from the car. She detached herself from André.

'Of course. I remember — the netball queen. Hi Chloe.'

'In Rainbow maybe — and in my younger days,' Chloe

said, acknowledging her netball renown, and then moving onto Ella's. 'Page one huh? exciting for you. We hear about your journalist achievements. Everyone around here is proud of you.'

'Really?'

'Of course. It's a country town. You know how that works. Anyway, I'll leave you two to it. See you in town this arvo André.'

'Okay. Thanks for the lift.'

They watched the dust plume stretching back down the driveway.

'So, what's happening?' Ella asked.

'Nothing yet. I'm gonna get cleaned up and go back into town to marshal the troops. The park ranger is supposed to be organising a fire-fighting helicopter that drops guys in on ropes. They'll clear a space to land. Then we've got to ferry a team in. Nothing's gonna happen before tomorrow though. And Alex is coming up. He's staying at the Eureka.

'Does it need both of you? Are you happy with that?'

'It's fine. Alex is fine. At least he didn't send Cockburn. And Alex will need to take a statement from you. I can't do it.'

'I'll bet you can. I'll tell you everything you want to know,' she teased.

'Are you okay to hang around here?'

'Only for a day, and only if I keep getting the inside story. I'll have to put off sorting out any of the farm stuff and get back to work. That's not gonna be such a problem because, like I told you, probate takes forever. Months usually. Anyway, most of the legal things can be dealt with remotely.'

It was time for André to herd the elephant into the room.

'I just ran into Lila.'

Ella lost her smile … and her voice.

'She looks like you,' he offered.

Ella thought intently, and long.

'It doesn't matter,' she concluded. 'She'll be gone by the time I go. I'll make sure of it. It's full steam ahead with plan A.'

Bewilderment spread across André face, and not for the first time that morning.

'What?' Ella demanded with feigned innocence.

'What what?' I just met your sister for the first time ever. *You've* just met your sister for the first time since I've known you. Don't you have some catching up to do? Or stuff to sort out at the very least. You've just buried your mother. Her mother. I've got no idea what's going on but I can tell you one thing. She made it quite clear that *she is* not going anywhere.'

'Is that what she said? What else did she say?'

'She said you're in denial.'

'I'm in denial!' Her voice rose. 'I'm in denial?'

Ella swung away from André.

'Hey. Don't blame me. I'm just saying … '

'You're just saying what André?'

'I dunno, El. You've never told me anything about her. How could I possibly know what this is about. Now I'm suddenly the enemy. I only spoke to her for a minute through the window of her car. But she's your sister. And she looks so much like you — a bit older maybe — I mean actually. It's a no-brainer to me that you should be getting together. I know she was a no-show for the funeral, but she's here now. What's so bad that you can't … don't you *want* to be friends? Or even sisters? Surely you got on at some stage.'

Ella looked at him. She drew breath and covered her mouth with the fingers of both hands. Her fingers shook a little as she looked at him — then looked away from him — then at him again. She had to prepare herself.

'She left me when I was only ten, "A". She was way older than me and she got to do all the big-kid stuff, and she was good at it all. The clothes she was into. She and her friends talking about and doing all the adolescent things. They were so cool before I even knew what cool was. It wasn't like I was envious though. It was stuff I was too young to aspire to. I was content simply idolising her. She was my real-life close-up view of what life ahead held. I felt smug that she was part of my world. It was something I had that none of the other kids I knew had. Anyway, that's how I saw it as a ten-year-old kid.

'And there was family stuff too. She was Dad's shadow on the farm. The substitute son after our brother Vincent died as a baby … and I came along as a girl. Whatever Dad's reasons were, she got to drive the ute. Help him round up sheep. She even got to do roustabout stuff in the shearing shed. When the shearers came, I wasn't allowed near the place until years later. By then I'd lost interest.

'Then she left and never came back. Just like that. When Dad died a year or so later, I thought she'd come back then. I prayed she'd come back. But she didn't. Not even for his funeral. Just like she didn't come to Mum's.

'Mum fell in a heap after dad died. She threw herself into running the farm and struggled for years to get on top of things. And still no Lila. She robbed both of us back then, and she hasn't stopped robbing me. There's nothing for me to want back. Can you think of a worse time than now for her to show up?'

They looked at each other, still apart. André went to speak.

'That's really heavy shit El. Maybe … '

'Can we just leave it, "A"? I've lived with it for too long.'

She stepped closer and placed her hand on his arm. He looked at her hand and wondered.

'Let me deal with this, huh?' she added.

André gave an acquiescing shrug, albeit reluctantly.

'It's not my fight, but it's hard to watch, El. I just don't want either of you to get in the way of yourselves — of what most of us value most — however it comes about. Especially now you've both lost both your parents.'

'Hmm.'

She put her arm around him, rested her head on his chest and let the argument die out. It soon felt safe for him to ask, 'Is that that then?'

'I'll say something to her, if only to shut you up.'

The possibility of a détente nevertheless seemed a vain hope. She drew herself away from his chest and screwed a face.

'You smell! You have a shower. I'll make coffee and read my page one masterpiece again.'

Attention successfully diverted, she added in after thought.

'But leave the three-day growth on, it's kinda sexy.'

Desire collided with his bafflement.

André's eyes closed against the sting of sweet tank rainwater streaming shampoo foam down his face. In his temporary blindness he felt firm curves fold around his lathered torso.

'Hey, who is that?' Aren't you already clean?'

'It's tank water. You can't waste it.'

Elation sex, André contemplated. *Now that can't be bad.*

Chapter 7

A white board on wheels was all that transformed the windowless dining room of the Eureka Hotel into a briefing room. Chloe Lane had written "Detective Sergeant André Marshall, Homicide Squad" in red marker pen. The board was otherwise blank.

André arrived in a tee-shirt, many-pocketed hiking shorts and closed-toe sports sandals. He made his way round the room meeting Crime Investigation Unit members who'd driven up from Horsham. They were dressed down for a day in the bush. Chloe, the sole female officer present, was still in uniform. Detective Senior Constable Alex Castellanos from the Homicide Squad had arrived in a collar and a tie and quickly discarded the tie. Alex's driving fatigue evaporated when — contrary to André's intel — he spotted an espresso machine behind the bar.

The mood was upbeat all-round. Word had spread that there'd be no action until the next day, so beers had been taken with lunch. The publican's offsider Gwen was collecting finished plates from the tables. The pub might have been the last watering hole standing, but a not too recent reno averted signs of decline that inevitably befell opposition establishments. There was even a slice of inner-city grunge with wall-plaster chipped back to bare brick.

The "Metropolis of the Mallee" — as Rainbow was once dubbed — was on the brink of a silo-art led revival. It was not immune from the tourist phenomenon of transforming wheatbelt landscapes with murals painted onto the omnipresent high-rise silos. Rainbow's planned contribution was to turn the concept inside out. *Their* mural would be painted inside the silo with a lift installed to a viewing platform on top — the ultimate desert view. Nor was it a pipe dream. Visionaries with clout managed to twist government arms for a whack of $2.1 million.

André tapped a glass to get everyone's attention. When that only half worked, he announced loudly, 'If we make this quick, the rest of the day is yours.'

The chatter ceased and André was true to his word.

'I'm assuming you've all seen the photos by now — and you've probably heard that Blair Hope, the acting park ranger, is precious about every blade of grass in the national park. So, we need to be on our best behaviour. I'm totally fine with that and I don't want anyone giving him something to complain about. Okay?'

André paused for the silent response he expected.

'With a bit of argy-bargy, Blair Hope gave the okay for us to chopper in tomorrow morning with what he refers to as a minimal presence. If you are wondering what that means, my interpretation is: we'll be taking in whatever and whoever we need to get the job done. Okay?'

This time the "okay" was even more rhetorical. No pause

was offered — or wanted.

'Blair Hope will be there at ten a.m. with a chopper and rappel crew to clear a landing site.

'The pathologist team aren't here yet, but don't worry, they'll be flying up in the morning. There's a dirt airstrip out the road, although they'll probably land at the proper one in Hopetoun. Who can liaise and pick 'em up?'

A local CIU hand went up.

'Good man. Now, when we get there. We think the body was dropped from a plane so we don't expect to find anything other than the body. We'll search a tight area around the remains nevertheless. Basically, the hollow between the dunes. Like this.'

André erased his own name from the whiteboard and drew a mud map. An X in the centre of the board marked the body. Wavy lines above and below it represented the nearest dunes. He drew a child-like helicopter shape on the outer side of the bottom dune and joined it to the X with a dotted line.

'Blair Hope and I will do an outer circuit to make sure there has been no vehicle access into the area. It's a safe bet there hasn't been a vehicle within thirty ks. You'll see what I mean when you get there.

'The media are already sniffing around. That's a local issue for you blokes. About all you can tell them is a dead body has been found in a remote part of the national park. Everything else is unknown at this stage. Any questions?'

'I see in this morning's paper that your girlfriend found the body,' one of the local detectives said.

'That's right. Detective Castellanos will be taking a statement from her. She and I were together when we found the body. I can vouch that everything she wrote is correct.'

'Cosy.'

'However you want to see it, a body has been found and we all have a professional job to do. Anything else?'

After due silence he asked, 'Anyone for a beer?'

André rode up front with the helicopter pilot. Blair Hope and the two Parks Victoria rappel crew were in the rear. The GPS took them to the point where André had placed his finger on the map. With only a few wisps of cloud about, André's orange tee-shirt shone like a beacon. When the time came, the leather-gloved rappelers barked commands at each other and slid down ropes like SAS commandos, fully armed, with chainsaws on their tool belts. A one-hander model dangled from a carabiner on their belts and an even smaller cordless version was fastened into a holster. Beneath their helmets, both had the dark good looks and no-nonsense professionalism of a movie version SAS squad. Their Stihl one-handers were soon carving a swathe through the spindly Mallee shrubs. In the meantime, André had the pilot take him up to see the view from body-dropping plane height and beyond. At 2,000 feet, the desert was a sea of black-green with the whitecaps of occasionally exposed sand ridges. No white threads of sandy vehicle tracks were visible in any direction. The pilot was unwilling to take it higher and they returned to the orange speck to christen the newly cleared landing pad.

André and Blair Hope made a hunched exit, crossing paths with the hunched rappellers under the rotor. They turned to watch the newly trimmed scrub being enveloped into a swirl of leaves and bark as the helicopter rose and headed for the horizon to collect the crime scene team. From the top of the dune, André pointed for Blair Hope.

'Down there. We'll let forensics go in first.'

'I read what your girlfriend wrote in the paper,' Blair Hope said. 'She hit the nail on the head. This is beautiful. I'd be happy to be placed out here whenever I drop off the perch.'

'That's exactly what Ella said.'

Silence.

It was the first time they were alone together and neither liked having something in common. André was first to think of something to say.

'Could you tell from the air if anything came in by land?'

'I was looking,' Blair Hope answered. 'I'm already with you on the plane theory. You wouldn't get within a bull's roar in a four-wheel drive and you'd give up before you even came over the horizon on a dirt bike.'

'You and I can check on the ground when we get things set up here. How do you want to tackle it?' André asked.

'I'll do it now. I'll keep away from the hollow with the body. I'll come and get you if I find anything.'

'You'll need someone with you, won't you? You were the one that told me how dangerous it is.'

'I've got what I need in this day-pack. You stay here and stick to your knitting.'

Ouch!

Blair Hope turned to end the discussion and sloped into the Mallee scrub with the agility of a rock wallaby.

The "minimal" presence André had negotiated with Blair Hope and his regional manager included two gazebo fabric shade roofs. The bright blue added an alien splash of colour. One was erected over the body, the other beside the landing site. A local detective stretched crime scene tape from Mallee tree to Mallee tree in a wide barrier around the body.

'Keeping the roos out?' André quipped.

'Procedure,' came the deadpan reply.

Leave it rest, André bade himself with Glenevis's words ringing in his ears.

The local team and Alex scoured the hollow, drew a blank, and retired to the shade. Job done.

'Should have brought a pack of cards,' said one detective constable. 'Can't even get mobile reception.'

Blair Hope reappeared and joined their number after a three-hour absence in the scrub.

'Nothing been within five kilometres of here since the Pliocene Age. When this was a seabed.' He handed André a chalky shell-like scrap. 'Not even an Aboriginal grinding stone or flake in sight.'

The focus of attention had narrowed to the actual remains. The forensic pathologist and trace evidence technician were crouched over the body on plastic ground sheets. A photographer hovered among the mounting collection of evidence bags. They were now below the surface, proceeding slowly with an archaeological-dig trowel and soft-bristle brush.

Conversation had become low in the late-morning still. A murmur of even softer insect hum and distant bird chatter settled over the group. It was the least likely prelude to two rapid gunshots within the camp.

BANG. BANG.

A bedlam of reactions saw several bodies hit the deck and at least two guns drawn in instinctive response. The direction of the sound had all heads facing the local CIU detective beside the second gazebo. He stood peering at the ground directly in front of him — pistol in his hanging right hand.

'Snake,' he said.

'You stupid fucking arsehole,' André, who was standing closest, snapped. 'That's a Butlers legless lizard. It won't kill you.'

'Not now.'

'How did you know it's a legless lizard?' quizzed Blair Hope who had jumped up to examine the reptile in its writhing death throes.

'It's not the first one I've seen this week. I googled it.'

'Then do something and get this clown out of here. I could have him under the Wildlife Act of 1975, you know?'

'A legless fucking lizard,' the detective constable protested. 'A legless lizard is what a fucking snake is, isn't it? How the fuck was I supposed to know? I was only trying save your fucking lives. Fucking thanks I get.'

The argument lapsed with his mates' laughter.

'Okay' André said to Blair Hope. 'You fly back with this lot. I'll stay here with the pathologist's team. They should be able to wrap it up today. Come back for us before it gets dark.'

André was thankful to have the scene to himself. Enough had been done to placate the local CIU. Deflecting any resentment away from him to Parks Victoria didn't do any harm either.

André settled down on the fringe of the pathologist's ground sheets and retrieved a snack bar from his pack.

He watched Doctor Sophie Conan Doyle lift a rib bone with tongs, brush it clean and place it correctly in the skeleton jig-saw she was assembling on a sheet of plastic. Sophie had worked on several of André's cases and she was already his pathologist of choice. Not that he normally had a choice. His colleagues favoured the more experienced hands. Sophie was closer to thirty than forty but had impressed him with her persistence and reluctance to make assumptions. She swore to him that her ancestry could not be traced to Sir Arthur Conan Doyle, the famed creator of Sherlock Holmes. André suspected she said so to escape over expectation — *there can't be that many Conan Doyle's on the planet.* He found her to be hungry for information about cases in order to have a complete canvas on which to paint her report. Conan Doyle or not, Sophie was the most sleuth-like pathologist he knew at the Institute of Forensic Medicine.

Sophie and he attended court for the verdict of the Zhirinovsky case in which she had given the pivotal evidence. When the conviction was announced, they rushed off for a celebratory drink. The adrenalin careening through their veins could not be ignored. A pally bond was seeded.

'Anything so far, Doc?'

Sophie smiled without looking away from the bone she was dusting. Her brown hair was tied back and her fair skin had reddened slightly in the heat.

'Female, which you already know.'

A long pause to concentrate on her brushwork.

'Nothing from the clothes but we'll check them back at the lab. Expensive though. I like the shoes.'

The second female to praise her clothes, André noted.

'Anything else?'

'There are a few traces of blood left here and there on bones. Probably mummified. It might tell us something back at the lab — if it's not too old. She's probably been here about six months, but don't quote me on that.'

'That confirms another opinion I've had,' he said.

Her head lifted from the task and gave an inquiring expression through her glasses. André told her about Ella's assessment.

'The footprint across the tibia looked too small to be yours. Did she leave the flowers too?'

'Uh-huh.'

'A rare humane touch in this job. Not that I condone people getting that close.'

'It wasn't by choice.' André defended. 'I reckon the body would have been here for eternity if Ella hadn't come along and stepped on it.'

Quiet settled for a while. Neither was hurried.

'Can you tell if she fell? From above, I mean,' André asked after he watched a few more rib bits being placed in the puzzle.

'Not much doubt she fell from a great height. It looks like she landed on her back. A few of the ribs have fractured or broken across the back. And the back of the skull is cracked. I expect to find that all of the breaks occurred upon landing. You're lucky that the bones have not been scattered. Eagles did most of the dining is my best guess. There's a lot of what could be beak scrapes on the bones. Possibly some rat-sized animals too, but no evidence of foxes. They tend to drag bits all over the place.'

'I noticed there's been a fox baiting program.'

'Lucky.'

'Anything to show if she was dead or alive when she fell?'

'Nothing to go on here. No bullet damage to the bones and

any stab marks will be hard to detect among those made by animals. Something might show up in a post mortem of what's left. I also think it's unusual that the body landed back first, not feet first or head first. I'll need to chase up a paper that was written a couple of years ago about damage sustained in falling fatalities. A lot of stowaways were dropping from the wheel housing of planes flying into America.'

'Mm.'

'Any idea who she is?'

'None at all. I presume you can extract some DNA and dental records?'

'There's plenty for odontology to get their teeth into if you know who you're looking for.'

'As a stand-up, you make a darn good pathologist, Doc.'

A contented smile spread as she brushed another bone. André smiled unthinkingly at her smile. His phone rang.

'Huh?'

There was supposed to be no reception. The screen told him it was Ella.

'Hello?'

Nothing.

'Hello Ella? Can you hear me?'

More nothing.

He looked at the screen again.

'Bugger. I haven't even got one bar but it made a connection,' he told Sophie. 'There's not supposed to be *any* reception here. I'll try on top of the dune.'

It rang and Ella picked up.

'Are you still out there?' she asked.

'Yeah. I'm not sure if the call will last though. I'm at the body, on the dune, and I've only got a quarter of one bar — if that.'

'God, I wish I was there. I don't mean with your work buddies. I just mean out there. Is it good?'

André did a quick 360 on the dune top. If he ignored the speck of human activity in the gully, it was just him, dune scrub to every horizon, and an endless sky.

'Yeah,' he admitted, feeling the guilt that he was there and Ella wasn't. 'What're you up to?'

'I'm going back to Melbourne.'

'Today?'

'Yeah, now. I'm assuming you can get a ride back with Alex. Is that okay? I've left some food in the fridge.'

'Yeah. Okay, I suppose.' He was trying to sound like he wasn't trying to get his head around being there without her. 'What about Lila?'

'Uh. She's still holed up in the shearers' quarters. I was going to tackle her about not staying here, but Auntie Glad showed up. She'd heard Lila was back. Things were tense for a while. She hasn't seen Lila for twenty years either. Now Lila's gone back into town with her. The whole thing will have to wait for now. I'll call her.'

'So, Lila will be there when I get back tonight?'

'Yes. Trent knows, so you don't have to talk to her or anything.'

'Uh huh.'

'No. Let me re-phrase that. Don't talk to her.'

'Can you hear yourself, El?'

'All right. You can be polite if you bump into her. But you know what I mean.'

'As if I want to be meat in that sandwich.'

Ella decided to change the subject.

'*What's news with the body then?*'

'Slow going really. The pathologist is pretty certain she fell from an aircraft. She won't be able to confirm that until she's back in the lab, though. Not much else I can tell you.'

'*So, "it is suspected she fell from a plane".*' She spoke it newsreader style.

'Yeah, but you didn't hear it from me.'

'*And you aren't wondering "Was she pushed"?*' The same newsreader voice.

'"All possibilities are being considered",' he answered in his own mock interviewee voice, ' … and I didn't say that either. You can write whatever you want about the actual crime scene because you were there. But don't make anything sound like pillow talk or you'll really get me in the shit.'

'*I like the sound of pillow talk.*'

'Me too. I should be back home by tomorrow night. Love you.'

Silence.

'Hello? You there, El?'

He looked at his phone. No bars.

Chapter 8

Lila was in Ella's cane easy-chair on the back veranda, waiting for him. André waved goodbye to Alex and wandered over. She was halfway into a second Corona stubbie. An empty sat on the side table, along with a cutting board, knife, and the unused portion of a lime.

'You want one?' she asked.

'Have you moved in all ready?'

'Nah. I came over here because I wanted to make sure I didn't miss you.'

He moved into the other cane chair.

'In that case, you've wasted your time. It's not my battle. You and Ella are on your own.'

She took the time to take another swig.

'That's fine. I wasn't expecting any buy-in. More than that. I don't want to go behind Ella's back in any way. But I do want to talk to *her*.'

His eyes shifted to the Corona she had placed back on the table. It looked good after a long day in the desert. The beads of icy water still clung to the glass bottle. She noticed his gaze shift to the Esky tucked on the other side of her chair.

'You sure you won't have one?' she asked.

'What do you want, Lila?'

'I need to talk to Ella and she's avoiding me. Trent tells me she's run off back to Melbourne and I don't have her number — or her address. I'm happy to talk to her in Melbourne — if I knew her number or where you guys live. She asked Trent not to say.'

André looked nonplussed.

'You don't know what any of this is about, do you?'

'You're talking to a cop. We know how to respect peoples' boundaries, especially in an estranged situation. And she's my partner. I'll give you my number, you give me yours. I'll pass it on to Ella. If she wants to meet with you, I'll let you know. Or maybe she'll do that herself.'

'I'll do that if you hold off mentioning it to Ella until I'm actually in Melbourne. I'll be there for work before I head home to SA. Then, if she still avoids me, you'll know how shy she is about sorting anything out.'

'I'm not going to collude against her. What do you think I am?'

Lila gave the question some thought.

'Honourable, it would seem.' She held her Corona up as a salute to him.

'To my newfound, honourable, estranged, de facto, brother-in-law.'

He smiled.

'Okay, we do it your way,' she agreed. 'Now, do you want me to knock the top off one of these for you or what?'

'One. Then I've got work to do.'

Fear of where to tread made for laboured conversation. One

stubbie was indeed enough. Lila's parting comment nevertheless took one step extra.

'I know we're avoiding the elephant on the veranda … ' she said, ' … but I have one thing to say that I want you to pass on to Ella. Tell her I did it for her.'

Chapter 9

The lights were on when André arrived at the office early. At the far end of the workstation cluster, Inspector Rab Glenevis stood staring at the display board on which André had begun a link diagram. He noticed Glenevis's hands instinctively feeling for his pockets, of which he had none. He was wearing a kilt — the red and blue MacPherson tartan of the Victoria Police Pipe Band uniform.

'Afore you start hangin' it on me, a few of us are playin' at Paul Bernardi's funeral this afternoon. A retired inspector … afore your time … an' mine for tha' matter,' he explained.

'Uh-huh,' a duly nullified André said.

'An' nae mention o' me bein' a Cameron Clan man wearin' MacPherson tartan. Where were Cluny MacPherson and his army when 300 of our finest laid down their lives for Bonnie Prince Charlie at Culloden. Eh?'

The history was as unknown to André as the Yao Africans of Lake Malawi, but he sensed enough to treat the question as rhetorical. He shrugged.

Glenevis turned his attention back to the board.

'Ha' you nae got more than this?' he asked.

At top centre of the crime board was a generic photograph of a light plane. An arrow ran from the plane image to a photograph of the skull peering from the Mallee sand. There was more than a metre of blank space on both sides of the images.

'Well you know, identity can take a while, starting from scratch like this. We're in the same boat as the WWI bodies they're still unearthing at Fromelles — and you know how long DNA can take on top of everything else. We do however have the advantage of modern-day dental records. That'll speed things up bit. We're working our way through about a dozen possibles that fit the timeline and gender. Just the Victoria ones at this stage. If it's not one of ours, it'll start all over.'

'Well at least get a few of those likelies up on the board. Ah want ta see that somethin' is happenin'.'

'Okay Boss,' André said. He slipped the backpack off his shoulders and sat at his workstation. Glenevis settled his bum onto the opposite workstation.

'Do you nae have somethin' from th' autopsy?'

André locked eyes to avoid the distraction of Glenevis's sporran and his hairy white legs.

'I've got a meeting with Sophie this morning to pick up the report. She already agrees that the body came from above. I'm not hopeful we'll get more than the basics about the body. Height. Maybe a rough age.'

'Will she actually say tha'? That th' body fell from an aircraft?' Glenevis asked.

'More like: "Damage consistent with having fallen from a great height." I'd say.'

'Okay. But let me know. This has captured th' media's

attention. There's already plenty o' speculation aboot the body bein' tossed oot of a plane. Ella's article dinnae leave much doubt.'

'She was there. She's only reporting what she saw.'

'Ah know, but Ah'm nae comfortable aboot you and her becomin' th' news. Let Alex do any media — or get me. Ah dinnae want ta see you bein' quizzed on camera aboot your involvement. Get Alex to have a word ta our comms people.'

'Right.'

'One more thing André.'

'What's that?'

'Next time you go on leave, can you go somewhere interstate? We've get enough comin' thru our door without you addin' ta the pile.'

Sophie was already seated when André arrived for coffee. The café meeting was Sophie's suggestion. *Nothing to show and tell at the lab*, her email read, *only need to hand over the autopsy report. See if you've got any questions.*

Maretto's was below a Bourke Street glass-tower home for high-profile legal firms. Its elegant interior of timeless dark timbered walls was a step into a refined European world. The solid timber tables stood comfortably apart from each other and the dense dark blue carpet softened conversation — enough for each table to enjoy an invisible cone-of-silence. The crowded clamour of its glass and polished concrete cousins in shopfronts along the rest of the street was a world away. There were a few lone device readers, even a couple of actual newspaper readers, but most tables were occupied by two or three suited men and women intensely discussing docs, — paper and digital. Perhaps the place was designed by the building's lawyer occupants. André had not previously heard of or been to Maretto's.

A slim A4 envelope sat on the mahogany table in front of Sophie.

A table-service waiter took their coffee orders, which arrived with the tiniest possible biscuit on the saucer. A mini star of chocolate chip.

Their catch-up conversation was about their shared appreciation of how remarkable the Mallee desert was.

'But it's a day's drive for a proper coffee,' André lamented.

'You can't have it all,' Sophie mock-sighed, as if her whole life had already been defined by such truism.

'So, this is it,' he said, picking up the envelope. 'Everything you told me but in writing?'

'Pretty much. Nothing from her clothing. We've recorded makes and sizes where we can. An upmarket dresser, like I said. She may or may not have been dead when she left the plane. There are traces of flunitrazepam in what blood we could recover — over 100 µg/L. The sample was scant, so that might not be entirely accurate. At the very least she was deeply sedated when she hit the ground.'

'What's flunitrazepam?'

'It's in date rape drugs like Rohypnol, easily dissolvable in drink. Typically causes sedation, confusion, amnesia. It can last for twelve hours.'

'Do you know when she died?'

'My best guess is six months ago, maybe a little longer. She's 167 centimetres tall. Natural hair a bit darker than what you saw. Age is a tough one because of fauna-teeth and beak marks on critical bones. Probably 39 to 44 years old, although the report says 35 to 45 — to cover my bum. DNA, dental photos and blood type are all in there. No fingerprints, of course.'

'Brilliant. Dental *and* DNA. We can get to work with that.'

'You can thank the perpetrator for that. If they're careless enough to leave a body lying around, there'll always be crumbs.'

The black screen stared at Detective Senior Constable Alex Castellanos. Its imagery had disappeared entirely when the desktop PC dived into a data-base to gather his latest request. Alex was left gazing at his own reflection. It was late morning and he was caught by surprise to see his facial stubble was already prominent. Why didn't his head hair grow as fiercely he contemplated, then shifted his gaze to the sparse crop above his forehead.

The screen flashed back to white life. The chance for Alex to contemplate his face/head hair imbalance vanished as quickly as it came. His brain was now challenged by a long table of female names and their personal details. He resumed his staring competition with the screen. This time Alex blinked first. He released the mouse and placed his finger-entwined hands on his bristling scalp. Lifting his gaze, he saw André come into the open-plan office carrying a buff A4 envelope. His stride betrayed smugness.

'How's it going?' André asked in a suspiciously jaunty tone.

'As my Nonna would say, "like looking for fleas in the straw", mate. I think the list has begun to breed in the computer. You'll need the entire office wall if Mr Edinburgh Tattoo wants names on the board.'

André smiled. 'I hope that doesn't mean you hung shit on Glenevis. He's kilted-up for a funeral he's playing the pipes at.'

'Oh fuck. No wonder I got the ray. And he piled it on for

me to get this done.'

'Well *"Hang on, Help is on its way".*'

André sang the Little River Band tune while holding opposite edges of the A4 envelope and cocking it from side to side to the imagined beat.

'The autopsy report. You've been flirting with Dr Sophie, haven't you? That's why you're so chipper.'

'I *have* had a professional meeting with Sophie as it happens, but it's what's in the report that's floating my boat. Your list is about to shrink big time, Aristotle.'

'Yeah?'

'39 to 44 years old, height 167 centre metres, light brown hair dyed blonde, dead about six months, DNA, blood type and dental details. That gonna narrow it down a bit?'

'Give me two hours.'

Two hours became two days. Alex arrived early to find the office lights already on and André gazing at the crime board — one hand in his pocket, the other wrapped around a takeaway cup.

'Morning, Alex. Got it down to three, I see?'

The three names were written in Alex's hand beside the desert skull photograph — Portia Meredith, Suyin Lijuan and Helen Lawless.

'Mornin', mate. This is only the Victorian ones. We're not going interstate at this stage. These look likely enough for starters.'

'Have you got a favourite?'

'Not yet. They're all married women, no kids. Not sure we can read anything into the demographic, though.'

André nodded in sage agreement.

'All three were on Missing Persons books. All still missing. The hard-copy files will be here this morning.'

'Then there's a good chance we'll already have some sort of DNA on file. Want a stab on which one it is?' André asked.

'D'you want to make it interesting, mate?'

'Okay. A slab of Coronas. You can pick first.'

'"Every hand's a winner" … baby,' Alex kinda sang. 'So I choose Portia Meredith.'

'Hot Chocolate?' André asked incredulously.

'Nah. You're thinking of "Every-*one's* a Winner". I'm talking The Gambler — Kenny Rogers.'

'I'll choose Suyin Lijuan then,' André said.

'Ooh. You can buy those Coronas now,' Alex said with glee.

'The bet's off if that's insider-trading talk.'

'No. It's the Asian name, mate. Less likely to use a plane to dispose of a body, I reckon.'

'We're supposed to be guessing the kill-*ee*, not the kill-*er*. But okay. I'll go for the other one instead.'

'Too late. Ah'll have tha' one,' said an approaching Rab Glenevis. 'Is she blonde?'

'Why?' André and Alex responded in unison. 'Have you got your own prejudiced theory as well?' André added.

'Alfred Hitchcock reckons they make th' best victims. "Like virgin snow tha' shows th' bloody footprints".'

They both gaped with bemusement until Alex asked, 'How does that work then? If you're right, do we both buy you a slab?'

'Unless Nonna Castellanos has a better system. A "*better*" system,' Glenevis repeated, realising his unintended pun.

André and Alex groaned dutifully.

'A'right then,' he said with a mock hurt face. 'Tha'll be th' end o' th' week afore you get a match from forensics. Aristotle can keep goin' through th' files. In th' meantime André, you can give Fi a hand with the dead girl a' Keon Park. An' no goin' near any o' those possibles until we have a match.'

Ella sipped the chilled New Zealand sauvignon blanc and watched. André was trimming steak for a stir-fry on the opposite side of their kitchen bench.

'When will you find out?'

'Not long,' he answered. 'Make the most of it. I might not be around to cook when this thing gets legs.'

'I'm more interested in having something to write. Rita wants an angle to keep it alive. She wants to keep milking my own involvement. I don't want to waste the chance either, so right now, anything to hang my hat on would be nice.'

'It should only be days. We've honed the long list right down, but there's always a chance nothing will match. And you know we can't start talking about any of the likelies. Imagine if we put stuff like that in the public domain. We'd have false-alarms and bushfires breaking out all over the place. We'd be crucified.'

'That hasn't stopped the Sunday tabloid speculating, has it? Is it one of the parade of faces they came up with?'

'Nah. Their scattergun approach went too far back. Your estimate of being dead for six months was spot on.'

'Really?' Ella beamed. 'It just shows you. You can take the girl out of the country … wait a minute, maybe I can use that. How long she's been dead, I mean.'

'You can't. I never told you.'

'No? I told you. You just said so. I was the one who told you how long she was dead. You can't stop me quoting myself.'

She looked smug.

André lifted his hands slightly in mock surrender, knife still in hand, then finished slicing the meat into strips. He looked up.

'All right then, country girl. When are you going to bite the bullet on Lila?'

'Jeez, "A". You slipped that in from nowhere.'

'Well?'

She huffed dismissively.

'I've given you her number, and nothing's happening. She wants to speak to you. *You* need to speak to her, even if it is only to give her her marching orders. Are you avoiding it?'

'It's my problem, "A". I'll deal with it when I'm ready. You know I've got a lot on.'

He put the knife down to make a serious announcement.

'I brought it up because I got a text from her today. She's coming to Melbourne.'

Ella stiffened and began tapping her teeth with a thumbnail. André filled the void.

'I can arrange a meeting if you like. Not here, of course.'

More teeth tapping.

'You really need to do this, El, even if you don't want to connect on an ongoing basis. You're the executor of your mum's will and despite what Miriam wanted, or what you want, as Miriam's daughter she *will* probably have grounds to challenge. Not that I have a clue about whether she even wants to challenge the will or not.'

The teeth tapping stopped.

'This isn't about money "A".'

'No? Last time you mentioned the will you were pretty determined that Lila gets nothing.'

'That's because of what she did. She doesn't deserve a cut. In any case, Mum didn't include her, so that should be the end of that. Who am I to go against my mother's wishes?'

André cocked his head sceptically.

'Well, she doesn't deserve a cut,' Ella responded.

'Maybe she does or maybe she doesn't. Or maybe it doesn't matter anymore. From what I can tell, you don't know anything about her. You don't know where she lives or what she's been doing for the past twenty years. Is she rich? Does she have a partner? Has she got any children? You may have nieces and nephews you don't know about. You might really like her partner. Don't you have a scintilla of curiosity? Don't you want to hang onto what family you have left in the world? And even if it's not about money, these are things that still need to be sorted. It's all too weird. Don't you think you ought to un-weird it? Even a little bit?'

He sounded like he'd exhausted his persuasion but had one more up his sleeve.

'You know the last thing she told me at Rosenfeld was: she did it for you.'

Ella went wide-eyed with feigned surprise.

'She did it for me. Oh really. She disappeared out of my life — for me?'

She stood up, paced 360 degrees and placed both her palms on the bench to address André.

'Okay. You organise that meeting. I wanna hear her tell me exactly how I benefited from her disappearance.'

Chapter 10

Glenevis, André and Alex struck the pose. Hands in pockets looking at the story being constructed on the crime board. A photograph of a woman's face had been added beside the bare skull in white desert sand. The name Portia Meredith was written immediately below. The other two names had disappeared from the board.

The forty-three-year-old was attractive in an unobvious way. A face more long than round. Hair to her shoulders. Soft hazel eyes. The restrained smile in the photograph hinted at a composed and determined disposition.

'She looks betta in flesh,' quipped Glenevis.

André and Alex exchanged obligatory side glances before Alex got down to the serious business.

'So that's a slab each then? Good. I'll leave one here and take one home,' he said.

'Just tell us aboot her. What kind o' name is Portia Meredith anyway?' Glenevis asked.

'A Sydney money name. She was Portia Sutton before she married John Meredith. They lived in Beaumaris. He still does.

Reported missing last March, a week after he flew to London on business. She drove him to the airport. No kids. At the time, he reckoned she left him and he couldn't care less. Her cards and phone stopped being used within a week of him flying out. A suitcase and some clothes gone.'

'What's he do?'

'He's a corporate lawyer turned developer. Apparently, he figured there was more money in owning projects than preparing contracts for them.'

'What d'ya mean apparently? Who ha' you spoken ta?'

'Deborah Harvey.'

Detective Sergeant Deborah Harvey was a widely known veteran with Missing Persons.

'She said Meredith was a hard case. He refused to go on TV to appeal to the public. But his story checked out. If he did do it, he would have been pulling the strings from overseas. If he plugged into the criminal world to do it, there wasn't so much as a squeak from anyone. It all went cold.'

'Weel a body an' all this media will warm things up a wee bit,' Glenevis said. 'Meredith will be expecting a visit, whether he killed her or nae. But let's keep him guessin'. Dig up as much as ya can aboot him afore you do th' next-of-kin thing. I dinnae care how many days th' announcement is delayed. And Ah want every media outlet ta find out at th' same time, André,' he added pointedly. 'We dinnae play favourites without good reason. An' you getting' on a promise is nae good enough reason.'

'If it does leak it won't be from me,' André protested.

'All th' same … ' Glenevis said. Then proceeded to ram the point home, ' … dinnae take your work home until this is safely in th' public domain.'

The room fell silent.

'An' one more thing, André. Take Deborah with you when ya do see Meredith. She can tell us whether Meredith's demeanour has changed now we've found his wife's body.'

Deborah Harvey drove via St Kilda, skirting Port Phillip Bay clockwise. The foreshore soon cast a spell over André, sitting in the passenger seat. Pockets of windswept tea-tree, she-oaks and banksias stretched, off and on, in a thin belt of vegetation on the beach side of the road — all the way to the bay's head. Some of the bush was buffed but plenty remained in the natural state that William Buckley would have encountered — the first European to make the trip, albeit on foot. Convict Buckley escaped from the short-lived pre-Melbourne bay-side settlement near Sorrento. He survived with aborigines until Europeans had another crack at permanent settlement, thirty-two years later. These days, the occasional interloping genus of palm tree, brick barbeque, car park, and rotunda fused into the bay's fringe of remnant scrub.

Being on Beach Road in a suit and tie was anathema to André. He knew it as a childhood summer escape, albeit shared with thousands of others. These days it was the weekly backdrop for Ella's and his bike training. He had completed several Around-the-Bay-in-a-Day rides — one with Ella — as well as running a marathon on the bay-side road from Frankston to the city. What luxury, to sit in the sun behind glass and enjoy the endless waterside vista rolling by.

The road rose gently over cliff tops and dunes that hid the renowned Brighton bathing boxes and suburban yacht clubs. Lower sections held glimpses of sandy beaches, groynes and the ever-present horizon of water meeting sky. Two container ships silhouetted without perceptible movement.

Deborah noticed André's absent gaze before speaking.

'You won't be able to read this guy, you know? He'll be charming enough, but absolutely unforthcoming about the matter at hand. You'll see why he does all right in business. You'd want him on your side if you were negotiating a pay rise. He's the complete package.'

'What did you tell him?'

'That we have developments to update him about.'

'Did he ask what?'

'No.'

'Do you expect him to be surprised that we found her? That she was the body in the desert?'

'Not if he killed her … and not if he didn't kill her. You'll see.'

They passed through the scrub of Rickets Point and began looking for house numbers on the inland side of Beach Road. Over the decades, all but a scattering of the esplanade's single-story homes had been sacrificed in favour of two-storey mega homes in pursuit of bay views. An odd few even managed to incorporate a third storey rooftop deck or folly to guarantee a line-of-sight that cleared the beachside trees. It was said that some homeowners resorted to furtive tree-lopping raids by night. Large signboards offered a reward of $25,000 for nailing the culprits.

Deborah found Meredith's house number and they entered the driveway to a stark tinted-glass edifice. A clone of itself stood as its right-side neighbour. To its left, a homely post-war clinker brick abode awaited the fate of other former single storey hangovers from the past. The iron gate had already been electronically retracted behind a high, rendered garden wall in anticipation of their visit.

John Meredith opened the door.

To André, he looked a well preserved fifty something. Solid of build, a firm face carved in warm sandstone with reticent eyes, paler than blue. His light brown hair was grown to a length that could be pulled back from his forehead in a handful and planted behind his ears. The thick quiff was trimmed just above the collar. He dressed plainly but expensively in a crisp white shirt and dark suit-trousers. Altogether, a larger-than-life figure despite his average height and lack of a jacket and tie — yet to be donned for the office.

'Come upstairs, can I get you a coffee?' The voice was deep and commanding.

John Meredith parked them in an upstairs lounge room with a full-height glass wall facing Beaumaris Bay within Port Phillip Bay. He left to get coffees. *The bridge of the Queen Mary — without the wheel,* André mused as he began making mental notes. The panorama and passing road traffic was silent behind the double-glazed expanse. *How idyllic. A Brett Whitely-worthy bay within a bay,* André kept observing to himself. Indeed, a post-impressionist depiction of the view hung on the wall beside him. *How odd when you can simply turn your head to see the real thing?* The obligatory telescope on a tripod shifted his thoughts. *A telescope shop would have to be a goer in this neck of the woods.*

Meredith returned with a plunger of coffee and cups and saucers on a tray.

'We've got an espresso machine but that takes me forever.'

He seated the detectives on the pale leather lounge and took the matching single-seater for himself. He didn't wait for milk and sugar niceties to get on the front foot.

'So, you're with Homicide, Detective Marshall. Is that significant?'

André followed Meredith's lead in not beating around the bush.

'It is, Mr Meredith. I'm afraid I'm here because we've found your wife's body and we think she's been murdered.'

They watched Meredith put his cup and saucer back on the coffee table and then place both hands, palms face-down, on the wide arms of the chair. He looked past André and Deborah Harvey at the bay and audibly drew in and exhaled a long breath.

'I'm not shocked you're telling me this. I'm sure I would have heard from Portia if she was alive, even though my thoughts until now were that she'd left me. How was she murdered?'

'We don't know yet. I'm sorry but the body was in a decomposed state.' André said.

'I see. Is it the body you found in the desert?'

'Yes,' André answered, noting, but not unnerved by Meredith's polite directness.

'Are you sure?'

'I'm afraid the body is beyond recognition, but the DNA and dental records are a match. Do you have any idea why she might have ended up dead in the desert, Mr Meredith?'

'Shouldn't I be asking you? I hope you are not treating me as a suspect. You know I was overseas when she disappeared. When can I have the body for a funeral?'

The request surprised André. He became more defensive than he wanted to sound.

'I'm asking you about your wife because I assume you are concerned that she was murdered. If she had enemies, we

would expect you to know and want to help us find the killer.'
He paused before responding to Meredith's particular question.
'You'll need to speak to the Coroner's Office about releasing
your wife's body.'

'I *am* concerned about her death Detective Marshall. The desert
thing is incomprehensible to me. But I went through everything
I know with Detective Harvey when Portia disappeared.'

'Detective Sergeant Harvey was dealing with a missing
person. We now have a confirmed murder investigation and
I'll need to go through everything again … and more. Without
pre-judging anything, involvement in foul play cannot be ruled
out by being overseas. We'll need to account for everything you
were doing at the time.'

'That sounds precisely like you *are* treating me as a suspect.
Should I have my lawyer here?'

'That's your prerogative if we do a formal interview. The
purpose of this visit is to let you know about your wife. We
also need to warn you that your wife's name will be released to
the media tomorrow. You can expect the media to be on your
doorstep and you might want to take measures. Someone else
is letting Portia's mother know as we speak.'

Meredith sat thoughtfully silent.

'We'll also need to come to your office to gather details about
Mrs Meredith's and your affairs. I understand your wife is the
other Meredith of Meredith and Meredith Developments.'

Gave his development outfit a law-firm style name, André
thought. *Once a lawyer always a lawyer.*

'I'll have my lawyer there to help you with what you have
authorisation to be provided with.'

'We hope that doesn't mean we cannot rely on your co-
operation, Mr Meredith.'

'I said my lawyer would be there to *help*, Detective.'

André let the matter end and gave Deborah the ready-to-go look. Meredith picked up on it.

'All right then. If that's all for now Detective Marshall,' Meredith said in a tone a little too crisp. *Maybe we have succeeded in brushing a nerve or two,* André speculated in his mind.

'No. That's fine for now. And it's Detective Sergeant, by the way,' André said without showing umbrage, and stood to leave. 'Cracking view too, I have to say. Especially with that convenient gap in the mature trees.'

'Yes it is,' was all Meredith managed to answer with a deadpan glare. This time, André scored his own surprise hit. *How well the cap seems to fit* he reflected, despite having not known if a bothersome tree once stood between where they stood and the bay. It was a backhander André considered worthy of Meredith's blatant smarminess. He reached the door and turned back for a final ruffle.

'There is one other thing you should be able to clear up before we leave. You said earlier that, "*We've* got an espresso machine". Who is *we?*'

'My partner,' uttered Meredith with a slowed distrustful monotone.

'Their name is?'

'Eve Delmonte.'

'Did you know Ms Delmonte before Mrs Meredith went missing?'

Meredith glared before deciding if and how he would respond.

'Eve is a long-time colleague who also knew Portia. She has been supportive. We were supportive to each other when Portia went missing. She'll help me get through this too.'

'Right.'

Things came to a final end with a staccato exchange of looks between all three.

'Thanks for the coffee, Mr Meredith,' Deborah began and ended her contribution to the visit.

They observed the protocol of waiting until they were in the car.

'Guilty,' proclaimed André. 'You?'

'Guilty,' Deborah replied, pressing the ignition button.

'You'll have your work cut out, though,' she added.

'At least I've improved your stats — got Portia Meredith off the missing persons list.'

'We'll have to send you on holiday more often,' she laughed.

'Who is she then?' asked Ella.

'I've been told in no uncertain terms not to tell you. You'll have to come to the media conference in the morning.'

She paused, open mouthed, before announcing: 'Wow! What a splendid way to honour the trust and fulfilment we provide for each other. Why don't we wait until morning and hold our own media conference thingy the next time you'd like to visit this side of the bed.'

She rolled away and turned off the bedside light.

Ella and André sat apart on the couch in their loose house duds watching the late news. The head of John Meredith's lawyer protruded above a sea of lapping arms and hands holding microphones with media logos, mobile phones and micro-recorders. Platitudes spilled forth.

'Mr Meredith asked that his privacy be respected in this time of grieving. Mr Meredith is shocked to learn that his wife has been murdered. Mr Meredith hopes the police will do all they can … '

Footage followed, showing Meredith's black Mercedes driving into his Beaumaris home and the iron driveway gate rolling shut behind. The flash of someone's head behind the tinted window was unrecognisable. Footage of Meredith from the time of his wife's disappearance was re-used to show the man. The more recent footage of Wyperfeld National Park ran as the reporter's voiceover linked the two events.

Ella snapped to life with the excitement of seeing the familiar on screen. 'There's the information centre. And there's you beside the helicopter. You're on TV again.'

The footage hit a mellow nerve.

'It was good being up there … apart from the funeral … and finding a body. Wasn't it?'

André smiled back without revealing his relief that she was talking to him again.

'What's he like in person? He looks a bit larger than life to me.'

'He's got something, but I'd be careful about getting too close.'

'You think he did it?'

'I'm keeping an open mind.'

'You *do* think he did it, don't you?'

'Let me put it this way,' André said. 'You remember the *Spicks and Specks* TV quiz show that had the *Rock Star or Serial Killer* segment? The one where they show a photograph and contestants have to guess if that person is a rock star or serial killer?'

'Yeah.'

'Well. I don't think Meredith would be much of a singer or guitar player.'

'I don't think I'll be getting too close in any case. We tried for an interview and got nothing. I'm writing a full-page spread for the Saturday edition.'

'Didn't you hear his lawyer say he wanted his privacy respected?' André teased.

'I had to try. *You're* not telling me anything,' Ella said, reminding him that her sore point was still a sore point.

'He's got a new girlfriend,' André offered.

'Really? Does this mean I'm off the blacklist?'

'You've never been on my black list,' André said, moving closer on the couch to put his arm around her. 'But you're going to have to verify that info. I didn't tell you.'

'Who is she?'

'One of Meredith's employees. Eve Delmonte.'

'So, he would have known her before his wife disappeared,' Ella said.

'Goes without saying,' André shot back.

Ella frowned.

Chapter 11

'We're gonna have to dig a lot deeper because, right now, we've got nothing to grill Meredith about that Missing Persons didn't cover six months ago.'

André stood beside the link diagram. It still hadn't grown beyond the before-and-after photographs of Portia Meredith and a generic, light plane. He hesitated about where to place the photo of John Meredith that he was holding.

'He's screwing one of his employees. That's new,' Alex reminded André.

'Have you found out what Ms Delmonte does at Meredith and Meredith?'

'She's a project manager, mainly dealing with fitouts on commercial developments. It's a sizable part of the empire.'

'What do you mean empire? I thought Meredith and Meredith was a small outfit.'

'They are in the sense that there's less than a dozen permanent staff, but what they accomplish is substantial. All the technical and hands-on personnel they need are contracted in … architects, engineers, quantity surveyors. They have their favourites but there's plenty of consultant turnover nevertheless, especially on interstate jobs. Same with the construction outfits they use. They also form companies left, right and centre for different projects. There's big money flying around — plenty of opportunity to hide dodgy payments. If Meredith paid a hit man, there's a good chance a forensic accountant would never trace it.'

'Where are these projects?'

'Office blocks in and around town, some apartments complexes on the New South Wales coast and Lakes Entrance. Something in Adelaide.'

They stared at the link diagram.

'Have you seen Eve Delmonte yet?'

'I've seen her at Meredith's office but I haven't spoken to her. She's like a younger version of his dead wife.'

'Remind me about Portia's family in Sydney.'

'Father dead. Her mother, elderly and in a care home but still compos — power of attorney hasn't kicked in. No brothers or sisters. Portia came to Melbourne to work straight out of uni. Did legal work and met Meredith in the world of corporate-legal. Her father's business was sold after his death. That left the mother with plenty, including an almost-harbour-view house that is leased out. Plenty of money that I imagine won't be left to John Meredith. He's got his own hefty pile and he'll probably get Portia's share of their joint assets as well. Millions mate, although, you can't afford to let your guard down in his world, things can nosedive in no time flat.'

André had done his own bit of reading.

'From what I saw on the missing person file, the Merediths have few close friends, but can rustle up a decent crowd among their professional network,' he said.

'Pretty much. Portia's inner world was not particularly big,'

Alex confirmed.

That exhausted their intel. André studied the board, alternating between tapping his chin with the marker pen and chewing the end of it. The combination soon yielded a change.

'Okay,' he said, and began prising the photographs off the panel and erasing the few bits of text and arrows.

On the newly blank canvas, he drew three broadly spaced parallel black lines from one side of the board to the other. He placed Portia Meredith's photo alongside the top line, and John Meredith's against the second line.

'I want a photograph of Eve Delmonte here,' he said, tapping third line. 'Until something else throws up, we only look at these three bods.'

He then added vertical lines to create a table. The central vertical line was drawn in red.

'The red line is when she was reported missing. Either side of that are the four weeks prior and the four weeks after, with a separate timeline for the three of them. Laying it out in a grid like this might help us narrow the time-of-death-window that Sophie estimated, from weeks to days.'

Alex nodded.

'Witnesses won't be as reliable after this long, so we concentrate on all the hard data we can lay our hands on — phone records, bank cards, CCTV, toll use, security systems, social media, email — whatever we can get. Confirm everything. We get Zac and Sue to give us a hand. If any other suspects show up, we'll add a row.'

Satisfied with the plan, he asked Alex, 'What have we got so far?'

'The most obvious thing is John Meredith flying to London the week before she disappeared. His passport checks out.'

'Right,' André said and wrote "UK" on the John Meredith line — left of the red line.

'He spoke to Portia on the phone a couple of times during the first few days after he landed. Phone records tally. His calls started going to her voicemail for a day or two before he reported her missing.'

André made a note on the Portia line — also left of the red line.

'Anything else for Portia Meredith? What was she up to back here in Melbourne?'

'She drove him to the airport in her Beamer. Phone and cards stopped being used a few days later. Her hand bag, wallet, mobile phone, suitcase and some clothes were gone. Car still in the garage. He reported her missing five days after their final conversation. She's not on Facebook or Insta but Meredith and Meredith do have a corporate site.'

'Hmm. You better get all that onto an Excel version of this, with a more detailed breakup. Put the crucial bits up on the board.'

Alex nodded and added, 'Delmonte's a blank at this stage.'

'Let's interview her *after* we've spoken to Meredith again. Get what details you can about her movements in the meantime.'

André and Alex strode through the forecourt café umbrellas to the building foyer. The medium rise office block was set back from the St Kilda Road footpath. Its dark grey rendered exterior gave nothing away, other than the street number in shoulder-high stainless steel. The directory board in the foyer told them that Meredith and Meredith Developments resided on the third floor. They rode the lift with a girl holding a cardboard tray with four takeaway cups. Its doors parted to a blank third floor wall, save for a discreet sign directing them to the right. The coffees continued their upwards journey.

Their final hurdle was an electronically locked door to the glassed fronted foyer of Meredith and Meredith Developments. A softly lit stylised version of the company name stared back at them from the wall behind an unmanned inner reception desk. Well-tended indoor plants stood sentinel. Aubergine carpet showed how easily things can date in the chrome and glass world.

Alex had been before and knew the routine. André caught Alex's arm before he could press the buzzer and proceeded to read the long list of company names written in small frosted lettering on the side glass panel. The list was headed with the words *"Registered office of:"*. Most of the names were *"something"* properties, holdings or investments. Some had names that didn't look or sound like real words.

'Okay,' he eventually decided. Alex pressed the buzzer and they waited for a coolly groomed woman to appear from a door beside the reception desk. She led them to the oversized meeting-cum-interview room off the reception area.

'Take a seat and I'll get Mr Meredith. Tea or coffee?'

'Not for me thanks.'

'No thank you.'

The detectives sized up the view to the adjoining office building and took a side seat at the large beech table. The heavy swivel gas lift chairs tilted back when sat upon, conveying an instant feeling of importance to the sitter. André stood back up to be upright when Meredith entered. An all-white architectural model on a corner table caught his attention. André suspected the six-level building with curved front balconies was an apartment block designed to spoil some coastal hamlet.

'It's a dying art. These days, they model everything in electronic three-D,' Meredith told André as he entered the room. The bold hair, pristine white shirt and subtle grey silk tie reminded André how effortlessly he carried the weight of his success. His suit jacket had been left on the coat rack in his office.

'Can't beat something tactile, I imagine.' André replied.

'Depends who's going to look at it. That one didn't get out of the ground. It was meant for Lorne.'

'Bad luck.' André said, with barely concealed sarcasm.

'Not necessarily. We harnessed a reliable new investment source in the process.'

'Not a world I know much about,' André admitted.

'Then what can I tell you? I've already provided the information Detective Castellanos has asked for. Is this to be the formal interview? Should I get my lawyer?'

Meredith gestured for them to be re-seated and took what seemed like his accustomed place at the head of the table.

'No. This is still information gathering. We'd like to speak to staff members and we hope you can also fill a couple more gaps while we're at it.'

'Well let's see just how innocent this can be. Fire away.'

'Were you in a relationship with Ms Delmonte before your wife disappeared?'

André had taken a dive in the deep-end nonetheless. He was counting on Meredith's hubris to deal with the situation without playing the lawyer card — notwithstanding that Meredith was himself a lawyer, albeit in property. André counted on right, although a slight pause and tilt of the head from Meredith appeared to be recognition of the strategy. The contest was back on.

'We had a short affair,' Meredith delivered with calm.

'Had? How does that tally with you living with Ms Delmonte now?'

'It hasn't been a constant. The first time around, it ended about three months before Portia disappeared.'

André nodded.

'Did Mrs Meredith know about the affair?'

'You would need to ask her if you could. We never discussed it.'

'Can you tell me how it was then, Mr Meredith?' André asked with a wearied tone.

'I was reluctant to take the thing with Eve anywhere. I wasn't unhappily married. Portia and I had our moments but we shared a buzz running this business together. If you don't know this game, that might not sound like love, but it always stopped us drifting apart. To tell you the truth, I was more worried about hurting Eve. It might sound messy to you but there's no motive to be had. Of course, it would be a different matter if *I'd* been knocked off.'

André didn't know what Meredith was hinting at, so ignored the jibe.

'Portia was hands on then?'

'For certain projects. There were none current when she disappeared, though.'

'Your projects are far and wide I believe.'

'By and large they're in and around Melbourne. Some on the coast. The odd interstate job.'

'Did you and Ms Delmonte travel together?'

'Sometimes. Sometimes Portia and I travelled together. Sometimes Portia and Eve. Often, we travel alone or with the consultants we bring in. Our inner team is a lean operation.'

'Did Mrs Meredith ever have an affair?'

'If she did, she was discreet.'

'In the absence of a "no", I'll take that as a yes.'

'That's an unbased assumption, Sergeant — one I never made myself.'

'So, you're telling me you don't know if she was having an affair when she disappeared?'

'I'm saying it was not a habit she had. Nor I, for that matter.'

André's right brow involuntarily raised itself.

'When she went missing, you were asked if she had enemies. Any further thoughts in light of her murder?'

'I've asked myself that, to tell you the truth. There's nothing more I can come up with.'

It always amused André to hear people unthinkingly trot out the homily, "to tell you the truth", when they were being formally interviewed, or actually under oath.

'Surely you have business adversaries?'

'Of course. "If you want to make enemies, try to change something" — according to one former US president. That's our reality; we're developers. Collaterally, we're always turning somebody's world upside down. However, most of those things eventually blow over. And I must say, we also heed the maxim that we can learn from our enemies. It's a business where it's better that we make an agreement than an enemy. The only time I've seen it get really ugly is when companies go under. In fact, that happened to a corporate real estate firm that Portia was unwillingly involved with in Sydney. About a year ago.'

'Unwillingly? Can you tell me what happened?'

'Portia always looked after the projects we had in Sydney. It gave her a chance to see her mother. At the time we were using Pritchard's exclusively for our corporate real estate in Victoria.

Pritchard's franchised their name for an arm's length operator to set up a branch in Sydney. The franchisee assumed our contract with Pritchard's Melbourne office would automatically apply in Sydney. It didn't. We were careful about that because Portia had no intention of using them. She had a long-standing contract with CRK Property Consultants, an old Sydney firm with connections to her family. Pritchard's in Sydney nevertheless got their hands on the property details from their Melbourne parent office, who were free to field inquiries in Victoria, and began selling them off the plan. When Portia realised and did something about it, the Sydney operator ended up going under before he got off the ground. He ended up losing his home, reputation, everything.'

'And he blamed Portia?' André asked.

'He confronted her in a rage at her hotel. Threatened her in front of hotel reception staff and a couple of guests. The police were called. It really shook her up. She took out a restraining order against him. I'm surprised you haven't unearthed all this, or don't the states' police data bases talk to each other?'

The dig confirmed their sub-text battle. André shunned the bait.

'I'm sure we can extract it. Can you tell me the person's name, please?'

'Simon Stone. My PA, Ros, might still have his details in our system.'

'Thanks, Mr Meredith,' André nodded. 'Did Mrs Meredith leave a will and can you confirm that her share of the business will pass to you.'

'We are both lawyers by profession, so of course she had a will. I'm surprised you haven't asked about it already. Portia's will provides for her mother to have a modest percentage if she preceded her. I can confirm, however, that both our wills provided for the majority to go to each other, or any children we were yet to have. We also have a financial power of attorney for each other. There's nothing complicated about it.'

'I imagine you stand to gain a lot of money, Mr Meredith.'

'If that's supposed to be a question, I'll answer it by saying I already have a lot of money, and in any case, it's money we already shared, Detective Marshall … sorry. Detective Sergeant.' Meredith all but smiled his apology. André allowed a pause.

'When you reported Mrs Meredith missing, you told Missing Persons, she probably left you.'

'Yes.'

'Which is a far different scenario to what we're dealing with now.'

'Of course it is, but she had left me — un-intentionally as it now turns out — and that's all I knew at the time. In my mind, she must have learnt about me and Eve. For me, the affair wasn't without feelings of guilt and hurt, and the prospect of having to face her with whatever acrimony she might bear. I only allowed my thoughts to deal with what I thought the reality was.'

'And the fact that she never re-surfaced?' André asked.

'To be honest Sergeant, it was some months before my mind began to wonder and go to darker places. But by then, it was hard to shed the bitterness that had set in.'

'Because you thought she'd left you?'

'Mmm.'

'Mmm,' André responded in kind. He wasn't counting, but Meredith had just dismissed Portia's extended demise with a neat twenty-five-words-or-less kind of explanation. Hardly justification for promptly putting it all behind you and getting on with life, let alone the lack of curiosity or concern about what befell the wife he "wasn't unhappily" married to. Regardless, André decided he'd dug as deep as he should at that stage.

'As I said, we'd like to speak to staff members including Ms Delmonte. Do you mind if we stay here and use the meeting room?'

'You can use the room by all means, until a meeting that's scheduled for three o'clock. But Eve's in Adelaide.'

No loss, thought André. *You'll no doubt have your stories synchronised.*

'And by the way,' Meredith added, 'Eve is not pleased she's being dragged into this publicly. Nor am I. Do you know how that came about?'

'I'm afraid it is the least you can expect. The media are unbelievably resourceful.'

'And well connected,' added Meredith with a pointed glare.

So, he knows about Ella, André noted.

Eve Delmonte surprised them by coming to police headquarters to be interviewed. She no longer lived in her own apartment at Docklands as the Missing Persons records showed, and André supposed she did not want to be interviewed at Meredith's house or at the office. He only knew Portia Meredith from photographs but he judged Eve Delmonte to be more striking, and obviously reflective of John Meredith's similar taste in partners. Fewer years gave Eve the edge. Her face was the kind that makeup manufacturers like to use in print advertisements. A distant, unsmiling, flawless visage of impenetrableness.

Eve Delmonte arrived in a belted, dark grey overcoat that she removed to reveal a female business-version of John

Meredith. A black skirt and jacket. Not tight, but not so loose as to conceal curves. Dark stockings and heels, her white shirt worn with the collar out.

'We had a brief affair before Portia disappeared. It was never going to last. John was not unhappily married and I was racked with guilt because Portia is, was, a friend.'

Not unhappily married, the exact words Meredith used. *Too well rehearsed* André observed. He joined in playing their game.

'And you comforted each other when Portia disappeared?'

'Yes.'

The same brusque answering — *they were made for each other.* André exchanged a knowing look with Alex.

'When did you move in with Mr Meredith?'

'Three months ago.'

'Yours and Mr Meredith's phone records show constant contact in and out of office hours.'

André waited, finally lifting a brow for a response.

'Sorry. Was that a question?'

'It's conversation,' André shot back.

'We had an affair,' she delivered wearily. 'We work together. I imagine even you and Detective Castellanos phone each other from time to time.'

'Were you surprised to learn Mrs Meredith's body was found abandoned in the desert?'

'Flabbergasted. Like people who didn't even know her were.'

André noted that she did not question: *abandoned in the desert.*

'And apparently you were the last person to see Mrs Meredith before she disappeared. Now the last person to see her before she died.'

'Don't you mean the last person other than the killer?' she corrected him.

Chapter 12

'Tha's more like it,' Glenevis said, observing the crime board, now a busy collage of photographs and a spaghetti of arrows and notes in coloured marker pen. 'You boys ha' been busy. Tell me what it tells me.'

He took a chug of tea from his mug bearing the slogan, "If It Isn't Scottish, It's Crap" written in gothic font.

'You go Alex,' André said.

Instead of assuming a lecturer position beside the board, Alex remained seated, raised his arm to direct a laser-beam spot onto the board with a pencil-size pointer.

'Ooo, new toy,' Glenevis quipped.

'Portia Meredith,' Alex began, with the red dot hovering jerkily on her photograph. 'Nothing new there. Credit cards and mobile phone all go cold five or six days after John Meredith left the country. Before that, she drove him to the airport. Car detected on the tollway. Last photograph of her was from an ATM camera in Castlemaine, the weekend before he flew out. She and John Meredith had a weekend away. After that weekend, her credit card and phone use drop off a bit. And interestingly, not the pattern of previous months.'

'In what way?' Glenevis asked.

'Not her usual supermarket, different service station,' answered André. 'Not I'm-planning-to-get-killed behaviour, though. More I'm-planning-to-do-a-runner if anything.'

'Might she ha' left him? Was there anyone else on th' scene?'

'Not according to John Meredith and not that we've found. But one of the staff members was more suspicious of Portia having an affair than of John Meredith's liaison with Delmonte. We're working our way through Portia's phone records. Any regular calls to blokes appear to be genuine work stuff. There weren't too many of those however, she was between projects. If there was someone else it was well hidden and without smell.'

'Go back further an' also get onto tha' staff member who reckons Portia Meredith was playing aroond. Apply a bit o' pressure,' Glenevis said.

'We also need to speak to Simon Stone,' André said.

Alex laser-spotted the name written along the Portia Meredith line. 'He's the bankrupted Sydney estate agent that she took out an intervention order against. I spoke to the New South Wales coppers and read their report. It seems to have all come and gone with the dispute. But we're not discounting it, just concentrating on things closer to home at this stage.'

'What aboot Eve Delmonte? Missing Persons never looked at her,' Glenevis asked.

'She's a cool cat too,' André chipped in. 'In fact, I reckon the whole three of them are, were, whatever. She had a bit of an affair with Meredith but slickly explains it away. Now she's living with him. Nothing we haven't seen before, but the way they can describe it and dismiss it so clinically is just too … I dunno. It's like Grace Jones and Miles Davis were rooting each other and then broke up. Neither would be likely to admit it mattered to them. Only, in Meredith and Delmonte's case, they *have* ended up together. It did matter to them. I don't think it stacks up.'

'Pretty skinny stuff — nae matter who Grace Jones an' Miles Davis are,' Glenevis observed.

'Err … maybe that one *is* a bit obscure,' André shrugged.

'There's phone calls and texts between Eve and Portia. Maybe it was a three-way.' Alex said, directing the laser-dot to a note on the board. 'Eve Delmonte and John Meredith call and text each other at all hours too. She said it's work. Probably no more than we phone and text each other, as I was told. Her phone was oddly quiet the weekend the Merediths were away. Perhaps excluded from the threesome.'

'Or included,' added Glenevis. 'What did staff have ta say aboot the John Meredith an' Eve Delmonte thing?'

'Some admitted suspecting the affair but were reluctant to say so. I had to draw it out of them. Although they're a small close-knit team, I got the feeling they all go their own way out of hours. Other than Delmonte, as it turns out.'

'And John Meredith. Wha' did he have to say?' Glenevis asked.

'He threw up the least new stuff.' Alex said, switching the laser back on. 'He's still at pains to emphasize he was out of the country. Phone calls to and from his wife from London. He left messages on her voicemail until he realised she'd dropped off the radar. We tracked down the details of his and Portia's weekend break in Castlemaine.'

The red dot wobbled over the note that said "Ostler's Cottage".

'That's the Airbnb they stayed at, and it checks out too. Just the two of them, I'm afraid,' André added, spoiling Glenevis and Alex's salacious speculation. 'They dined on her card.'

'To be honest, Boss, the board's not telling us much at all,' André continued. 'There's a veneer here that we haven't cracked. We need to find out more about the Castlemaine weekend. Why are they having a cosy weekend away if she's about to leave him? How does that work?'

'Ah agree.' said Glenevis. 'And where's th' picture o' th' light plane you had up on th' board? Get tha' back up there. You need ta track down tha' flight — even if you figure oot who killed her. That's th' only way we'll ever link the killer ta her body.'

'Meredith and Meredith Developments regularly charter flights to places that are off the commercial routes,' Alex hastened to add. 'They use a company called Hyetts' Aviation, based at Moorabbin Airport.

'We're also going through air traffic control records for flights within cooee of the Mallee during the three months after she disappeared. Nothing so far, but its uncontrolled air space and lodging flight plans is not compulsory.'

'Wha' d'ya mean, uncontrolled air space? How the fook do they stop planes crashing into each other?' a bemused Glenevis asked.

'Maybe they have rear view mirrors,' Alex quipped.

It fired Glenevis up.

'I suggest you do more than check Hyetts' Aviation's records. Find out just how chummy they an' th' Merediths are. There're nae many businesses around tha' provide a service for jettisonin' dead bodies. Keep checkin' other operators too. Th' small aeroplane world cannae be tha' big.' He paused for thought. 'It wouldnae hurt ta ask our own air wing. Find out how they'd go aboot dropping a body from a plane. It cannae be an easy thing ta do.'

'What about the one you told me about. The body dropped from a helicopter in Glasgow. The one that landed at your local. Do you know how they went about it?'

'When did Ah tell you aboot that?'

'When I first phoned you about finding the body.'

'Oh yeah,' Glenevis said slowly, as the memory re-emerged. 'Well, we never found oot. They got away with tha' one. We thought they'd loaded th' wee chopper they used into a container lorry and we pounced on it heading south on the M6. But tha' were nae chopper in it. There's nae chopper wee enough to fit in a lorry. It were all staged as a decoy while the real one got away. They did their homework an' we fell for it. They dinnae get away th' next time, though.'

The room fell silent as Alex and André digested the yarn.

'Righto, Boss,' André said. 'I'll speak to the airwing. We've also had bean-counters looking at Meredith and Meredith's business. No shortage of suspicious money movement but more of interest to the tax office and the feds. Pandora Papers territory, or Operation Wickenby if you remember that far back. There's enough funds held offshore if untraceable remuneration was needed for a foul deed. A D&B credit report confirms the business is healthy enough. Plenty of moolah for both partners while they stayed together. The bean-counters also reminded us that it's an industry where cash flow stakes are high. Things can go downhill quickly if you get it wrong. If it did happen to go off the rails, Meredith has structured things to protect his own assets. Others would bear the brunt.'

'Charmin',' Glenevis noted. 'Wha' did you mean by "plenty of moolah for both partners while they stay together?"'

'The company is basically a partnership between John Meredith and Portia Meredith. If they fell out and one wanted to, or needed to buy the other out, neither would have had the capacity to do so.'

Silence signalled that their thoughts about the case were exhausted.

'What advice would Nonna Castellanos have to offer Aristotle?'

'I'd have to default to Socrates on this one. "The only true wisdom is in knowing you know nothing".'

'Well thanks for nothin', Socrates — literally. We already know we know fook all aboot nothin', an' fook all help that turns out ta be.' Glenevis said.

'At least we have some deep thinkers. The best your mob can throw up is Billy Connolly.'

'Well if Billy's genius is lost on ya, Ah'd recommend you give th' Clan Cameron motto a go: "Sons of the hounds, come hither and get flesh".'

André and Alex turned to each other in dismay.'

'Er, handy to know,' André offered.

Chapter 13

'Remind me why I'm here.'

"B-e-c-a-u-s-e … ' André stretched out into a filibustering drawl.

'Can you be a bit more specific, please?' Ella hustled him.

'Because you keep ignoring that which shouldn't be ignored.'

' … and a bit less esoteric.'

'Because this always ends up with you getting cranky at me whenever I mention it. As if it's somehow my fault that your long-lost sister landed on your doorstep.'

'She wasn't long-lost, she was long gone. Saying she was lost implies she has been missed. She wasn't.' Ella argued.

'See. You've got your back up and it's me copping it … again.'

She grabbed his arm and cosied up to atone as they walked into the café.

'Sorry "A". It's not your fault. I'll try to stop doing that. Okay?'

'Okay. Let's just have the conversation with her and take it from there.'

They were too early for bustle in North Melbourne's Auction Room Café — just as André had calculated when he chose the location. He already knew he could rely on the coffee. The urban legend was once dubbed Melbourne's best in the *Age Good Café Guide*.

Lila had sent him a text. She said she was staying in Melbourne and wanted to sit down and talk to Ella. Ella still didn't want Lila to have her phone number or address. It was not without some arm twisting from André that Ella acquiesced to the meeting, so long as Lila continued to go through André and they met elsewhere. Anywhere but at their flat.

The Auction Room Café was ideal neutral ground. Its twin vintage shopfronts offered plenty of space with plenty of spaces. If there were no suitably-private nooks on offer inside, the weather was fine enough to sit streetside. Plan B became surplus however when André pounced on an empty inside table where the front window met the side wall. With precisely three chairs, it was made for the job at hand.

They stuck with table water while waiting for their "companion" — André's choice of word to the waiter after a deliberating pause. It was Ella's first visit. She raised her head, checking out the décor. Chic fittings melded onto an un-fussily aged canvas — the adjoining shells of two classic buildings. Inside was dominated by the lack of ceilings and stripped back brickwork strewn with remnant render. Its chunky floor timbers were worthy of a road-bridge deck. Outside, the beyond-faded blue frontage wore a barely legible former signwriting job as a badge of honour. She began writing a review in her head: *Stellar inner city … contemporary urban … something like that.*
And then Lila arrived.

Greetings were low key. Both wore long-sleeved black tops

with a jacket and scarf. André noticed that they both noticed. Lila sat in the remaining empty chair, facing Ella. Before it could begin, small talk was cut off with the arrival of a young waitress. It never resumed after the waitress scurried from the tense-est coffee ordering of her short career.

André looked from one sister to the other to confirm neither intended to go first.

'Okay then. How about I get this show on the road?' he announced.

'Sure,' Lila said.

'Thanks, Lila. As you already know, I'm a copper working in homicide. I'm Melbourne born and bred and now I work in Melbourne. Outside of work, my obsession is adventure racing. Long distance trekking, running, kayaking, cycling, that sort of thing. It doesn't leave much time for anything else. That's how I met Ella, over three years ago. She's into it too, but that's her story to tell. We're partners now, so I'm a potential brother-in-law. What about you, Lila? How has your life turned out? What are you up to these days?'

He could feel Ella's scorn at him resorting to a trite professional training-course ice-breaker.

'Right,' Lila surmised, sensing the ice had in fact thickened. She pressed on regardless.

'These days I live in South Australia and I manage a winery in the Barossa Valley. Hence the van you saw me driving at Rosenfeld. Actually, I've been in South Australia ever since …' She looked at Ella. 'Since … you know, I left.

'One way or the other, I've been on the land all my working life. Well, *all* of my life, actually.' It came out as a self-realisation. 'I also have a few acres of my own over there where I grow organic wine. That's my obsession. That and playing bass guitar. I'm in a local roots-music band. I also have a partner of about three years. His name is Beau. He's in our band too. He's a winemaker but at a different winery. We're not married but we plan to one day. No kids. No surprise nieces or nephew yet I'm afraid, but we're talking about that too. In fact, we're trying. I'm older than you, Ella … you know … biology doesn't wait.'

'Oh,' Ella sounded taken aback that a new, frank and interesting life had just stepped out in front of her. She hadn't thought that far ahead.

Lila sat back. André put his hand on Ella's hand.

'Ella?'

'Sorry "A". I'm not playing that game. I'm not at work now. She knows where I was born and grew up, and now I'm a journalist in Melbourne. Why did you leave, Lila? Why didn't you ever come back? Not for Dad's funeral. Not for Mum's funeral. Why are you here now? As if I have to ask.'

She crossed her arms as she finished, then looked down and realised she'd instinctively crossed her arms in anger. She chose to leave them crossed.

André, as the self-appointed mediator, was suddenly obsolete. This was Ella's call. This was why they were here. Ella had cut to the chase. He, too, turned to Lila.

The moment had arrived and Lila knew. She looked at the table and gripped it, took an extra moment, then raised her eyes to Ella. She tried to say something, but it wouldn't come out. Tears began to well in her eyes and she tried again. Then it did come out, in a rush.

'Dad was abusing me.'

Her eyes dropped again and their table of three froze. Café clamour rushed in to fill their stunned silence. Babble, the clatter of cutlery being gathered, the milk frother shrieking, the growl of coffee being ground. A nearby door emitted an infinitesimally short squeak, just before it clunked itself shut.

'What?' Ella eventually asked, as if she hadn't understood the four words. Lila lifted her eyes from the table. 'No,' Ella followed up and gestured "no" with both hands. 'I know what you said. But … '

Lila and André let Ella find her thought.

'Did that happen and no one ever told me? Dad? Dad abused you? Even if he did, surely Mum knew.'

'She knew,' Lila said softly, looking at the table once again.

'What do you mean, "She knew"? She wouldn't have put up with that. She would have done something about it. What did she do about it? Did she report it? Did you report it?'

Lila looked up, registered Ella's accusatory glare, and struck back.

'She did something about it all right. She sent me to boarding school. The only time the police became involved was when I ran away, and it wasn't mentioned then either.'

The coffees arrived.

'Flat white?'

Ella turned her head sharply and transfixed her attention to the window. She let André and Lila direct the coffees and croissants to their rightful placings.

'Did it really happen? You weren't overreacting or anything?' Ella resumed.

Lila shook her head slowly and long.

'It happened. When he and I were out on the farm. The hay shed. The ute. One day he couldn't help himself. He went all the way. That was it. I was so scared I'd be pregnant. I couldn't stay. I was too young to have a licence but I'd been driving for yonks on the farm. It wasn't hard to find a car in Rainbow with the keys left in it. I was gone. That's how I ended up leaving.'

Ella turned back to the window. There were far too many thoughts to gather. André still had his hand on hers. He squeezed again but she was beyond tactile consciousness.

'You're telling me my dad wasn't who I thought he was. My mum wasn't who I thought she was. You aren't who I thought you were. In one fell swoop. That's my whole family. My whole fucking family … that I don't have a fucking clue about.'

Some nearby heads ate more determinedly to avoid turning to look. Ella turned back from the window to implore both of them.

'I'm thirty years old and now I suddenly find out I've spent all that time in some kind of bubble. How am I supposed to deal with that? Huh?'

'Would you really have wanted that burden though, Ella? Knowing about it wouldn't have made your life any easier or better. Having said that, now that you know, it's in your head for life. The best hope I can give you is: you learn to move on … in some respects.'

Ella was beyond being mollified.

'And Mum. Why didn't she confide in me? At least after Dad died. Why didn't she reach out to you then? I don't live under a rock, you know. I'm in the media and I see stories like this. I hear how some mothers can be conflicted, or be in denial or whatever. God, I've even written about it like I know stuff. But this is my mum. Couldn't you and her have sorted something out?'

The questioning disbelief stayed on her face.

'I don't know Ella. She didn't contact me after Dad died. At the time I assumed she was grieving, so I waited. And then … I don't know. Maybe because it had already become so unspeakable between us. In the end, neither of us reached out. But I'd thought about it again lately. Before she died. I thought I might be able to change that if I have a child. But now … '

Ella didn't reflect on Lila's "what if".

'I'm sorry I can't deal with this. Not Mum. Nor Dad for that matter. I was young when he died, but he has always been my hero.'

'I know, Ella. He was my hero too. I loved being on the farm with him, before he turned into what he became. I loved the farm. As weird as it sounds, I mourned losing him even before he died. And then I mourned not being on the farm any more as much as I mourned no longer being part of a family.'

Ella shook her head slowly and silently. Lila gathered herself.

'Look, I needed to tell you that and now I have. But I'm gonna go now. This will be so confusing for you. You might need to see a counsellor or something. I did, although not until later in life.'

Lila placed her hand on Ella's hand and Ella let her.

'I'll be in town for a few more days. So let me know if you want to see me again. If you want to ask me anything else. Anything. It would be good to talk, once you … you know.'

Lila rose to leave. She gave Ella one last touch on the shoulder.

'See you, André.'

André stood. 'Bye,' he said without otherwise acknowledging the situation. He too was stunned to quietness.

He resumed his seat as he watched her leave. 'She didn't drink her coffee,' he said out loud to himself. None of them had.

'Do you believe her?' Ella asked him.

'I think I do. Yeah. Do you?'

'Yes. Well maybe.' Ella said quietly, like she was confessing to a crime. 'In some ways it fits how things were. The sadness I'd see in Mum. She had a brave face, as you know — but there were other times, when people weren't around. I always put that down to her losing Vincent when he was a baby. He was before me. Then Dad dying, Lila running away … for good. Mum's life was not short on tragedy. How much worse that must have made her suffering?'

They both absently picked at the croissants as they pondered the question. André went to the counter and ordered fresh coffees.

'They don't have a whisky.' he told Ella. He'd actually asked. She ignored what he said as a comment.

'What am I supposed to do with this?' Ella repeated.

'Jesus, El. What can you do? Maybe … '

He drew a blank. She answered for him.

'What? Be civil? Befriend her on Facebook?'

'I suppose. Especially if you want to become Aunty Ella when her and Beau become pregnant.'

That sank in. Lila had given them a glimpse. Ella cocked her head to retrace their conversation.

'She does play bass in a band,' she weighed up.

'Maybe they're on YouTube. I should have asked her the name of the band,' André said.

An up side was coming out too easily — and too soon. It halted Ella in her tracks.

'Hang on. "A". I can't even think about playing happy families until I reconcile all the serious shit. That's if I want to reconcile it. If you haven't already forgotten, she just turned the family I thought I knew and loved on its head.'

André gave a helpless gesture.

'I dunno. It still feels like there's something else. We didn't talk about why she showed up. Why now, after she's had the past twenty years to do it? She avoided answering that question. There must be other stuff too. Heaps.'

'You couldn't have covered anything more today, El.'

'Maybe. Maybe not. All I know is that now, after she drops a bombshell like that and runs, I feel more alone than I ever have.'

Chapter 14

Any Australian pub named "The Commercial" has a built-in identity dilemma on its plate. In a domain where wonderfully-offbeat monikers have sprouted forever, it is an indictment on the country's history that a name as monumentally drab as "The Commercial Hotel" is so omnipresent. Laws must have been enacted to have one in every town. It can even be considered non-naming in the sense that every pub is innately "commercial" in any case. Every one of the 100-plus surviving Commercial Hotels in the nation represents an opportunity gone begging to wet one's whistle at a Hope and Anchor, a Loaded Dog, a Black Stump, a Hit or Miss, a Tasmanian Miss, a Bunyip — or if you were Inspector Glenevis, at Posie Nancie's in Glasgow.

The suburban Commercial Hotel midway between the Meredith and Meredith office and Charles Lyon's Templestowe home suffered an identity crisis greater than most. The classic, nineteenth century two-storey corner design battled its 1980s tacked on drive-through bottle shop to retain some gravitas among neighbouring low-rise shopfronts. The bottle-shop had recently lost its battle with the local Dan Murphy and transitioned to drive through coffee. Now it relied on customer reticence to leave their vehicle to overcome the pub's stark lack of coffee cred. The establishment's most enduring and attractive feature was the ornate glazed tiles wrapped around the lower street-side walls — ostensibly, so the piss could be hosed off after the stampede of drinkers eager to get as many beers in as possible, were compulsorily kicked out at six o'clock. The madness of Victoria's "six-o'clock swill" laws lasted until 1966.

The Commercial's battle to survive continued inside where Alex made his way through a dining room full of stained pine colonial chairs with spindly turned-legs. He found Charles Lyon in the bar, sitting on a window-bench stool. Alex took it to be Lyon's regular stop off point after a hard day at the office, although none of the evening regulars seemed to know him. He was drinking Coopers on tap and bought another for Alex.

'Cheers.'

'Cheers.'

Lyon had racked up at least sixty years on Earth and like the pub, was an aging blend. He wore a weary expression, a navy-blue suit of some years and a tie that had been on special with the shirt. The utilitarian business-wear belied someone still on top of their game, even if his best efforts were behind him. His grey-free black hair grew naturally into a 1950s style and his reddened elfin face bore a constantly alert expression. Charles Lyon appeared confident that he remained an asset to Meredith and Meredith Developments.

'You had a problem with me seeing you at work again. You're not a suspect, you know.'

'I should hope not. I want to be helpful but being seen having a long chat with you is not going to go down well with

John Meredith. Better that he thinks our ten-minute chat at the office was the beginning and end of it. I'm good at what I do but I don't want to be looking for another job at this stage of my life. I've been with M and Ms since they started. Not that it's always appreciated.'

'M and Ms?'

'It's what they're known as in the industry.'

'What do you mean: "not appreciated"? Aren't they a good company to work for?'

'Can I speak off the record?' Lyon asked.

'If you tell me anything, then I know. But I'm not writing anything down.'

Charles Lyon was not assuaged.

'I don't want Meredith to know I spoke to you again and I don't want to make another statement.'

'It might not be a problem, Mr Lyon, I only wanted to see what more you can tell me about Mrs Meredith. You hinted that she might have had an affair.'

'She did. And call me Charles, seeing that we're having a beer,' he justified. 'The affair was a couple of years ago. Her and James Hyetts.'

'Okay Charles, and it's Alex by the way.' Alex reciprocated. 'So, I presume James Hyetts belongs with Hyetts' Aviation?'

'You know about Hyetts?' Charles sounded surprised. Alex nodded and waited for Charles Lyon to continue.

'I'm not sure John Meredith ever knew about her affair for certain. I was probably the only person in a position to notice. Portia was pretty much working full time then and I was supporting her on most of her projects. One in Mount Gambier, another in New South Wales. They were all charter plane trips, and overnighters. You notice stuff when you're working that close. Dining as a group. Staying in the same hotels. The smug smile on Jimmy's face the next morning.'

'Did it have an end?'

'I don't know. I'm not sure how or if it ticked along after those particular projects ended. If it did, I was no longer close enough to see.'

'You said Mrs Meredith was working full time back then. I've been told that when she went missing, she hadn't been coming into the office because she was between projects.'

'I reckon she lost interest when the Eve Delmonte John Meredith thing began.'

'I thought that was a brief affair.'

'Brief affair? Is that what they told you? It never ended,' Lyon said, and not without some venom.

'How so?'

'Me and Eve Delmonte are the experienced project managers on the team. Trained professionals if you like.

'I've been with them since they began. I cut my teeth on office towers in the CBD, some early Docklands things. What Portia and John brought to the table back then was good noses for business opportunities — conceiving corporate property projects with strong institutional investor appeal. What they hadn't learnt however, was the complexities of delivering the actual projects on the ground, and the subtleties and cunning of construction companies, unions, and councils. That's where you need people who know what they're doing. Me and them worked hand in glove through those tough, formative years.

'Eve came later with a degree and a couple of years of doing apartment blocks with Belconnens. She's handy enough, but since her and John Meredith began rooting, the criteria for allocating projects is more to do with opportunities for them to be together. The crumbs fall my way. Take it from me. Their affair might not have been common knowledge until they shacked up, but that thing never stopped.'

'Another Coopers, Charles?'

'Thanks.'

Alex glanced at Charles Lyon from the bar as he waited for the beers to be poured. *Sour grapes coming home to roost. Was it that straightforward?* he speculated.

Alex sat the two schooners on the table and asked, 'Do you think Meredith killed his wife?'

Charles Lyon took the directness in his stride.

'No. I'm not saying that at all. John Meredith was in London when she went missing. We were dealing with him daily for the whole two weeks he was away. He was locking in investment for the Lorne project. Portia going missing became part of all that during the second week. He was noticeably unsettled in the Zoom conferences. So was Eve. Sounds twisted, doesn't it?'

'How is morale at the office? Is there any discussion about what happened?'

'When it was a disappearance, we were all supportive. M and Ms might not be a socialise-out-of-work kind of place, but we are still tight-knit. Now that it's a murder, no one knows how to feel. No one wants to believe John did it but I think some of the staff are reflecting uncomfortably on him and Eve becoming an item. She's even driving Portia's car now. That BMW Coupe was special to Portia. Her pride and joy. I reckon we're all experiencing delayed grief for Portia. The business is strong but the place will never be the same for most of us. I guess we will all be relieved if you can find out what happened.'

Alex could not hide the swagger of his entry to the office.

'To quote a fellow countryman, "Eureka",' he said, not without smugness.

André looked up from his screen. 'You were born here. You can't claim Archimedes as a countryman,' he said.

' … of Greek extraction, as you and Glenevis never cease to remind me.'

'Whatever. So, to what do we owe this euphoria of discovery?'

'I had a drink with Charles Lyon last night. The M and Ms project manager.'

'M and Ms? Is that what they call themselves?'

'Apparently it's how they're known in the industry. Anyway, one disgruntled employee injected with Coopers truth-serum has unearthed gold.'

'How so?'

'It appears that the John Meredith and Eve Delmonte affair never waned or ceased and Portia Meredith was probably aware of it. I'm not sure how that alters events but at least we know that they've been lying. And there's more.

'Portia Meredith was also having an affair a couple of years ago. Even more interesting is, she was shagging pilot James Hyetts of Hyetts' Aviation.'

'Portia Meredith and Hyetts' Aviation. An aircraft link. Now we *are* getting somewhere. Great work.'

'I thought that might sizzle your bacon, mate.'

'And why is Charles Lyon disgruntled?'

'Meredith started playing favourites when he and Delmonte began screwing.'

'Not just sour grapes from Lyon then?'

'A vinegar-vat full of sour grapes, but genuine nonetheless I'd say.'

'What messy lives people lead.'

'Keeps us in a job, though.'

The traffic was no heavier than you'd find in a country town when André and Alex drove into the nation's second busiest airport. That claim had everything to do with Moorabbin Airport's overall flight numbers. Had they relied instead on passenger numbers, it wouldn't have cracked the top fifty. The suburban small plane mecca's sheer volume of flights derived from flying lessons, charters, joy flights, aero clubs and helicopter businesses.

Commercial wonts of the twenty-first century was seeing the airstrip's once respectfully distanced ring of golf courses and commercial and industrial barns edging scarily onto the runway surrounds, as well as upwards into formerly hallowed air space.

Hyetts' Aviation office was in the old quarter of detached low-profile, flat-roof aviation premises amid the inner sanctum of perpetually mowed vastness. The building would have looked all of its fifty odd years had it not been for a recent makeover and updated corporate signage. Hyetts' logo was also splashed across the mini-bus parked out front. The crowning glory of the otherwise pedestrian building was its profusion of full-height windows. Most faced the runway and its apron crammed with small planes. The engrossing view could even be admired by looking right through the building from the carpark.

Inside, the reception area had been expanded to become a mini passenger lounge. The company's fleet of small aircraft featured in photographs mounted around the walls, along with pilots in epaulette-ed uniforms, gold braid and winged badges. James Hyetts' photograph was captioned *"James (Jimmy) Hyetts', Managing Director"*. André and Alex were surprised to see a man in his sixties, bearded with a full head of grey, fluffy hair in need of product, and half-rimless glasses. He arrived beside them before they had fully taken in his image. In person, Jimmy had the same reassuring pilot smile as his picture and the same short-sleeved white shirt with navy epaulettes. He ushered them to his office without discussion about why they were there.

'Sorry about the mess.'

With a compact printer beside his document-cluttered desk, Jimmy appeared to be doing more than his fair share to stave off the paperless office. The glass office front allowed him to enjoy a runway view. On the other side of his desk, his seated visitors had the pleasure of observing Jimmy's collection of framed certificates mounted on the wall. Among them, André noticed the logo of Ansett airline, a much-lamented Australian favourite before its inglorious descent into administration in 2002. Jimmy recognised the look.

'Ansett,' he acknowledged. 'Their demise was the best thing that happened to me. That's how all this began.'

'Uh huh,' André said, nodding.

Still the conversation failed to kick off. Jimmy had dragged a competent looking middle-aged woman away from reconciling a pile of documents and an Excel spread sheet. She took their order for teas.

'Thanks, Margaret.'

Margaret gave a quick smile and retreated.

Jimmy was ready to talk.

'I presume you came to see me about Portia. I've been thinking about contacting you.'

'Why is that?' André asked.

'I've been a close friend over the years, closer than many. The only reason I haven't contacted you is that I don't know what light I could shed on the matter.'

'Would I be right in saying you and Mrs Meredith have been more than close friends?'

'Someone's told you that? Is that why you've come to see me?'

'We're speaking to everyone who knew Mrs Meredith. When did you have a relationship with Mrs Meredith?' André persisted as the last traces of cheeriness evaporated.

'About two years ago. I was flying her and a couple of others to a job in Mount Gambier, every few weeks. We usually stayed overnight and it just happened. You know. Like a shipboard romance.'

'And were you seeing Mrs Meredith when she disappeared?'

'No. Well not like that. We tried to keep it going in Melbourne when the project ended, but it wasn't the same. We had our lives here. Partners we cared about. But we did have coffee from time to time. We talked.'

'So, you were on intimate talking terms with Mrs Meredith when she disappeared and you didn't speak to the police when they were looking for her? Don't you think you could have shed some light on her state of mind?'

'She had a husband who would know her state of mind better than I … and … who might not appreciate me presenting myself as an expert on the matter.'

'So, what's different now, Mr Hyetts?'

'It's a murder. She obviously hadn't simply taken herself off somewhere. There's a murderer to be found, isn't there?'

'Taken herself off somewhere?'

'That was my initial thought when she went missing. I don't wish to flatter myself but I think our fling opened her mind, or at least led her to question her own situation.'

'Can you tell me now how Mrs Meredith was, leading up to her disappearance please, Mr Hyetts?'

'Jimmy's fine,' he said, grudgingly.

'Okay, Jimmy.'

Alex added 'Jimmy' to the notes he was taking.

'Portia and I had coffee about three weeks before she disappeared. I think she had been troubled by the affair she was sure John was having with Eve Delmonte. I suppose you've found out about that. Portia and John were due to go away the following weekend, purportedly for together time. I think she was sceptical but not unwilling. The John and Eve thing had not been revealed or broached by her or John. Portia was still playing it straight, but she was far from settled. Others might not see that. She kept things close to her chest and was very considered in dealing with most situations.'

'And what about after that?'

'I called her after her weekend away. I left a message but never heard back from her before she disappeared.'

'What about John Meredith? What do you have to do with Mr Meredith?'

'Business mainly. The odd flight here and there.'

'You understand that Portia Meredith's body may have been dropped from a plane?'

'I can tell you, no one's that good a friend that I would do that for them,' he said with a look that veered from concern to vexed.

'What about your other pilots?'

'I'd be insulting them to even think about it.'

'We have to ask the question, Jimmy.' Saying *Jimmy* felt awkward to André.

'Look, I think I've been more than helpful. Is there anything else?'

'Not for now,' André said.

Margaret arrived with cups of tea and biscuits on a tray.

'Anyone for an Iced VoVo?'

This time André didn't wait to get in the car.

'I want every Hyetts' Aviation flight since Portia Meredith's disappearance checked against the records of whoever keeps flight records. Make sure every flight went to where they said it was going and there are no variations. If there's no confirmation of arrival for any flights we want to know why. We're not eliminating Jimmy.' He added with emphasis, 'Somebody flew a plane that the body was dropped from.'

'What are you going to do?' Alex asked.

'I'll be visiting the police air wing. Then I'm off to Sydney. As soon as the New South Wales police notification stuff can be organised.'

'Her mother?'

'And Simon Stone, if we can track him down.'

However many flight numbers Essendon airport lagged behind its fellow suburban strip at Moorabbin, it could still hang its hat on having once been Australia's second international airport. It nevertheless needed all the cachet it could get since Tullamarine took over Melbourne's international mantle in 1970. These days it was being taken back to its farm paddock roots with a re-badging to *Essendon Fields*. And it, too, faced creeping commercial encroachment of its runway fringes, along with an ensuing road network. André navigated it to the Police Air Wing hangars.

He was directed to Pilot Senior Constable Terry Jones who was fossicking around in a Leonardo AW139 helicopter parked on the hangar apron. The beefy senior constable with side hair buzzed to zero jumped out of the passenger door holding a clipboard.

'Detective Sergeant Marshall … André,' he clarified as he extended his hand. 'Big up close, aren't they?' he added as their hands locked.

'Senior Constable Jones, call me Terry. And yeah, the

Leonardos usually surprise people when they get this close. This one's about to head off on a targeted patrol, but *I'm* right to hang around and talk.'

'Thanks.' André said, and watched him dart over to a uniformed female pilot and female observer approaching the helicopter. He wrote details they gave him onto his clipboard and came back to André.

'I'm all yours now. Let's head inside, away from the noise.'

André stood his ground.

'Mind if I watch?' he said, keeping his eyes on the Leonardo.

Its rotors flopped into a slow turn that gradually became a blur. The whine rose to ever higher pitch for a good two minutes before the chopping sound of the blades signalled lift off. The helicopter rose to a bellied silhouette and drifted off at a forward angle as quickly as the eagle André had watched at Wyperfeld. He made the association in his mind and felt focused for the discussion.

'I suppose you've had a bit to do with these in your caper,' Terry yelled when hear-ability returned.

'We retrieved the body from Wyperfeld National Park in one that Parks Victoria organised — more of a workhorse unit to my eye. Other than that, I've never been close up or in one like this.'

'You should have said. They could have taken you for a quick spin.'

'Next time.'

Terry drifted into the hanger as they spoke. They headed to a couple of plastic chairs in deep shade beyond the shaft of intense daylight that pierced the hangar mouth. André's concentration battled the regular stream of planes coming and going between them and the horizon of suburban rooftops.

'Have you given any thought to how someone would go about dropping a body from a plane in the Mallee?' André began.

'It's no easy task,' Terry said, 'Even if you have the wherewithal. Just getting a body into an aeroplane without being seen could be difficult. Most airports are public places. It would be easier with a helicopter because you can put one down just about anywhere. Finding a helicopter pilot to do something like that wouldn't be easy, though. You'd have a better chance of finding a fixed-wing pilot. There's plenty of them. It's not like you need a university degree to get a licence. You can start learning when you're fourteen, you know?'

'Fourteen? You're kidding me.'

'Nah. Your killer might even have a pilot's licence. If he did it himself, or herself, it would be one less person to rely on to keep quiet. Although … ' Terry began to question himself, 'You would need a minimum of two people to do the job.'

André mulled Terry's response before asking his next question.

'There are private planes and airstrips around the countryside. Couldn't something like that be used? What about crop dusters, they seem to land in paddocks anywhere?'

'If they used a private setup, you'll have no hope of tracking it down through records. The pilot is not going to come forward. And what are his neighbours going to tell you? That Joe Blogs flew his plane like he always does.

'However, if you want some good news, you can cross crop duster off your list. They're usually single seaters with no room for a dead body and an extra person to do the chucking out. Crop dusters are also low wing. You need a high wing plane. One with the wing above the cabin. A clear space between the door and the ground.'

'Well, someone did it, so it must be do-able. How would you go a-b-o-u-t i-t?'

André tailed off as he asked. An engulfing combination of whine and hiss foreshadowed a Phenom 300 luxury business jet creeping down the runway that the hanger abutted. Terry plucked two pairs of protective earmuffs from nowhere and passed a pair to André. Nothing was said. They walked out of the hanger door to stand and watch.

The inspired eleven-seater creation made a U-turn on the spot and halted in front of them, facing the runway, ready. Cranking up to full power took under five seconds. The craft was unleashed and off the ground in a further fifteen.

'Fuck me,' André mouthed.

Terry laughed.

'They're something, aren't they?' he yelled.

'Fuck yeah. How fast is that?' André yelled back, rhetorically.

The rumble that followed it into the sky began to fade, enough to remove their ear muffs. Terry smiled and got back on track.

'If it was me, I'd use a helicopter. But like I said, I think you can probably rule that out. The Mallee is a long way off and you would have range and refuelling issues. A helicopter would also attract attention in that neck of the woods, whereas a light aircraft wouldn't rate a second glance.

'Me and my mate would hire a high wing Cessna. Something like a Cessna 172 would get you there and back from here or Moorabbin. We'd select the plane's departure location carefully, looking for somewhere to lift a body into the plane unnoticed. Somewhere we could drive our car right up to the plane to load luggage. It would take some daring, you know, a bit like

Weekend at Bernie's — with a plane. Actually, a lot like Weekend at Bernie's, with the dead body in the co-pilot seat. You'd choose a time when the least number of people are about. To load the body, I mean. A country airport might be the best fit for the job.'

'So you *have* thought a bit about it?'

'Yeah. And there's more.'

'Please … ' André encouraged.

'I'd have no hesitation in lodging a flight plan because we would be confident the body would never be found. More chance of the flight coming to somebody's attention if you flout aviation requirements. But then again, if you flew from a country airport, it's uncontrolled air space. You wouldn't be obliged to lodge a flight plan.'

'Shit,' André said. 'Way too many variables.'

'Dead right. But that's what you're dealing with.' Terry gave an apologetic grimace. 'When we got to the drop zone, I'd cut the throttle right back and bring it down below a thousand feet. Legally you can go to five-hundred. The less wind speed the better for opening the door. My mate would push the body out of the co-pilot seat. If I banked the plane, the body would probably topple out under its own weight. Close the door, job not quite done.'

'Not quite?' André's voice rose questioningly.

'I'd fly to my flight plan destination. You couldn't nominate the middle Wyperfeld National Park as your destination, but you would need to be flying somewhere. Somewhere in the vicinity, like Mildura say. That would be ideal and any variation from the flight plan would not be too noticeable,' he clarified.

'Fuck. What an undertaking.'

'It wouldn't be daunting for someone who knows that world, just well thought out.'

André nodded his appreciation at Terry's thoroughness.

Something distracted Terry. He had turned in the direction of the main passenger terminal.

'Have you got a bit of time? I can show you,' he said.

'Show me what?'

'Surf Flights have got a Cessna 172 over there. It looks like someone's packing it up for the day. Probably Justin. I can take you over for a close up and a bo-peep inside if you like.'

Terry was pointing to a flock of small planes further along the tarmac. They wandered over.

Justin was a thinner version of Terry — the same tight haircut and shades, but wearing the familiar white, short-sleeved commercial pilot shirt. He faced them and waited as they approached.

'What's happening, mate?' he asked Terry once they were in earshot.

Terry told him.

'I guess that'd be funny if it wasn't real. I've been reading about it … and thinking about it, to be honest,' Justin told André.

'Good. You'll be up for a bit of role play then.' Terry said. 'You can be the stiff.'

Justin and André smiled and wondered how Terry was going to handle this. He started with André.

'Imagine you've driven your car here to load your cases and stuff onto the plane. Justin is the dead body. All you have to do is lift him out of your car and into this co-pilot seat.'

He opened the door to the co-pilot seat.

'About waist height. It shouldn't be too difficult with a helper. As I said, your biggest problem is not being seen.'

The three of them stood in the shade of the red and white

Cessna's wing. They were the only souls in sight. They peered pensively at the beige vinyl pilot and co-pilot seats through the open cockpit door.

'The second person. The other live person,' Terry clarified, 'Sits in a back seat. When the time comes, they reach forward and un-clip the seat belt, open the door and push the body out. This wing strut is forward of the door,' he emphasised by tapping the strut he was leaning on. 'Nothing for the body to hit except the ground.'

André nodded gravely. Terry was less solemn.

'How much would you charge for a job like that, Justin?' he asked. He and Justin smiled.

'You're talking about my early retirement to the south of France. A four-bedroom villa perhaps.'

He was still smiling, and then his face lit up a level.

'I know. Let's do a practice run. If we can get this right, I'll add the service to our website.'

They all laughed.

'Now?' André said.

'Sure. I've got time if you have. My run to Albury has been cancelled. I can show you how an *expert* gets rid of a body.'

They'd simply been three blokes peering under a bonnet discussing how to fix the problem. Now, out of the blue, they were given a chance to get hands on. They jumped at it.

'You sit in the back,' Terry said to André. 'I'll be the stiff.'

André gazed below at the patchwork of vineyards in the Yarra Valley — each vineyard a slightly different shade of green. Terry peered at him around the headrest of the co-pilot seat and told him, 'You can drop me off here, thanks.'

'You like a red then?' André said loudly above the engine noise.

Terry smiled and nodded. He tapped Justin on the shoulder. Justin wore a pale green headset into which he occasionally spoke *delta foxtrot* and *thousand feet* jargon. He nodded back to Terry and cut the engine back to an easily talked-over level.

'Not yet, wait till he takes it down a bit,' Terry said to André.

Detail materialised slowly from the ground. Cars in front of a cellar door. Other coloured rectangles moved silently on slot car roads. The glider like lull was broken by howling air when Terry pushed the door open without warning.

Justin watched, smiling. He banked the plane with the opened doorway pointed earthward. André felt his body lean unwillingly towards the unobstructed Google Earth live view and instinctively braced himself on whatever his hands and legs could reach.

Terry shouted.

'Now all you need to do is unbuckle my seat belt and let me fall out. Give me a shove — if you need. Like a first-time skydiver that freezes.'

André's response came only when the plane was righted and the door re-closed.

'Gotcha. Too easy when you put it like that.'

Chapter 16

Manager Gilda Wynne strode down the hallway towards Shoaltide Rest Home reception area like Senator Michaelia Cash fronting up for an interview — right down to her swinging arms and sharp-cut trouser suit. Matron Gilda — as she probably would have preferred being called — may have been the only lanyard-wearing staff member not in carers' scrubs, but she wore her own one-of-a-kind uniform like a general. It almost prompted André to check whether lapels with pips had been added to the shoulders of her jacket. Instead, he concentrated on not dropping his jaw.

'Detective Sergeant Marshall,' she beamed. 'I was wondering if one of your number might pay Valerie a visit — and here you are. How good of you to come. Especially after we had to fight off the media last week. I'm sure that Valerie will take some comfort from you travelling all this way to see her.'

Her intense smile lingered.

'I hope so. It has after all become a murder investigation, so I do need to ask Mrs Sutton about Portia … and I'm sorry you had to deal with the media.'

'They got short shrift, never you mind,' she said with fervent pride.

Exceedingly short, André fancied — and nodded.

'We've taken Valerie to the music room. No one will bother you there. Come with me.'

She turned sharply on the spot and began marching back down the corridor. André took a skip to catch up.

'I love the building,' he offered as small talk — and meant it.

The ultra-modern fitout of an extensive former family residence belied the 1950s provenance still evident from the building's exterior. The high-hedged perimeter and well-established gardens also hinted at mid-twentieth century beginnings.

'You're in Walter Burley Griffin country in Castlecrag, detective. He designed the whole suburb with its bushland setting in the 1920s, as well as doing a lot of the initial homes. All of them were uniquely modern, even back then. Most of them still are — a century on. Sadly, our own building is not a Burley Griffin, but it was designed in the fifties by one of the modernist architects that paid homage to his Castlecrag vision. The extension however is a bit of a misfit.'

'He did houses too?' Andre responded. 'I only knew of Walter Burley Griffin as the American town planner who designed Canberra.'

'Oh yes. Here in Castlecrag, he did both. Sadly, in our own corner of the suburb, we don't have his trademark harbour view.'

It was about all they lacked, André observed as they made their way through an interior that could easily serve as a high-end boutique hotel. So far, only banisters along the corridor walls and a mission statement plaque hinted at its actual function: *Observance of moral and ethical boundaries conducive to residents.*

Gilda Wynne leant forward to swipe them into a deeper section of the home with her lanyard pass.

'To keep them in as well as keeping intruders out,' she smiled with the lassitude of an oft told joke.

The first sign of life appeared as they passed through a common room without windows. A handful of residents silently watched a home-cinema sized television showing an advertisement for an abdominal-reducing exercise apparatus, procurable with four easy instalments. Walking frames were parked beside each resident. A couple of the women turned their heads to offer coy smiles to André. Most viewers dressed in day clothes, one in a dressing gown, all in slippers.

When an unfamiliar smell began to permeate, André knew it would stay with him for life, lingering in his brain to trigger these images whenever his nostrils were to catch its waft again. What money would buy for his final years.

Manager Wynne paused outside the door to the music room.

'She's still very heartbroken. Try not to upset her.'

The music room resembled a piano bar without the bar. A black baby grand took pride of place among skilfully positioned lounge seating with low tables. As well as the missing bar, a few high-back electric recliner chairs scattered among the lounges also gave the game away. The room did however have a bank of full-height windows that looked onto the spray of a statue-ed fountain in the tranquil grounds. A half-played game of scrabble was laid out on one of the tables. *Perhaps my wait in reception was to hunt the other occupants out, resulting in a slow-motion walking frame race down the corridor* André mused.

Valerie Sutton sat on an upright chair at a table by the window with an untouched cup of black tea. Her thick silver hair sat aloft like an oversized 1950s Elvis quiff. Valerie's clothes sense was somehow the antithesis of Gilda Wynne. A gum leaf green cardigan and frilled shirt with a sensible skirt. Valerie, too, was slim like Gilda Wynne.

'Valerie, this is Detective Marshall.'

'How do you do? Mrs Sutton, and please call me André. I'm sorry about Portia and I'm sorry to have to talk to you about her today. Just say if you would like to take a break at any time.'

Valerie had already worked out what she wanted to say to André, and it didn't include small talk.

'Of course. I want you to do your job,' she told him determinedly.

'I'd like to ask you things about Portia that might help us with our investigation. Is that all right?'

'You won't have to investigate far. John Meredith killed her,' Valerie said in a clipped voice that matched her stoic posture.

'Take a seat Detective Marshall and would you like a cup of tea?' Gilda Wynne asked in a voice well practised in ignoring inmates' outbursts.

'Thank you,' André said and took the seat opposite Valerie.

'Why do you think John Meredith killed Portia?' he asked after Gilda Wynne had left the room.

'He's a cold fish. Always has been. According to Portia, his own brother and sister have disowned him. There's only one person he has time for and that's himself.'

'I see,' André said, sensing that useful clues or evidence might not be forthcoming.

'He came to see me after she disappeared, you know, smiling through gritted teeth when he realised he had to deal with me about Portia's affairs.'

'What did he need to deal with you about?'

'There were formalities for administering her affairs when she officially became a missing person. I sent him off to see my lawyers about all that. They told me he already had Power of Attorney and there'd be no point in taking issue. They did, however, advise me to change my own will so that Portia's inheritance would only go to her if she was found alive — otherwise it could end up passing on to John Meredith at some point down the track. I can tell you he won't be getting a cent of the Sutton money when I go.'

André was pleased to observe that Valerie had her wits about her. Relieved that she was miles from any sign of dementia.

'Does John Meredith know you changed your will?'

'He certainly does. I took great delight in telling him. I'm only sorry Portia didn't change *her* will when she spoke about re-doing it.'

'She spoke to you about changing her will? Did she say why?'

'She never tells me details like that. But something John said, or did, had upset her before she came to Sydney. That was about a year ago. I knew something was up when she told me she was having lunch with Rachael.'

'Who is Rachael?'

'Rachael Martin, she's Portia's best friend from uni days, she's a lawyer too. I'm pretty sure Portia was catching up with her to pick her brain about the will.'

André could see a rabbit hole presenting itself.

'I'd like to speak to Rachael if I could. Do you have her number?'

'No, I don't. But she works with Millar Comyn McPherson in the city.'

Valerie seemed satisfied that she had told André what she had, and that he would be taking the matter further. She un-stiffened enough to take a sip of her tea.

'Thanks, I'll chase that up,' he said. 'I know you've been asked this before, but can you tell me how Portia was the last time you spoke?'

A pained silence fell as Valerie's lips began to quiver.

'We didn't speak,' she said, but couldn't go on without sobbing.

'It's all my fault. I should have called her,' she finally blurted and buried her nose in a hanky.

The sobbing slowly lessened.

'I know it's hard, but you can't blame yourself, Mrs Sutton,' André said, putting his teacup down and standing to comfort her with a hand on the shoulder.

'You don't understand,' she said jerkily. The words and breathing competed with her sobs. 'Portia's last call came while the home had its afternoon nap. She called the landline and the girl at the front counter took the message. Portia knows not to call me then. It made me angry and I refused to call her back. If I had … maybe she knew she was in danger … '

The sobbing erupted again.

'Please don't blame yourself, Mrs Sutton. If Portia thought she was in danger she would have come to the police. You know that. Let us find out what really happened. There might be aspects … things that can put your mind at ease.'

'I'll never be at ease. Not now.'

Another silence settled, save for Valerie's sniffing. André sat back down and let it subside.

'Tell me how Portia was when you did speak to her.'

'She would always phone me on Saturday afternoon, after nap time. She and John were having a long weekend away at Castlemaine. She mainly chit-chatted about where she had lunch, the market she went to. I probably prattled on about who was displeasing me most at this place.'

Gilda Wynne re-appeared.

'Not you, Gilda,' she was quick to add. André couldn't tell if her clarification was made in fear or sincerity.

'I knew this would upset you,' she said when she saw Valerie's distressed face.

'It's to do with the phone call, isn't it? She can't be consoled when she starts going on about the phone call,' Gilda said — as if Valerie was not in the room. 'Let's hope Detective Marshall can get to the bottom of it, eh?' Now speaking as if André was absent.

'Shall I get nurse to run you a bath then?' she said.

Something for me to look forward to, André thought — *being bathed by someone else — again.*

'What do you know about the phone mix-up?' André asked Gilda Wynne as she escorted him back to the reception area.

'There was no mix-up.' she clipped defensively. 'Portia called at two-ten, which is during our nap time. The receptionist took the message and told Valerie. Valerie did not return the call because she was miffed. It was most unusual. Portia knew our routine and she never got it wrong. Valerie thought Portia did it on purpose. I'm afraid the aged mind can dwell too much on the merest trifles. It's the bane of our lives here.'

'A set nap time for everyone sounds unusual in this day and age.'

'Shoaltide Rest Home has been having nap time between one o'clock and two-thirty since it began in 1971. Even those who insist on having mobile phones are required to observe nap-time. We might have a modern setup but our practices are traditional and that's exactly how our guests like it. If you end up here late in life, Detective Sergeant Marshall, then I can assure you that you will be enjoying nap time every day.'

André felt a shudder at his core.

'Here's my card, Ms Wynne. Please let Mrs Sutton call me if she wants to know how we're getting on. I'll try and call too, after two-thirty.'

Chapter 17

'Do you miss me?'

'Yeah. It's bin night,' Ella said into her phone.

'And that's what you miss most about me?'

'Pretty much. Last night I got to hold the remote in my own hand. I even figured out how to use it. So, I can cross that off my bucket list.'

'All right. You could try and cheer me up after the day I've had,' André said as he sat on the hotel bed, flicking between channels with the mute on.

'Why should I? I'll bet you're using the remote control as we speak.'

He dropped it and announced, 'I can honestly say I'm not. I'm just pondering the mini-bar list and a page of pouting escorts I have to choose from.'

'Oh-yeah? So why did you choose me to phone?'

'I miss you even if you won't admit that you miss me.'

'I miss you too,' Ella said with mock emphasis. *'Why was your day so bad?'*

'I finished in time to try running some of the City to Surf

course and I got lost. Earlier in the day when I saw Portia Meredith's mum, I brought her to tears. And now I have to stay an extra night to meet with one of Portia's school friends. I think I do need to hit the mini-bar.'

'What happened with Portia Meredith's mum?'

André told her.

'That's not right,' Ella said. *'Portia phoning the receptionist when she knows her mum can't take the call. Women don't get things like that wrong. A bloke might, but not a woman. She must have done it on purpose for some reason.'*

André mulled the sentiment. None of it made sense.

'Why would she do that on purpose? Even if she did, it doesn't mean someone was going to kill her.'

'You're the detective, but I don't think it's insignificant.'

'Thanks for making the fog thicker.'

'I don't think you need my help. How did *you get lost on the City to Surf course? I've run that a few times before I met you. Where did you go wrong?'*

'Somewhere near Vaucluse. I know you've done the run too but that would have been on a race-day when you simply follow the crowd. It's different in normal traffic. I was also tackling it from Surf to City which made everything look different. I ended up returning to Bondi and doing the run to Bronte and back.'

'So where are you off to tomorrow?'

'Camden. About sixty ks southwest. These days, Simon Stone hangs out at an airfield down there.'

'Another airfield, eh?'

Ella's lapse to nonchalance gave André pause.

'You haven't asked me who Simon Stone is. Or where all this is headed, or what developments you could write about.

Are you okay?'

He thought the phone call had gone dead.

'Are you there, El?'

'I'm here,' she said quietly.

'What's wrong, El?'

There was another pause. This time he knew to wait.

'I can't get her out of my mind, "A". It's all I've been thinking about. I can hardly string two words together on the screen at work. I'm scared I'm losing it. I have to see her again. There's too much I need to know.'

'Oh.'

'I've arranged for her to come round here before she leaves Melbourne. Before you get back. Just her and me.'

'Oh.'

'Is that all you can say?'

'No. It's just … '

Whatever "just" was, wasn't coming out.

'Just what?' she demanded.

'I'm just surprised. I didn't see that coming. Not after you were so stand-offish when we met her. How did you get her number?'

'It was on her van when she first showed up at Rosenfeld. I put it in my contacts then.'

André thought aloud. 'All this time, you were saying one thing and doing … You know, if I thought about it, I would have realised it'd be on your radar somewhere down the track. But not this soon. But … that's good. All good … at least that's what I reckon.'

'Yeah. Well, we'll see.'

'So, she's coming round there then?'

'Yeah. I'm not doing a meal or anything. I just need to talk to her without being in a public setting.'

'Uh huh.'

'Uh huh?'

'I mean yeah. That sounds good too. Will you be having a drink? Does she drink?'

'She manages a winery. What do you reckon?'

Another silence landed. The phone call had come 180 degrees.

'Are you okay, "A"?'

Airfield panorama was becoming way too familiar, even the tea room within a hangar. From its inner shade, André gazed once again to a mega-door vista of flatness. The occasional student aircraft took off or approached with wings tilting this way and that into a tentative landing.

Simon Stone had not shed the confident look of a real estate operator, even though the role had shed him. Grey hair had been kept at bay into his early fifties, in spite of his bankruptcy. Although he eschewed the obligatory epaulet-ed shirt, a set of wings on his plastic name tag divulged his current vocation.

'The body in the desert made the news in *Sydney*. But I didn't know it was Portia Meredith until you told me now,' he told André.

'The body was dropped from the air. Probably a light plane.'

'And that brings you here?'

'No, funnily enough. Not you being a pilot. Not initially. You became a person of interest because of the intervention order Portia Meredith took out against you.'

'This isn't a good look then, is it?' Stone admitted, rolling his eyes towards the tarmac. 'But I didn't kill her. The episode I had with her was a one off. I've moved on since then.'

'How can we be sure of that?' André asked.

'I got shat on by everyone, not just Portia Meredith. Pritchards were just as much at fault. I assume you know they were the commercial real estate group in Melbourne that I agreed to franchise in Sydney. I was actually doing them a favour. Using my networks to give them their first foothold in the market up here. Pritchards were the ones who believed that the contract they had with M and Ms in Melbourne was universal — that it would also apply to M and Ms Sydney properties. I wasn't acting off my own bat. It was Pritchards head office that set me up to sell M and Ms new Sydney apartments off the plan. How else could I have completed transactions like that? It was supposed to be their kick-starter for the franchise.

'When Portia pulled the plug on that, Pritchards didn't have the guts or the will to challenge them. John Meredith was a sharp corporate lawyer in his pre-developer life. He wrote the book on that stuff. He dug up a mountain of fine print and went gung ho. He had to because Portia had already signed up her Sydney mates to manage the sales.

'I was Pritchard's first foray into franchising their name. It wasn't the auspicious start they had hoped for, so they cut their losses before their name could be dragged into the mire. I was disposable. A write-off, literally and literally.

'They poached me from Latimer-Rydge at the peak of my powers. When they pulled the rug, I'd already entered a lease for new office premises and fitted them out … as well as forking out for the franchise and all the other establishment costs. Pritchards did some money too, you know. They lost their only chance to expand to Sydney. A lot of old-money

Sydney people saw what was going down, and the shutters went up. But the way they so willingly snuffed me out allowed Pritchards to keep their Melbourne contract with M and Ms. That's why they survived there. I, on the other hand, never stood a chance. You probably know, I lost everything. My home, my reputation, then my family a bit later.'

'Plenty to be angry about then,' André said.

'Yeah. And I did get angry. It's all on the record. I released that anger though, admittedly to my peril, but I'm not a brooder. The court sent me on an anger management course. I can give you my counsellor's details. They'll tell you where my head is at. The only time I feel remotely angry is when I talk about it like this and have to re-live it.'

Simon Stone had finished making his case and reached for his cup of coffee — instant, and now cold. André wasn't ready to acknowledge how convincing it sounded.

'So, what are you doing here?' he asked.

'The one thing I didn't lose was my pilot's licence. I've known Greg, who runs Nepean River Flying School, since we did flying training together. We both joined the same flying club after we got our licences. He chased flying work around Australia and eventually started his own business here. Greg gives me work as an instructor and doing joy flights. He can do me a bit of cash in hand too, which helps in my situation. He's been a real friend when I needed one.'

'I hope his flight records are not so casual. We'll be seeking details of everything you've done since Portia Meredith disappeared.'

'Check away, I've got nothing to hide.'

André found Rachael Martin at the pinnacle of the Sydney legal world, physically if not metaphorically. Millar Comyn McPherson had set up camp on the forty-fifth level of a shiny tower in Phillip Street. Other legal firms may have occupied skyscraper floors closer to the sun, but that seemed a moot point to André as he gazed down upon roofs of lesser towers and the icon fringed harbour beyond.

He had navigated there in the manner of a tourist. First enjoying a ferry ride and then negotiating Sydney's CBD street canyons via Google Map on his phone. The maze of express lifts travelling to various batches of levels within the skyscraper challenged him further.

The firm's upscale waiting area of marble and French inspired timber-trimmed tub chairs could not be fully appreciated before André was led to the harbour-view meeting room with leather-topped table and bold mono-print wallpaper. The receptionist offered him café-style choices of tea or coffee. His flat white was delivered with a European sparkling mineral water for the yet-to-arrive Rachael. The fashion-runway coolness of the receptionist had him expecting Wonder Woman lawyer.

Wonder Woman failed to emerge. Instead, a version of her secret civilian persona arrived — Rachael Martin, wearing an unassuming mid-length red woollen cardigan over her usual lawyer-busting regalia of a black pencil skirt and white long-sleeved blouse.

The dressing down touch, if that's what it was, worked. It came with an engaging smile and handshake that definitely belonged to comfy-cardigan-Rachael. André felt his face ease.

They took seats across the corner of the table. Rachael allowed André to have the view.

'Thanks for seeing me on short notice,' he said.

'I'm pleased you came. I've been half thinking about contacting the Victorian police since Portia was found.'

It was becoming a mantra amongst those he interviewed.

'Not when she went missing?' he found himself saying to yet another interviewee.

'Then too, I suppose. But I'm in Sydney. It isn't as easy as popping down to the local cop shop, and I doubted I could offer much in any case. *Is* there some way I can help?'

Rachael's business card told André she was a senior associate specialising in property and infrastructure. With fine dark hair placed delicately behind each ear and a quizzical tilt of her head, André imaged her and Portia prizing each other's secrets since they roamed the schoolyard together. He was counting on it.

'Yes. Mrs Sutton told me that Portia may have spoken to you about changing her will.'

'That happened when we had lunch about a year ago. Portia often contacted me when work brought her to Sydney. We'd do lunch if we could. Totally personal, our professional lives never overlapped. It was almost like talking shop was a no-go zone for us. And with Portia also being a qualified lawyer, and married to a lawyer, it's not like she'd seek professional advice from me. She's also smart enough not to do business with friends.

'On that day however, which was the last time we saw each other, I do recall her straying into what was an untrodden territory for us — legal stuff.'

André raised an eyebrow.

'Strictly hypothetically,' she quickly justified to André's eyebrow. 'Or that's how it began. By the end of our discussion, it was pretty thinly veiled. I was definitely a sounding board.'

'Do you remember specifically what she asked?'

'The things that concerned me most were about her will.

Mrs Sutton was right about that. Portia wanted to compare notes about the mechanics of how a new will revokes an existing will. She already had a will that John had prepared. She wanted to clarify whether the law required John to be informed if she had a new will.'

'But she didn't ask you to prepare a new will for her?'

'No. That would never happen. But I know Portia and I could tell that she was in gathering mode, assembling facts in her mind. She is a very considered person and I would not have expected her to decide or act at that stage.'

'But I assume you were curious?'

'Oh yes. I grilled her as much as I could. She was obviously considering the possibility of no longer being with John. The will was only part of it. She was workshopping how she might extract herself from the business, although, she didn't mention divorce. Not specifically.'

'Perhaps she considered the legalities around divorce to be common knowledge,' André suggested.

'Maybe. She focussed on the business side of things, including how difficult it would be to set up her own operation in Sydney.'

'She mentioned coming back to Sydney?' André asked eagerly. Rachael realised how loaded her statement must seem to a Homicide detective.

'It wasn't as cut and dried as I'm making it sound. It was more a case of her thinking out loud. By the end of the meal, we did get down to some girly tin tacks. She told me she had had a brief affair and it caused her to question her own marriage. She suspected John had not always been faithful, but she nevertheless considered their relationship was not necessarily a lost cause, for no less reason than their stimulating business bond. Despite the situation, she still took a lot pride in what they'd built together.'

Rachael lifted her head in a vacant gaze, assembling her own thoughts for summary.

'She had some serious things bubbling below the surface and no simple solutions staring her in the face. But I don't think Portia was hellbent on action. Not at that stage.'

'And what did you think when she disappeared?'

'I didn't know she had disappeared until a long time afterwards. My first impression was that she had left John.'

'And now that she's dead?'

'I'm gobsmacked of course, but what doesn't surprise me is that she was dropped from an aeroplane. She and John have been mixing in flying circles since they first knew each other. It won't be a stranger who did this.'

Lila brought wine, a whole case resting at her feet. That's where Ella's eye fell when she opened the door.

She lifted her gobsmacked face.

'I took you for a white drinker,' Lila said. ' … and I brought you these.'

She held her hands out with flowers. Ella's eyes dropped again to take in the flowers. Roses, in a compact bouquet. No florist's filler of baby's breath. Just a simple mixture of white, pale pink and apricot roses. Just as their mother would pick each summer for the dining room table at Rosenfeld.

Ella's plan to remain cool — at least for now — was challenged. She rallied nonetheless and took the roses nonchalantly.

'Thank you. Come in. I'll find a vase.'

She left Lila to pick up the case of wine and find her way to the living area of the modern second-storey apartment. She plonked the box on the end of the marble-look benchtop. Ella already had a vase out. She was filling it with water at the other end of the bench.

'This is a semillon sauvignon blanc. It's not what we're

famous for — or even grow ourselves, but we manage to source some choice grapes from smaller vineyards in the area. It's another arrow in our quiver.'

'Hmm,' Ella said as she teased the roses into shape.

The tension had Lila prattling. 'To be honest, it's not pure Barossa. There's a bit of Adelaide Hills in there too. That's why I'm in Melbourne. For the winery I manage … which I think I mentioned when we met in the cafe. I've been over here selling it into specialty wine shops. We don't do the likes of Dan Murphy. You probably don't know the label.'

Ella gave Lila a glance and placed the vase between them in the centre of the bench. She stood back and looked, gave the vase a final quarter turn, then faced Lila again.

'There. They look nice, don't you think. Thank you, Lila.'

'Glad you like them.'

Lila opened the box and took out two bottles.

'I chilled these two. Would you like a drop now?'

'I'll get some glasses. Take a seat.'

Ella nodded towards the black wooden table and chairs between the bench and the lounge area. Ella's own smaller vase of flowers graced the table. Natives with a couple of proteas.

'Oh. They're nice too, Ella.'

'Thanks.'

'I like your apartment too.'

Ella gave an acknowledging smile of pride. Her sole disappointment in the flat was their second-floor vista of suburban rooftops. But it was night time and Hampton's lights twinkled magically through the glass doors opening onto a deck.

'Do you own it?'

'André and I bought it not long ago. He grew up near here.'

'I guess that was a serious step for you both to take.'

'I suppose.'

Nothing was being given away. She placed two wine glasses on the bench and picked up one of the two chilled bottles.

'Neu Hass Winery,' she observed out loud. There was a note of wonder in her voice, a question that had been on her lips since she first saw the name on the van at Rosenfeld. 'Are they the same … ?'

She didn't have to say more. Her and Lila were three generations on from the surname of Hass and the story of their great grandparents Conrad and Zelda Hass's journey from the Barossa to establish Rosenfeld was family legend.

'They are. Probably not that-distant relations.'

'And do they know who you … ?'

It was another sentence she didn't need to complete.

'No. I've never told them. They employed me without knowing.'

There was a silence as Ella poured the wine. The silence became louder as she handed Lila her glass and sat down.

'To … ?' Lila prompted.

'To Mum,' Ella responded quickly.

'To Mum then.'

Ella wondered if Lila was accepting her choice of toast without necessarily agreeing.

Clink.

They both sipped and sat back in their chairs. The moment they both wanted so much had arrived.

Lila broke the ice.

'So. You want to know everything?'

'If that's all right with you.'

Ella took more than a sip of the semillon sauvignon blanc as soon as she said it.

'That's all right by me. But you have to take on board that I've never told anyone before. I haven't even told Beau, and we're talking about having kids. So, this is hard for me. I've got no idea about how well it's going to come out, even though I've been thinking about it for days. But …' she paused to emphasise what she was about to say. 'Right now, there's nothing more important to me in the world.'

This time Lila took more than a sip. Ella waited, not knowing if she should respond. Lila took yet another bracing breath, and started.

'Before he, Dad, started it all, I used to love the farm and doing farm stuff with him. I really loved it, you know … '

She stopped herself and held her hands out to gesticulated a "no".

'I've already told you that. Let me start again.

'Back then, while I was still at school, you would have been too young to know, and too young for me to share it with you — even if I wanted to — but me and Bevan Grant had sex. It was back when Lake Albacutya had water in it, which you probably do remember. A lot of us would camp out there in the summer holidays. It was so idyllic with its sandy beach and shady gums. At our age, we took it for granted that it would always be there — full of water. Anyway, it wasn't hard for Bevan and me to end up in a tent together, even with the odd adult coming and going to keep an eye on the group.'

She saw the look on Ella's face.

'Hey. Don't judge me for that. You grew up there. You know that can happen. There's usually someone you know who is first to "do it". In my time, it was your sister. Anyway. The reason I'm telling you now is because Dad suspected and he made me tell him. After that, he couldn't constrain himself. He somehow felt … entitled. Entitled to go all the way I mean. He'd already been taking advantage of me, doing other stuff, you know. By that stage, I reckon Mum would've had to know.

'I began making excuses to not go with him. On the farm I mean. And when I couldn't get out of it, I couldn't look her in the eye when I came home. That's when she must have got her way and I was sent to boarding school in Adelaide. It wasn't his decision but I don't think he would have dared argue against it in any case. He would have suspected why she wanted me to go to boarding school. If he pushed back, it might have forced her to unleash the genie from the bottle and I don't think either of them could face that conversation. It was a pretty moot situation in any case. Boarding school merely gave me respite during school terms.'

She paused to take another drink. Ella remained solemn faced.

'As I said, it happened that summer when Bevan and me were spending time at the lake. That's when he, Dad, forced me to go all the way. No protection like Bevan and me used. And that's when I took off. As soon as I got home, I was out of there. The car I took was Bevan's brother's Mitsubishi Magna. He would drive us out to the lake sometimes and I knew he usually left the keys in it. You know what people are like in the country. He probably figured out it was me that stole his car when word got out that I had shot through. But I don't think he ever said. Maybe other people in town figured out what was going on. I dunno.'

She stopped again to drink.

'Where did you go?' Ella asked. It was her first buy in and that didn't go unnoticed. Story telling became a little easier for Lila.

'I went to Adelaide. I was heading to my boarding school friend's home, Alysha McGuinn. They lived at Clare — more than 100ks north of Adelaide. For most of the trip, I was shitting myself that I'd be pulled up by the cops for driving underage and without a licence. I don't think it occurred to me that I was committing the even greater crime of stealing a car.

'When I reached Adelaide, I left the Magna with the keys in it and took a bus to Alysha's. I had stayed there during a term break and I knew the drill. I don't know if Bevan's brother ever got his car back.'

'I wouldn't worry about that. Last I heard was, he runs pubs down on the surf coast.'

Lila smiled quickly.

'They tracked me down, of course. I'm not sure if it was with help from the local cop or if Mrs McGuinn wanted to let Mum know.'

She paused as she topped up both their glasses.

'So why didn't they bring you home?'

'They couldn't do that. Not legally. Not if I didn't want to go … and if I was safe. I was over sixteen at the time.'

'And were you safe?'

'I have Alysha's mum to thank for that. She didn't take sides of course, but she told me I could stay if I wanted to. She knew I didn't want to go back and she was happy to tell the cops that. I think she knew why I ran away. She must have known. Alysha must have worked it out and told her. I never asked. If they knew, I didn't want to be told.'

'But wasn't there something Mum … or Dad could do?'

'To begin with, they wouldn't have been dealing with it with a united front. She would have been furious at him. Blaming him for causing it but not daring to challenge him outright.

She was probably too afraid to know how bad things got. He was probably afraid that she would challenge him or that I'd spill my guts, which I never did … until now.'

She gave an apologetic look and continued.

'If either of them did want to force the issue, it would have become public knowledge, no matter how hard the system would try and supress the matter. Once you're in the system, other human beings know. And if one human in a small country town knows, everyone knows.

'I reckon the local cop was reading between the lines when he questioned me, but he didn't want to touch it with a barge pole. Messy domestic stuff that no one could prove or disprove. If it ever was brought into the daylight, imagine how that would have played out for your life, let alone theirs.'

Ella stared at her — stupefied. It was all too credible and incredible, all at the same time. She wondered how Lila handled it.

'How did *you* feel?'

'I was full of emotions. Angry at the cop for not doing anything, because I could tell he figured it out, even though I didn't tell him anything. Angry at Mum to be honest, for giving up on me. I felt abandoned as well as being relieved that I had escaped. I felt grateful to Mrs McGuinn. I also felt really homesick. I didn't miss Dad, though. Not ever. But I did miss the farm. I missed you. I really missed you.'

She wiped a tear. Not crying. Just one tear.

'Sorry. I told myself I wouldn't.'

Ella reached out and placed her hand on Lila's.

Lila's lone tear was joined by a couple more as she tried to smile. She reluctantly withdrew her hand to produce a tissue and wipe her face.

'I said I wasn't going to cry, but I brought tissues anyway.'

She looked down and shook her head.

'Sorry.'

'No. You've never told this to anyone. Do you want to take a break? Then you can tell me about the last twenty years. Come and sit on the sofas and I'll crack the other bottle.'

Lila moved to the well cushioned corner sofa and watched and wondered while Ella retrieved the other bottle. *She's expecting more. Apart from putting her hand on mine, she's being too reserved.*

'Are you all right, Ella? Me telling you all this? It's major, major stuff to take on.'

'I know Lila. But I need to hear it. I've hardly slept since we met at the café. You need to tell me about when Dad died. Why didn't that change things? Why couldn't you come back then?'

Whoa. No trauma pains there. The journalist has a list she's working through.

'I will have that drink, please,' Lila said in her out-loud voice. She took a chug and set off on round two.

'Before I get onto Dad dying, I'll tell you how it worked out for me at the McGuinns. They let me stay there and finish high school. At the public school. It was a bit weird with Alysha still going to boarding school, but we stayed best friends and we still are.

'I didn't stay with them long. I only stayed there until I got my year 12 certificate. Which was long enough for the authorities to stop checking on me. Then I moved out. I was worried about wearing out my welcome at the McGuinns. Having said that, I've spent many a Christmas with them. That's when I wasn't overseas.

'I left home, their home, for a job at a Clare Valley winery.

A few years later, I put myself through Roseworthy Ag College, which is what I always wanted to do. I've been working in agriculture off-and-on ever since.'

She paused and took a deliberate breath. Ella sat and sipped attentively with her legs beneath her on the couch.

'Okay then,' she said to get back to the matter at hand. 'When Dad died, it was only about a year after I left. Mum contacted me to tell me. As far as me going home was concerned, I wasn't ready to go back there, even if she had wanted me to. Not that soon. There was no great shouting match and I never heard from her after that. We were two immovable objects that somehow remained immovable. I sometimes wonder if deep down, there's a part of her that blames me for letting him do it to me in the first place. Maybe she's never forgiven me. Or maybe she was dealing with shame or guilt. I dunno Ella. It was a messy time and I was still young. I don't think either of us recovered from that. I know I didn't. I thought she owed me and she probably thought I owed her.'

Ella shook her head. 'And neither of you tried again after that? You *were* after all, mother and daughter.'

'Maybe we both got used to things being how they were.'

Ella dropped her head.

'It unfolded how it unfolded. I've learned to live with that, Ella.'

'Well, I never did. For twenty years, all I ever wanted was for you to come home, Lila. Now I learn that neither of you tried. I never knew that all that time, she knew where you were. If only she had told me that much. Maybe *I* could have done something. At least I would have tried.'

'Don't go there, Ella. It is what it is.'

'It is what it is? What a fucking trite saying that is. As if that ever explains anything. Look, I get you're a victim, I feel for you, I honestly do, and I don't want to devalue that, but you've had twenty years to deal with it, Lila. I've had five minutes and it sucks. The whole fucking thing sucks.'

Ella wrung her arms and began to cry. Lila moved beside her and held her. She let herself be consoled.

'I'm here now, Elly.'

As soon as she said it, Ella stopped crying and pulled back.

'No one else ever called me that. I'm ten again.'

They smiled at each other and held each other's hands.

'It's just you and me … Elly.'

'Mm,' Ella answered while nodding agreement.

They sat silently drinking in twenty years of missing each other. It was Ella who broke the spell. She stood to get a tissue and wipe her own tears. She returned to sit across from Lila again on the corner lounge.

'You're not in the will, you know,' she told Lila.

Lila instantly sobered. *Ella's still not done. She's returning to her list.*

'I didn't expect to be. But that's not what this is about, Elly. This is about you and me.'

'I know. But Dave Urquhart, that's Mum's lawyer, is the executor of the will and he's already asking me stuff. Things I'll have to deal with. It's something we have to talk about.'

'Well, I can tell you now that I am not after money.'

'Maybe you should be, Lila. By the time I sell the farm, we're not talking peanuts. Just because Mum left you out of the will doesn't mean I don't want to do what's fair. I do want you to have what's fair. And even if I *didn't* want to do what's fair, you're probably entitled to challenge the will in any case.'

Lila shifted from feeling affronted.

'You're selling the farm?'

'Not straight away. Apparently probate stalls all that for months. So that money will be a long way off.'

'Right,' Lila said in a concerned way. Ella felt compelled to reassure her.

'We'll be sharing it, though.'

'I thought I already got a share, Elly. Here tonight, I mean. I got a sister back. I won't be challenging however my little sister decides to divvy things up.'

'Yeah,' Ella smiled. 'I guess you can't write feelings into a will.'

They enjoyed another moment smiling at each other.

Ella tilted her head and said, 'It will be sad to sell the farm, though.'

She felt a shift when her nostalgia was not reciprocated, then alarm as Lila sat up, straightened herself solemnly and held both hands out in readiness to utter something of import. And then she did.

'Here's the thing Elly. I don't want you to sell the farm. I'd like to run it for you … or for us both. That's one thing I would like. Really like.'

Ella pulled a stunned face before she spoke.

'Are you serious? Could you even do that?'

'Of course, I'm serious. Agriculture is what I know. It's how I've spent my life. I think I mentioned that I'm into organic agriculture with my own modest vineyard. That's where I think the potential is in the Mallee. Nearly all of the current Mallee farmers can only produce crops by spraying — which I'm sure you know is getting more on the nose with consumers as time goes by. Farmers around here have all become slaves to those massive boom sprays. But there are a few pioneers amongst them, trying to do things organically and biodynamically. I reckon we should have Rosenfeld join them at the vanguard. I'm not talking alternative wacko stuff, Elly. The European Union is demanding limited pesticides and environmentally sustainable products in trade agreements, and so are our own supermarkets.

'And it's not just the farmland we can protect. I notice Mum resisted clearing or selling the thousand acres of scrub we have bordering Wyperfeld. I know it's marginal for farming, but we can make sure it's protected from clearing forever by whacking a Trust for Nature covenant on it. And there's other bits that we can revegetate and do something about Mallee fauna becoming rare … '

Lila noticed Ella's head shaking in amazement and stopped.

'I didn't see any of that coming.'

'Sorry, I'm starting to rave. But I can't say I haven't thought about it,' Lila admitted.

'It hasn't crossed my mind that I *wouldn't* sell the farm. You know Trent Hofner is counting on it coming onto the market.'

'Yes, I know. And I can tell that you're no farmer. But you are a Hass descendant, and Rosenfeld was Mum's farm. Dad only married into it. Before that, it was Grandma's farm and Grandpop married into it then. Now it's your farm Ella. The will says so. You're the third generation of the Hass female legacy. Between us, we can keep that legacy alive. You don't have to cut me in if you don't want to. Just let me run the place for you.'

'Jeez, Lila. You're all over this. Keeping the farm … that's nowhere near where my head's been since Mum died. I'll have to take all that in. I'll see what the executor has to say about it. If it's possible for him to distribute the will differently I mean.

But whatever I, or we, end up doing, your fair share will be factored in. Okay?'

'Thank you for the last bit, Elly. And with the farm, what have you got to lose? If I fail to make a go of it, the real estate will still be there to sell.'

'Let me think about becoming a farmer then.'

Chapter 20

Ella and André peeled off from the peloton of cyclists grinding city-ward along Beach Road for the reward of sitting at a bay side café in Lycra and downing espresso coffee. The Saturday morning training ritual normally served to exorcise the week's work demons and leave the mind unoccupied for the weekend ahead. On this occasion it failed.

'Why have we stopped?' Ella asked, as she extracted a plastic drink bottle from its cradle. She was stopped from throwing her head back to drink from the bottle by the Port Phillip Bay seascape. Several yachts were out early, before the sun rose enough to transform the water from grey to blue. Its faint aura still bathed everything in a soft orange glow.

'Gee. You don't see this with your head down in that pack, do you?' she said.

The whoosh, whoosh of several cars broke the calm.

André clutched his bike on the esplanade's thin shoulder of grass and pointed inland.

'That's Meredith's place.'

'Oh my. I only saw the driveway on TV. He gets to wake up

to this every day? Lucky bastard.'

They stood in their ribbed helmets looking thoughtfully at the house-wide glass facade.

'He *must* be well-heeled enough to have a body dropped from a plane,' Ella said. The sweat had been rising in her face since they stopped.

A blonde female figure strolled onto the glass balustrade-ed upper balcony, cup in hand. She wore Lycra pants to below the knee. The dark patches on her singlet top hinted at a treadmill session.

'That's Eve Delmonte,' André said.

'So why have we stopped exactly? Are we on a stakeout?' she teased.

'I dunno,' André said glumly. 'I just thought I'd show you while we're passing. We've dug up a bit of stuff. A lot of dots, but nothing joining them yet.'

'Well at least you've got a body. I know that's stating the obvious but without a body you wouldn't even know there was a killer to be found. You know. Whoever did it, has had their world rocked. They thought they had nothing to worry about … ever. Now, they suddenly have gaol hovering on their horizon. You need to take advantage of that. Maybe you need some more media speculation,' Ella ended, with a conspiratorial smile.

'Not yet. There are still a few things I want to follow up before we resort to that, but listen to you. You sound like you've got your mojo back. I wish I'd been there when the Richie sisters made up.'

Ella gave him a disgruntled stare.

'What? Did I get that wrong? You told me you made up. Right?'

'Kinda. It got complicated.'

'You've lost me.'

'Yes, we did make up and I told her we share the inheritance. She is Mum's daughter after all is said and done. Whatever went down between them, she's earnt it. That's beyond discussion in my mind and I told her so.'

'And you can do that, even though the will says otherwise?'

'Apparently. I checked that out with Dave Urquhart. He's Mum's lawyer in Horsham. He's also executor of her will. As long as Lila's happy to become a claimant and she and I sign an agreement, he can distribute everything accordingly.'

'I knew you were leaning that way, and it all sounds do-able, so don't tell me Lila had a problem with that.'

'Not exactly. What I didn't see coming was, she wants us to keep the farm. Me and her. She wants to farm it. That's her thing. She went to ag college early on and has been working on the land ever since. She wants to keep the family farm legacy going. I would become a silent partner.'

'Jesus. That's big. Tying all your money up like that. Your only option will be to keep on working.'

Ella gave him a wry look.

'I hope you're joking "A". It's not like I would retire even if I could. I love what I do. I've got my dream job. And if we don't sell the farm, Mum also has a sizable super account. So, it's not as if I won't be able to upgrade our house, or travel or whatever. All you have to worry about is me being better off than you.'

'Hey, I don't have a problem whatever you decide. It's not my call. I was just saying … you know … making sure you're okay with everything.'

'I think I'm okay with the idea of keeping the farm. At least I don't have a problem thinking about it. As far as I know, there's no major loans associated with the enterprise so, if Lila's any good at running it, there's no reason why it won't keep generating a handy income for both of us. If she did happen to make a meal of it and things went pear-shaped, we could still sell the real estate down the track. And you and me can still go up there to stay, of course.'

'I can't argue with any of that. It seems more of a hard call for Lila to make than for you. She's the one who has to give up her job and the life she has. Pulling up stakes and moving interstate. That's major, El.'

'That's what she really wants to do "A". But do you know what's odd after all these years?'

He shrugged.

'I still don't think she's telling me everything. I realised that after she left the other night. In the old days, before she ran away and her life used to fascinate me, I always used to badger her about what she was up to, especially the dodgy teenage stuff. Stuff I could tell she didn't want Mum or Dad to know about. She used to fob me off of course, as you would, with a prying little sister. However, I might have only been ten or something, but I could tell when she was up to something. You know. I'd overhear what she'd say to her friends and stuff like that. I'd know when she wasn't telling the truth.

'After she left our flat the other night, I realised I still do. That's one dynamic between us that hasn't changed in twenty years. Isn't that amazing?

'I guess. But what is she lying about?'

'She might not be lying but there's something she's not telling me about why she and Mum didn't make up after Dad died. I can't see that it would change anything, but she was fudging when I asked her about it, the exact same way she fudged things when I was ten. *"It just is what it is"* my arse.'

'I don't know what "it" you're referring to, but everything is what it is,' André laughed.

'Exactly,' Ella announced, as if André was confirming everything that she just said was precisely correct.

André sought what he thought would be safer ground.

'Well, for what it's worth, I could handle being the partner of a farmer, albeit a silent one. A "Collins Street Cocky" as you would have been known back in the day.'

'Hmm. So, you're saying we should keep the farm?'

Ella cut him off as he opened his mouth to answer.

'Looks like they have a visitor,' she said.

The Hyetts' Aviation mini-bus straddled the nature strip to park in front of Meredith's house. André recognised Jimmy Hyetts' shock of white hair as he walked to the gate. An exchange of more than Jimmy's name took place on the security intercom before the gate was released for him to enter. Eve Delmonte disappeared from the upper balcony as soon as Jimmy entered.

'Jimmy Hyetts,' André said. 'Perhaps he's here to join some dots.'

'How does he fit in?'

'Meredith and Meredith regularly use his company, Hyetts' Aviation, getting to some of their regional projects. Anyone with an aeroplane is more than a person of interest. Let's sit on the grass. I want to see how long he stays.'

'Wow. It is a stakeout.'

Chapter 21

André and Alex sat in Hyetts' Aviation mini passenger lounge. They awaited Jimmy Hyetts return in the mini-bus from ferrying passengers to the terminal for a flight to King Island.

'Come through,' Jimmy Hyetts said to them without stopping when he entered through the front door. He strode ahead to his office in the bowels of the building. No pilot smile was on offer this time. Margaret was nevertheless summoned to make teas and coffees again. *More for Jimmy Hyetts' benefit*, André surmised.

'What now?' he said with impatience. 'I have to rush off for a pick-up soon. We're a man down this morning.'

'I'd like to know why you went to see John Meredith at his home on Saturday morning.'

'What?' Jimmy said sharply and rose to shut the office door. 'What's that got to do with you or anyone else? Have you got me under surveillance? It's bad enough that you're going through all our flight records. You've got the Civil Aviation Safety Authority looking down their nose at us, and now this!'

Margaret returned with the tray of tea and coffee. Strident

silence prevailed until she scurried to leave without making eye contact.

'You're not under surveillance, Jimmy.' Calling him Jimmy still grated. 'Your van was noticed inadvertently. As for the flight records, we make no apology. You own a fleet of light aircraft regularly accessed by a murder victim. A murder victim who just happened to be dropped from an aircraft. We are obliged to eliminate any connection as thoroughly as we can. The fact that you are seeing the victim's husband out of hours does bugger all to rule out possible complicity with John Meredith.'

'Complicity. Hah. I went to see Meredith for bringing this upon me. You might have gathered that I am none too happy to be drawn in to the matter. And that's on top of losing a friend.'

'And how did John Meredith bring this upon you and what did you expect him to do about it?' André asked. 'Is there something you haven't told us?'

'I wouldn't be surprised if he did kill her. I don't know how, because he was overseas. I'm not going to say that on the record either and can you not write it down?' he said turning to Alex.

'Why are you being so sensitive about John Meredith?'

'I might have said too much when I went off at him on Saturday morning. He came back at me with the same questions as you. "Why am I blaming him?" He and I go back a long way and we still do business. He's also a lawyer.' Jimmy added with a weak smile.

Everyone's rattling his cage, André thought.

'What do you mean you and he go back a long way?'

'John and Portia and I go back to our Bayside Aero Club days. In the 1990s.'

'You didn't tell us that when I asked you about your relationship with John Meredith.'

'You didn't ask me that. You asked me what I have had to do with John since Portia died. Check your notes Detective Castellanos,' he said turning to Alex. Alex stopped writing.

'And I'm not just being cute about it. I thought that's all you were interested in.'

'Okay then. How come John Meredith was in the aero club? Don't tell me he's a pilot too?'

'I thought you would have known. That's why he uses our company. He knows we'll let him have a go at the controls. He loves flying. If you're checking anybody's flight records you should be checking John Meredith's.'

Alex watched André gripping the steering wheel with both hands, staring hard at Hyetts' Aviation office … yet to press the car's start button.

'What?' he asked André.

'Three pilots. Now we've got three fucking pilots and two aero clubs.'

'Are we going to see Meredith?' Alex asked.

'Not yet. What can we ask him? Can you fly a plane? We know he can because Jimmy Hyetts just told us so. And so what? He was overseas when it happened.'

'Maybe he has other aero club connections. "Birds of a feather flock together", they say — or Plato did.'

André was too riled to play the proverb game.

'See what you can do to get a list of members *and* ex-members. Try and find out if any of them are still on Meredith's Christmas card list.'

André brought the engine to life.

André began warm-down stretches from his regular lunchtime dash around Docklands. There was no Melbourne Tan parkland escape for joggers within cooee of police headquarters. Nearby pedestrian and shared cycle/pedestrian paths did, however, offer water frontages around Victoria Harbour and along the Yarra River, as well as striking icons like the sculptured Webb Bridge. He spotted Alex strolling back to the office with lunch in a paper bag.

'Anything awry in the Hyetts' flight records?' he asked.

'Still checking. So far not every flight went to plan but usually with good reason. Bad weather; passengers changing their minds or getting COVID; everything checks out. Maybe Jimmy used someone else's plane. Zac and Sue are checking what we can.'

'Any links from his aero club days?'

'I've got some old members' lists from the club sec. She tells me there's hardly any members from the early 1990s still around. The only way to find a connection will be to track down some of those former members and ask them.'

'That'll take too long. I'll grab a shower while you eat your lunch. Then it's time to speak to John Meredith again.'

The smell of asphalt filled the car as Alex drove at snail's pace between the orange plastic bollards. Diesel fumes from B-double Kenworths front and back contributed to the burnt fossil fuel cocktail dragged in by the car's air conditioning system.

'Why don't they do it at night?' Alex complained. 'Especially on this road.'

The four south bound lanes of the Melbourne-Geelong freeway had ground to ten kilometres an hour gridlock, five kilometres before the road works came into sight. Their destination was the seaside township of Queensliff on the western headland of Port Phillip Bay.

'This is bullshit,' André said. 'Not the roadwork. I mean Meredith making us come all this way to see him. Drop into the Geelong cop shop and see if we can swap cars for a lights and sirens job. We'll make sure our visit doesn't go unnoticed.'

Alex spotted the historic two-storey hotel at the other end of the Queenscliff street. It too was cordoned off with temporary bollards and fencing for serious renovations. He turned and smiled cheekily to André.

'Siren time?'

'Two bursts should do it.'

Alex parked by the No Parking sign, watched by leather-gloved demolition workers who paused from manhandling torn pieces of fibrous plaster and Masonite into a dusty skip. The tanned and tattooed all-male workforce wore a uniform of hi-vis vests over bare skin, filthy shorts and dusty steel capped boots. Kiss's *I was Made for Loving You* came on the builder's boombox. The army of Village People construction workers moved back into life.

The siren burst also stopped the pacing of several tradies on mobile phones and drew John Meredith from within the building. He emerged with a man carrying a bundle of A1 plans under his arm and Charles Lyon in tow. *Their* pristine hard hats and fluro vests were worn over shirts and ties.

'What the hell are you doing coming here in that thing and using a siren?' Meredith demanded.

'We drive a company car as I presume you do. And as for the

siren, we noticed an errant driver we needed to warn. I thought you'd appreciate our concern for the community.'

'All right. You've made your point. I'll meet you at Maddy's Café in ten.'

Meredith and Alex both ordered macchiatos. The other customers sat outside to enjoy the morning sun. Meredith led them to an inside table away from windows.

'A reno like that is not your usual style,' Alex said. A surprised André and Meredith both turned to him quizzically.

'Nothing new gets built in this town.' Meredith offered, caught off guard. 'Except for some Government stuff. For years, the place was full of retiree professionals with the wherewithal and connections to resist anything. The borough was the only municipality in the entire state not rationalised under Kennett's hatchet job in the 1990s. They won't take kindly to police arriving ostentatiously either.'

Alex nodded.

'Is this part of your enquiry or detective version of small talk?'

'Just interested. My father's firm do some developments.'

'What company?' Meredith asked.

'Used to be Castellanos Concrete. Now they're just Castellanos.'

'A good outfit, we use them sometimes.'

'So Dad tells me.'

A smiling Alex and the interruption of coffees being delivered focused Meredith on the matter at hand.

'I can see why Jimmy Hyetts is annoyed with you lot,' he said.

'We're not enamoured with Jimmy ourselves and as much as we like a day at the beach, we don't appreciate being dragged all the way down here to talk to you.'

'Well, I'd appreciate it if you could find my wife's murderer.' Meredith countered before checking himself and glancing around to see if others were in earshot.

'We can't do that without speaking to you from time to time, even when it's just letting you know developments.'

'What developments?' Meredith pounced.

'The fact that you and Jimmy Hyetts are more than just business acquaintances. The fact that you have a pilot's licence.'

'None of that is news or secret. I'm relying on you to ask me what's relevant. You're the supposed professionals.'

André ignored the dig.

'Anything to do with flying is relevant when a body has been dropped from a plane.'

'Well, you're barking up the wrong tree with Jimmy,' Meredith came straight back. 'He's been a pillar of the Bayside Aero Club and his community. He is more than offended that he's being dragged into this by association. He's no murderer and if he had been approached by anyone to drop a body from a plane, the police would have been the first to know about it.'

'And what about you, Mr Meredith? When was the last time you flew an aeroplane?'

'You know I was in London when all this happened,' Meredith said, reverting to a rehearsed and weary monotone.

'When?' André persisted.

'Last year, but not since Portia disappeared.'

'Where did you fly?'

'Portia and I flew to Mildura for a long weekend.'

André and Alex looked at each other.

'Mildura? With Portia?' André asked incredulously.

'Yes.'

'You would have passed where Portia was found?' André said.

'We flew from Bendigo. Our route was well east of the Big Desert.'

'I wouldn't say that's entirely out of the ball park for someone in an aeroplane. Were you surprised that she was found near where you had flown?'

'Surprised? I was surprised when she disappeared. I was surprised that she was murdered. By the time I learnt that she had been dropped from a plane I was way beyond surprise. There's no words for it.'

'Hmm,' André said with a slow nod to show he was considering the truthfulness of Meredith's reply.

'When was this flight to Mildura?'

'Last April. We spent a night at Castlemaine and flew from Bendigo to Mildura for an extra day's break.'

'What plane did you fly?'

'This is all history,' Meredith said offhandedly in a vain attempt to have André back off.

'The plane?'

'We hired a Cessna from another old Bayside Aero Club friend who now lives in Bendigo. His name is Robert Woodruff. Now I don't want Bob put through your mill like you did with Jimmy. I can understand you checking Jimmy because we do business all the time. But Bob is an old and dear friend.'

'Have you hired Mr Woodruff's plane before?'

'Once or twice. Certainly not often and not since Portia disappeared.'

'Have you hired any other planes?'

'Only the business flights with Hyetts'.'

'As I said, anything to do with flying is relevant when a body has been dropped from an aircraft. And the more we look, the more planes and pilots we seem to find. I can tell you, we will be checking each and every one of them without fear or favour, including Mr Woodruff.'

André began the car conversation. 'Why didn't that show up on flight plans in the vicinity of Wyperfeld?'

'She was still alive then. We didn't go that far back.'

Chapter 22

'Look at this mess,' André said, waving at the crime board. 'The more we dig up, the less we get to the bottom of.'

Alex offered a helpless gesture.

'No pithy Greek saying?'

'Funny you should mention it, mate. Nona used to tell me, "When you don't know what to do, cough".'

André didn't bat an eyelid.

'Well, you give that a go. I'm having one last crack at getting this board to make sense. Alright?'

He proceeded to take down every photograph … again. Then he re-erased the marker-pen information, a tad too vigorously.

'Back to basics,' he said out loud to himself and set about placing the photo of Portia Meredith alive and the photo of the plane, side-by-side, top and centre. In a row below that he attached photos of Simon Stone, John Meredith, Eve Delmonte and Jimmy Hyetts, as well as two separate silhouettes labelled U1 and U2.

'See if Glenevis is around to lend some Scottish wisdom for

a recap. I'll get coffees in for you and me. It could take a while.'

'Scottish wisdom?' Alex muttered as he left.

Alex and Glenevis sat at the small round table and watched sugar sink slowly into the crema on Alex's coffee.

'I still dinnae know how this whole fookin' city drinks th' stuff.' Glenevis commented.

'I asked the barista to do one in batter for you, but, you know … ' Alex shrugged.

'You couldnae find enough batter in all o' Melbourne ta make tha' taste good. Ah'll stick ta ma Irn-Bru — th' best thing Woolworths ever put on their Australian shelves.'

Glenevis held up the distinctive orange and blue can of Scotland's other national drink, after whisky. A carbonated soft drink that, depending on who you ask, "tastes like the colour orange", or "kinda like rust and battery acid, and it's magic".

'You know that's got caffeine in it too, don't you?' Alex retorted.

'This is made in Scotland from metal girders and if you want proof, it says so in the ad. Tha's wha' you two need ta get inta ya.'

Alex shook his head.

André placed his own half-finished takeaway cup on the table and picked up the marker pen.

'This is our suspect row,' he began, tapping the row that began with Simon Stone's smiling real estate shot. 'At least three of them are pilots, including this bloke. Simon Stone.

'He lives in Sydney, which is where he very publicly accosted our victim about sending him bankrupt. She had an intervention order placed against him. These days he's picking up casual flying-instructor work from one of his mates at an airfield on the outskirts of Sydney. He has access to light aircraft. That's motive and means right there.'

Glenevis and Alex nodded and sipped. André drew a line from the plane to Simon Stone before he continued.

'He says he's trying to move on after his fit of rage against Portia Meredith. His anger management counsellor confirms that. His movements around the time of her disappearance can largely be accounted for. If he *did* do it, he would have had to fly a round trip from Sydney to Melbourne and back to Sydney via a very long detour over the Big Desert, having collected Portia's dead or drugged body along the way. Apart from the enormity and the cost, and the complexity of all that, there are no flight records to support it.

'Alternatively, he could have driven from Sydney to Melbourne and back, abducted or killed Portia Meredith, then took her body straight back to Sydney to fly it to the Big Desert at his leisure.'

André turned to Glenevis and Alex for comment.

'Not at his leisure if she was drugged and not yet dead,' Alex offered. 'And way too far-fetched. Why fly the body all the way to Victoria from Sydney. It's out of range. He'd have to refuel somewhere. That's just asking to be detected if you ask me.'

André agreed.

'It's not something he's likely to do with an accomplice either. The whole from-Sydney thing is too big an ask,' he said. 'And don't forget she took a suitcase of clothes. How would that fit in?'

'Okay,' said Glenevis. 'Let's leave him oot of th' picture for now. These things usually happen close ta home.'

'Let's look at Meredith then,' André said and pointed his

marker at the media picture of John Meredith. 'He probably realised that Portia Meredith was leaving him and wanted out of their business. Behind his back she was thinking out loud about going back to Sydney and setting up shop on her own. That would make it struggle-ville for him. Her mother says she intended to change her will. If John Meredith knew Portia had not yet changed her will, it might have suited him for her to go missing. That could buy him years before she was eventually declared dead. More than enough time to get the business sans Portia onto a sound footing.

'Plus, if that wasn't enough motive, he had moved on romantically to Eve Delmonte. For him, Portia was already dead to him. Money, love *and* vengeance. Take your pick.'

'He's also a pilot, but he was conveniently out of the country, so he was not around to do the deed himself,' Alex reminded them.

'Did he have her murdered then? And by whom? That's the question as far as Meredith is concerned. He's not out of the picture by any means. Agreed?'

Both Glenevis and Alex nodded again. André drew a link from Meredith to the first question-marked silhouette.

'U1 represents a possible hired murderer-cum-pilot — "Unknown One",' André explained. 'Of course, U1 and Hyetts' Aviation could be one and the same. I'm not ruling out that Meredith used them for the job. Meredith and Jimmy Hyetts have been pretty cosy for decades.'

'Tell me what you found oot aboot Hyetts then,' Glenevis asked.

'As you know, Meredith's chartered Hyetts' Aviation flights for regional projects. We since discovered that in the course of doing so, Portia ended up having an affair with the owner,

Jimmy Hyetts. Jimmy and Portia and John Meredith all go back to their aero club days in the 1990s. The affair supposedly ended before our victim disappeared. But who really knows. For mine, all of that leaves a big question mark over Jimmy Hyetts.'

'Agreed. Next.' Glenevis said.

'Eve Delmonte. Did she kill Portia in cahoots with John Meredith, or even with Jimmy Hyetts? According to Charles Lyon, Meredith and Delmonte never ceased their affair before Portia disappeared — as they both claim.'

'So, she's nae a standalone suspect? Her involvement would be in league with Meredith and whoever flew th' plane?' Glenevis asked.

'That's about the strength of it. She didn't have an axe to grind with Portia, but she had clandestinely replaced her in the relationship. Could she have been enticed by Meredith to replace Portia in the company as well? Could *she* have persuaded Meredith to do something about ending it with Portia?'

The questions were hypothetical for now. André drew a link between John Meredith and Eve Delmonte.

'There's a few possibilities of how it could have played out with Eve. We know that she visited Portia while John Meredith was away. That gave her an opportunity to spike Portia's drink. As you pointed out, she would also need a pilot to fly the body over the Big Desert — U1. John Meredith's mate Jimmy Hyetts, for instance. Or did Eve put the body into cold storage until John Meredith returned from London to dump the body himself? I admit it's hard to see that happening, but let's note the possibility anyway.'

'Un-fucking-likely is an understatement, mate,' Alex said. 'The logistics of accessing cold storage and storing a body undetected and un-rotting are off the scale. Even if it was kept in cold storage somewhere, the perpetrator would be faced with getting a stiff stiff into a plane seat. She would also need to get the body out of the house on her own before Portia was reported missing.'

'Mm,' André uttered grudgingly. He nevertheless drew lines from Eve Delmonte to Jimmy Hyetts, to Meredith, and to U1, the prospective pilot-for-hire.

'It's all getting too farfetched and your crime board is lookin' like a fookin' spider web again,' Glenevis said. 'Who's this U2, other than Bono, who Ah assume was at home in Dublin at the time.'

'Not bad for an old bloke,' Alex said. André grinned.

'Fook you guys. The eighties is *ma* era. I've still got th' cassette for The Joshua Tree.'

'I rest my case,' Alex grinned.

André pressed on.

'U2 is "Unknown Two". It's possible that someone we don't know about yet killed her. Maybe a random killer. Someone *she* didn't even know.'

'Come on, André. You're nae that desperate, are you? There's nothing random aboot something this elaborate. This took plenty o' planning. You need ta keep looking close ta home. You've already got three proper suspects who are pilots. More than enough. You can get rid o' U2,' Glenevis said.

'The way this is shaping up, U2 is our most promising lead. The harder we look at everyone else, the colder the whole thing becomes. Every extra detail we uncover seems to strengthen their alibis. Another phone record, tollway record, CCTV, traffic camera footage, security system printouts. We're building everyone's defence and watching our case evaporate.'

'Then just leave it for a while,' Glenevis advised. 'If you have nae noticed, murderahs have not been on long service leave while you two ha' been tryin' ta figure this one out. Fi has still got her hands full with th' Keon Park thing and Ah got a call this morning from uniform aboot a bag snatchin' near Windsor station. Th' elderly victim fell an' is on life support — aboot ta die. It'll be certain manslaughter. You go ta th' hospital André, and this time, *you* can give Fi a hand Aristotle.'

André didn't see it coming.

'What, drop the whole thing?'

'Course nae. But someone has to keep tha show on th' road. It'll take your mind aff it for a few days. Come back fresh. Nae?'

Glenevis and Alex watched André frown and try to get his brain around Glenevis's order. Alex thought he could help matters.

'Want to swap?' he asked.

Alex's offer re-focussed André's attention.

'No way. That Keon Park murder is gangland related, right up Fi's alley. She thinks the Armed Offenders Squad still exists and she's running it. She's a mad woman who's likely to get you killed.'

'I tried. Your call.' Alex shrugged.

'So, we just drop the Meredith thing?' André said, turning back to Glenevis.

'You can walk and chew gum, cannae ya? While ya dealin' with th' woman on life support, you can also organise follow up press for Portia Meredith in th' weekend papers. See what tha' prompts.'

'The net of the sleeper catches fish,' Alex philosophised.

'Exactly, Aristotle. Throw some juicy titbits ta Ella.' Glenevis told André. 'See if getting you into her good books kin cheer you up. Let it be known that th' police are baffled. Come clean tha' Portia Meredith was dropped from a plane, tha' she is connected to a prominent Melbourne aero club. Her husband who was also a member of th' aero club was on business overseas an' is nae suspected of killing his wife. Give Meredith a false sense of security. Maybe aero club members will be disgruntled an' come forward with somethin'. Let's see what it stirs up.'

His logic appealed to André.

'Aye boss,' he nodded thoughtfully.

'Now you're talking,' Glenevis shot back at André's unintended Scottish-ism.

Chapter 23

The ward station woman lifted her eyes from a screen and nodded wordlessly to André in the direction of a waiting area at the end of the hospital corridor. He spotted Senior Constable Brendan Luxton with a double take. It was the domain of rookies to look like they are still in their VCE year — not a senior constable in uniform. *Fuck. I've got "cop" written all over me and my understudies are all growing younger. What hope have I got?*

Luxton rose and came to meet him along the corridor. Pleasantries were dispensed with in favour of a rundown in truncated cop-speak.

'Her name's Ivy Varrenti. Daughter and her daughter's husband are in the waiting room. Sandra and Ken Burch.' Luxton told him. 'They're waiting for bad news. Turning off life support at best.'

'Teenagers?'

'Yeah, but not ID'ed yet. It happened quickly and they probably don't even know she's injured and dying. Poor descriptions from the only bloke that admits seeing it happen.

There'll be a bit of leg work to do, but we *will* be able to track them down.'

'Then I need to speak to her daughter and son-in-law now. Has the hospital got a room we can use?'

'Hello Mrs and Mr Burch, I'm Detective Sergeant Marshall.' He left out the bit "from the Homicide Squad."

'I'm sorry to hear what has happened to your mother. I know this is the worst time for you to speak to me but I need to ask you a few things that can help us catch the people who did this.'

Sandra Burch was frozenly attentive to André from the moment he spoke. Her breathy near-sobbing paused and she held a handkerchief mid-wipe of the cheek. Now calmed by André's concern, she told him, 'She caught the train to see her specialist at The Avenue Hospital. Now she's across the tracks in The Alfred. What do you want to know?'

Ken Burch comforted her on the shoulder.

'I understand your mother had credit cards and a mobile phone in the bag that was stolen?'

'Yes, and six hundred dollars in cash.'

'Have you reported the stolen credit card to the bank, or done anything about the phone?'

'We haven't had a chance … ' Sandra Burch began anxiously.

Ken Burch finished his wife's explanation.

'We came straight here, Ivy's the most important thing right now.'

'I'm not being critical,' André said. 'I need to know the state of the credit cards and her mobile to help track down the culprits. If the card and phone remain active, they'll try to use them when the cash runs out. They're only teenagers from what we understand. They might be dumb enough to leave a trail, especially because we don't think they know they harmed your mother, let alone how badly. They've probably already used the cards, maybe online, or phoned their mates on your mum's phone.'

'So, you don't want us to cancel them?' Sandra Burch asked with dawning awareness.

'No. Let's leave it for a while, but we need to get those details right away, please.'

'I can give you Mum's mobile number. She's with Telstra. I know she banks with ANZ but I have no idea about the card number.'

Brendan Luxton wrote down the mobile number.

'I can give you a key to her unit so you can look for the credit card details there.'

'We'll see how we go with the bank first, Mrs Burch. Do you know what other cards your mum carries? Medicare? Myki? Driver's licence? Other bank accounts.'

'She definitely has a Myki and Medicare. Other than that, I … '

Sandra Burch sobbed at her own helplessness.

'That's all helpful,' André reassured her. 'The other thing I'll be doing is trying to keep this out of the media. I don't want the culprits to be spooked by knowing the extra trouble they are in. Not yet. That's not an easy thing for us to do without your help though. We'll do all we can to keep media people away from you, but if anyone does happen to ask you about this, tell them they need to speak to the local police — Senior Constable Luxton. And it's not just the mainstream media. Social media will also be our enemy. So don't be drawn into discussing or answering anything with anyone. Tell them "No comment" if you have to, no matter how rude it may seem or how nice they are.'

Sandra nodded without lifting her head from sobbing into her handkerchief.

'Thank you, Mrs Burch. I'll leave you with Senior Constable Luxton and get things actioned. Stay strong,' he said, touching her on the shoulder. He also offered a tight-lipped nod to Ken Burch before turning to leave.

The woman at the ward station raised her eyes once more as he passed, scrolling his mobile phone contacts for Georgie from Communications.

'This is a No Mobile Phones area.'

He nodded an apology and waited until he reached the lobby before pressing the Call button.

'Georgie. It's André Marshall.'

'Hi André. What have you got?'

'A bag snatching that I need to keep out of the media.'

'You do realise I'm the person to call when you do *want something "in" the media.'*

'Ha. Ha. With this one, the victim fell and is about to die from the injuries.'

'Tragic, but straightforward. You're gonna have to spell it out. What's the problem André.'

'We don't think the kids that did it looked back. They won't know they left a life in the balance. A potential manslaughter. They'll try and use the phone or cards, if they haven't already done so. A few days to make sure will be handy.'

'Do you realise what you're asking. Media outlets are one thing, but I've got no control over people's mobile phones and social media.'

'I know all that, but there's still a chance it hasn't travelled far. Even though an ambulance attended, witnesses probably don't have a clue about how badly the victim ended up. I said potential manslaughter but realistically, life support might have already been turned off. It'll miss the main TV news bulletins at this hour but anything you can do using your networks to keep a lid on it might help. We need to give these kids a bit more rope … '

She sighed.

'I'll do what I can with the main outlets, but short of a court order, you've got no hope of holding anything back — real, fake or otherwise. Seriously, André. The Dutch boy with his finger in the dyke was a nineteenth century fantasy. These days, news at every level is a tsunami.'

'Thanks, Georgie. That's all I'm asking. I'll text you the details.'

'Okay, detective sergeant. Say g'day to Ella for me.'

Her tone was weary.

André was quick to escape the lecture from Georgie and texted the details. *Windsor. Mrs Ivy Varrenti. The Alfred Hospital. 5.20 pm. Senior Constable Brendan Luxton. South Yarra station.*

Chapter 24

Ella felt him peering over her shoulder in the small bedroom study in their unit. The rapid soft clicking of the laptop's keyboard came to a pause-button halt with her fingers still splayed across the keyboard.

'I hate that,' she said through gritted teeth, not bothering to look up. 'I said you can read a draft when I finish.'

André ignored her.

'Have you got plenty of stuff about the aero club connections? We're not gonna solve this until we find out about the flight. It's over six months ago, so we need something that jogs peoples' memories.'

'It's a full page spread in the weekend supplement. There'll be photos of planes with their doors hanging open and shots of the desert.' She thought for a moment and added, 'Are you sure you want us to say you're baffled though, even if it's true?'

'It does stick in the craw, but we actually want you to say baffling. Just don't attribute it to us directly. If you need to put words in our mouth, use the usual cliches instead. "Continuing to investigate; following leads; confidentiality; privacy concerns;

hopeful". You know.'

'Maybe I should interview John Meredith,' Ella said, testing the waters.

'You won't have any luck there. His only public statement was spoken by his lawyer. When Portia disappeared, he wouldn't have a bar of making an appeal on camera. You'll need to get the word count up without anything from him.'

'What about Eve Delmonte?'

'You've got even less chance of interviewing her.'

'What I mean is, should I rub that in Meredith's face? The old brigade of the aero club won't like their Portia being replaced by a younger version. Maybe that will loosen tongues.'

'It's all part of the exercise,' André said as he watched her resume typing at speed.

She slowed and hunched slightly at his continuing presence.

'What?' she finally stopped to ask.

'Nothing. Just thinking.'

'Well can you do it somewhere else, please?'

She resumed typing.

'Have you decided what to do with the farm?

'No, I haven't. Are you going to let me finish this or what?'

'Will you be long?'

She abandoned typing and turned in her swivel chair to look hard at him. She smiled.

'You're horny. Aren't you?'

He hesitated.

'It has been a while.'

'No, it hasn't. Have you already forgotten this morning?'

'Oh yeah. But it is getting late.'

'You're such a romantic.'

She smiled and turned back to the keyboard, and began to

type slowly.

He clasped each of her shoulders from behind and started massaging, unable to delve lower without awkwardness. Ella's hands came to a halt again over the laptop keyboard. She waggled her shoulders slowly into the motion of his hands and finally leant back in the chair, closed her eyes and sighed breathily.

Still trapped behind the chair, he said 'You've got no bra on. You are ready for bed.'

'Just let me shut this down.'

'Don't you have to press the start button first.'

'Already done.'

Ella was surprised at her own uncomfortableness. She sat at the Meredith and Meredith Developments board room table, waiting for John Meredith to finish a phone call in his office. The door opened and her heart sped. His PA entered to tell her he would be a little longer. 'He apologises.' Would Ella 'like a drink?'

'Yes please. Some water.'

This is stupid, she told herself. *I've interviewed the Premier and Sting. John Meredith is merely a business man,* she reassured herself. *Keeping me waiting is just gamesmanship.*

She was surprised that he had taken her call. Even more surprised that he agreed to see her — if she could come to his office straight away. *Was that strategic? If it was it was working,* she thought. *Calm down. You'll be all right when he gets here. This is what you do.*

'Hello Ella, I'm pleased to meet you.'

'Good afternoon, Mr Meredith. You're a familiar face, even

though we haven't met before.'

Handshake over, he gestured to her to sit down. His tallness, chiselled face and copious flowing hair drew her gaze to his coolly appraising eyes. *It was tactical,* she fathomed. She had arrived unprepared about what to ask, then had to wait.

'I read your work. I thought you were unusually sensitive about the discovery of Portia's body. I appreciated that.'

'I'm sorry about your loss. If it's some consolation, Mrs Meredith was found in a beautiful and peaceful place. I was able to leave some flowers there before she was retrieved.'

'Thank you,' Meredith said.

'Do you mind if I record this?' Ella asked and dug a micro recorder from the handbag at her feet.

'Let me see,' said John Meredith and held out his hand.

An astonished look formed on Ella's face as she found herself placing the recorder in his palm. No interviewee had ever wanted her recorder. Nor could she imagine handing it over if they did.

John Meredith studied it enough to find the record button and turned it on. He placed the recorder on the table between them.

'There,' he said.

'Thank you,' Ella replied — left in no doubt that John Meredith considered himself to be in charge.

'As I told you on the phone, we're doing a story in the weekend paper. The police have also agreed to provide comment. I think they believe an update and review might elicit additional information from the public.'

'I'm sure they need all the help they can get.'

'It's a baffling case.'

'So, what can I tell you that's not in the statement I already issued?'

'Were you surprised to find out your wife's body was dropped from a plane into the Big Desert at Wyperfeld National Park?'

'Surely that's a rhetorical question. Something so inconceivable is shocking for anyone to imagine. What I can tell you is, the loss of my wife has pre-occupied my thoughts. How all that might have happened is too surreal to get my head around.'

'Are you disappointed that the police have not made progress?'

'I'm afraid I haven't been kept up to date by the police. If you are telling me they have not made progress, then of course I am disappointed. I think the whole community will be rightly disappointed with the police, in that case.'

'I understand that you and Mrs Meredith's friend, Eve Delmonte, are now together?'

Meredith drew breath audibly to compose himself.

'Yes, Eve has helped me get through the loss and I think I have been a comfort to her. You'd already know she and Portia were colleagues. Unless you have been in this situation you won't appreciate how rare and valuable such loyalty can be. We are there to help each other day by day and I know we will get through it together.'

'You say it's too surreal to get your head around, but surely you wondered how your wife's murder came about?'

'I honestly try not to go there. But my staff and I have told the police everything we know. Portia is not the kind of person who made enemies and was much loved in our circle of friends and business. I hate to think what heinousness the police investigation will eventually be led to. Let's hope it's soon.'

'Indeed. Is there anything else you think is important to be said?'

'I think that's clearly the call of those tasked with the job. I'm afraid any closure for me still rests in the hands of the police. Let me know if they think I can say anything else to help.'

'I will,' Ella said, finding herself too readily agreeable as well as being short of further questions. Even more annoyingly, John Meredith knew. He picked up the recorder and said:

'If that's all then?'

Without waiting for an answer, he hit the Off button and handed it to Ella.

She looked at the recorder in her palm — pissed off. She squeezed out a stiff smile.

'Thank you. I'm sure we'll be able to do something useful with that.'

It wasn't the best comeback she could ad lib but enough to keep him guessing. It *also* pressed a button, as she found out when they rose for a final brief handshake. With hands still held, John Meredith's face fell unfamiliarly hard and fixed Ella's eyes chillingly.

'Be careful what you write, Ella. You don't want to get yourself pushed out of a plane as well.'

Blood was quick to flee her face. The only reaction she could muster was to snatch her hand away. John Meredith's face just as quickly softened to its former charm. His weapon holstered; its aim having been true.

'We all have to be careful with the killer still free,' he added, as an innocent explanation for the words they both knew were anything but.

Ella fumbled with her bag and left. Wounded and numb.

Where are you now?' André asked.

'I'm in front of his building in St Kilda Road.'

'Walk to the next corner towards the city. I'll pick you up in five.'

They took an inside table. The weather was warm and most customers were outside. On any other day, the experience was to be savoured. Bad coffee was unknown at any of the cafes on the Albert Park strip.

'I saw inside him and I saw her skeleton in the sand. He wanted me to see it again. What he's capable of doing to a woman. It was faster than a camera shutter, a look so quick I can't be sure it happened, except for the image left tattooed on my brain. But I can tell you, he did it. He absolutely killed her. He wanted me to know, and he wanted me to know so you know he did it. And that look. I think he did it himself, no matter how much sense that doesn't make. He's taking pleasure in this. Not smiling pleasure, evil conceited pleasure. He thinks you've looked everywhere and come up with nothing. He thinks he's untouchable.'

'Untouchable! The gloves are off. He hasn't seen how hard we can play.'

'With the cards he's holding, you'll need to do more than simply rise to the bait.'

'I know. But look, you're still shaking. If he tries anything else on you, he's likely to become a victim himself.'

'What? You'd risk prison for me? Would you have my picture on your cell wall? You could get an inside tat job. E-L-L-A. A letter on each knuckle.'

'Okay. I'll be smart too. Are you gonna be okay?'

'The way I see it, he just confessed, albeit invisibly. It was worth it as long as it helps you figure it out.'

'How was the interview part?'

'It's on tape. You can listen to it if you like. He's too smooth to leave a trace of anything. Smarm embodied. He'll eat you if you try anything stupid. He's like a QC-cum-spin doctor wrapped in the body of a used car salesman. KC, I should say.'

'All that and he's not a politician. Seems a waste.'

'Yeah. Well his threat has backfired. He won't be getting off lightly when I write this story. Can you drop me back at work? I need to hit the keyboard.'

'Be careful what you write.'

'Not you too.'

Chapter 25

The headline and lead paragraph:

DEAD, CENTRE OF NOWHERE
The body of a pilot's wife was found dropped from a plane into Victoria's Big Desert. Our reporter Ella Richie, who happened to discover the body, has been following this baffling case.

The fourth paragraph continued:

John Meredith (pictured above left) was in London when his wife, Portia Meredith (pictured middle left), was reported missing. Police believe she was murdered at that time and dropped from an aeroplane over the Big Desert in Wyperfeld National Park (pictured from the air - below left). Mr Meredith is well connected in the flying world. He was an active member of the Bayside Flying Club for many years and has a pilot's licence himself. Police said they do not have reason to look at Mr Meredith's movements at the time of his wife's murder and are currently investigating other leads in the flying community. John Meredith told this reporter, "I hate to think what heinousness the police investigation will eventually be led to. Let's hope it's soon." Will that world be a world John Meredith is familiar with — Melbourne's bay-side flying community? It is understood that police have so far questioned three pilots and are scrutinising flight records, both in Melbourne and interstate.

As previously reported, Portia Meredith's friend Eve Delmonte has since become Mr Meredith's live-in partner at the home of John and Portia Meredith. Mr Meredith agreed to be interviewed and said, "Eve has helped me get through the loss and I think I have been a comfort to her. Unless you have been in this situation you won't appreciate how rare and valuable such loyalty can be. We are there to help each other day by day and I know we will get through it together." There is undoubtedly a lot they have gone through together.

'Not with your Greek colleague today? What should I make of this?'

André stood in the meeting room of Meredith and Meredith Developments. John Meredith sat down at the head of the table. Drinks had not been offered. John Meredith anticipated the gloves-off encounter.

'I noticed that this room is equipped with cameras. Do you film meetings with visitors?'

'Not without telling them. Our cameras are for video conferencing and presentations. Why? Do you want to tell me something that cannot be repeated?'

'Did you film your interview with Ella Ritchie?'

'I think you know that your girlfriend taped the interview.'

'Not all of it. You chose to impart advice to her that sounded to me like a threat. A threat that begs plenty of questions about why it was made.'

'Say what you mean, the cameras are not on.'

'You don't deny it then?'

'I warned Ms Ritchie about the risk that's out there because of your lack of success. There is a killer on the loose at a time she was setting forth in print, I presumed to rattle their cage on your behalf. I think that's a dangerous position for you to place her in. A perfect murder has been committed. The perpetrator might need to commit another.'

'You spin it however you wish. But if you go near her … '

'What? You'll assault me? You'll fabricate a case against me for murdering my wife? Grow up, detective. Why would I go near your girlfriend? She came to me. She sat right there, in front of where you're standing now. She listened to my advice and failed to heed it.'

'Failed to heed it? Failed to heed it?' he repeated. 'As far as I can reason, the only person who'd see Ella's story through those eyes is the murderer.'

'That's enough, detective. I resent that you accuse me of threatening your girlfriend. And now you're intimating I murdered Portia. I've let you have your little chest-beating session, now fuck off. Don't come near me again without allowing me time to have my legal representative there first. And even then, I'll be treating it as harassment. If it's like this meeting, I'll also be looking at slander and false accusation. You might want to bring your own lawyer along.'

Meredith's words were delivered with the chilling ray he had flashed at Ella — but with wasted effect on the homicide detective.

'You said it's a perfect murder. Hardly the boast of an *innocent* man, hopeful of justice for the murder of his wife.'

Chapter 26

Senior Constable Luxton and André entered the security office within the bowels of the shopping centre. Its only window was onto the cement-block corridor that led beyond the public toilets. They watched Donata Sanoulay searching CCTV views of store fronts.

'Werribee is the last place I expected this lot to rear their heads.' Luxton said to André.

'Me too. The totally opposite side of the bay. There's no quick or easy way to get to South Yarra from here — by car or train. And what's the attraction for teenagers anyway? Chapel Street is only a shadow of the hip fashion mecca it was in my day. They say it's gone further downhill since COVID. It's not like they don't have all the in names over here these days anyway. H&M, UNIQLO, Billabong?'

Donata and Luxton both turned their attention from the screen and grinned at each other.

'What? Am I that far off the mark?'

'As a fashionista, you make a pretty good cop,' Luxton laughed.

Donata re-focussed.

'Dune Break wasn't it — the surf wear shop?'

'Yeah,' Luxton said.

The solid over-tanned security guard with bunched back yellow-blonde hair leant further in and glanced between the two monitors.

'This camera is your best chance,' she told him, indicating the right-hand screen.

'That's Dune Break, next to the hairdresser. What time are we looking at?'

The frozen image showed three shopfronts with Dune Break the closest and the most clearly in focus.

'It was a Visa transaction three days ago. Eleven seventeen a.m. They would have left within a minute after that. They were too hoodied-up and head-down on the in-store camera, so we're hoping they let their guard down when they left.'

'Three days ago!' Donata said with alarm. 'How come you're only looking now? Didn't you have the bank monitoring the card?'

'It was a stuff-up by the bank. Whoever put the monitoring in place left the default on the *weekly notification* setting. Lucky I chased them up when I didn't hear from them sooner,' Luxton explained.

'Bummer. Let me see then.'

Donata said it slowly as she sped up the superimposed date/ time display in the top corner. The readout flashed by like petrol pump figures until it passed eleven o'clock. After that, she slowed the footage to recognisable fast-mo imagery, and finally to shoppers strolling by at normal speed.

'Eleven seventeen is coming up now.'

Luxton and André leant in.

'There.'

She paused the screen.

'That's them. Two girls and a boy. I'll take it frame by frame for you.'

'Nice work, Donata,' André said.

The image had frozen with one girl emerging from the shop carrying a Dune Break shopping bag, its logo of a stylised dune and wave clearly visible. Another hoodie-wearing girl and a boy were close behind and visible through the shopfront glass. None of the three looked older than sixteen.

The bag carrier was the fashion conscious one among them. She wore black leggings and a tight brand-name printed singlet top under a white embroidered jacket. There were clusters of bangles on both arms, coloured earrings and chains around her neck. The other two both wore tight black jeans — the female with a printed black and white tee-shirt under a black hoodie. He, in an almost plain grey hoodie with the hood raised.

Each click of the mouse brought them further out of the shop in staccato poses.

'Go back one,' said Luxton. 'That one shows all their faces.'

'No. Back one more.'

'That's it. Can you screen snap that and email it, please?' Luxton asked.

'You don't happen to recognise them, do you?' André asked.

''fraid not,' Donata said. 'I can ask the other security guys if you like.'

'That'd be good. Let Constable Luxton know what you find.'

André didn't give her his own Homicide Squad card.

'I presume they stole the credit card?' she asked.

'Exactly.'

'What about the other purchase at Dark Odyssey? Do you want to check that too?'

'Yeah. If you could, please. We need to make sure we have a match.'

Dark Odyssey was another teen clothing shop. The shopfront display on screen was predominantly black and featured antiqued silver skulls, chains and crosses.

Footage showed the same three people emerging after a purchase. This time, the second girl held a black unlabelled shopping bag. All three smiling.

'Now I know what they look like, I can see if there's any better footage on other cameras.'

'Thanks, Donata.'

'I knew it wouldn't take long,' André told Luxton as they reached the marked police car in the shopping centre car park.

'They must be from down this way,' Luxton speculated. 'The mobile phone was used down here too.'

'I reckon they rode the trains over to Chapel Street for the day. They look more like kids wagging school than street kids. They were right down near the station at Windsor when they snatched the bag. They probably thought they were home and hosed when they jumped off the train back in Hoppers Crossing or Werribee.'

'We could get footage from those stations but I don't think we'll need it. If we give these pics and footage to the local coppers, I reckon they'll have them within twenty-four hours.'

'I hope you're right,' said André.

'Do you want to check out the house where they used Ivy Varrenti's mobile?'

If "Back to the Future" was being re-filmed, then Michael J Fox could be zapped back to 185 Jubilee Parade. Beyond Werribee, beyond Wyndham Vale, beyond Manor Lakes to Melbourne's westernmost frontier. The near-empty housing estate looked no different to the subdivision on the outskirts of Hill Valley where Marty McFly gazed nonplussed at the bare and empty-paddock expanse where his parents would later build the house he grew up in. The sparse housing also allowed precise triangulation of the mobile phone.

André and Luxton drove the few hundred metres beyond the recently occupied 185 to where the sealed road came to an abrupt end on Melbourne's doorstep to the Werribee plain. The sky stood tall above a road-less, tree-less vastness stretching halfway to South Australia.

They did a slow crawl back past the isolated, still garden-less home. It stood vacant lots apart from a few bare house-frames and other half-built single-storey homes of the future neighbourhood. Number 185 would soon erupt into incriminating despair when "Wyatt's" parents answered their door to uniformed police. Would Wyatt, as he referred to himself in texts, be the one looking at a manslaughter charge or would he merely be a friend of those that were?

'Not what I expected,' Luxton said.

'No. And we won't be what they're expecting either.'

'I guess not.'

'I think we can hand this over to the local squad now. Then we'll head back to the Burch's. I think it's time to cancel their mother's credit card and phone.'

They crossed under the city through Burnley Tunnel and took Burwood Highway to Vermont.

'The funeral is in two days,' Luxton said when they arrived in quiet residential streets to find the Burch family home.

'It's never a good time to do this,' André said.

The long street was a collection of post-war brick veneer homes with well-established gardens. A few now had non-original high fences facing onto the street and a couple of houses had extended upward, or been replaced altogether with a two-storey version.

Ken Burch was at work. Sandra Burch had told them she was not going back to work until after the funeral. There were signs of kids too. Most likely back at school. She invited them into her lounge room and they allowed her to make them tea. She welcomed a delay.

The newish leather lounge suite and large screen sat among artefacts dating back to the 1970s — a small wood grain bookcase, a mosaic coffee table, a nest of occasional tables and a magazine-free magazine rack. Plates on display racks completed the story of the room's evolution.

Sandra Burch brought tea and biscuits to the lounge room on a tray.

'I don't know how to feel, whatever news you have,' she said.

'I know it won't help how you're feeling, Mrs Burch, but I can tell you that things have gone in our favour. The card and phone have been used and it's given us enough evidence to identify and locate those who did this to your mother.'

'Thank you,' she said quietly and held her mouth.

André was unsure what she made of the news.

Luxton placed his cup on the coffee table and waited for the right time to take a sip.

'I expect an arrest will be made within a day or so. I'm afraid there will be media involved this time. You may or may not want to deal with them. Senior Constable Luxton can help you with that if you like.'

'Thank you,' Sandra Burch whispered again and made a concerted effort to compose herself to talk.

'Who did it?' she asked.

'Two girls and a boy. We have their photos from cameras at the shopping centre where they used the card. They all look about sixteen. We don't think they're street kids. More like kids wagging school we reckon. Going to Chapel Street for the day.'

'Goodness. That sounds tragic too.'

'We're yet to find out their story. But that's not your concern. You won't be one of those families left empty — without justice.'

'I haven't got to those emotions yet. I'm still dealing with the fact that I'll never be able to pop over and see Mum again. Nor will she see her grandkids again.'

She lifted her hand to cover her mouth again, shakily.

'We can cancel your mother's cards and mobile phone now we have a trace on the offenders,' André said. 'Do you want to do that yourself or would you like Constable Luxton to look after it?'

'The statements have already come for both of those. Mum was too old-school to switch things to on-line,' Sandra Burch said, regaining her composure. 'They were in the post I collected from Mum's this morning. Mind you, it was only the end of the month yesterday. They're quick off the mark to get money off you — even when you're dead.'

'Can I take a look at them, please?' Luxton asked.

André had drifted out of the conversation to examine the mantelpiece photograph of Mrs Varrenti.

'Of course. I've already seen that the card and phone have been used since Mum died. That's why I expected you to have news.'

'You've opened them?'

'Yes. With the phone calls and the credit card transactions still appearing, it looks like Mum never died.'

André looked up from the photograph. 'What did you just say?

Chapter 27

André drove Ella's Subaru XV to pick her up in the city after work. Their double kayak was strapped to the roof for a training session on Port Phillip Bay. The long sliver, with a pair of lithium carbon paddles strapped to its hull, hung well over each end of the SUV's cabin.

He nosed into the Collins Street extension where Ella waited, away from the solid stream of peak hour traffic in Spencer Street.

She smiled at the sight of him and weaved through the parked cars to slip into the passenger seat.

'Being on the bay is just what I need after the day I've had.'

'Stressful?'

'Flat out.'

'Newspapers are supposed to be frantic, aren't they? I've seen those old black and white movies.'

She smiled.

'There's still plenty of that. Some days more than others. The budget leaks came a day early and everyone was chasing angles from your "average taxpayer". You try finding someone average.'

'Are leaks so acceptable they have a recognised schedule?'

'I don't need you getting cynical on me. Not today. On top of all the work stuff, I had a Zoom meeting with Max — Mum's accountant. He wanted to talk to me about when to put the farm on the market.'

'What did you say?'

'I had to fudge. I inferred there were going to be more probate delays. He was still pretty keen, though. According to him, it's been a couple of good years — weather and crop-wise. With the place travelling so well and the books looking good, he thinks there'll never be a better time to have it on the market.'

André turned his head briefly from the road to look at her.

'If you're not going to sell, why don't you just tell him.'

'Because Max's accountancy practice is local and I don't want other people hearing that I'm thinking about not selling. At least not until I'm definite about it. If Trent Hofner gets wind of it, he's likely to drop the ball managing the place. That's the last thing I want right now.'

'When could Lila take over if you do go ahead with things?'

'God, we haven't even discussed that. And I don't want to. Not until she and I sort out everything. God knows when we'll get a chance to do that now. She's gone back to South Australia.'

'I thought you and her were sorted. Can't you deal with anything else as you go along?'

'It's still niggling at me that she wasn't completely up front about her and Mum. It might not sound like something that should stand in the way but ... '

She glanced at André.

'I dunno why, "A". I'm just not ready for her to get everything her own way — on a platter.'

André drove in silent thought.

'How was your day?' she said as a full stop to their discussion about Lila. It was Ella's cue to extract training gear from her backpack and begin changing in the car. When André stopped at lights, Ella was down to her black bra and slipping on a bright training top.

'Ella. They're looking at you.'

'They're women, *and* I'll never see them again.'

Now she had her skirt off and was wiggling into Lycra shorts.

'The light's green, André.'

He reverted his eyes back to the road and gave an apologetic wave to the toot-er behind him.

'My day?' He emphasised his words to herald something profound. 'I reckon I figured out how Meredith did it.'

'Really! How? Can you prove it?'

'Not yet. 'So far, it's only my how-dun-it solution to a locked room mystery. If Glenevis and Alex buy it, *then* we can begin evidence testing.'

'Locked room mystery? It was the middle of an absolute wilderness. It couldn't have been less locked-room if you tried.'

'You know what I mean. Do you want to hear my theory?'

'Do you want to share this kayak ride with me?'

'Since you put it like that. My theory is that John Meredith killed his wife on the weekend *before* he went to London. He deliberately flew to Mildura that weekend so that he could drop her body in the desert en-route, never to be found again. Eve Delmonte would have gone with him and passed herself off as Portia Meredith for their night in Mildura. When they returned, Eve used Portia's mobile phone and credit card until after Meredith was safely out of the country. All the while, Portia appeared to be alive. Electronically, she still existed.

'The beauty about the plan was, Meredith could do it all himself. No need to engage other pilots or freeze the body, or anything complicated. Just him and Eve.'

He glanced at Ella for a reaction.

'I don't know about calling it beautiful, but … how elaborate. How conniving. How …' she gestured for a better adjective.

'Ingenious?'

'That's too much of a compliment. The question is, will the theory fit with what you have?'

'It's only in my head so far. I actually saw an example of this today where a woman's card and phone were used after she died. Anyone reading the monthly statements would assume she still lived.'

'So, you can chase all that card and phone activity down and you've got him?'

They had joined the slowly moving four lane peak-hour congestion passing over West Gate Bridge as they headed to the former port of Williamstown. André lifted his hands from the wheel in frustration.

'It might not be that easy. Glenevis hates anything that sounds more like a movie plot than reality. "Dead woman killed in the future!" That kind of thing. He's old school when it comes to murder. It happens close to home and killers usually slip up. Leave that over-egged stuff to Colombo.'

'But he'll be okay with you investigating the possibility, surely?'

'I'll run it past him in the morning. We'll need to check it out in any case. He should be all right with it. As long as we keep plugging holes and not creating new holes.'

'You know what my considered opinion is?'

'Tell me.'

'As a mystery solution, it appeals to the writer in me, but I also think it has a plausible ring to it. I had John Meredith eyeball fear into me. In that moment, I saw that he was capable of something like this. The lawyer in him is more than capable of covering his tracks in such a contriving way. And the whole thing is such a riddle that the solution has to be something …' She searched the space in front of her eyes again for the right word.

'Unorthodox?'

'Nothing as orthodox as unorthodox. You're dealing with utter callousness.'

Chapter 28

Although Rab Glenevis milked being Scottish, André had seen the ephemera on display behind his desk too many times to be transfixed. His office couldn't be more Scottish if that country's top TV sleuths, DCI Jimmy Taggart, Constable Hamish MacBeth and DI Jimmy Pérez, had all moved their desks into the room with him.

All available shelf space was taken. A framed photograph of the Victorian Police pipe band flanked by the figurine of a piper in a kilt; a "Scots Dictionary"; a mini blue and white national flag, and a tartan coffee mug bearing the Cameron clan crest — obviously not for drinking out of. The drinking version bearing the slogan "If It Isn't Scottish, It's Crap" lived on Glenevis's desk, as did his name-plate. In case his name didn't sound Scottish enough, someone had added "Mc" by hand in front of Glenevis. Only the Scots Dictionary held lingering intrigue for André. Could it be as loony as he imagined?

'I have a theory,' André said, once he sat down in one of two chairs on the visitor's side of Glenevis's desk.

'You dinnae look too pleased about it,' he responded. 'I take it this is aboot Meredith.'

'Yeah. It's only a theory at this stage, but if you reckon it's got legs, I'll start chasing down evidence and testing it.'

'So nae exactly your traditional trace, investigate an' evaluate methodology then?'

'More analysis of a hypothesis, if you like.'

'Well, Ah'm nae gonna know whether I like it or nae if you don't tell me.'

'Okay. I reckon John Meredith killed his wife and got rid of her body before he flew to London.'

He paused a tad. Enough to see if Glenevis reacted so far. He hadn't.

'It would have happened when he and Portia supposedly flew from Bendigo to Mildura the weekend before he went to London. Eve flew with him with Portia's dead or drugged body also on board. Eve helps him drop the body along the way. Then, for the rest of the trip, Eve acts the part of Portia. They kept conspiring to fabricate Portia's existence until he's out of the country. Nice and clean. No other players needed.'

Glenevis leant back in his chair and clasped his hands behind his head.

'Fabricated her existence. How would they do tha' exactly?'

'Used her credit card and phone. Stuff like that. Remember how her mother never actually took the call when Portia phoned the nursing home.'

'An' have you checked? Nothing wrong with a theory if there's some hard evidence,' Glenevis said.

'We haven't been looking in this space, but the bits we do know, fit. The rest of it is going to take more work. The most compelling thing is that there are no actual sightings or photographs of Portia Meredith since she and John Meredith flew to Mildura on the weekend before he left for London.

'It's possible that Eve Delmonte joined Meredith at Bendigo airport to help load a drugged Portia Meredith into the plane. She takes over being Portia after they drop the body and land at Mildura — where nobody knows either of them. Apparently the two women were not unalike.'

Glenevis held his cheek thoughtfully. André could see he wanted more.

'They would also have jettisoned the case Portia packed for the weekend away. The missing case of clothes was a prop to look like she left him of her own accord. It was however real and it had to be got rid of. It's probably still out there in the desert.'

'What does Deb Harvey say? Did Missing Persons check any o' this out when she first went missin'?'

'I haven't asked her yet. I wanted to run it past you first. It's really plausible to me but, if I'm honest, there is a television plot-ish element. You know, "He travelled back in time to kill his wife." What do you think?'

'See if Deb is around an' get her in here. We can ask her now.'

Deborah was summoned and André explained his theory — with more hesitation than enthusiasm.

'We didn't investigate that exact scenario,' Deborah admitted. 'But we did what we could to verify all of Portia's movements leading up to her disappearance. We went hard on CCTV and resorted to warrants if we thought it could yield a response. In the end, it didn't yield anything incriminating. We thought the matter was settled with toll-point pictures of Portia Meredith driving her husband to the airport and going back to her home without him. But I have to tell you, it was the middle of the day and reflection on the windscreen obscured the image. Finally, we got a finger print match on the driver side door handle, and from the steering wheel. After that, that was pretty much that.'

'How could you get a finger print match? She wasn't on record, was she?' André asked.

'The car prints matched those on personal stuff in the house. Make-up. That sort of thing. Also, there were people from the office that phoned her that week too. It sounds like an appealing conspiracy, but from what we found, I don't think it stacks up.'

'Did you know that Eve Delmonte and John Meredith were having an affair at the time?'

'No. But we put it on file when they later got together. There was no sniff of that at the time. Of course, Portia was not known to be dead at the time, either.'

'Maybe that's part of it. Staff were too loyal or sympathetic to John Meredith to voice suspicions when it was believed Portia had left him,' André said. 'Staff have been more forthcoming since Portia's body was found. And knowing that Eve Delmonte has shacked up with John Meredith.'

'Maybe. But you're not simply arranging the pieces in order to fit the theory are you André? If you're right, it's an extremely elaborate crime. Maybe too elaborate.'

'Good point, Deb,' Glenevis contributed at last. 'Short of a photo o' John Meredith flyin' a plane over th' drop site, I cannae see how we can pin this on him. But thanks for th' input, Deb.'

His conclusion seemed to dismiss the idea, and Deborah.

'No problem,' she said, sounding vindicated.

Glenevis waited for Deborah to leave his office before telling André: 'Check it out.'

'But you just said … '

'Ah was appeasin' Deb's professional jealousy or whatever shite that was. Ah actually like your theory. She reckons they went hard. You an' Alex go harder. Okay? If you have to, you walk, drive or crawl the exact trail he followed. From when Portia was last seen ta when she got on that plane. See first-hand if he couldnae pulled it aff like you're sayin'. You know what Ah'm sayin?'

'Yeah. Okay.' André said.

'One other thing. Keep it low key an' well under wraps. Whatever you do, dinnae go anywhere near Meredith. Ah dinnae want ta give him ammunition ta ridicule us publicly. You only question Meredith if you have everything locked down. If this is th' MO that Meredith an' Delmonte used, then they will ha' slipped up somewhere. You're talking aboot keeping a charade going for a week and a half. So you should be able ta find somethin' bulletproof. If nae, find another theory. Got it?'

'Got it.'

André sat on the end of Alex's workstation expounding his theory. He liked Alex's nonchalant response.

'Feasible, I suppose. So, what now?'

'Those tollway pics of Portia Meredith going to and from the airport to drop her husband off — the ones we saw on the missing person file?'

'What about them?'

'Chase up an electronic version and get Jennie from IT to see what computer magic she can weave on the windscreen glare. See if it really is Portia Meredith.'

'Right.'

'Ideally, we also need to speak to M & Ms staff again. According to Deb Harvey, they spoke with Portia Meredith sometime between the Mildura flight and John Meredith's London trip.'

'Too easy.'

'Not easy. I'm under strict instructions not to do anything that will alert Meredith to this line of inquiry.'

'I can try Charles Lyon. He all but wore a disguise so that Meredith wouldn't know he spoke to us.'

André thought for more than a moment.

'All right then. As long as Glenevis doesn't get a sniff. And let's re-check every credit card transaction, road toll registration, social media post and mobile phone call Portia Meredith supposedly had after the Mildura flight. Double check for CCTV or witnesses.'

'Right,' Alex said, adding the task to the list in his notebook. 'And what about Eve Delmonte. She wasn't in the frame when the Missing Persons Unit did the initial investigation. We should re-check what we have on her and account for her movements over the Castlemaine weekend and beyond.'

'Dead right,' said André.

'That could be our motto,' Alex said. 'And it's not even Greek.'

'I'm afraid this is the best I can do,' Jennie said to André and Alex. They leant over her shoulder to examine the tollway photo of Portia Meredith's sapphire black BMW Coupe on one of the two oversized screens at Jennie's desk.

'This is the one on the way to Tullamarine Airport. You can see a man I presume is John Meredith in the passenger seat.

And this … ' John Meredith disappeared with the click of the mouse, ' … is on the way back.'

'It doesn't look any clearer than the printouts of the Missing Persons Unit files.' Alex said.

'I'm sorry, but that's timing for you, or Murphy's law. The sun is reflecting off the windscreen in both directions and the driver's sun visor obscures nearly all her face in any case. The visor is positioned way forward. She might even be wearing a cap but with all that happening, there's no way of telling. You can't pull up your socks if you're not wearing any.'

'Now there's a good Aussie saying for you,' André said to Alex.

'I'm Australian too, I was born here you know.'

'There's something else I found out too,' Jennie said, ignoring André's and Alex's proverb battle. 'I thought they might have retrieved better examples from other traffic cameras along the obvious routes back to Beaumaris.'

'And?'

'Nothing. The driver, whoever she was, joined the M2 freeway to the airport just before it passed through the final toll point. Either the Flemington Road or Brunswick Street on-ramp. The same thing happened on the way back. They would have used the same entry/exit, possibly to make sure they only passed through one toll point. Between there and Beaumaris, they appear to have avoided conventional routes altogether. Like the Bolte Bridge and tunnels to the eastern suburbs.'

'So, what you're saying is, this could be a carefully calculated part of my theory that they fabricated Portia Meredith's existence. They allowed a single, staged, toll record. They know that having no toll record on an airport run is not credible, so they limit it to one toll pass in each direction, thereby minimising the kind of scrutiny we're giving it right now. Is Meredith that calculating?'

Jennie had an answer.

'I don't know anything about Meredith, but they could have gone via the CBD or to any of the million-plus other places in our state's capital city. I've heard that people actually do that for any number of reasonable reasons.'

Alex shot her a wry face and asked, 'Can you go back to the first photo?'

'See that,' he pointed. 'John Meredith has not put down the passenger side visor. Maybe he wants to be seen clearly and maybe the driver has lowered her's because she doesn't want to be seen clearly.'

'That may well suit our theory Alex, but unless we come up with a recognisable photograph of Eve Delmonte driving, nothing changes. Don't forget Deborah Harvey's mob found Portia Meredith's fingerprints on the steering wheel.'

'Well, that's odd then,' Alex said. 'Go back to the second photo again,' he asked Jennie.

John Meredith's image disappeared in favour of the driver's side close-up.

'Look, the driver's hands are not on the steering wheel.'

'So they aren't.' André marvelled. 'Do you reckon she drove with her knees all the way from Beaumaris and back, just to retain Portia Meredith's finger prints on the wheel?'

'It's odd, whoever's driving. I don't know what to make of that.'

'Another baffling tangent. Just what we need. Thanks for your help in any case, Jennie.'

The lift door closed behind André and Alex on the IT bunker level. They watched the rising floor levels illuminate above the closed doors. Alex spoke after three floors of lift silence.

'You know, this theory of yours. It might explain some of the blanks I've come across for Eve Delmonte, mate.'

'Yeah?'

'Yeah. I'll show you back at the office.'

The lift doors opened to their own level and Alex was soon entering his computer password and navigating to a folder labelled "Delmonte". He clicked to open a spread sheet of dates, times and activities.

'This is a four-week timeline for Eve, leading up to when Portia Meredith was reported missing. What I found is: there's nothing that shows she was anywhere other than in Melbourne from when John and Portia Meredith left for Castlemaine.'

'And that fits how?'

'There is no record of Eve Delmonte being *anywhere* on the Sunday and Monday that John and Portia Meredith flew to Mildura. She did not use her credit cards. Her phone appears to be turned off. There is no toll-road use. There's a complete electronic hole in her life. That's not an easy thing for anyone to accomplish in this day and age. Not without trying extra hard. If she did accompany John Meredith to Mildura, she would not want any calls to or from her mobile that would tell us so.'

André nodded sagely.

'I reckon you might be on to something with this theory of yours, mate.'

'Good. Welcome aboard. Keep checking everything Portia was supposed to have been doing since that Castlemaine weekend. And don't forget to have a word with Charles Lyon again.'

'Okay. But do you want to stick your neck right out?'

'You mean speak to Eve Delmonte and risk the wrath of Glenevis?'

'No, no, no. I don't mean interviewing her as a suspect. I'm not suggesting that at all. But what about as a witness. What if we had a tip-off that Simon Stone did come down from Sydney to do the deed and had been seen hanging around the Meredith's office. We should check whether other people noticed him in the area, shouldn't we? Glenevis would want us to do that.'

Chapter 29

'Thank you for coming in again, Ms Delmonte.'

'I'll do what I can to help find Portia's killer.'

'We're trying to establish Mrs Meredith's state of mind at the time she went missing. I know the Missing Persons Unit went through this with you at the time and you told them, "There was nothing out of the ordinary."' André said, having opened the manilla folder before him and reading from the topmost page.

'That's right. I visited her, on Tuesday night I think, because she was on her own while John was in London.'

'On the Friday before that, Charles Lyon spoke to her on the phone. He told the Missing Persons Unit that she seemed unusually jolly. Did she seem that way when you saw her on the following Tuesday?'

Eve's face registered a sharp pause.

'Oh? She seemed fine,' she said, seemingly surprised to learn about Charles Lyon's phone call.

'Nothing you've thought of since then that might have seemed unusual?'

'I'm afraid not.'

'Mm, there's something I want to show you,' André said, flicking further into the manila folder. 'I must have left it on my desk. I won't be a minute.'

André returned with a glossy A4 photograph of Simon Stone.

'Here it is,' he announced, holding it out for Eve Delmonte. He let go before she had hold of it completely and she lunged to catch it.

'Sorry,' André said. 'Do you know this man?'

'Only from photographs. It's Simon Stone. He's the estate agent from Sydney that Portia took a restraining order out on.'

'Yes. We're asking employees if they happened to see him in the vicinity of the office or the Meredith home around the time Portia disappeared. Did you?'

She took time to give it considered thought.

'Mm. Not that I noticed specifically,' she said. 'I didn't have reason to be suspicious at the time so he might well have been there without me noticing.'

'So you didn't see him?'

She studied the photograph again.

'That may have been when I noticed a New South Wales car in the street. I know that's not the sort of thing that normally stays in your memory, even though their number plates are yellow and stand out from the crowd. But there was one that showed up a few days running. Not that I gave it any more thought than that. I mean I wouldn't have made a connection or bothered taking the registration or anything.'

'And this was at the office or when you visited Portia at Beach Road?'

'I'm talking about when I went to Beach Road.'

'What about around at the office? We understand he might have been in Melbourne the previous week and may even have visited the office on the Monday that John and Portia Meredith were in Mildura.'

'I'm afraid I was in the field that day.'

'You can remember that exact day after such a long time?'

Some imperceptible movement told André an alarm set off in her head. Perhaps there *was* no movement. Maybe only the steadying of her head, or her mouth becoming slightly more fixed. She had been drawn unexpectedly into the six-month old alibi she had rehearsed in her head about that Monday. She had forgotten about it until this moment. The day her phone was switched off. *How did it all go?*

'I think something important arose about the Queenscliff project and I had to interrupt John on this extended weekend break.'

'So that would show on your phone record?'

'No,' she hastened to say — too quickly. 'I accidently left my phone at home on the charger that day and had to borrow someone else's on site.' André watched the wheels turn in her head as she dug the hole deeper. Eve Delmonte had the same sense of her own unravelling — enough to stage a recovery.

'Does it matter what I was doing? Isn't Simon Stone the one you're after? All this thing with John might have happened on a different Monday. Like you said, it's a long time ago now.'

'Was John away on other Mondays?'

'I don't remember. He must have been. I'll have to check my diary. He may simply have been away from the office on a project. It might not have been a Monday. Or it might have been the Monday that I was home sick.'

It was not going well. She made to escape.

'Is there anything else?'

'No,' said André slowly, 'I think you've told us enough. There's nothing else is there, Detective Castellanos? You've got all that in your notes?'

'I have,' Alex said with his best unsettling smile.

'Well thanks for coming in again Ms Delmonte. There's nothing else you'd like to tell us while you're here, is there?'

'Not if that's all the questions you've got.'

'Of course. Can you show Ms Delmonte out, please, Detective Castellanos.'

Alex returned to the interview room, closed the door, and gushed.

'We could have shot that alibi down big time if we didn't back off. Could she have wanted to have seen Simon Stone any more or what? A car with a New South Wales number plate indeed.'

'I don't know why I didn't think of this before. We should get this photograph checked for fingerprints.'

André held up the A4 high-gloss photograph of Simon Stone by the tip of one corner — the smeared fingerprint of Eve Delmonte's reflex catch indelible on Mr Stone's forehead.

'If this whole thing is as elaborate as I say it is, I think Eve would have been ultra careful about leaving prints in Portia's BMW. But check it against the ones Missing Persons found. Just in case.'

'Sure,' Alex said with a worried look. 'Won't Delmonte and Meredith realise we are not interested in Simon Stone when they discover we haven't asked their other staff if he was seen in or around the building on that Monday?'

'I hope so. Let them know we know how they did it.'

Chapter 30

This time Alex arrived at Commercial Hotel before Charles Lyon.

'I'm on the Coopers again. Same for you?' Alex offered when Lyon found him on a stool at the same window bench.

'Thanks.'

'Getting anywhere?' Lyon asked Alex when he arrived back at the table with two schooners.

'Starting to piece it together,' Alex said.

'Not saying then?'

'No. I mean we're starting to piece it together.'

'Fair enough,' Lyon accepted. 'So, what piece do you want from me?'

'Mrs Meredith's state of mind leading up to her disappearance. In the Missing Persons report, it says that you were on the phone to her on the Friday. The day before John Meredith flew to London.'

'That's right.'

'Can you tell me how she seemed.'

'She seemed jovial from memory, although I didn't actually speak to her directly.'

'What do you mean, you didn't actually speak to her?'

'I was writing up some meeting minutes for a Sydney project. Portia was not working on the project but I wanted to make sure I got the politics right because the consultants and investors were part of her Sydney network. I was in John's office and mentioned to him that I hadn't been able to get Portia on her mobile. He said she was having some problems with it and that he would try her on their home phone for me. He had to speak to her in any case.'

'So, he rang Portia at home on her land line while you were in his office?'

'Yes. It was one of those things where the person holding the handset conducts a three-way conversation. I remember plenty of jocularity. John told her of my concerns about how the Sydney consultant would react if I minuted what was actually spoken — without spin. He uh-huh–ed through her reply and relayed to me that Portia called the Sydney consultant a pedantic old woman, and not to worry about him. It went on like that for a bit. I remember because Portia was not usually so frank about her fellow Sydney-siders.'

'And John Meredith never passed the handset to you to speak to her directly?'

'No. But I can tell you she was in good spirits.'

'Uh-huh.'

'I tried to speak to her again the following week but I only got her message bank. Then a couple of days after that, no one could find her.'

'Yeah. We know how it went from there,' Alex said.

'So, Fi's got you sniffing around St Kilda … and she hasn't managed to get you shot at yet. It can't be all bad.'

'Yeah-nah. I reckon she's going to get a result too mate,' Alex told André.

It was mid-morning at the St Kilda beach-side café. They strolled beyond the cafe's late breakfasters to drink their coffees sitting on the lip of the passing boardwalk, their feet dangling above the sand. The mid-week bayside trail traffic was sparse with relaxed walkers outnumbering earnest cyclists and runners, an occasional stroller-pushing-mum-runner among them. Perhaps the weather had something to do with it. The grey bay reflected an overcast sky.

'I still miss seeing the Tasmanian ferry over there,' Alex told André as he looked west along the shore to Port Melbourne. In recent times, the tall Spirit of Tasmania had abandoned its original mainland berth for the regional bayside city of Geelong.

André had his own distraction.

'How can they do that in this weather?' He watched two Speedo-clad ancient leather bodies wade into the water and dive under.

'Fucked if I know.'

The vista lent itself to savouring hot coffee. Their takeaways were empty when Alex filled André in about Charles Lyon.

'He's convinced he and John Meredith were having a phone conversation with Portia Meredith,' he concluded.

'You didn't suggest otherwise to him.'

'No. I wanted to see if he had any suspicions himself. He had none. If John Meredith faked it, he did a convincing job. Charles Lyon is no fool.'

'He probably had Eve on the line. That would make the conversation sound natural,' André suggested.

They lapsed into contemplative silence as they watched a frustrated poodle and an even more frustrated boxer fight their leashes to sniff an aloof border-collie.

'Have you looked at Portia Meredith's supposed movements again?'

'Yeah. It's all very interesting and serendipitous in its way.'

'Serendipitous for who?'

'For us. There's far less than her usual credit card use after the Mildura flight. It's all contactless, of course. Nothing large enough for a PIN number.'

'Of course.'

'Buys food at a small supermarket — also without cameras where you need them for something like this. Some purchases in Acland Street, but it's too long ago for the shop people to remember her. There might be some street CCTV we can track down and trawl through. Zac and Sue will start looking at it when they're off Fi's thing. No petrol station purchases where it's usually CCTV city. If Portia's car did need a top up, I suppose they could do it with a container or simply use cash.

'Same scenario with her phone. Plenty of incoming calls, most going to her voicemail. The few answered calls and outgoing calls could easily be staged by Eve Delmonte and John Meredith. Eve probably took the calls from John Meredith in London when he supposedly spoke to Portia. Interestingly, a couple of the calls and texts between Portia and Eve are from the same tower.'

'I guess it's not impossible for Eve to be making a call to Portia in Portia's neighbourhood, but she lived in Docklands at that time. She could however be calling Portia's handset in the same room — setting all this up.' André said.

'Exactly.'

'And the fingerprints?'

'That's the bad news, mate. Nothing Missing Persons found in the BMW match Eve's prints. As far as your new theory goes, that's your biggest spanner in the works. The fact that Portia's prints were on the BMW's door handle and steering wheel after the airport run. Everything else can be easily construed to fit the hypothesis — but not Portia's finger prints.'

André sat and stewed. Alex buckled as silence grew.

'It was a long shot,' he said.

'No, it wasn't. This isn't construing things to fit. We simply identified the most logical explanation for the way all these things unfolded. When you take into account how incongruous most of these things were, they had to be staged. There's no other reasonable explanation.'

'Except for Portia's finger prints. The only hard bit evidence in all of this,' Alex persisted.

'Yes. But only the prints on the steering wheel. With the door handle prints, you could avoid disturbing them by opening the door from the other side. The steering wheel however — that's a trickier proposition. There has to be an explanation. We just haven't found it yet.'

'You reckon? So how do you propose doing that.'

'By taking a road trip.'

He chose his moment. Lying on the couch together, scrolling through Netflix. Ella's choice.

'How would you like a change from training on Beach Road this weekend?'

'I can feel an ulterior motive coming on' Ella sang to the ancient memory of a Four-X beer commercial.

'Sure, but you'll get to ride country lanes without traffic lights and without cycle-raged motorists. The only traffic is likely to be a tractor and you'll be the one doing the passing for a change.'

A suspicious, 'And … '

'And a romantic country cottage.'

'Really?' she said, sitting upright on the couch to examine his expressions. 'You can't un-say that. What's the deal?'

'I'm thinking of going to Castlemaine and Bendigo to kind of re-enact the Portia Meredith thing. See with my own eyes. The Airbnb they stayed at in Castlemaine is free and I've got a reserve on it. What do you reckon?'

'You're offering to take me on a romantic weekend in Central Victoria to kill me?'

'Pretty much. We'll take the bikes and get our training in up there — do a winery crawl on two wheels.'

'Is that before or after you kill me?

'Before, of course. I'm a gentleman.'

Chapter 31

'I know we're going to Castlemaine for you to kill me, but I still think this is romantic.'

'What can I say?' André said, turning to look at Ella behind the wheel. 'I'm a new age kind of guy. I wouldn't kill you just anywhere. I've got style.'

André began chasing radio stations as 3-RRR reception faded behind Mount Macedon and Hanging Rock.

'Bugger, I love triple R.'

'Play my phone instead and stop being bored,' Ella scolded.

'I spy with my … '

'Piss off. I'm not ten.'

'I'll look online where we can do a ride then,' André said, and retrieved his phone. Their mountain bikes peered through the back window from a towbar mounted rack.

The dual carriageway of the Calder Freeway ran all the way to Bendigo. André watched the roll-call of bypassed towns on the big green exit signs. Diggers Rest. Where would-be miners once put their feet up after a hard day's slog walking to the goldfields. The staging post was now less than half an hour's drive out of Melbourne. Then Woodend, where the original route ran through the once-feared Black Forest. The foreboding stretch of fire-charred mega eucalypts and deep undergrowth was once the home of bushrangers. Today the autobahn bypass through steep pine plantations evoked its German namesake. There was an irony in there that André couldn't put his finger on.

Bleak flats and more lost city radio reception gave way to rolling countryside near the turnoff to Daylesford — a celebrated spa town escape. By the time they reached the Castlemaine exit through native box-ironbark forest, vineyards were visible on the shoulder of Mount Alexander.

'Do you want to drive so I can navigate to the Airbnb?' Ella offered.

'It's in the GPS when we need it,' André came back. 'Let's head into town for a coffee first.'

Castlemaine was heralded by Chewton on its outskirts. Its scattered, historic-ness and hilly charm was not lost on creative emigres and city commuter tree-changers. Original Castlemaniacs observed with interest as hipsterism challenged their country town ethos and house prices ran off the leash. Ella drove directly to the cafe strip despite André's directions.

'It does feel like a holiday town,' Ella said as she waited at the tiniest of footpath tables for her coffee and pear cake to be delivered.

'It's more of a bob-each-way for me. Good coffee with that farm ute and onboard kelpie parked out front. Like having Degraves Street in Dimboola.'

'After growing up in Yaapeet, this is like another country to me.'

'Anywhere's another country after Yaapeet. Hey. See that ATM over the road. It took the last photograph we have of

Portia Meredith. She withdrew four hundred bucks.'

'Your mind never leaves the job, does it?'

'You're right. Let's get to the Airbnb so we can get on the bikes and see the place properly.'

'Give me a look at the map first,' said Ella. 'I want to get there today.'

'You're forgetting I won a navigation award for the event at Bribie Island,' André said in his own defence.

'That was on foot. On roads you're hopeless without the GPS.'

The winding out-of-town lanes told the opposite rural tale to Ella's Mallee roots, where neighbour bought out neighbour in an exponential attempt to make broad acre cropping viable. Here, among hilly pastures and trees, holdings were shrinking. Fledgling olive groves sat cheek by jowl with artist studios, alpacas and the occasional shed and caravan of aspirant owner-builders. The bucolic nirvana was a harsh mistress for some, with "For Sale" signs on several front gates. Their greyed half-built timber skeletons and neglected vines represented romantic enterprise gone wrong. Divorce, job-redundancy, or the realisation of just how hard building a house can be.

'I have a theory about houses that start out with people living in a shed like that,' Ella said.

'You have a living-in-a-shed theory?'

'Yes I do. My theory is that Australians love living in a shed. See that caravan and shed on our left?'

Ella slowed for André to take in the caravan beside a colour-bond double-bay shed with a protruding wood-heater flue, a plastic water tank, and television aerial.

'Suburban-house designers have refined those elements into a brick veneer version. You have a look next time you're in a new estate. The facades are dominated by a giant remote-controlled double garage door with a front door and a one-window room tacked onto its side. It'll go down in history as shed-ism, or the shed period. They should preserve that caravan and shed as a heritage embryo of our era.'

'See. I told you we were coming to a historic area,' André quipped.

They ruminated shed-ism silently until André consulted the map and declared, 'Turn left after this bridge.'

The white gravel road crossed a single lane timber bridge. A sign to Ostler's Cottage was fixed to a redgum on the far side. A hand depicted on the sign literally pointed left.

'The owner's house is along this road on the same side before we get there. We need to call in and collect the key from Molly. Her place is called Lochleven.'

Weather-worn piers stood at the entrance to Lochleven and a long drive led to what appeared to be an original homestead. Elaborate chimneys sprouted above its high slate roof. Bay windows protruded from walls of handmade red bricks along the timbered veranda. The resplendent detail kept presenting — fretwork, finials, stained-glass window trims …

Molly was there to greet them where the formal gravel drive formed a roundabout in the lawned front grounds.

'Ostler's Cottage is where the station's horse keeper lived when our family first settled the place. They had a contract to provide changeover horses for Cobb and Co when the route ran through the property. It's about half a kilometre further down the road. Most people don't know that an ostler is a stableman.'

She led them through the wide entrance hall into a side

room with an antique desk and chairs. Ella and André dawdled after her, their heads swivelling at the high pressed ceilings, friezes and the elaborate mantelpiece in the office.

'This is great,' Ella said, striving not to gush.

'Thank you. We're lucky to have kept it in the family. We don't have much land any more but Paul and I love doing this. We do accommodation in this house as well as the cottage.'

She produced the key from a drawer as she spoke and held it out for Ella to take.

'Should we drop it back here when we go? How do you normally do it?' André interrupted.

'We're usually at the farmer's market on Sunday mornings, so leave the key on the kitchen table and close the locked front door behind you. There's everything you need for breakfast in the cottage — cereal, bacon and eggs, bread, coffee and tea. No other meals, though — as you would have read. If you don't want to go into town to eat, you can do something on the barbeque.'

'Oh, we're organised,' Ella said, 'We did our homework.'

'Lovely. I hope you have a nice stay.'

'Before we do go,' André said. 'I have a particular interest in coming to Ostler's Cottage. I'm with the police and I'm involved in the case of the woman who went missing not long after staying here with her husband back in April. Someone would have contacted you about her at the time. You probably read that her body was found in the desert not long ago.'

'Oh. Right.' Molly said with obvious surprise at the shift in conversation. 'I do remember. Not that it's a selling point for us.'

'This is not an official visit,' André reassured her. 'But I would like to ask you a couple of questions while I have the opportunity. If you don't mind. Here's my ID.'

'Yes, of course.'

She didn't sound completely at ease. André pushed on nonetheless.

'I know you were asked this when she first disappeared, but do you remember them staying here?'

'I remembered them coming here but nothing else. They collected the key when they arrived, like you're doing now. I didn't see them leave. Nor did Paul. We might have heard or seen their car leave from a distance. They both stood exactly where you and Ella are standing now. They would have left the key inside when they left. They already knew the drill.'

'Why? Had they been here before?' André asked.

'Oh yes. That was their second visit. I remember looking that up. Their first visit was about eighteen months before that.'

'Do you remember what car they drove?'

'Not the first time. But I remember their second visit. They came in a black Mercedes with tinted windows.'

'And there was nothing unusual about how they left the place.'

'No. There was nothing noted in our records. It was a straightforward stay as far as we were concerned.'

'Do you know what they did for an evening meal?'

'Only what I might have said to the police when she first went missing. I can't even remember what I told them. It's so long ago.'

'Never mind. That's okay, and thanks Molly. I'm sorry to mix business with pleasure but this is an inquiry that would have brought me here anyway. Sadly, it's a case of mixing pleasure with business.'

'I'd do something about that if I were you,' Molly said, turning to Ella with a knowing look.

'Oh, my goodness,' said Ella and braked to a stop at the gate. 'It's a genuine rose covered cottage.'

Too many tantalising details began to emerge from the overgrown cottage garden, still in flower. White multi-pane window frames against warm stone walls; a hand pump to an underground tank; freestone garden walls and a dormer attic window overlooking the jungle of traditional plantings; the veranda-end overgrown by a climbing banksia rose. Two elms and two palms at the front and a mulberry tree behind the cottage attested to the garden's many decades.

The gravel drive led to the rear of the cottage where a white framed conservatory opened onto an arrival area that stretched to the treed creek line and rolling pastoral panorama beyond.

Modernity prevailed in the conservatory's living area with a lush brown leather sofa and solid sideboards in fine natural timbers. Further in, bare wood floors and staircase had been brought back to life without losing their original patinas. The main bedroom took up the entire upstairs section. It was decorated by an altogether different hand. An elaborate carved mahogany giant four poster bed with canopy overwhelmed its surroundings, as did a spa bath and en-suite.

'Wow. A four-poster bed,' exclaimed Ella, 'That'll be a first. I'll bet it wasn't like this when the ostler and his family lived here.'

'Hmm.'

'Did you see the hamper of local nibbles downstairs, and the open fire?' Ella enthused. 'And this spa bath. I'm having that when we get back from our ride.'

'Okay.' André answered distractedly.

Ella paused, stopped in her enthusiastic tracks.

'Stop investigating the crime scene. This is too romantic. In fact, I'm starting to doubt your theory. How could anyone bring their partner to somewhere like this to kill them? It beggars belief.'

'It's perfect.' André said. Ella came to him with a smile and wrapped her arms around him — too soon.

'It's out of sight of anyone. He's been here before and knows he won't see or be seen by Molly or Paul once he collects the key. Portia speaks to her mum in Sydney on Saturday. On Sunday morning they cook breakfast here. He drugs her tea or coffee with Rohypnol. The Mercedes has tinted windows so no one can see a drugged Portia Meredith when he puts her in the car. It's so perfect.'

Ella stood back, opened her mouth and gave him a stare and a head shake.

'That's it,' she said. 'You haven't heard a peep out of me about Lila. So how about you return the favour and zip it. You've had your go to get it off your chest. That's it. No more John and Portia Meredith for the rest of our stay. Okay?'

'Sorry. I'd forgotten about Lila. Have you decided what you're going to do?'

'I'm going to see her after this getaway. And that's all I'm saying. And that's all you're saying. This is our getaway. Okay?'

'Yeah. I'm done if you are.'

He moved closer to hold both her hands.

'Don't forget we've got an open fire, a spa and a four-poster bed to experience before you drug me at breakfast.'

'All in good time. Do you want to know what I found on-line while you were driving?' He waggled his phone and continued. 'We can have a crack at La Larr Ba Gauwa — the mountain bike park at Mount Alexander. It's just down the road. It's supposed to be awesome. And there's a winery we can swing by on the way back. Grab a local shiraz to go with all those things on your checklist.'

'So long as we add one other thing.'

Chapter 32

'This guide describes Bendigo as Vienna-in-the-bush. Another bloke called it, "As flash as the centre of Paris". So, if you apply that logic in reverse, the city of love mustn't be short on used car yards,' André concluded from the passenger seat.

Ella negotiated the double lanes of traffic through the long, suburban approach to downtown Bendigo. Their country cottage adventure of yesterday was suddenly a world away.

'You haven't been to Bendigo before, have you? You'll see what they mean when we get to the centre of town. We used to come here when I was little and have Christmas with my uncle René and Aunty Lucy. And my cousins, all six on them. I think most of them still live here.'

'There it is,' André interrupted as they waited for lights to change where the architecturally sharp, angular looking police station stood.

'They say the design is based on the peak of a police hat.'

'Oh yeah. I can see that.' Ella smiled.

'So can I, but I'm not sure I like it.'

'Is this more your style.'

Ella pointed to the imposing gothic cathedral that came into view on their left.

'Too polar opposite. Although … they don't make them like they did in the nineteenth century any more, do they?'

'I hate to disappoint you, but that didn't get finished until the 1970s,' Ella said, not without smugness.

'*Here*'s Vienna-in-the-bush.' She announced at the main set of traffic lights. The classical city streetscape unfolded before them.

Massive Alexandra Fountain stood in the middle of the intersection with its elegant semi-nude Greek goddesses — Princess Psyche among them — atop dolphins and mythical seahorses with tridents. A vintage tram trundled by, bearing modern advertising. The quintessentially European Rosalind Park gardens and opulent nineteenth century architectural marvels radiated ahead and leftward up View Street.

'Oh, yes,' André said with genuine admiration. 'Do they do good coffee too?'

'I know just the place.'

Ella parked opposite the elaborate four-storeyed Shamrock Hotel. From there she led him to a coffee haunt down a pedestrian lane — pure Melbourne CBD in appearance *and* taste.

Seated and with double shots ordered, Ella asked, 'So you think John Meredith met Eve Delmonte in Bendigo and joined him and a comatosed Portia in his Mercedes, heading to Bendigo airport.'

'Yes.'

'No ifs or buts about that bit, then?'

'No. We'll find out how do-able it all was when we go to the airport.'

'What if they needed a coffee stop?' Ella said, trying hard to breathe life into her question.

'Eve would have to pick up takeaways for them. John Meredith wasn't parking anywhere with people around. Not with a drugged wife in the car. My guess is: he had Portia in the back seat. Not in the front seat where she might be seen when he stopped at traffic lights. And he wouldn't chance having her in the boot. That would be beyond explaining if he did happen to be pulled over. Unlikely, I know, but why take that risk? It would also be easier to manhandle her onto the back seat. Woman-handle.' He corrected himself.

'What you're saying is, the last people to see Portia alive were Molly and Paul. On the day they arrived at Ostler's Cottage.'

'That's about the strength of it. I'm not expecting to find any more sightings, but I have to follow this trail and make sure. I'll give Darcy a call. Let him know we're here.'

'Is he the one you were at the academy with?'

'Yeah, He's in the CIU up here. He set this up for me.'

He listened to his mobile ringing out.

Detective Senior Constable Darcy Ireland was waiting at the newly expanded Bendigo Airport passenger terminal. The airfield itself was carved out of the surrounding box-ironbark forest. For decades, spasmodic attempts to establish a passenger-flight service to Melbourne fought a losing battle with cars as the freeway crept ever closer to town. It wasn't until a runway extension allowed Qantas to introduce a service to Sydney, that public air travel took off in Bendigo.

The airport had nevertheless been growing over time to accommodate a range of other private and government operations. At least a dozen single-engine planes were parked on the tarmac apron, one, an old fighter plane. Most were tied down and some had custom made weather covers lashed around the cockpit like blindfolds. The layout of the place conformed to type — windsocks, cyclone fences, scattered hangars and dongas in a mowed expanse of internal roads. A couple of helicopters were parked where several larger commercial premises had sprung up.

'M-a-a-t-e.'

'M-a-a-t-e.'

The handshake lasted as they grinned at each other.

'I can't believe it's been this long,' Darcy said.

'Yeah. You oughta come to the big smoke a bit more often then.'

'I do. But I'm always flat chat with something.'

'I make time to see you when I come to Bendigo,' André goaded.

'For the first time in your life … and it's work,' Darcy defended. He gave a mock punch to André's shoulder.

'At least I'm here. Darc, this is Ella.'

'Pleased to meet you, Ella. If you start getting serious about this bloke, ask me about when we shared a place in Richmond. His room was called the abyss.'

'It might be too late for that,' she smiled.

'You two should come round to my place, after this. Have a drink. Meet Claire.'

'Sorry, Darc. We're in training. We're riding the O'Keefe Rail Trail before we head back.'

'Well at least you're doing adventure racing *with* someone these days. That's good.'

'Yeah, we think so,' André said. 'So, what have you teed up here?'

'I thought I'd take you for a look around first. Robert Woodruff said he'd be here in half an hour. I can guarantee he's an innocent party in this. I've met him. He's a pillar around these parts. He steers clear of the city council but he's on any number of other organisations. He's even been a member of a Community and Police Consultative Committee. Any of our blokes that have dealt with him won't have a bad word said. He'll be shattered if it turns out that his plane was involved in a crime.'

'I'll play that down,' he assured Darcy. 'No sense upsetting your "pillar" if he genuinely was clueless.'

'It's more of a concern than you realise. If it turns out his plane *was* used, there are those who think highly enough of him to try and keep a lid on it. Not kept out of your investigation of course. Just out of the media.'

'I don't need to put that sort of detail in the public domain. But this is a country town. What comes to the surface in your patch is your lookout.'

'Thanks, mate. Jump in mine and I'll take you to the hangar. That's where he's meeting us.'

They drove away from the terminal to an isolated cyclone-fence gate. It was accessed by punching a code into a keypad on a pillar positioned for use from a driver's window.

'Robert gave me the code when we set this meeting up,' Darcy explained.

Through the gate, the road made its way to a bank of hangars further along the airstrip. Robert Woodruff's Mercedes sedan was already parked when they arrived.

Post middle-aged, Robert Woodruff greeted them with a politician's affableness. He even wore the kind of neat casual that politicians favour when interviewed on Sundays.

'Thanks for seeing us on a Sunday, Mr Woodruff,' André said as he shook his hand. 'Ella and I are up here for the weekend and I wanted to use the opportunity to see the Bendigo set-up first-hand.'

'Impressive dedication, Detective. Call me Bob.'

'Thanks. I'm fine with André.'

'I'm uncomfortable that you want to look at it at all, André.'

'We're hoping it won't have any bearing on the case,' André lied. 'But our procedures require that all possibilities are investigated and eliminated.'

Darcy joined in the stroking. 'This is normally something we could tick off with a phone call. It's just that André happened to be in town.'

Robert Woodruff shrugged.

'When John Meredith or someone else hires the plane, do you usually provide them with the code to the security gate?' André asked.

'With John I did. We go back a long while and he knows the ropes.'

'And that's what happened in April?'

'Yes.'

'Okay then. Can we have a look in the hanger please, Bob?'

Robert Woodruff thumbed through a cluttered key ring as he led them to a side door. A white Cessna 172 with minimum blue trim stood in the centre of an expanse large enough for two such craft. Some folding camp chairs, an esky and large nylon bags were piled in a corner near a tall cupboard, sink and fridge. The plane's VH number was emblazoned in large letters on the rear half of the fuselage. André photographed it.

'We shared the hangar with another local owner until he sold his plane about a year ago. Only our baby in here now.'

'When you head off somewhere, where do you load and unload your stuff?'

'I normally drive in here to unload from the car if we are taking luggage with us. I leave the car in here in any case and lock the hangar while we're away. Do you want me to open the main door?'

'Thanks.'

Conversation paused as they watched daylight creep under the oversized front door creaking into an upwards fold.

'When did John Meredith book the plane?' André asked.

'Oh, about three or four weeks beforehand, from memory. Said he was going to do the Mildura trip again.'

'Again?'

'Yes. The time before last, he and Portia also flew to Mildura for a couple of days' break.'

'So, you've dropped me out of the plane. You've had a stay in Mildura. You've flown back to Bendigo and now you're making your way back home. If your theory is correct, this is John Meredith with Eve Delmonte, driving back to Melbourne.'

Ella took her eyes off the Calder Freeway to see André answer.

'Not necessarily. I could be driving back on my own, having dropped Eve back to her car in Bendigo. If she went there by car.'

'Then there could be traffic pics of John Meredith and Eve Delmonte together on their way back to Beaumaris. There could be toll registrations.'

'Yes!' said André with sudden glee. 'That's if they came back into Melbourne on the Tulla Freeway. There's several options to do Bendigo to Melbourne, though.' he added with equally rapid deflation.

'Or Eve travelled to Bendigo by train and came back in his car with him. If that's the case, you might also capture Eve on train station CCTV.'

'We're in the middle of checking all that, but I'm not putting it past them to have thought it through.'

'Would that be enough to nail them?'

'A photograph of John Meredith and Eve Delmonte returning from Bendigo in his car? At that time? Yeah. I reckon that could do it.'

'Then I'm betting they *did* think of it,' Ella said. 'Can't you nail them without it?'

'It's getting hard. The Missing Person's Squad found Portia Meredith's finger prints on the steering wheel of her car, which she supposedly drove John Meredith to the airport in. In my theory, Eve Delmonte is driving that car to the airport, a week after Portia was chucked out of the plane. That's baffling.'

André went on to tell Ella about the hands not being visible in photos on the top half of the steering wheel.

'Maybe they fitted a tractor steering wheel spinner,' Ella said.

'What's that?'

'It's a knob that tractors have fitted to their steering wheel. When you're doing a tight turn at the end of a row, you need to spin several rotations of the steering wheel really quickly. If you want to, you can use it to keep driving the tractor one-handed all day, from one end of the paddock to the other without ever touching the actual wheel. You could drive a car the same way if it had a tractor steering knob fitted.'

'Fuck. I have to come up with the most absurd solutions to make this thing hang together.'

'I'm trying to help, you know.'

'I know. But it would have been a red flag for Missing Persons if the steering wheel had been altered in any way. I'm not saying it's impossible. It's just that Meredith and Delmonte haven't put a foot wrong. Not a phone call out of place. No ATM pics, tollway registration or credit card mis-used. Now this. Just when you think nothing can be that well executed or fool proof in the electronic age.'

'Well, you work it out on your own then.'

After due silence, Ella turned music on. Neither spoke until they changed drivers at Woodend.

'Do you realise we won't be that far apart tomorrow? You and Lila at Rosenfeld. Me in Mildura. What's that as the crow flies? A hundred clicks?'

'And the rest.'

'Oh.'

'Have you decided how you'll play it with Lila?'

'Hmm,' Ella answered dreamily and lapsed back into her car reverie.

'Not saying?' André said when it became obvious that she intended to ignore the question. She turned to look at him.

'If you are interested, we have had a couple of phone calls. I haven't told her yet, but I'm not gonna deny her. Wanting to run the farm, I mean. I quite like the idea. Actually, I like everything about it. Keeping it in the family. Keeping that line of female ownership going. That's pretty unique and special. So is Lila's passion about organic methods and for preserving the scrub block. It will also be great to have her living in the house. It takes all the pressure off sorting Mum's stuff out. We can take our time with all that and do it together. And it's my home. I know you leave home when you grow up, but, like I told you, I'm not ready to face not having Rosenfeld to return to. Not yet. Not with Mum gone. Not this soon. The farm's all I've got left … and Lila, I suppose. Am I talking sense or have I just given up, "A"?'

He took his eyes off the road for far too long to look at her.

She watched the windscreen, oblivious, or perhaps knowing, that he might be welling up.

'That makes perfect sense to me. That's the way families are supposed to work, El. I'm proud of you.'

She turned to him, but now his eyes had returned to the road. Having this conversation during a car trip was doing neither of them any favours.

She slapped him on the shoulder. His head spun back in her direction.

'What the … What was that for?'

'For not telling me so while I was worrying myself sick about all that.'

He shook his head. His eyes firmly on the road.

'And *she's* not off the hook either. I still need to get to the bottom of her and Mum's falling out. She can't fob me off like I'm ten anymore.'

Chapter 33

Ella and Lila had tucked themselves onto the adjacent couches in Rosenfeld's lounge room. The open fire was into its second large box tree log for the evening. Lamps poured further quietude into the indoor idyll. Both dressed aptly in loose house wear. Trackpants with Ella in a crew top, Lila's with a half zip. Lila had just topped their glasses from the second bottle of Neu Hass Winery contentedness — semillon sauvignon blanc.

Ella was holding Lila's phone, looking at a picture of Beau.

'Are you going to marry him?'

'I might now I have a bridesmaid,' Lila smiled.

Ella gave a dry smile in return.

'Nah. I suppose we will, because we talk about having kids. But getting married? It hardly comes up. We're usually too busy. What about you and André?'

'It's not something we talk about either. We're pretty settled and committed with jobs we enjoy too. I guess we both presume we will but at this stage, I don't think either of us want to be the one driving it. You know?'

'Yeah. I do know. I suppose when you have enough going

on in your life, you kinda have enough. Deciding to have kids is a different thing of course, because that clock keeps ticking. And then you wonder if you're gonna be one of those couples where it doesn't happen and that makes you wonder: have you been wasting your chance … or have you let it go by already?'

Lila's eyes widened with realisation.

'God, I've never said this stuff to anyone. Not even Beau.'

'Should you be drinking if, you know … you're trying?' Ella asked.

'I don't usually. That night at your place. That's the first drink I've had for about a year. That's not easy when you work at a winery. But I needed it that night. Boy, did I need it.'

'And tonight?'

Lila smiled contentedly before she answered.

'Because this is special, this is to savour. You and me. Being back here. The farm. The adventure that will be — even for you as a silent partner. I feel proud for both of us. I couldn't deny myself the moment. But I'll be well and truly back on the wagon after tonight.'

'We are lucky, aren't we? I can't believe I even considered selling it.' Ella said.

'You were grieving. And you didn't have the hands-on involvement to envisage keeping the farm and running it.'

'I know. But this is home. I love this place. I don't know what I was thinking.'

'Hmm. We *are* lucky, aren't we.'

They watched the fire in comfortable silence.

'Did Mum go out with anyone else after Dad?'

Ella thought before she answered.

'I could tell there were a few who were interested. Interested enough for me to try and scowl them away. Maybe she did go on an actual date when I went to uni, although I doubt it. There was nothing she ever mentioned. She was a pretty self-contained person when I think about it. Maybe because of the tragedies in her life. Vincent. Dad … you leaving. And now, the stuff I never knew about that happened to you. But I don't really know if she was always like that. I was too young to really know her otherwise.'

'That's a shame. She was young enough.'

'And pretty enough. But I never saw it through those eyes. Or maybe I didn't want to. It was always just me and her.'

'I suppose,' Lila said and cast her eye about. 'When did she buy this sofa?'

'Oooh. Probably ten years ago, or a bit more I'd say.'

'And the carpet?'

'Around the same time. After the millennium drought broke. The worst was behind her and it was a kind of a celebratory lash-out.'

'I wish I could have been there to support her. Farm-wise, I mean.'

'You could have been.' Ella said.

'Technically. But no.' Lila answered.

'Not technically. You could have been.'

Lila sat up from her comfortable position on the couch.

'What are you saying, Elly?'

'You and Mum. After Dad died. I still don't see why either or both of you didn't jump at the chance to be together again.'

'I explained that. And I'm here now.'

'It didn't explain anything to me, Lila. There has to be more to it. I know it's been twenty years and I was only ten back then, but I know you. That dawned on me after the last time we met. I knew you before you left, and realised I still do. Back then, we didn't talk about things you were up to … or *you* didn't talk about it. But I picked up on stuff. Stuff you and your friends went on about. Especially the teenage taboos that excited you all so much. Smoking. Drinking and boys and talking about sex. You were so into everything. But when I quizzed you about anything like that, you knew how to fob me off, which was fair enough, I was only ten. But the way you fobbed me off. It's the same now. I just know.'

Lila gave her a long hard stare.

'I really don't think you want to know, Elly.'

'So, there is something?'

Lila looked down; shook her head slowly.

'Believe me, Elly. You don't want to know. This … ' She cast her head around the room. 'This is perfect. I know Mum is gone, but you and me, together. That's as much as I want going ahead. I can see it means a lot to you too. Anything else has nothing to do with it. Believe me.'

'I want to know.'

'Then I'll say this once. I told you what happened with Dad and me — what drove me away from here. You know that was as bad as it can get. You're the only human being I have ever spoken to about that.'

'Me *and* André,' Ella corrected her.

'Well yeah. Back then, others might have guessed, or assumed they knew what happened, but you and André are the only ones I have ever actually told out loud. It took me twenty years to do that. And when I decided to tell you, I knew that would bring you pain, and I knew you deserved to know. Not just deserved to know, but you should know. You needed to know.'

Lila stopped to drain her glass.

'There *was* another dark thing that happened back then and I'm asking you to trust me. It really is something you don't need to know. If I told you, it would bring a whole different level of pain. Not pain you deserve to experience or that I have any desire to inflict. In fact, the opposite is true. Please, Elly. Some things need to be let be.'

Lila's entreaty did not give Ella pause.

'I want to know,' she repeated.

Lila examined her emptied glass intently, placed it on the coffee table with a resigned shrug, and braced herself.

'All right then, if you really are that determined … I came back once, about a year after I left. But not here to the house.

'What happened is, I stole another vehicle in Clare, a four-wheel drive with a kayak on top. Even though I'd done that once before, I can't believe I did it again. I saw it parked in the same driveway for days, and when I looked, the keys were in it. So, I just took it one night and drove back here and camped on the lake. I bush bashed the thing into the point on the other side. I was homesick and believe it or not, camping there on the beach really helped. The next morning, I took the kayak out. I wasn't far from where dad used to drop his yabbie nets. His secret spot, he called it. It was late January and I knew there was a good chance he'd have the nets in to get a feed for Australia Day.

'So, I paddled there and of course, the nets *were* in and he was there too. By himself in his tinny with its outboard motor. He was put-putting from one drop net to the next, pulling each of them up and dropping his catch into the boat. They were his yabbie nets in his secret spot and he was there.

'I couldn't believe he actually was there, even though I thought he might be, but I wasn't deterred from going over to him. My biggest fear at that point was that things would play out in a way that exposed me as having stolen the four-wheel drive. My worst fear was I'd end up in jail for that.'

Ella had assumed a dumbfounded look.

'I got nearer and nearer without him noticing me. The outboard motor was idling and he was turned away from me pulling up nets. I paddled right up to the tinny before I startled him.

'He sneered as soon as he saw me. "You!" he said. He couldn't even utter my name. I wasn't his daughter anymore. He told me to piss off to whatever rock I now resided under. It sounds weird, but even when he raped me, I never experienced rejection from him. That was something new, a pain I shouldn't have felt, but I did. He said other stuff too. That he didn't need me anymore … "Because" … and that's when he threw in the kicker — the way he let me know that I was obsolete. "Because … it wouldn't be long before Ella … "'

Lila couldn't finish what he had said. Ella began to shake.

'When he said that, I didn't think, Ella. I just lost it. I lifted the kayak paddle and lashed out towards him. I wasn't close enough to hit him but I gave a mighty swipe in any case. It was sheer anger. The blow hit the boat and slid along the gunwale to the outboard motor. As it did, it knocked the gear lever that sits up like Jackie on the tiller handle.

'I don't know if you know, or if you remember. Outboard motors have a short flexy cord called a lanyard attached to an engine kill-switch. You attached the other end of the lanyard to your belt. That way, if you fall overboard, the cord reaches the end of its stretch and detaches from the switch. That stops the engine instantly and prevents the boat disappearing over the horizon and leaving you stranded in the water.

'The thing is, you can't move around the boat to raise and

drop yabbie nets unless you detach the lanyard from your belt. Which of course he did … Look it wasn't something I thought through. There was no time for any wilful cause and effect. But that's what happened.

'He was on his feet at the front end of the boat with the safety kill-switch lanyard disconnected. When my wild paddle swipe collected the lever, it slammed into gear. The boat took off and threw him out. The whack from the paddle also knocked the tiller onto full steering lock. That set the boat in a tight circle pattern. He surfaced just in time for the back end of the boat to sideswipe him on the head. That alone was enough force to do him in, but at the same time, the propellor must have sliced into his body or legs because blood also came from below the surface … '

'You killed him?'

Lila gave a grim tight-lipped nod.

'You killed him?'

'Not on purpose, Ella.'

'But there was a coroner's inquest. André dug out the finding for me a while ago. It said there was nothing suspicious.'

'Of course there wasn't. No one could set out to do someone that way on purpose. It would be an absolutely impossible thing to plan and execute. The investigators wouldn't have had a clue anyone else had been there in any event. The only explanation they could come to is: he was thrown overboard when he put the boat into gear without having the engine kill-switch lanyard attached — which is not an uncommon thing for someone on their own to do when they're idling in neutral and pulling yabbie nets up in dead-calm water. But that's what happened.

'I knew he was dead straight away and I bolted. Someone

else found him. It wouldn't matter how soon they did, I would have been halfway back to Clare in South Australia. I was so scared and fucked up.'

Ella bit her thumb nail and thought.

'But Mum knew or found out ... didn't she?' she guessed.

'I phoned her along the way. At a phone box. We didn't all have mobile phones back then. I couldn't tell her what was wrong but I was so upset and I blurted out that I was sorry. That was probably before she even found out he was dead. When I got back to McGuinn's in Clare, they told me she had phoned. She might have only been phoning to tell me Dad was dead, but she would have realised from that call that I hadn't been in Clare when it happened. The reason why I was in a state and had phoned her earlier — it would have all dawned on her. She was smart enough to put two and two together. When we did catch up on the phone, she didn't say anything about being suspicious. She simply said, "Stay away". I was too afraid to say anything to her, and we never spoke again. She said it so fiercely that for years, I thought she'd dob me in if I went near her, and I'd go to jail.

'She was the only one who could have put two and two together. No one else knew I'd been to Victoria. It ended up being a secret she took to her grave. I don't know why she decided that's how it should be ... because I was responsible for a death? Was it because I took the man she loved from her, despite how contemptible he had become? Maybe she resented being faced with turning her daughter in for being a killer. Which she never did. Maybe she realised that that would have a toll on you. Probably all of that. I don't know, Elly. I'm sorry, I didn't want us to have secrets but I thought what I already told you was more than enough for you to know what I dealt with. I really didn't want you to have to carry this as well.'

'Did they catch you for stealing the four-wheel drive?'

'No,' Lila barked. 'Is that the only thing you're concerned about?'

'Jesus, Lila. What am I supposed to say. I find out my father was a sex offender and now my sister killed him.'

'I didn't want to tell you.'

'It doesn't matter. I know.'

They both stewed.

'And André's a cop,' Ella said.

'So? He was there when I told you what Dad did to me. He didn't exactly fall over himself offering support or justice from the system.'

'So, you have it in for André too?'

'Of course not. This is way beyond cops becoming involved. It's not what any of this is about any more. It's about you and me. Our lives now, going forward. Look, Elly. André's a great guy. I'm looking forward to getting to know him. Honestly. And I know how much you'll need him now.'

Ella's pain stretched beyond speech.

'I can't deal with this. I can't talk to you about it. Not now. I'm going to bed.'

Chapter 34

Ella's mind may have been preoccupied, but she was experienced enough to know that, like exhaustion, being overly distracted was also a risk. The Big Desert would be too unforgiving if she navigated off-track and got it wrong — especially solo. She stuck to paths on a circuit through the dry Black Flat Lake and back to Wonga Camping Area via Cameron Track. The maelstrom of questions in her head drowned out Wyperfeld National Park's gnarled beauty.

She killed him. My sister killed my father. She did it for me. Would he have begun molesting me? Was he just saying that to spite Lila? Would Mum have looked the other way ... again? Would she stand up to him this time? Did Lila also save me from boarding school? Maybe I would have liked boarding school. What would it be like living a whole life knowing you killed someone? What will it be like for me, knowing Lila killed Dad? How did Mum live with that? What would have happened if she had taken it to the police? How would my life have turned out then? What if Lila had been found out? What if she had gone to prison? How would Mum have coped with that? The same blood that courses through my body, the blood of a sex offender, the blood of a killer … probably a manslaughterer if it had ended up in court. It was an accident … wasn't it? Could it be construed as not an accident? What does that do to me? Is that the genes I'll pass on? Should I tell André? Could I not tell André? Will he be able to tell something is up by how I act? Would he feel compelled to act? …

She ended the run atop Mount Mattingley, a kilometre short of the camp ground where she was parked. It seemed a colossal misnomer to call the slightly highest dune a mountain. It nevertheless enabled a 360 view from its galvanised-steel viewing platform. Nine hard kilometres, a big sky and horizon to horizon pristineness did something to take the edge off the voices in her head. She leant against the railing and felt the storm within ebb to simmer.

Another desert-Eden moment stopped Ella in her tracks on her cool-down walk back to the SUV. She stood watching a pair of grasswrens on a feeding mission flitter in and out of a massive porcupine-grass ring. Tiny feet prints in the sand attested to others sharing the micro-climate sanctuary within a species that tortured settlers' horses and tore their clothes to rags. Maybe the prints were that of a ningaui — a mouse-like marsupial — or perhaps a Mallee dragon lizard. An emerging cypress-pine and wildflowers had also found protection amid its spiky fringe. The interaction and dependency of life, thriving among the inhospitable.

She arrived back at the information centre to find a four-wheel drive Volkswagen campervan and a Nissan Pathfinder had joined her SUV in the car park. Their four occupants were blokes somewhere near retirement age. They were heading to central Australia on a boys' trip.

'What brings you to the Big Desert?' Ella asked in the easy

conversation of passing travellers.

'The birdlife,' said the tallest of them. 'We came around Lake Albacutya yesterday. Saw regent parrots straight off. I've been trying out my brand-new Canon RF 800mm telephoto lens. Got some brilliant shots of an eagle on the wing. The autofocus can track them on the move.'

'I just love it here,' said the most verbose of their number. 'We'll check out Pine Plains and Snowdrift before we press on. You don't look local either with gear like that,' he added.

'I used to be,' Ella said. 'Now I just visit. I try to get a bit of adventure race training in when I can.'

'I've done a lot of wilderness stuff on foot over the years. Not as energetically as that, though. I like a pace where I can take everything in. We hope to do some trekking in Kalamurina Wildlife Sanctuary when we reach Warburton Creek. It's running now.'

She learnt much more about them than they about her before she finally wandered into the un-manned information centre on her own. It was midmorning and already warm. Dark shade within the mud brick building offered cool respite.

She gave the now-familiar displays and visitors' book a miss and half-heartedly studied the wall map. The gentlemen of leisure could be heard heading off to continue their road trip to Warburton Creek — the respite of distraction gone with them. That left Lila.

Their conversation happened as Ella carried her bags to the car — Lila following.

'I still can't talk about it, Lila,' Ella said without turning back to look at her.

'So, you'll call me? Right?'

'I don't know. I have to think.'

'What am I supposed to do in the meantime. Put my life on hold for another twenty years?'

Ella slammed the back door of the SUV and spun around.

'How the fuck do I know? Let me get my head around this. Right now, I have no fucking idea about how to deal with it. All right?'

'Look, Elly … '

'Don't "look Elly" me. I just can't have this conversation now. I'm not talking about the farm thing. I don't have a problem with that. Sharing the inheritance. Keeping the farm. I already decided all that. It's just … ' She slowed pace. 'Maybe it was an accident, but it happened. You and him. It was enough of a nightmare before this … Just let me get used to carrying all that around in my head for the rest of my life … Surely you know what I'm faced with.'

It was a point Lila couldn't argue. She didn't argue. She watched Ella get in the car and leave.

Chapter 35

Not for the first time, it occurred to André that this case involved more airports than any case he'd ever worked on, or even heard of. This time, he was fronting up to Melbourne's International at Tullamarine, Terminal 1, Gate 56. *Did they really have that many gates?*

The trek to his departure point snaked the full length of the domestic terminal arm. Beyond the alcoves of seating at every other gate where Boeing and Airbus jets nosed up to the window and peered in. Beyond aerobridges that took passengers to the front door of the plane without ever being exposed to weather.

Gate 56 was a flight of stairs to a ground level exit-door and out the very end of the building. André followed his band of fellow passengers through the door and onto the actual tarmac. They took the painted yellow path to the shrunken version of an inter-city domestic jet aircraft — a Dash 8 with actual propellers and scaled down Qantas livery. Inside, seating was in twos, each side of a centre aisle. *Capacity of about fifty* André calculated and took his window seat. The aisle seat remained empty for the flight.

An hour later, at over 20,000 feet, the only sense of Mallee below was a gradual change to dark green from the emerald green of the south. Melbourne to Mildura in an hour twenty-five. Its boast of having Victoria's busiest regional airport was more likely a result of being twice as distant from Melbourne as any other city worthy of the title.

It was arranged that Detective Senior Constable Lyn Olsen would meet him at the airport.

He instantly rued not having his sun-glasses handy as he ambled down the boarding stairs and followed his fellow passengers across the tarmac to the terminal building. Because he and Lyn Olsen had never met, he wondered if she would have a cardboard sign with his name on it — even as a joke.

Once inside, he blinked away the dazzling glare and was stunned to see Ella waiting for him and looking anxious. Before he could take it in, the woman standing next to Ella produced a card with ANDRE MARSHALL written on it. He stopped in his track to begin a game of eye hockey.

Ella looked at André. He looked back and then shifted his eyes to the sign to the right of Ella, then raised his eyes to the sign holder — Lyn Olsen. Lyn looked back at André. He shifted his gaze to Lyn's left. Lyn followed his gaze and looked at Ella. Ella turned her own gaze to Lyn, then dropped her eyes to the sign Lyn was holding.

'Oh, I'm sorry,' Ella blurted to Lyn. 'He didn't know I was going to be here. I'm Ella.'

André rushed over.

'You must be Lyn. I'm sorry. I wasn't expecting Ella to be here. Ella's my partner. What are you doing here, El? Sorry.' He leant forward and kissed her.

'I can … ' Lyn began to say. Ella cut her off.

'I need to talk to you "A".'

There was urgency in her voice.

'I'll wait over here then,' Lyn said and headed towards some seating.

'Thanks, I'll just be … ' André blurted.

'Take your time,' Lyn added and began scrolling her phone as she walked away.

André turned his attention back to Ella and put his arm around her.

'What's wrong? Is it Lila?'

She nodded.

'I needed to be with you.'

She held him with her head on his chest, and kept holding on. His gaze wandered aimlessly within the terminal building.

'Have you got time to talk before you go and do your thing?' she said from within their embrace.

He pulled back from the hug to respond.

'Err. I'm in Lyn's hands and I don't know how she has planned this. Wait here and let me talk to her. Is that okay?'

Ella nodded. André walked over to where Lyn was still scrolling her phone.

'Good to meet you, Lyn, and sorry about this. It's a family thing. Ella lost her mum a week or two back. Her mum lived on her farm down the road near Rainbow. Ella's been up there dealing with the stuff you deal with. It's become an emotional time.'

'Good to meet you too, André … and don't apologise.'

'I need to … you know … help Ella deal with stuff that came up. Do you and I have to be somewhere?'

'Yeah, but nothing's locked in. We've got the rest of the day if you're flying back tomorrow. You do what you have to do, then give me a call.'

She handed André her card. He looked at it and told her, 'I'll try not to be too long.'

'All good. Catch you later.'

He knew she meant it by the touch she gave him on the forearm. He looked over to Ella.

The incoming passengers soon dispersed and no departure flights were pending. That left plenty of seating options they could have to themselves in the near-deserted café. They found a couch with an outlook onto the tarmac. He fetched coffees.

'This is so ridiculous,' Ella said and shook her head.

'No. Tell me,' André said.

'Okay, but let me have some of this coffee first. It's been a rough however long it's been.'

Andre watched her savour the coffee as it composed her.

'I kept pushing Lila until she told me — she told me everything. Why she took off like she did. Why she and Mum fell out.

'She shot through to South Australia because the molesting built up to him full on raping her, "A". That's why she jumped in a car and drove as soon as she could.'

'Christ.'

'And she and Mum never actually fell out … they just never got back together. It was all to do with how Dad died.'

'What about how your dad died? You had me to dig out the police version of events as soon as you knew me well enough to ask. He had a messy end, but how the accident happened was straightforward enough. He wasn't the first person to come to an end the exact same way, and he probably won't be the last. No one had reason to question it … you included. So what's different now? What does Lila know that no one else does? From what she told me and you, she was in South Australia. She had been for over a year.'

Ella was holding her coffee cup with both hands. She raised her eyes, gave him a serious look and pointedly said nothing.

'What? Lila *was* there?'

Ella hesitated further.

'If you don't want to say, El.'

'I want to say, "A", but I'm confused.' She looked confused.

'Then don't say. But if she was there, was it still an accident?'

'The pertinent thing is what he said to her,' Ella said.

She welled up and André waited for her to tell him.

'He told Lila he didn't need her any more … '

Her speech faltered and André made to comfort her. She stopped him.

'Let me say it … he told Lila he didn't need her anymore because it wouldn't be long before … he let her know that he was going to take up where he and Lila left off … but with me as Lila's replacement.'

This time she did let him comfort her.

'Jesus, El.'

'I know. I had to tell you that. You're all I have now, "A".'

She sighed shakily after another long embrace and reached forward for the last of her coffee.

'What am I supposed to do with that?'

'What? That your dad was like that, or that Lila was involved in what happened to him. Was she?'

'I want to tell you, "A".'

She let him make of that what he would.

'Okay. Say she was there then. Would she have been in the boat with him?'

Ella shook her head "No".

'So, if she was there, she was in another craft,' André said in Police speak. 'Was it still an accident?'

Ella nodded "Yes".

'But it happened because Lila was there. She was driven to lash out and that's when something happened. That's how he fell out … accidently.'

Ella looked hard at him with tears in her eyes.

'That probably saved me, "A". That saved me from the same fate as Lila. She thinks Mum guessed how his death came about and that's why she never spoke to Lila again. But nor did Mum say anything to anyone else. She'd already been keeping Lila's torment secret … vainly bearing her absence … then Dad dies on her, and then she works out how he died. So much she kept bottled up to take to her grave. I don't know how she did that and carried on normal life. Such a big fucking mess … and it engulfed my life without me ever knowing. I haven't been able to process it, "A". I had to come and see you.'

'You did the right thing. I'm here … we'll get you through this together.'

'You know, the more I think about it, everything could have played out in so many other ways — none of them good.'

'It's head spinning.'

'I'll have to try getting used to my dad being … you know … what he was. And how my mum was somehow wanting in the whole thing. And Lila. Is she more than a victim? Is she my saviour "A"? All of that. You know?'

'That's all on top of your mum dying. And then you go and trip over a dead body. Maybe we'll need to get you a counsellor. In my game we know the good ones.'

'Hold on, "A". This is not something I want to be discussing with a stranger. And you know as well as I do, it's not stuff I can tell anyone else. I'm in the same boat Mum was in. I just needed to talk to you about it. We're still normal, aren't we?' Ella asked.

'Better than normal, I'd say.'

'Not like Lila. She's lived every day of her grown-up life with this hanging over her head. She'll probably ask me if you … you know … know.'

'I only know what you told me. Personal family stuff that was going on at the time. Nothing contradicts the coroner's finding that your dad was alone in his tinny on Lake Albacutya and fell overboard by some accident or other. That's not so uncommon and not normally fatal, except, his un-manned boat managed to plough into him. After all this time, the take home message has not changed. Your dad would probably still be alive today if his kill-switch lanyard was not unattached. Everyone knows boat owners do that so they can move about and do stuff. End of.

'And don't worry about Lila. She sounds like she's learnt to live with things the way they are, and still find a life. A winery manager in the Barossa, with a boyfriend and playing bass in a band. Not a bad start. I'm still looking forward to getting to know my potential sister-in-law.'

'Potential?'

'Is there a word for more than potential?

'Hmm.'

He squeezed her tightly with the arm he already had round her shoulder.

'Thank you,' she said and hugged him. It lasted.

Ella separated first.

'I'm gonna go back now so you can do what you came here

to do,' she said.

'Hey. You can't drive off on your own after all this. It's massive. Stay here. I've got a room.'

'As good as that sounds, I feel fine. I've had the conversation I needed to have, with the person I needed to have it with. That came in handy for saving my life, or at least getting it back on track, so well done and thank you. Now I'm back to being a functioning human being again. See.' She spread her arms out to show him, then gave him a quick kiss. 'You've got a job to do and the last thing I fancy is hanging round Mildura on my own all day.'

Her flippancy failed to allay. 'I'm not comfortable with this. Not at all.'

'I'll call you down the track. And don't worry. Look at me. You were here when I needed you. We can pick up on this back home. Don't worry.'

He worried. His face didn't lie.

Take two. It may have been his second encounter with Lyn Olsen, but he was seeing her for the first time.

Lyn was of the preceding generation of detectives.

'Been in Mildura forever,' she joked.

André knew that when members rise to CIU at a regional centre, they dig in for life.

A smart dresser in a skirt, shirt and jacket, but somehow more rural than city style. It wouldn't surprise André to learn she was married to a cop — or had been married to a cop.

'I heard Chrisso shot a legless lizard at Wyperfeld. Wished I hadda been there,' she said as they waited in line for André's second coffee.

'Scared the shit out of everyone.' André said.

'It's legend up here. Chloe Lane told me the stand-in ranger wanted him charged under the Wildlife Act.'

'Blair Hope? He didn't make it easy for any of us.'

'Not a local,' Lyn said as a say-no-more explanation.

City-boy André smiled.

'Were you able to find out about Meredith's flight?'

'Yeah. They arrived on the Sunday afternoon in a Cessna. Flew back to Melbourne late morning on Monday. I've got all the details and the precise times for you. I'll email them through.'

'Thanks.'

'He parked the Cessna on the southern apron in a tie-down bay. I can show you before I drive you into town. He hired a car. He would have walked over here from the plane to pick it up before driving back to get his luggage, and passenger.'

'And then drove to the Mediterranean Sunset Resort?'

'They like to call it a resort. It's a motel with a pool, a tennis court and some palm trees. I'll take you there next.'

'Aren't you supposed to be promoting the place?'

'The locals are country. We leave the pretentious stuff to the pollies and tourist operators.'

Mildura was reclaimed desert, all the way to its CBD on the Murray River's southern bank. On the northern side, the New South Wales outback stretched all the way to Queensland. The river's junction with the equally iconic Darling was a mere twenty kilometres downstream.

The magic combination of water and desert manifested immediately on the drive into town from the airport.

Agriculture block after agriculture block of verdant vineyards — some swathed in a sea of protective white netting — and not a house without the healthiest lawns this side of Wimbledon. Arrival at an oasis was underscored by omnipresent palm trees in the lawned centre strip of a boulevard, long and wide enough to rival Canberra. Quirkily, the cross streets had been given numerical names in the manner of downtown New York. No doubt, a product of the town's American planners.

The Mediterranean Sunset Resort held a prime early position along the grand entranceway. More palms and inviting leafiness abounded.

Lyn parked and led André into the large reception foyer that was enjoying mid check-out/check-in calm. The smiling receptionist summoned Lyn's friend Wendy, the on-duty manager.

Wendy, who wore a badge with only her given name on it, led them into an empty bar lounge that adjoined a restaurant. They sat at the nearest table.

'I've printed out a record of Mr Meredith's stay,' Wendy told them and handed André a single page. He scanned through it as Lyn and Wendy chatted about the new motel they could see being built across the road.

'I've heard they'll be catering to budget travellers,' Lyn said.

'Theo is not pleased,' Wendy responded.

André read on — Meredith and Meredith Developments. Their St Kilda Road address, check in date/time, check out date/time, evening meal, breakfast, champagne, room 95.

That'll be a first for the tax office. Claiming killing your wife and celebrating it, André thought.

'The meal?' André asked. 'Did they eat that in the restaurant?'

Wendy reached for him to hand her back the printout. She

glanced at it and told him the obvious.

'It doesn't say. But it might be recorded on the computer, I'll check.'

She disappeared beyond reception.

'Wendy and I used to play tennis in the same team,' Lyn told André.

'You don't play anymore?'

'I started feeling the heat as I got older. It's bloody hot here in summer … and there's much easier ways to spend a Saturday afternoon.'

Wendy returned and sat down again before addressing André's query.

'Everything was room service. The meal, the champagne, breakfast. They had a spa suite.'

Wendy cast a knowing look to Lyn.

'Can you show me please?'

Wendy led them through to a central outdoor space with a bar, a tennis court and a pool. They crossed via a path to a two-storey row of rooms facing back to the main building. Room 95 was on ground level. They entered through the double glass doors that fronted the pool. Inside, André was overwhelmed.

The room was dominated by a huge white multi-person size spa on a platform. A king-size bed and an oversized television screen filled the remaining space. The staid bedspread seemed oddly out of place.

André summed it up after a long pause taking everything in.

'So, it's not fitted out for your lone travelling salesman then?'

'Not necessarily. Not if they order in takeaway,' Wendy said. She pulled a face at Lyn to emphasise the innuendo.

André peered into the bathroom, then opened a rear door. It opened directly onto a lane of car parking. Suburban Mildura began on the other side of the lane.

'Guest parking,' Wendy told him without being asked.

'Only likely to be seen by other guests, if at all.' Lyn added.

'I guess so.'

'Has Mr Meredith stayed here before?' André asked.

'I can look it up for you. It won't take a minute.'

They wove their way back to reception and Wendy disappeared again to consult "the computer".

Lyn slipped into country-town small talk again with the receptionist while André leafed brochures disinterestedly.

'So, you must be Brian's niece,' she established before Wendy returned.

'We have one other booking for Mr Meredith of Meredith and Meredith Developments. About eighteen months before. For two people. Here are the details.'

Wendy handed him another A4 printout, and a key.

'What's the key for?'

'Lyn booked you in to stay here tonight. Room 95 was vacant. That's an upgrade. On the house.'

Back at the car.

'That's about it for me. I'm done. Thanks for arranging all this, Lyn.'

'No problem. Do you mind if I ask what it all means?'

'You just led me through a perfect template for John Meredith to fly to Mildura, literally drop off his drugged wife Portia along the way at Wyperfeld, without landing the plane. He arrives here with another woman who he expects any casual observer to assume is his wife. Spends the night celebrating with champagne and departs without anyone seeing enough of her to testify that she was not Portia Meredith. At the airport, they arrived away from the terminal building and take the much more expensive hire car option instead of a taxi, for such a short stay in a motel. They don't even walk to the motel restaurant to eat. Room service everything.'

'Is that what you think happened?'

'You tell me. We've both done the walkthrough of John Meredith's trip from the moment he landed. What do you think my chances are of finding a witness that can remember seeing the woman that accompanied him, and could they positively identify her as Portia Meredith … or even as someone who is not Portia Meredith? Is it worth trying?'

'When you put it like that,' Lyn said.

'Having said all that, it's just one of the scenarios we're exploring. Things are a bit more complicated at the Melbourne end. A lot more complicated actually. Up here would have been a breeze for John Meredith and his companion.'

'We aim to please,' Lyn joked before noticing a dark look on André's face. She decided a bit of humouring might be in order.

'I suppose if they did take a taxi from the airport, they'd *both* be dropped off at the front door of the motel and end up passing through reception, and the rest of the place. Not the sort of close-up exposure they would have wanted.'

'Exactly. What we've established here this morning is: if it wasn't his wife who was with him in the motel room, then their movements, or lack of movements, made sure no one else was any the wiser.'

'Nor would anyone else be any the wiser if it was his wife.'

'No, but that's not what we're testing here.' André explained.

'So, you now know that it could have been someone else, or it could have been his wife,' Lyn re-interpreted.

'Yes, but … '

André's "but" stalled on his perplexed lips. Lyn realised her humouring was not humouring.

'You said it's a template. What did you mean?' she tried.

André recovered, but in a tone far less assured.

'It's a replica of the same trip John Meredith and his wife did the year before. My only problem is that this particular trip — the second one — took place a week and a half before his wife supposedly disappeared. We're still working on how it fits in.'

'Good luck with that then,' an even more confused Lyn said, hoping it would end the discussion. It did the job. With no further clarification or buy-in coming her way, she was ready to resume normal operations.

'Seeing it's your first visit to Mildura and you're already checked in, do you fancy a Cook's tour of the place.'

André stood paused in blank silence. His thoughts hadn't moved on from their circular conversation. His mobile rang.

'Hi Alex.'

'How are things at club Mildura, mate?'

André gave an update.

'That's all good, isn't it?'

'I suppose. Did you get any traffic pics of Meredith on his return journey?'

'Yeah. That's why I called you. It shows Meredith driving back from Bendigo with a female passenger. I couldn't believe it was that easy.'

'And?'

'That's the bad news. Inconclusive. Whoever she is, she's curled up sleeping with the seat reclined. Someone blonde.'

'How better to stage it. To make it appear your dead wife is still alive.'

'Or simply asleep.'
He looked at the phone, and then at Lyn.
'How come I'm starting to feel outnumbered?'

His phone rang as soon as the flight attendant announced they could turn their devices back on.

'It's me. I'm at the airport to pick you up'

'Really. I thought you went back to Rosenfeld. Did you drive all the way from Mildura yesterday?'

She ignored stating the obvious.

'I've parked in the main car park. Meet me at the footbridge. The terminal side.'

'I won't be long. I've only got carry-on.'

In ten minutes, Ella and André had their arms around each other in an airport hug. André released himself and held her apart to judge how she was holding up.

'How are you now? You sound like a different person. Not weighed down at all.'

She disregarded his question, too eager with news.

'I've got a surprise for you.'

'What?'

'I'll show you when we get to the car,' she said and bustled him across the concourse to the car park. 'Tell me how your trip went. Is everything still falling into place?'

The joy of their reunion drained from André as he told her.

'It's like at Castlemaine and Bendigo. Everything fits perfectly. They parked the plane away from the main airport terminal. He fetched a hire car and they went to a motel where she can stay in the car while he checks in. He's been there before, so he knows he can drive to the rear-lane car park to enter the room. They have room-service meals and drinks in a room made for sex. Eve Delmonte is enough like Portia Meredith, if ever they were observed, which they wouldn't have been. That's how you celebrate killing your wife.'

His despair was not anticipated.

'Isn't that a good thing? You didn't want anyone witnessing Portia Meredith after John Meredith left Ostler's Cottage and that's exactly what you've got.'

'As my colleagues point out, it also fits John Meredith taking an innocent trip to Mildura with his wife, before she was reported missing.'

They had reached Ella's SUV.

'Well maybe this will cheer you up. Take a look,' a beaming Ella said. She opened the driver's door, stood back, and gestured towards the steering wheel in the manner of a game show hostess showing off the grand prize.

André lit up.

'You've got the tractor steering knob. Wow. How did you manage that?'

The black gear-stick like knob was clamped to the steering wheel in the six o'clock position.

'I got it before I went to Rosenfeld. It's from a shop in Nunawading that sells disabled aids. You can also get them on eBay. I got this version because it's held on with a simple strap that you tighten with an Allen key. There's no need for a fixed attachment or screw holes or anything like that on the steering wheel itself. When you remove it, no one can tell it was ever there.'

'Nice. Really nice.'

André nodded appreciatively.

'I thought you cops would have known about something like this.'

'The traffic guys probably do.'

André felt the knob and spun it on its inner spindle.

'It's brilliant to use,' Ella enthused. 'I might leave it there. Hop in and I'll show you.'

She fired the motor, moved the gearstick into reverse and one-handedly spun the steering wheel into a sharp backwards exit from the parking bay. Into Drive, and they were soon winding down the carpark exit ramp — all courtesy of the spinner knob. Ella brushed her hair back with a spare hand to prove a point.

'Easy, Oscar Piastri, you're not on the tractor at Yaapeet now.'

She laughed. 'Do you know how mixed metaphor-ish what you just said sounded?'

'It does look like it's pretty handy,' André said.

'I drove all the way here one-handed,' Ella boasted. She turned to see if he looked pleased.

'I suppose they could have done it like this.'

'Suppose?' Ella protested. 'Haven't I just put the missing piece of the puzzle in place for you? This is your theory proved right. Everything fits. Where's the excitement. A thank-you would be nice.'

'I know. I've had two days of it. Everything fitting so perfectly. Just like this does. But I realised as I was explaining it to Lyn

Olsen — everything can also be as innocent as John Meredith chooses to paint it. Everything is as non-incriminating as it is incriminating. If I throw in something like this … ' he gestured to the spinner knob, '… my theory sounds as desperate as his explanation sounds plausible. Absolutely normal behaviour.'

They neared the interchange where the Calder Freeway from Bendigo joined the Tullamarine tollway to the city. It prompted Ella, who wasn't as ready to concede defeat.

'Were you able to catch his trip back from Bendigo to Melbourne on camera?'

'We did actually. Alex phoned me yesterday. It shows a female passenger resting or sleeping on a pillow with the seat reclined. Facing away. Could easily be Eve Delmonte or Portia Meredith. Could be staged for the benefit of any potential investigation. Could also be someone who is tired, having a snooze.'

'But we know he did it. He intimated as much to me. Actually, he more than intimated. He tattooed it on my brain. Can't you bring him in and put him through the wringer … or whatever you do?'

'Sure. He and his lawyer would enjoy that. All we'd be doing would be building a case for them to claim incompetence, harassment, desperateness — you name it. They could argue it's not even circumstantial. Just a man and his wife having a weekend away.'

'So, you cast all this aside. Just like that? Didn't you have Glenevis on board?'

'Glenevis said he liked the theory. That doesn't mean he's not expecting a grain of hard evidence … as a minimum. Something that irrefutably links Meredith and Delmonte to the theory. There's still a chance we'll find it though,' he added to mollify Ella. 'No coverup can be that watertight. We just have to keep looking. Longer and harder. That's where we're at now.'

'Oh yeah. And where is that?'

André's tone became methodical.

'Firstly, although the autopsy doesn't give us an exact day or even a week that Portia died, it does not rule out that she could have died prior to being reported missing. So, at least on that basis, the theory remains in play.

'Secondly, John Meredith does not dispute that he flew to Mildura that weekend. However, we also have to accept that we'll never be able to prove he detoured over the Big Desert enroute. No one ever looks up. We'd need a witness at a thousand feet above the national park for that.'

'What do you mean, "no one ever looks up"? Is that a thing?'

'Apparently. People look left and right, down and they look under, but never up. They'll usually focus on the middle of their vision. Look it up. That's not a pun by the way,' he added, and moved on.

'Thirdly. All of that means we shift our focus to Delmonte. Eve locked herself in as being home and sick on that Monday. That's the window we work with to link her to the wrong place at the right time. A chink that will have her travelling to Bendigo. CCTV from a railway station or traffic camera. Maybe she hired a car or got an Uber to Bendigo. It's not a big window. Maybe she also went to the shop where you brought this steering knob. If anything turns up, she's gone. And if she is incriminated, she'll take Meredith down with her. As shifty as he is, there'll be no room left for him to wriggle.

'Anyway, we need something as solid as that because, even if Portia was dropped out of the plane while you and I were actually training in the Mallee, we wouldn't notice unless she landed at our feet, at that very moment. If we did hear a plane, we'd probably dismiss it without thinking. Just someone having a squiz at the desert. With the naked eye, you'd have no idea.'

Ella drove in stony silence — pondering. André moved on.

'Any way, how are you? Did you see Lila on your way back?'

'I wasn't ready for that. I drove straight home.'

'That's a long drive with a lot of thinking time.'

'I listened to a podcast.'

They passed under the Big Cheese Stick freeway sculpture in further silence. It wasn't until they had crossed the Bolte Bridge that Ella glanced at André — long enough for him to see her quiet-time had gestated into a question.

'You're not worried about any of the Lila stuff, are you?' she asked him.

'Worried? In what sense? About it affecting you? … which of course I'm worried about, or about what actually happened? Her being abused or what may have happened to your dad? Whether I should do anything as a cop? Is that what you're asking me?'

'All of that.'

André sensed it was mostly about him being a cop. He thought before he answered.

'Look. I was there when Lila first told you about what happened with your dad. It went without saying that it was a private moment among the three of us. Sharing that with anyone else never entered my head at the time, and that's still the case as far as I'm concerned — cop or no cop. I understood the reason she told us was solely to let you know. The fact that I'm a cop, was just happenstance. If she wants to leave it in the past, that's entirely her decision. If she needs to talk more about it with you, I'm happy for that to be a matter that stays between you and her — so long as *you're* not beating yourself up about any of it.'

She kept her eyes on the road and placed her left hand on his. They both remained silent until they exited the freeway onto Kingsway and crawled to a halt in gridlock.

'Any other concerns come out of your long drive home?'

She was quick to say "No".

'If things do get too much, think about what I said about counselling,' he said.

'Maybe. Perhaps once I get my head around things.'

'Actually, it works the other way round, you know?'

'I know, but I have to go back to Rosenfeld. You've just reminded me there's something I should look up.'

Chapter 37

"It's déjà vu all over again".

It went without saying that the mangled saying spinning around André's head was coined by a sportsman. Before American Yogi Berra departed for the big baseball diamond in the sky, he'd made an art form of innocently juxtaposing the obvious. Among them: "You can observe a lot by watching"; "When you come to a fork in the road, take it"; and "Ninety percent of the game is half mental". Berra even had a Yogi-ism for summing the whole thing up — "I really didn't say everything I said". Not in André's case, however.

André found himself on a Melbourne freeway again, sitting in the passenger seat again, parroting everything he said to Ella the day before. This time, Glenevis was driving and the car's police siren was wailing.

'Is tha' where you've bin? You actually went ta Mildura? Hang on,' he added before André could answer.

They had slowed as drivers on Melbourne's M1 Monash Freeway panicked to near standstill as they tried to get out of the police car's way. The siren was having little effect in five packed lanes of traffic. Glenevis switched from the siren's long wail to a short burst of the far greater attention-grabbing yelp-yelp sound. It did the job, except for a recalcitrant truck with a trailer.

'Get tha' lorry's number,' he told André before the truck finally took the hint and set about barging its way into the adjoining lane. The sea ahead parted for Glenevis and they were back on track to a double-murder shooting at a service station. Uniform cops were already at the scene awaiting direction from Homicide.

'You went ta Mildura … ' Glenevis reminded André, above the wail.

'I did what you told me to do. I physically walked through every step from the last sighting of Portia Meredith at Castlemaine. To Bendigo, to Mildura, and all the way back to Beaumaris. I even used the spa that Meredith had in his motel room.'

'Yeah? Who with?'

'Sadly, I went solo. The point is, there's nothing about that weekend trip that doesn't fit. At every location they went to along the way, they didn't interact with others as a couple, to the extent that that in itself is suspicious. There are absolutely no witnesses, or record of any kind, that can confirm who accompanied Meredith on his trip. Meredith was, however, captured on a traffic camera when he was returning to Melbourne after flying the Cessna back to Bendigo. The pic shows a sleeping female passenger facing away from the camera. It is impossible to tell if the passenger is Portia Meredith or Eve Delmonte.'

'Anything more on th' time o' death?' Glenevis asked.

'Sophie can't rule out that she died that weekend.'

'Tha's good. And … '

'After their Mildura break came Meredith's trip to the airport for his flight to London. Portia supposedly drove him there in her BMW.'

'And Missing Person Squad found her fingerprints on th' steering wheel,' Glenevis remembered.

'Exactly. And we worked out that Meredith and Delmonte could have ingeniously made sure that remained the case when they drove the same car — after Portia died. That could be done by clamping a device called a steering spinner onto the steering wheel. They use them on machinery and disabled people use them in cars.'

They'd both been too gripped by the path Glenevis was carving F1-style through heavy freeway traffic, to shift their eyes off the road.

'I've got a picture here. Maybe I'll show you later … Jackie Stewart.'

'Jackie's a wee bit before ma time. Ah'm more a Colin McRae man, our world rally champion.'

André knew when Glenevis said "our world rally champion", he meant "Scotland's". He had already begun scrolling his phone for a picture of the steering wheel spinner.

'Give us a butcher's then,' Glenevis demanded above the siren, now back in its long wail mode.

He found the photo on his phone and moved it into Glenevis's vision. Glenevis nodded.

'Ella got one of these and tried it in her own car when she picked me up from the airport. Worked a treat. You can drive all day without actually touching the steering wheel itself.'

'Ella? Are we usin' consultants now?'

'You know she's still writing about the case. She's got more buy-in than anyone. She was the one who found the body, remember. The steering wheel spinner was all off her own bat.'

'So why dinnae you come up with tha'?'

'Shit, I can't win, can I?'

'Come on, André. Ah'm just having a go at ya. What else have you got?'

André settled.

'The steering spinner thing is kinda backed up by traffic pics we have. The cameras aren't set up to capture this sort of detail, but they do show the absence of hands where you normally expect to see hands near the top of the wheel. You can't actually see a spinner, but you'd expect it to be mounted out of sight in the six-o'clock position if you didn't want it to be captured on film. Conveniently, the driver's face is also not captured adequately. Glare, cap, visor … you know. So far, nothing much is working in our favour.'

André waited for Glenevis to process the verbal report with his mid high-speed-driving brain and a police-siren soundtrack. It wasn't a long wait.

'So, you're telling me you cannnae rule th' idea all the way in, even if you cannae rule it out. An' all your evidence is actually nae evidence at all. Nae witnesses in Bendigo or Mildura, Nae hands visible on the steering wheel. Nae spinner in sight. Nae passenger's face on the snapshot.'

André had not lost complete faith.

'Well, there is one other thing. If they wanted the airport drop-off trip to be credible and verifiable by us, they would need to pass through the Airport freeway's electronic toll point, which has cameras. They did that, of course, but not via the route you'd expect. We know that because they only passed through the toll point once in each direction. That kept any toll-camera scrutiny to an absolute minimum. Which again, is suspicious in itself. We don't know what the remainder of their route to Beaumaris was. We'll just have to keep searching traffic footage for other likely, or even unlikely routes. Tough, but not a complete haystack and needle.'

'So nae CCTV between th' freeway and Beaumaris to add ta your list o' nout. The fact that no one saw anything dinnae prove there *was* something ta see. You know tha', don't you?'

André raised both hands in an "I give up" gesture.

'Okay André. Ah *do* know what you're sayin'. But all the same, your pooshin' shite uphill if tha's all we have.'

'I know. But it's not so improbable that we ignore the blank spaces we haven't coloured in yet. We know they didn't take the predictable route home, but they did take a route. If we do clock them on CCTV somewhere unexpected, there's a good chance their guard will have been let down. Then we'll have them.'

'And you think that's not a haystack? What aboot using listenin' devices? phone taps?'

'I'd like to say yes but I think we'd be wasting our time. Missing Persons already went down that road. I had a listen and Meredith didn't give a sniff. It'd be that much harder now. Meredith and Delmonte are well beyond needing to discuss it with each other.'

For a short moment, it was just the sound of the siren.

'So tha's what it boils down ta. What aboot th' other suspects? Anything more?'

For the first time since their conversation began, Glenevis turned briefly to André to read him.

'We've pretty much ruled out Simon Stone and Jimmy Hyetts. It's all down to cracking John Meredith. We've already tried the media thing. We sailed close to the wind in that last story we gave Ella. All we got was Meredith arcing up and threatening us with legal action. I'll think of some other way to let him know we're still digging. Let him stew.'

'Good. Ah dinnae want this prick getting' away with it.'

The M1 traffic began slowing organically for the upcoming interchange with the South Gippsland Freeway.

'Fook,' Glenevis said and kicked in the yelp-yelp panic siren again.

'Havin' a go-slow phase might na be a bad thing,' he said to André. 'Because right now, I reckon you'll have your hand full sortin' this double-shootin' thing oot.'

<h1 style="text-align:center">Chapter 38</h1>

Rosenfeld had barely come into view along Hass's Road when Ella's phone rang in the SUV.

'*What are you doing back here?*' she heard Lila say.

'What? Where are you?

'*I'm in the paddock. In the harvester. I could tell it was your car a mile off.*'

Ella knew that on the Mallee wheat plains, seeing something a mile off was more often a truism than a pithy saying, especially if you were several metres above ground level in the glass cabin of a combine harvester. She shifted her gaze to see its moving dust cloud in the paddock behind the house.

'What are you doing? It isn't harvesting time.'

'*I'm learning to drive this fucking monster. Yee-ha. It's fantastic, Elly.*'

'Sounds like it.'

'*I'll bring it around to the main shed. Meet you there in a sec.*'

Ella drove up the driveway and turned away from the house to the sprawling farmyard of mega sheds, metal silos and unusually, only a few rusting relics. Pretty neat by most standards.

She arrived before Lila and hopped out of the SUV to stretch her legs. There was no time to savour familiar habitat. The thrum of the harvester heralded its imminent arrival before coming into view from behind the airplane-hangar sized machinery shed. The twelve-metre-wide monster straightened to enter the yard and idle up to the shed — or so Ella expected. What she didn't expect was for the business end of the harvester to suddenly fire up. The crop-header's innards kicked in with the whine of a rocket being wound up for launch. The wall-to-wall cutter bar began gnashing countless flailing finger blades as its massive reel twirled menacingly, ready to drag in and devour matter of any description in its path. The path Ella stood in.

It may have been the world Ella grew up in but, without her father being around, farm life had not been the hands-on experience Lila knew. Being this up close and personal to the pointy end of a combine harvester was as alien and menacing to Ella as it was to Lee Marvin and Sissy Spacek when one came after them in the movie Prime Cut.

She froze on the spot, helplessly allowing the colour to drain from her face.

Ella's inability to move off the spot sent Lila into a panic to halt the machine and shut down the thrashing header. The engine was still groaning towards complete quiet as Lila bounded down the ladder from the cabin and ran ahead to comfort Ella.

'I'm sorry, Elly. I wanted to put on a show for you. I thought you'd be impressed.'

She stood beside a still-in-shock Ella, holding her shoulders tightly.

'I've never been close up like this. Growing up here wasn't like that for me. You scared the fucking shit out of me.'

'I know. I know. I'm sorry, Elly. But this thing is fantastic. I love it. Come and I'll show you.'

'Jesus, Lila, I've just had my life flash before my eyes. And I've been driving four and a half hours. Let me at least calm down a bit.'

'Come on. It won't take a minute. You're here now, and all this is yours. Ours I mean. You need to know about stuff like this too. These things are worth more than half a mil, you know.'

'Half a million dollars? You could buy two decent houses in Rainbow for that.'

'Yeah. I know. Come on.'

Lila was holding Ella's hand to take her to the harvester. Ella acquiesced and let Lila lead her up the half dozen ladder steps to the cabin. Lila slipped into the operator's pillow-style red leather lounge chair with arm rests. That allowed Ella to step into the glass cubicle.

'Before you sit down, that's also a fridge. See?'

Lila lifted the seat of the basic passenger seat to reveal a built-in esky-sized fridge enclosure.

'For your sangers. Or a Carlton Draught or whatever beer they drink in the Mallee these days.'

She closed the seat-cum-fridge lid and Ella sat. There were no seatbelts.

'It's impressive, Lila. And high-tech by the look of the computer screen and controls. More like a PlayStation. And so high up. I wasn't expecting anything like this.'

The viewing height was akin to sitting on the three-metre board at the local pool.

'Operating everything is all screen-based, including calibrating the header. That took me all morning. Figuring out swaths and headlands. Even driving the thing runs on GPS. Now I've had a taste, I can't wait for harvest.'

'Mum did it sometimes, you know. She didn't leave it all to Trent. Maybe I should have taken an interest. It looks pretty comfortable in here. More like an office.

'I can think of worse work places. It's climate controlled of course. And it's got a decent sound system. Blue tooth to your phone. Although … ' She reached across the control panel for a CD case. ' … I've been listening to this. I found it in the house. The Lazy Farmer's Sons.'

'That's one of Mum's. They're locals.'

'What? You mean? Like, from the Mallee?'

'From Yaapeet.'

'You're joking. There's a band in Yaapeet? Playing these sort of gothic bush anthems? This is what the band I'm in try and do. It's great.'

'You probably remember Andy and Ben from school … hey.' Ella interrupted herself with a thought she just triggered. 'Does Trent know you're driving around in this thing?'

'Not if you don't tell him. He had to go to Horsham today.'

'Well, he'll probably find out anyway. There mightn't be many people around here, but nothing goes unnoticed. You should remember how that works. I'd better fill him in about us keeping the farm while I'm up here.'

'Is that why you came back so soon?'

'No. I'll only be staying overnight. I'm going to Wyperfeld in the morning and then heading back. I need to check out something for a story I'm working on.'

'You're still on the woman-flung-out-of-a-plane thing?'

'Yeah. The same case André's working on.'

'Uh huh. And you had to drive all this way just for that?'

'Uh huh.'

They looked at each other. Then looked ahead towards the house through the glass wall that formed the cabin's windscreen. Neither made a move to leave. They had both embraced the harvester enthusiastically as a diversion from their unresolved parting. Now the novelty was over. The moment to pick up where they'd left off had arrived.

'There is something else,' Ella conceded. 'And I didn't think I'd be having this conversation in a combine harvester.'

Lila recognised the solemn tone and turned to Ella.

'I don't blame you for killing Dad.'

Lila held her mouth with one hand and turned her face back to the windscreen.

'I can't,' Ella added.

'Did you tell André?'

'Not in as many words, but enough dots for him to join, Lila. I don't want to have secrets between André and me, even if it's your albatross, not mine. I know I can't unhear what you told me, about what happened to Dad, but that doesn't mean I want anything done about it. I don't. I absolutely don't. I've thought a lot about it; in fact I haven't thought about anything else … and I can't say I wouldn't have done the exact same thing if I was in your shoes. Especially if I had a younger sister, and in that instant, it was thrown at me that she'd be next. What happened happened, and I'm not troubled by André knowing what he knows. Until you showed up, he was the closest thing to family I have. If I have anything to do with it, he always will be. He's everything to me. He knows I've held back on detail because I never want to put him in that position, and he's comfortable leaving things as they stand. He absolutely respects it's a family matter, unless you think he should view it differently of course, which I'm sure you don't.'

They had both been talking to the windscreen. Lila turned to Ella. She had her hand back over her mouth and it was shaking. Ella reached across the padded armrest to embrace her crying sister. She held her tightly and let Lila cry until she stopped enough to pull away and look at Ella. Her lip quivered again. She gave up the attempt to speak and dived back into her sobbing hug.

'Oh, Elly,' she managed when she finally parted.

Ella tilted her head and rubbed Lila's shoulder.

'I know, Lil. I need you in my life.'

It was the first time she had resurrected the family's nickname for Lila.

'I know. And I've been waiting twenty years to be here … and to hear someone call me that.'

She rubbed Ella's shoulder as they faced each other, absorbing each other's absolute requitedness. It was left to Ella to break the spell.

'Besides, we're a farming partnership now. We need to get used to sorting things out in a combine harvester. Right?'

Lila gave a teary smile.

'You won't be able to get me out of here. I'm gonna make this my office.'

Chapter 39

Ella went directly to the information centre's visitors' book.

Been coming here for 41 years with our family and friends. Sometimes planted trees with Friends of Wyperfeld. Love it but miss the teas and damper and the lectures and slide shows the rangers ran.

Stalwarts, she judged.

Miriam, Judith, Kate, Shae and Alex. Last girls weekend pre-marriage. Can't wait to return.

Miriam. The same name as her Mum. She moved on.

Cool desert, Bianca Schulz, Dimboola.

Written in a young girl's hand. Probably oblivious to the ironic oxymoronic-ness of her entry.

Lachlan Schulz, Dimboola.

Her brother, with even less to say.

Love the quiet. Hope to come back with the caravan and stay. Betty and Gordon, Ivanhoe.

Day-trippers? Surely not. Not with a five-hour trip from Ivanhoe, she pondered.

Still bloody hot here, Dave Becker. Riverside Manor, Jeparit.

She recognised a local nursing home's moniker. It looked like they'd given the oldies a day out. It kicked off a mini-bus load of nostalgic contributions. As she leafed backwards, there were less birdwatcher entries than her previous browsing suggested there would be. She phoned André.

'How are things going? Are you and Lila good?'

'Yeah. All good. We're getting the farm stuff sorted. On my way home, I'll be breaking the news to Trent — that we're not selling. I'm not looking forward to that, but I suppose it has to be done. And Lila is all fired up. She was driving around in the harvester when I arrived.'

'It doesn't sound to me like it's still eating you up. Have things changed that much?'

'Possibly. I dunno. This sibling stuff is new to me. I mean, I have to accept what happened and that Lila didn't bring any of it upon herself. That's Lila's story and now it's my story too. I'm intertwined. I always was, even though I never knew. We didn't end up saying a lot, but we said what we needed to. Bottom line, neither of us want to spend another twenty years apart. If I'm honest, I think that sharing the farm will give us that life together that we've both secretly craved. I'm hoping so. Anyway, that's how I feel today.'

'And you've got me, El.'

'I know, "A". I know.'

Quiet erupted.

'When will you be home?'

'I'll be heading back shortly. I'll try and be there when you get home from work.'

'I don't have much to report on that front. Still digging away. Things will probably slow down for a bit on the Meredith front, though. I'm at a double murder shooting at a servo. You'll probably

catch it on the news.'

'Oh. Okay then. I actually phoned to find out what date John Meredith flew to Mildura. I'm working out my next article nevertheless.'

'April twenty-third.' He said off the top of his head. *'I don't think you should mention that date in an article, though. That'd be way too pointed.'*

'Don't worry, "A". I just want to get the sequence right in my head. I'll fill you in when I see you. Love you. Bye.'

An entry on the twenty-eighth of April struck potential gold.

Best week we've ever had here. A grey falcon, mulga parrots, black eared minor, azure kingfisher, splendid fairy wren. Too many to list. Best club turnout as well. Eight caravans. Renae Adams, North Melbourne Bird Observers Club.

It was possible. It all depended on whether the *"Best week we've ever had here"* stretched back to the twenty-third of April. It sounded like it could. She photographed the entry.

Mobile phone coverage was sufficient to bring up Google. The bad news — there were no contact details for the scant mentions of the North Melbourne Bird Observers Club — no Facebook page, not even an email address. It was time to pull in a favour. She phoned a research elf at work. He would call or message on her way back.

Next stop, Trent Hofner. Rosenfeld's part-time farm manager was about to become its no-time manager. She phoned ahead.

Chapter 40

Trent Hofner told her he was at the workshop on his own farm. It wasn't too long before he heard her car approaching. He came outside to greet her, wiping his hands on an oily rag.

'Servicing the side-by-side,' he told her with the greatest economy of words.

She was pleased she had recently learnt what a side-by-side was and could nod knowingly. She made a mental note to speak to Lila about getting one. A kind of cross between a quad bike and a golf buggy. The least piece of farm equipment a silent partner should have. A fun way to get around and inspect the place.

Trent was somewhere in age between Ella and Lila. They both knew of him from school days but were both separated enough in class years not to have been closely associated. He was dark-haired handsome and in dire need of a conversational transplant. When he interacted with other humans of his own volition, he'd probably relied on half a slab of beer to get him going.

Ella noticed his dearth of words had shrunk even more. It signalled to her that he knew why she'd come, even though she hadn't spoken to anyone local about not selling the farm. No doubt Lila's out-of-the-blue post-funeral appearance and ongoing presence at Rosenfeld was grist for the rumour mill. Whatever those rumours were, they didn't help.

Trent's initial non-word response of, 'Uh-huh,' sent Ella into over-apologetic mode. She could hear herself gibbering and hated herself — and still she couldn't stop. *Why am I like this? I've interviewed Julia Gillard. Shut up, Ella. Stop saying "sorry".*

She pressed on.

'We'll probably still need to call on someone on a casual basis to do jobs around the farm. Would you be interested?' she asked.

''spose.'

Ella couldn't resist sarcasm, at least in her head. *Double points for pruning that sentence of absolutely all unnecessary words and syllables.*

It was a different matter once she was in her SUV and driving out his front gate.

'Fuck. Fuck. Fuck,' she yelled out loud. She added a solid two-handed palm-thump of the steering wheel. The horn sounded unintentionally.

And now he thinks I'm giving him a friendly goodbye toot. Fuck.

One kilometre closer to Melbourne, she resolved the frustration in her head.

Note to self. Lila will be running the farm. Any hiring and firing will be her responsibility. After all, she'll be the one dealing with them face -to-face. From here on in, I'll be sticking to what silent partners do best — being silent.

It took until the outskirts of Ballarat for the newspaper's research elf to send her a text. It informed her that Renae Adams was still the secretary of the North Melbourne Bird Observers Club, although she didn't actually live in North Melbourne. Her address was in the coastal town of Ocean Grove and she was happy to meet Ella when she finished her nursing shift at four o'clock that day. Ocean Grove was well over an hour out of Ella's way but she had more than enough time to get there, *and* have a good coffee. She made for Ballarat's L'Espresso café.

The final leg of Ella's journey passed through the township of Meredith. She wondered if John Meredith had an ancestral connection. The township's renowned alternative music festival didn't seem like his cup of tea. The most recent line-up she could recall was headed by Yothu Yindi. Eve Delmonte would certainly be out of place, she decided. The long-distance runner's proclivity for reverie was taking hold.

Lapwing Street was in a neighbourhood of other bird-named streets in Ocean Grove. Perhaps the ornithological address was sufficient to have enticed Renae from North Melbourne. Number sixteen was a low angle roofed weatherboard on the lower side of the street. The house was not fully visible behind the street's avenue of random paperbarks and coastal banksias. The front lawn ran all the way to the kerbside channelling. Only the letterbox marked the formal boundary.

A red Toyota Rav4 sat in the carport. Ella peered beyond to see a caravan sitting on the back lawn. *Right house*, she noted to herself and rang the doorbell.

In her late forties Ella guessed when Renae answered the door. Thickening in the figure but not unattractively so. The friendly and efficient manner of a competent nursing sister showed through. Well-credentialed to be a club secretary.

The lounge room had been opened into the dining kitchen area sometime in the past decade. Renae chatted from the kitchen as she made tea. Children, but not home by the look of a gaming controller sitting idle by the TV screen. A husband too, owner of the size ten Blundstones by the back door. Also at-work or gone-fishing. He probably drove the caravan tow-er, which was not at home either.

Renae knew Ella was calling about the club's field trip to Wyperfeld. There were signs of bird observing in the room, but not overly so. Pictures of rare sightings mixed in with family photographs. Pride of place was a framed shot of a grey falcon in flight.

'It's a threatened species. I took that at Wyperfeld,' she explained to Ella as she poured tea from a tea cosy-ed pot.

When she settled in a lounge chair, Ella felt compelled to ask.

'How is it that you live in Ocean Grove and are secretary of the North Melbourne Bird Observers Club?'

'We're a bit like the South Melbourne AFL side moving north to become the Sydney Swans in the eighties. Unlike the Swans however, we hung onto our original name. For some reason, most of the older members migrated to this stretch of coast. Our meetings are now held in Geelong.'

'It's good when history is maintained,' Ella acknowledged.

'It's more than nostalgia, though,' Renae explained, 'I don't know if you know of Arthur Herbert Evelyn Mattingley … '

'I know exactly who he is.'

'Oh good. Well, he's like the club's patron saint and North Melbourne gave us a connection to him. He was born there in 1870.'

'Right.'

'You probably know he was the pioneer of Australian bird photography. He won gold medals at international photographic exhibitions. Mattingley was a member of the Zoological Society of London and a founder of the Gould League of Bird Lovers. He helped form the Bird Observers Club in Melbourne. He is also responsible for Wyperfeld becoming a national park, which is why you are here. I suppose you know, the highest point in the national park is named after him.'

'I do know,' Ella told her. 'I come from up that way originally and I've recently been back. I even ran up Mount Mattingley, although calling it a mountain is a stretch.'

'I know what you mean,' she smiled. 'Our club goes there on a field trip every two years. It's still one of the best bird observing sites in Victoria.'

'And the club was there on the twenty-third of April last year?'

'Yes. I've checked the dates since your researcher phoned earlier. We arrived the day before that on the Friday and left the following Saturday. That's when I wrote in the visitor's book.'

'What they probably didn't tell you on the phone is that the woman's body that was found in the desert may have been dropped from a plane on Saturday the twenty-third of April. Perhaps someone in your club might have seen the plane that day.'

'Oh!' she said with alarm. 'Did that happen when we were all there? I feel dreadful thinking about it.'

'The police are not certain exactly when it happened. But your club was there for a whole week. Maybe someone noticed a light plane.'

'I don't know,' Renae said, nonplussed. 'You occasionally see aircraft when you're bird watching but we don't usually take any notice. Some members get annoyed if one flies low enough to scare birds, like eagles maybe. But no one mentioned anything. Sometimes there are jet trails high above Wyperfeld.' She drifted off in search of memory. 'I'm not being much help, am I?'

'Perhaps you can ask other club members who went on the trip.'

'I'd be happy to. I think they will be like me, though. A bit disturbed to know that happened while we were there.'

'I'm sorry to sound like a policeman but I'd really appreciate it if you let me know anything they come up with.'

'Maybe you should talk to Henry Devine. He was there.'

'Why Henry?' asked Ella.

'He's one of the club's last remaining North Melbourne members. He doesn't attend meetings any more but he never misses a Wyperfeld trip. And when I think about it, he's a retired pilot.'

Chapter 41

'Where are you?'

'On the Geelong to Melbourne Road,' Ella told André on her mobile. 'I'm in the end-of-weekend traffic that's crawling back from the coast.'

'That's the long way back from Rosenfeld. Where have you been?'

'Ocean Grove.'

'How come?'

'Research,' Ella told him elusively.

'You must be knackered driving all that way. How long will you be?'

'I might be late. I still have to drop in and see someone in North Melbourne.'

'Can't you do that tomorrow?'

'You missed me?' she said.

'A bit.'

'I want to do this today. I'm back at work tomorrow and might not get a chance for a while. I haven't been driving all day though. I had a rest here and there.'

'Where?'

'Ocean Grove, Meredith.'

'Hope you weren't looking for clues in Meredith. That's not how it works you know.'

'No shit?' she said, calling out his condescension. He didn't have a comeback.

'I'll be as quick as I can in North Melbourne. Love you, "A".'

'Love you too.'

The Devine's two storey terrace was on the upper side of Chapman Street — more a boulevard, with its imposing lawned centre-strip of stately gums. The far-from-shabby neighbourhood was a collection of original small terraces and slate roofed Victorian houses, interspersed with the odd home of intervening periods, including a few new builds.

The Royal Children's Hospital being a mere block away caused Ella to drive laps battling hospital visitors for a non-resident parking space. If Henry Devine took a caravan to Wyperfeld, he did not park it around here, she surmised. On her second fruitless drive past, Ella hit the wall. *Perhaps André was right — I should leave this for another day.* She had left Rosenfeld soon after daylight and it would be dark again by the time she reached home, even if it turned out that Henry Devine was not in. There had been no answer when she phoned ahead earlier. Then, without warning, the tell-tale flash of a parked car's reversing light lit up. She pounced.

The iron front-gate squeaked predictably and Ella climbed the tessellated tiled steps to Henry Devine's door. The old brass ringer actually worked and was audible to the ringer, and hopefully the ring-ee.

Ella felt her face relax slightly when the muffled sound of

footsteps grew louder behind the door.

Henry Devine looked beyond retirement age but he somehow managed to retain an airline pilot's air of control and calm. The deepening lines and whitening hair merely added to his charm. A shade more travel-strain drained from Ella.

He led her through the elegant aged hallway to the obligatory modern living extension at the rear of the house where he and his wife Monique were enjoying a drink.

Cedar-framed double-glazed windows opened onto an outdoor deck with a Weber barbeque. A wide expanse of bookshelves ran along one side wall, interspersed with a modest size TV screen and an expensive-looking compact sound system. Like Renae Adams house, trophy photographs gave away his ornithological interest. Unlike Renae's however, were the accompanying photographs of aeroplanes.

'Renae told me you were a pilot. I see that it's more than a job,' Ella said, looking at a photograph of a slightly younger-looking Henry standing by a Tiger Moth bi-plane.

'The passion was there long before I became an airline pilot. There was no way that would die just because I retired. Would you like to join us?' he added, indicating the open bottle of wine on the table. 'We're halfway into a pinot grigio. From Tassie.'

The mere thought of a drink caused the remaining toll of a day-long drive to glide effortlessly from Ella.

'Yes, please,' came her eager reply.

Henry poured an extra glass as well as topping up his own and Monique's. Ella felt the first mouthful unclench her whole body. She became as one with the lounge chair.

'I don't mind his obsession,' Monique said with a soft European accent that Ella dared not try to guess. 'The way he still fixates over planes, he'll never be short of something to do in retirement.'

'How did you meet?' Ella found her newly relaxed-self asking. Monique Devine was as unmistakably a former flight attendant as was Henry indisputably an airline pilot. The hairdo and her bearing had not changed since she last trod the narrow aisle.

'Oh, I'm the biggest part of his obsession,' she replied. 'I was an airhostess, before we became flight attendants. We met at Orly Airport in Paris. I lived there at the time.'

'And do you go bird watching too, Mrs Devine?'

Her name is Mrs Devine, Ella realised, *how she must love that.*

'No. I'm the one he watches at home. I went to Wyperfeld once. The heat and flies were unbearable.'

She didn't ask me to call her Monique, Ella noticed. *Mrs Devine certainly does like being Mrs Devine.*

'She loves it when I go, though,' Henry was quick to add. 'And exactly what can I tell you about Wyperfeld?' he asked with curiosity rising above small talk.

Ella told him what she had told Renae Adams.

'Right.' Henry said thoughtfully. 'There *were* planes about that week, or at least *a* plane.'

'You know that off the top of your head? How can you be sure?'

'I can check if you like, I keep a diary of sightings … natural, *and* man-made.'

'Great,' Ella said matter-of-factly, trying to keep a lid on her budding excitement.

'Come to the study and we'll see what we can find,' he said calmly. 'Oh. And you've finished your drink. Another?'

Her answer was "Yes", and she brought it with her to Henry's study. He led her to a small room off the hallway, back in the home's old quarter. Monique stayed in the sitting room.

The computer was a beacon of modernity on an antique desk with an original banker's lamp. The room was dark with heavy wallpaper and ancient timber shelving. He beckoned Ella to sit in the wing-backed reading chair before leafing through a diary.

'Here it is. Saturday the twenty-third of April, two seventeen p.m., A white Cessna 172, blue striping, unusually low. Less than 1,000 feet. Flying out of the desert on a north-north-east course.'

'Oh, my God,' Ella gushed. She never considered herself to be an "Oh-my-God" kind of gal. She realised she'd watched one too many sit-coms and didn't have an alternative that sprang to mind. Her hands gestured fruitlessly. 'Really? You're kidding? Do you know what this means?'

Henry leant back in his chair grinning madly.

'Something good?' he guessed, enjoying Ella's inarticulate jubilation.

She nodded a grinning "yes".

'Let's see if I have a photograph then,' he said, and snapped forward to turn on his computer.

'No way! You can't say that unless you mean it. You're not having me on, are you? You have an actual photo of that actual plane?'

'Of course, I'm not having you on. I'm a bird observer. It's what we do. I always have a camera with telephoto lens in my hand. A b-i-i-i-g telephoto lens to be precise … and a monopod. That's a pole we use to steady long-range shots, and mid-air shots.'

He leant back into his chair again as the computer booted itself.

'They can put a man on the moon and look how long it

takes for a computer to start.'

Ella took another mouthful of pinot grigio and jiggled impatiently in uncharacteristic cliché. Her infectiousness had Henry smiling.

He dropped the smile to grab the mouse and began searching directories. He started talking to himself or the computer in the tone of a man not exactly as one with his machine. 'April … April … Wyperfeld … Damn. That was two years ago. Try again … That's better. Wyperfeld … April … Saturday. Ah. It'll be in this lot.'

Ella put her drink down, came behind the desk and leant towards the screen with both palms on the desktop. The directory opened with a full screen picture of a parrot bursting from a Mallee tree. The image was superimposed with the date and time in orange letters.

'A blue-winged parrot. Where's the forward arrow,' he said as he re-acquainted himself with the instrument panel.

'I preferred the earlier version of this program. I knew where everything was.'

He found the scrolling-forward arrow on the screen and clicked to an image of the same parrot, a micro-second later in flight. Then to a wedge tailed eagle with its wings spread to ride a thermal current. Thirty or so images appeared as Henry continued scrolling through the folder. Excitement had reached the verge of dropping off when a white aeroplane abruptly appeared on the screen instead of a bird.

'That's it,' he said. 'And if I zoom in like this, it gets a bit blurry, but we can still see the number clearly.'

He turned to look at Ella. She was frozen. A puzzled Henry said, 'If I … '

'Don't touch a thing,' she spat out so rapidly it stopped

Henry mid-reach to the mouse.

'Just leave it there,' she said with unapologetic fierceness.

How fragile it suddenly became in Ella's mind.

It's right there, now, on the screen in front of my own eyes … except, it's not a real thing. It's a virtual image that Henry can make appear and disappear at will with the click of a mouse. But what if he can't? What if it he makes a mistake … a wrong click or mis-keystroke that deletes the file … or kills his computer? We're probably not about to be hit by a meteorite, but a surge or overload on the grid could wipe everything out, couldn't it? Isn't that what the Wichita Linesman searches for? After all, the image is not a tangible thing, just a series of ones and zeros stored within. And those ones and twos are not a tangible thing either. Right now, the only object I could actually hold in my hand is a disc drive made of God knows what … and holding that up in front of a court of law is not gonna convince anyone about anything. The image can only be re-conjured from the magnetic disc when it's spun by a tiny motor within a computer connected to a chain of massive high-tension towers strung across the state to a colossus of power stations in Gippsland. If the court was on a desert island we'd still be up shit creek. Even with electricity, I'm relying on a man struggling to find the scrolling arrow on a basic media-player? He can get in the cockpit of a jumbo jet and get it to hurtle into the sky with 300 people on board. Shouldn't that have made him computer proof? Does he even have a backup?

She found a way to overcome the rampant paranoia in her head without slapping her own face.

'Just let me take a picture of it first,' she said, and began snapping several pictures of the screen image on her phone.

'Now do you mind if I copy it onto this memory stick and then I'd like to print a copy. Do you have a printer?'

Ella retrieved a memory stick from her bag. Her gravity was as infectious as her excitement and Henry fell into solemn obedience. He sat aside to allow a more experienced computer pilot to bring the jumbo in. He sipped his own wine as he watched and ruminated on her intractable purposefulness.

'I'm a bit of a fan of Diane Arbus, who you probably haven't heard of. She's an American photographer who says there are things nobody would see if she didn't photograph them. I think that's where we're at here, don't you think?'

Ella stopped mid-mouse task and looked at him with awe.

'She absolutely nailed it.'

He smiled and asked her.

'Can I get you another wine?'

He clocked her still gobsmacked face.

'Silly question,' he said, still smiling.

'I'm at Henry and Monique's place in North Melbourne and I need you to come and get me.'

'*Are you drunk? You sound tipsy,*' André asked.

'We've had a few,' Ella said with almost mustered solemnness.

'*Who are Henry and Monique? What's going on?*'

'They're a lovely couple I've just met. I'm at their house and they have a surprise for you.'

'*You haven't turned swinger, have you?*'

'N-o-o-o. Of course not. It's a good surprise. Not that … never mind. This will make your week. Your year. Your decade even.'

'*This better be good. I'll get an Uber over and drive your car home. What's the address?*'

She told him the Chapman Street number and added

cryptically, 'And bring a memory stick. You can never have too many.'

André stood behind the desk in the Devine study with his head swivelling between the screen image and the grinning faces of Ella, Henry and Monique. He bounced between the two like watching a tennis rally before finally fixing his gaze back on the screen. He shook his head in amazement before trying to utter words.

He opened his own phone and brought up the pic he took of Robert Woodruff's Cessna in its Bendigo hangar — the exact same Cessna with the very same VH number emblazoned on its side and underwing. He held it, face out, to Ella, Henry and Monique.

They peered forward and gave a resounding 'Oooo,' in wide-eyed unison.

'This is … it's … not amazing. There has to be a better word than that. I can't think of it, though. How did you do this?' he said to Ella.

'You told me that if we were at Wyperfeld when a plane flew over, we probably wouldn't notice because people don't look up and it would be unrecognisable to the naked eye if they did. When I tried to visualise Wyperfeld visitors in that situation, the first thing that came to mind were birdwatchers. The polar opposite of what you described. These humans *do* get around looking up, and they *are* equipped to see everything the naked eye can't. Every one of them is armed with binoculars and cameras with massive telescopic lenses.

'I tracked down Henry from the visitors' book in the information centre. That's where my morning started. Henry's a plane buff as well as a bird buff,' Ella giggled tipsily.

'I'm a double buff,' Henry said, setting himself, Monique and Ella off on well-lubricated laughing.

'You can never be enough buffs,' Ella added, extending the in-joke hilarity.

André was soundly glued to the screen in his own sober world.

'Have you saved a copy?'

His first thought mirrored Ella's. Suddenly this collection of digital bytes also seemed conjured from the ether. A butterfly, fleeting, with all the substance of a hologram.

'Ella wouldn't let me touch my own computer until she photographed the screen.'

'I've printed copies and have it on a stick,' Ella said, struggling to mirror André's soberness.

André handed her the memory stick he faithfully brought along. Ella let Henry try and copy it this time, satisfied that her own collected backup was protection enough.

'See, it's got the date and time and everything,' slurred Ella. 'It's what twitchers, I mean bird observers do. Henry prefers to be called a bird observer.'

'I'd love to accept your offer of a drink Henry. You don't know how much this gives me to celebrate. But I'm driving Ella home.'

'That means it's up to us to have another one for you then,' Monique giggled.

'You do know what this means?' André said. 'This solves the woman-in-the-desert murder. This is the silver bullet. We'll need to come back and get details and a statement from you in the morning.'

'Absolutely,' announced Henry raising his glass in celebratory fashion. 'Just have one André, to toast our success. To we four musketeer crime fighters who solved the latest Wyperfeld case.'

'The latest?' queried André.

'Oh yes. Check out the history as I did. You'll see that many were found dead up there when the white man first came, although not all of them so mysteriously.'

He hooked the little finger of his left hand to begin counting them off. His recall instantly began to battle the wine they'd all consumed.

'Some died of thirst … others from drinking too much … ah … and one was found in a dingo trap. What a way to go, hey? Suspected suicides and a supposed gun accident. They reckon a Chinaman died from want of opium. Wyperfeld was no stranger to death, my friend.'

The room was in danger of sobering. Henry continued regardless.

'It wasn't that many years ago that a guy fell overboard in Lake Albacutya. He was attacked and killed by his own boat.'

André turned sharply to Ella. He expected her to have a shocked look. The drink staved that off, but the remark registered nonetheless. She held a couple of fingers away from the glass she was holding to waggle her drink hand at André in a don't-go-there motion.

'Did I say something?' Henry observed with mock surprise.

'Nah, Henry. All the time I've been on this case, I never knew we were in such deadly territory,' André said.

This time, Ella did stiffen. The fun really *was* in danger of drying up.

'Okay then,' André announced. 'I'll join the toast and then I'd better get Ella in the car before I have to carry her out.'

He put his arm around Ella as they watched Henry and

Monique pfaffing around to find another glass and pour him a drink. He was embarrassed to see that it involved opening another bottle.

'To Wyperfeld,' André proposed with glass raised.

'To Wyperfeld,' they joined in.

'Hey, you've still got the tractor steering knob,' André said as he sat in the driver's seat.

'The "not-the-final-piece-in-the-puzzle",' Ella reminded him pout-ily. 'Have I got you the final piece in the puzzle this time then?'

André's response was too schmaltzy for the long consideration he gave to the question.

'You've always been the final piece of my puzzle.'

He nonetheless turned with a self-satisfied grin, only to see she had fallen asleep.

André listened to his phone connect and begin summoning Glenevis. It occurred to him that he might also be inflicting the Cock o' the North bagpipe ringtone on a sleeping Mrs Glenevis. He cringed. The ringing tone continued deeper into panic territory before Glenevis answered. Pleasantries were not needed. Glenevis's screen warned him who was calling.

'You've got me oot a bed on a Sunday night. If ya value your job, André, you'll be givin' this your best shot straight oof th' bat.'

Even in Glaswegian, Glenevis spoke with the un-mistakable drawl of someone who had just been woken.

'Okay. You know how you told me and Deborah Harvey that you couldn't see how we could pin the murder on John

Meredith … short of a photo of him flying a plane over the drop site?'

André could hear the wheels in Glenevis's half-awake brain groan into a few slow turns. It didn't seem to help.

'Ah do remember tha'. So, now you're going to tell me wha' other eleven-thirty-on-Sunday-night-worthy way you found ta pin th' murdah on him?'

André thought he'd just delivered an unambiguous, jubilation guaranteed statement of having solved the unsolvable. The last thing he expected from Glenevis was some obtuse misinterpretation.

'Err … no. That's not it, Boss.'

'Thirty-three minutes past eleven an' countin' —' Glenevis said with dangerously increasing cognisance.

'I found a photo of John Meredith flying a plane over the drop site,' André blurted to rescue his own euphoria.

André listened to the wheels turn a tad more freely. The silence stretched into panic territory again before Glenevis's answer came.

'My office. Eight a.m.'

Chapter 42

'So, this is what kept me awake for th' rest o' last night?'

André and Alex watched Glenevis gaze at the A4 photograph he was holding.

'Sorry. I had to tell someone. I was outta my skin.'

'Well, you're lucky I left mah skin on. I nearly called you back when it sank in — at two-thirty in the a.m.'

André grimaced apologetically.

Glenevis passed the photo to Alex and they watched him study it.

'You know the best thing about a picture is that it never changes, even when the people in it do,' Alex said.

'Is that what that well-known 500BC photographer Pythagoras reckons?'

'Ha ha. Andy Warhol. Greeks don't have a monopoly on wisdom, you know.' Alex said, and handed the photo back to Glenevis.

'And this is th' actual plane Meredith flew ta Mildura?'

'The exact same number. Henry reckons we struck it lucky, to have the numbers so large, the size can vary a lot. And to have the number on the underside of the wing. Apparently, that hasn't been a requirement for yonks.'

'And Henry is?'

'He's a retired Qantas pilot-cum-birdwatcher who was on a field trip to Wyperfeld National Park, equipped with a long-range telephoto lens, of course, and an irresistible curiosity about every plane he sees.'

'How did ya find him?'

'He was up there with a birdwatchers' club. Ella noticed an entry they'd made in the information centre's visitor book and tracked them down.'

'*She* tracked him down?'

André shrugged a yes.

'So, we have Ella ta thank, yet again?'

'She happened to be there yesterday.'

'That was handy,' Alex observed.

André shot him a *that's-not-helping* glare.

Glenevis summed his thoughts with a sceptical "Hmm" and shifted his attention back to the photo.

'Can you prove beyond doubt where and when this were taken?'

'Absolutely. I already know the meta data places it in a series of shots that are unquestionably on that day, at that time, and on that side of Wyperfeld. I'm sending Zac to Henry's place this morning to go through his camera and computer and authenticate all of that.'

'Okay. So Meredith cannae dispute this is him flyin' over Wyperfeld on his way ta Mildura in April, *and* descending to low altitude. But that's not th' main thing that kept me awake last night. What concerns me more is tha' Wyperfeld is not that far off-route ta Mildura. What? Less than a hundred ks?

Whatever it is, it seems pretty inconsequential on a trip tha' long — and up in the sky, like. If he gets wind o' this before you spring th' photo on him, he's goin' to say he was simply smellin' th' roses along th' way and meandered here and there.'

'You should have phoned me at two-thirty. I was thinking the same thing,' André said.

'And did ya think of how to deal with tha'?'

'With Meredith being as shifty as he is, I reckon he'll play into our hands … if we give him enough rope. As soon as I mention the possibility a plane flying anywhere near Wyperfeld on that day — before we produce the pic of course — he'll emphatically deny he was anywhere near the place. He'll think he couldn't be on safer ground to lie his arse off — thousands of feet above ground with the plane's ID way beyond range of the naked human eye, even when he descends a bit to drop the body.'

Alex opened his mouth to point out the incongruity of being on safer ground while in the air. Glenevis wasn't interested and cut him off at the pass.

'Then you better get him in here as quick as ya can. Before he gets wind o' anythin'. Ah'm the nervous type. To begin with, Henry knows, as does whoever else Henry happens ta chat to aboot it.'

This time André opened his mouth, to reassure him that Henry had been adequately briefed. Glenevis cut him off too.

'I trust Ella knows better than ta put this around at her work or anywhere else before we arrest this prick.'

'Yeah. She's cool with that. But she is writing this story as we speak. She'll be ready and wanting to press the "Send email" button as soon as we say so … which I reckon is fair enough.'

'You want us to play favourites?'

'No. She's already put herself in the position of favourite. She found the body and now she's found the witness. She's written the story, and, she's got a copy of the photo. On top of all that, she's doing the right thing, sitting on this for us. Her editor won't know until I say so. I just need to give her that nod while you're announcing a media conference to be held later in the day — preferably delayed until tomorrow.'

'She's got the photo?' Glenevis exclaimed.

'Of course. She was the one who found it and Henry. That all happened before I arrived. He was happy for her to have a copy.'

'And she wants ta print it?'

'Not before we give the go ahead. And it'll appear with the paper's watermark on it. But we can't stop her … can we?'

Glenevis held his jaw glumly.

'I'm not comfortable, André, an' Georgie in Comms is not going to like it either. She'll cop it from other media, ya know.'

'No one was stopping anyone else from tracking down a birdwatcher with a long lens.'

That was the clincher.

'O-fooking-kay. Arrest him then. Wait until he's at home, if you can. I don't want ta be defending this ta his lawyer or anybody else because we did it in an office building, in the full glare of people with their mobile fooking phones. Okay?'

André nodded — and then pushed things a step further.

'Still, if someone happened to be walking past his home when the arrest did happen. I don't mean a media cameraman or anything like that. Just an ordinary person with a mobile phone. Maybe even someone who knows the case well enough to be hanging around there on the off-chance. Well, we couldn't be held responsible for anything like that, could we?'

Glenevis threw his hands up in a gesture of surrender.

'Christ. In for a penny, in for a poond — just make sure that if someone is going ta do tha', it's not Ella. I don't want her anywhere near the place. Now get on with it and bring him in — and oppose bail. A n d ... ' he raised his voice to raise an additional concern. ' ... how do you propose dealing with Eve Delmonte?'

'She's a done deal once Meredith is in the bag. He'll be dishing up all the evidence against her that we need, faster than Portia fell out of the plane. What alternative will he have left, other than spreading the blame?'

'Right-oh. But monitor her movements from th' moment you arrest him. I don't want ya telling me she flew out of the country.'

There was an hour of daylight left when John Meredith and Eve Delmonte drove into the driveway of his Beaumaris home. The inconspicuous police observer waited until the electronic gate and garage door re-closed before she phoned the team waiting nearby.

'Go.'

John Meredith seemed genuinely surprised to see André and Alex with uniformed police on his doorstep. His head swivelled rapidly to take them, and the waiting police cars, in.

'I don't know what game you're playing here but this harassment is beyond the pale — although I'm not surprised, considering your starling ineptness at finding my wife's killer. Don't move an inch from where you're standing. I'm phoning my lawyer right now, as well as the people they know in Police Command. And don't say I haven't been warning you. To have you two drag the reputation of the State's police force through the mud like this, I'm sure that's something that won't be tolerated for a nanosecond. If I have anything to do with it, you two can expect a career change before you're eating your next breakfast.'

'Hold that thought about phoning your lawyer because, John Meredith, I'm arresting you for the murder of Portia Meredith on the twenty third of April. You are not obliged to say or do anything but anything you do say will be recorded and used in evidence against you at a later court hearing.'

'What the fuck are you talking about?'

'You have the right to contact a legal representative and you have the right to contact a person to let them know your whereabouts. Do you wish to exercise any of these rights before the interview continues?'

He stepped into André's personal space and raised his upper lip to deliver his response.

'Not just those rights, detective, but my right to sue you personally and keep on suing you for committing this fucking fuck-up of all fucking fuck-ups, until even your colleagues will want to hang you out of a police helicopter by your balls. You haven't even satis-fucking-fied the first or the second commandment of homicide — no one can have murdered someone who's not yet dead. Even if I managed to do that impossibility, I'd at least have to be on the same continent. The twenty third of April. What a fucking joke.'

'Can you turn around, please, Mr Meredith, so the officer can put the handcuffs on.'

Meredith tilted his head back in defiance and gave a laser stare. André gave a weary twirly sign with his finger.

'Around please sir,' he added nonchalantly.

'Sir?' Alex queried out loud — letting André know he was laying it on a bit thick. Meredith turned around for Alex to cuff him.

'I hope you don't intend to take me out of here like this.'

'We gave you that kind of consideration when we chose not to do this at your workplace. We waited for you to come home. And now we're taking you to be interviewed at the police centre in Spencer Street. Who would you like to contact to let them know that's where you'll be?'

Meredith looked up. Everyone else's eyes followed.

There was an architectural void above where they all stood in the entry hall. The void extended beyond the next floor to some even higher atrium skylight windows. Eve Delmonte was leaning into the void over an upper balustrade. *It really is a thing. We don't look up,* André noted in his head.

'Ring Kelvin. Now,' Meredith told her.

Alex held Meredith's elbow to lead him outside through the front gate to one of several marked police cars. A young guy walking a brown border-collie on a lead saw them coming out of the door. He held up his mobile phone and began snapping pics onehandedly.

'Look at that,' Meredith yelled at Alex. 'Grab his phone. I haven't given him permission to take my picture.'

'There's nothing illegal about … '

Meredith didn't wait for Alex's explanation.

'Hey you Fuck-knuckle,' he yelled after the dog walker. 'I've lived in this suburb long enough to know which house you live in. If I see any of those shots published … '

This time Alex cut *him* off.

'If I were you, I'd worry more about what our own internal cameras are catching. That is, if you don't want us to add *making threats* to your charge sheet.'

If André had to guess, Meredith would be flat out finding the dog walker's house in any of the fifty-plus suburbs this side of the Yarra River. Not if Ella had been thorough.

Night had set in but that was academic. There were no windows in the interview room. Had the architect engaged by police been instructed to position the interview room with a window, the view would encompass the massive corridor of western and northern rail lines funnelling into Southern Cross Station — not the leafy trees and parks in the interview room of John Meredith's St Kilda Road office. In this and every other way, the interview facility was the antithesis of the Meredith and Meredith version. No executive, high back, leather, pneumatic designer chairs, and nowhere to fit the beech-top board table without getting a chippie in to hack off a good three quarters of it and chuck that in a skip. Nor was there a head-of-the table position at the small laminate-top job jammed up against the wall.

The environment was as unfamiliar to John Meredith as it was familiar to criminal lawyer Kelvin Webb. 'Friends since law school,' Kelvin volunteered as he retrieved a legal pad from his satchel. André and Alex had already placed a manilla folder on the table. With only one piece of paper in it, it could easily pass as being empty.

The demeanour of John Meredith was no less emboldened than when he answered his door for André to arrest him.

'Can we get this over with. It's taken enough time out of my day already.'

'Certainly, Mr Meredith. Can you do the formalities please, Alex.'

Alex activated the video and voiced the where, when and who protocols before André opened serve.

'We want to ask you about the flight you took to Mildura on 23 April.'

'Why,' Kelvin asked. 'You know that was well before Portia went missing?'

'It's within the window the pathologist deemed Portia was murdered.'

'Nevertheless. We all know Portia was alive at that time. The flight you're asking about was a weekend trip John and Portia took to Mildura, and back to Bendigo.'

'*We* don't know that. So can you please let Mr Meredith tell us about the flight, Mr Webb.'

Kelvin Webb held up his hand to stop John Meredith and continued his conversation with André.

'As my non-pathologist mind understands it, when a body is exposed to the elements as long as Portia's was, it is impossible not to have a massive window for the date of death. A child knows that that doesn't make it possible for her to have been murdered before she actually went missing. Even if that were magically so, shouldn't you be checking all the sources you have available to you in this electronic age. At Mildura or at the airport, or wherever else this fantasy took place? I can see why John's so upset about this treatment.'

'You see, that's the thing, Mr Webb.' André said.

'Fuck all this. I flew to Mildura and I flew back,' John Meredith blurted.

Kelvin Webb held his hand up to John Meredith again.

'You don't have to go there, John,' he advised him.

'I'm not going anywhere. He's implying, because I flew an aeroplane to Mildura, I took a massive detour west to Wyperfeld National Park in the Big Desert to chuck my wife out of the plane. I didn't go anywhere near the Big Desert. We actually flew over Lake Tyrrell — the state's biggest salt lake. Since Chinese tourists put it on the map, Portia could never resist checking out the "sky mirror", as they like to call it.

'It may be a natural wonder to behold at ground level, but having a bird's eye of its endless pink expanse is beyond spectacular. And there we were. No need for us to take one of the local scenic flights on offer, we were already flying right over the top of it. That's a good 100 kilometres east of Wyperfeld. From there we took a bee-line to Mildura airport.'

'You remember all of that?'

'Have you been to Lake Tyrrell, detective?'

'Only at ground level.'

'Then you know how unforgettable it can be.'

'I agree it is special, but your trip was a while ago and you and Portia did the same trip not too long before that. Could you be getting confused?'

'Absolutely not. That only makes it easier to be certain, because we checked out Lake Tyrrell on both those trips.'

'You already suggested you didn't detour west as far as Wyperfeld on either flight to Mildura. Do you ever fly that way? Even accidently.'

'I'd never go that way if I can help it — to avoid using extra fuel if nothing else — and never accidentally. The only thing that'd get me that far off track would be to avoid a storm. If you check, you'll see that the weather was perfect on both occasions.'

André scratched his head and gave a pained look.

'The thing is, we have a witness.'

The suggestion didn't slow Meredith down.

'If you have a witness who thinks they saw a plane at Wyperfeld, there's no way it could be me. I'm not doubting people can spot light planes anywhere, there's enough of them about, but that was a clear day. We could see the Calder Highway like we were flying over a giant road map and we stuck to it like we were driving — way east of the desert, as you no doubt know. Like I said: check the weather records if you insist on dragging me through this farce.'

'I don't think I could have said it more clearly myself, detective,' Kelvin Webb added.

'The thing is — and forgive me if I keep saying that — our witness had a camera, and they took a photograph.'

'So? You'd need more than a mobile phone if you want to capture more than a white spec in the sky. The type of equipment you'd really need … '

John Meredith tapered off as André opened the manilla folder. The way André opened it — slowly, and calmly. It dawned on John Meredith that André had been acting way too cooly since he arrived on his doorstep at Beaumaris. The A4 photograph was still face down. He turned to Kelvin with a pleading *what-the-fuck* expression.

André flipped the photo and placed it on the table in front of John Meredith.

The silence of John Meredith and Kelvin Webb prompted Alex to say, 'For the purpose of the audio, Detective Sergeant Marshall has placed a photograph of an aeroplane on the table and recording of the interview is continuing.'

'Is this the aeroplane you used on that flight to Mildura, Mr Meredith?

'It's the same aeroplane but … '

'Leave it, John.'

Kelvin placed his hand on John Meredith's forearm to make sure he did in fact leave it this time.

'I presume you are alleging this photograph was taken at Wyperfeld National Park on the day you're talking about, and that you can authenticate that.'

'Indeed.'

André, Alex and Kelvin Webb all turned towards noises coming from John Meredith. They were all mesmerised to see colour had rushed from his face and his mouth was trying to utter words … and failing. As ideas to explain it away attempted to embark from his lips, those words stumbled over further advice from his brain about why each idea wouldn't fly. None found coherence before Kelvin Webb sparked back to life.

'Can we suspend the interview for me to further consult my client about this development, please.'

'Jeez mate, that was beautiful. You handed him enough rope for him to tie the noose *and* put it around his own neck,' Alex said in the corridor.

'Not only that. He also grabbed the lever and released the trapdoor himself.'

'How so?' Alex asked with genuine curiosity. André explained.

'He said Lake Tyrrell was glowing pink that day. Well, the carotenoids that produce that phenomenon only occur in summer. He's way fucked-er than he thinks.'

'I dunno if that's even possible mate — or even a word — judging by his reaction, which I didn't pick, by the way. Not him. D'ya reckon he's in shock?'

'Too right, but don't count on it lasting.'

'I'm so not counting on it not lasting. We want him at his slimiest best to spill his guts about Eve Delmonte's role.'

André looked at his phone.

'Let's have a coffee before round two. Can you get me one, I need to send a text.'

I'm gonna be home late tonight. If you also have some work thing you need to get off your desk, then now would be the perfect time ♡

Chapter 44

Ella and Lila passed through Antwerp on the hour-and-a-half drive from Yaapeet to Horsham — the closest place to do a "big-shop", and where the law firm of Baillie and Urquhart hung their shingle. The clutch of houses and a tin public hall was a far cry from the centre of the world's diamond trade, after which the hamlet's Belgium founder named the joint. These days, through-traffic only had to slacken off to eighty kilometres an hour. Nevertheless, a nineteenth century relic on the banks of the passing Wimmera River cemented Antwerp's importance in the echelons of Victoria's history — the restored remnant buildings of Ebeneezer Aboriginal mission.

'How long d'you reckon it'll be before they paint a mural on the silo here?' Lila said.

'Good call,' Ella answered. 'The next silo, ten ks up the road at Arkona, is my favourite. For mine, that one, and our local silo at Albacutya, are the only truly artistic ones. The rest are tea-towel art.'

'My, you are the critic. *You* won't be scoring a job with Wimmera Mallee Tourism any time soon — or later.'

'Ha ha. I didn't say there was anything wrong with tea-towel art. It has its place … '

'On a tea-towel, right.' Lila laughed.

'No. That's not what I meant. It's just that … Anyway, I already have a job that I wouldn't trade.'

'I know. I keep up with it all on-line, and when they had you on ABC radio. Next thing, you'll be doing TV talk shows.'

Ella drove without turning her head and gave a knowing smile to acknowledge Lila's comment. Lila knew the smile.

'You have? When? Did I miss it? Is it The Project?'

'Can't say. But it's next week,' she said and turned to Lila to give a bigger smile.

'You found the body, and then you solved the case. You deserve it. What does André think about all that?'

'It wasn't just me. We were both there when I stumbled on the body.'

'I know. But you were the one who solved it.'

'Not really. It was all part of a much bigger picture that he and his colleagues were constructing. I wouldn't have known what to do if I hadn't known how everything fitted in. Besides, what's the good of being a cop's partner if you're not getting some solid pillow talk. André's fine with it, actually.'

'You always were the smart one … and modest. I could tell you'd end up kicking some pretty impressive goals, even when you were ten.'

'Lucky for you. Otherwise, I might want to run the farm myself.'

'I don't think I'm in any danger there.' Lila quickly agreed, then just as quickly voiced a second thought.

'At least I don't think I'm in any danger. What do you reckon Dave Urquhart wants this time? He's already given you a copy of the will and we did that contested-will agreement thing for him. I think he's struck a problem. Maybe someone else has challenged it. Maybe he's come across debts nobody knew about and Mum's estate is bankrupt and we have to sell the place. Things like that combine harvester aren't cheap, you know. Nor are those mammoth sausage bags for that matter. Did she borrow money? Do you know?'

Ella wasn't expecting paranoia. She turned and gave Lila a hard look.

'You tell me,' Lila responded. 'Why would he want both of us there in person. This is no routine matter, trust me.'

'I dunno, Lila. None of that ran through my head when his PA called to arrange the meeting. I just accepted it as part of the process. Let's just wait and see. I don't know how all this stuff works, and neither do you for that matter. Calm down. You're starting to freak me out.'

'Well at least I'd think about it and ask questions?'

Ella found it was hard to harumph while driving. Silence lengthened as they passed through Arkona — a railway line and two houses on an unfettered 100 kilometres-per-hour stretch of the C277. An invisible, bespectacled, tennis-playing giant peered down on them from Ella's favourite silo artwork. According to australiansiloarttrail.com, the un-see-able sportsman was Roley Klinge — the late unofficial mayor of yet another German namesake locale.

The receptionist at Baillie and Urquhart ushered them into the bland client interview room before she set about summoning Dave Urquhart. A framed black and white photo on the wall depicted a dragon boat crewed by rowers with Baillie and

Urquhart's name emblazoned on their matching tops.

It wasn't Ella's first visit to the practice. Once again, she rued that Dave Urquhart didn't receive them in his personal office. The journalist within craved some clue about the polite, neatly dressed, middle aged man who managed her mother's legal affairs. In his office, there'd be things she could interpret. Like the coffee mug he chose, an artwork on the wall, family photos, a sports trophy, some goofy travel souvenir. Maybe a quote he fancied enough to frame. A framed copy of his qualifications would at least tell her where he studied. In the practice's client interview room, all she'd have to go on was his tie.

Dave arrived in a classic white business shirt that also gave nothing away. As she expected, his tie did all the talking. Silk, in an appealing deep burnt orange with micro white dots. It was a cut above anything acquirable in Horsham and served only to make Ella more curious about what artwork hung in his office.

'Can we get you a drink after your trip? Tea? Coffee? Water?'

Ella guessed that, "we", meant the receptionist.

'We're fine,' she replied on both their behalfs.'

Dave waited for Ella and Lila to sit down again before he took a chair opposite and placed a slim, tan, leather document-folder on the table. It took the tie and the elegant document folder to convey the standing of the organisation they were dealing with.

'Now ... ' he began, and then stopped. He noticed their expressions.

'You look concerned. Perhaps because you thought we'd already set things in train — as you instructed.'

'"Perhaps because you thought?"' Ella quoted him back to himself.

'Yes, Ella. Since I last briefed you and had you in here to sign things, a couple of matters we couldn't have anticipated have come to light.'

'Good things, or bad things?' Lila asked.

'I'll leave it to you to characterise, but let me walk you through it first.'

He began his explanation without opening the document folder.

'You will recall, Ella, that one of Miriam's significant assets is her personal superannuation account. She set it up a year or two after your father died. As you also know, there have been enough good years on the farm since then for her to build it into a very handsome sum.'

Ella nodded.

'Well, the thing with super accounts is, they sit outside of an individual's actual will. When someone with a super account passes away, it is the super company that decides who they pay the accumulated balance to. They do that in accordance with the account holders wishes of course, but that instruction is completely separate from a person's will.

'You'd be familiar with that requirement with your own superannuation. It's the *beneficiary nomination* form they send to you every few years to update.'

Ella nodded.

'I do know what you're talking about. Last time I renewed mine, I nominated Mum,' she said and dropped her head.

'Oh,' Dave said. 'We'd better deal with that a bit later then, but let me finish telling you about your mother's super.

'I have to tell you that there is an alternative to nominating an individual as beneficiary for your super. You can choose instead to have the account balance paid to the executor of your estate so that they, the executor, can then distribute the balance in accordance with your will. Had Miriam chosen to do that, then her super balance would have been paid to her estate, for which you, Ella, are named as the sole beneficiary.

'I say "had Miriam", because your mother didn't go down that road. She chose instead to retain her original nomination for the account balance to be paid directly to her daughter. At no point will that money come via me as executor of Miriam's estate.

'I haven't pointed out this distinction to you before now because you instructed me to divvy up all of Miriam's assets equally between you and Lila. I have taken that to mean all the assets sitting within Miriam's estate. Those subject to her will, as well as the money being paid directly by the super company.'

He sensed he might be losing them and hastened to check.

'Where I'm going with all this is: I had to contact the super company so I could gather everything and treat it as a whole. Do you understand what I have told you so far?'

Lila looked no less worried. Nor did Ella, although *she* was slightly amused that Dave strayed from legalese to use a term like "divvy-up". *A bit of the country boy* within, she thought.

'Yes, I do.' Ella said. 'That's exactly how we want this to be handled. I don't see the problem.'

'I'm getting there, I just want to make sure you understand.' He continued. 'Miriam's super account was something she, and presumably her accountant, managed. Miriam and I only discussed it in general terms in the context of preparing her will. Because she always said she'd rather leave her super account in the hands of the super company to pay the beneficiary directly, I never needed any of the details. That included the beneficiary nomination she made. I expect the beneficiary nomination was also something she didn't share with her accountant. As I explained, none of that was unusual. Nor is it normally a problem.'

'I still don't see that there is problem, and you're starting to worry me more,' Ella said, looking at Dave and Lila in turn.

'There's no problem as such about divvying up Miriam's assets equally, it's just that the mechanics — if you like — of going about that, are markedly different to what I anticipated. What I've only just found out from the super company is that Miriam's nomination didn't alter from day one. It was always the case that the whole of the balance be paid to her daughter. That daughter being Lila.'

'Me?' Lila said before grabbing her mouth and looking wide-eyed at Ella.

'Yes, Lila. You are the nominated beneficiary of Miriam's super account, via me as the person designated to locate you and let you know, which I'm doing now.'

Ella looked at Lila with the same gobsmacked expression.

'Lil,' she said.

'What does that mean?' Lila asked.

'In the first instance, the super money is all yours,' Dave said.

'No. I mean what does it really mean? If she thought this much of me, why didn't she ever contact me?'

'I don't know, Lil. But it's a good thing, isn't it?' Ella said.

'Would you like a glass of water before we go on?' Dave offered.

'Maybe a scotch,' Ella half-joked. 'But what do you mean, before we go on. Is there more?'

'There is. In the process of gathering all of Miriam's assets, the bank provided a safe custody envelope she'd lodged with them. I don't know if you know, but that's a paid service banks provide — keeping people's stuff safe in their vaults. It surprised me actually, because Miriam held all the usual safe custody documents with ourselves. Her will and powers of attorney. You know.'

Neither Lila or Ella spoke because Dave was opening the leather document folder for the first time. He produced a buff C5-sized envelope addressed in handwriting.

'This is addressed to you, Lila — again, for me to locate you and deliver it. It's sealed.'

He placed it on the table before her. Lila didn't reach out to take it. She looked at Ella and a tear came. Dave reached into his folder again. Ella and Lila stilled again, fearing yet another surprise.

'I'm going to leave you for a while, but here's a letter opener.'

Lila took the letter opener and Dave picked up his folder to leave.

'Do you want me to leave too?' Ella asked Lila.

'No. Stay, please, Elly.'

She sniffed and produced a tissue to dry her eyes. It took her a second go to get the shaking letter opener under the flap. Ella sat and watched her as she withdrew a two-page, handwritten letter from the envelope. There was also a photograph. She gave Ella a fighting-back-tears look and took her time to study the picture lovingly. The photo was of Miriam holding her dotingly as a baby. It calmed her. She handed it to Ella and began reading the letter to herself.

My Darling Lila,

I hope you don't mind that I have chosen to reach out to you in this way, for I fear your life might pass as unresolved as mine obviously has. You deserve more.

I have known for a long time that the way I responded to the tragedy and misfortune in my life has been wanting and has affected you unfairly.

You will be surprised to learn that it began much earlier than you think. You were too young to appreciate that, after Vincent died, I was in a near constant fog of depression until Ella came along. During those early years, your father assumed much of the mantle of your upbringing. You and he became inseparable in such a heartfelt way. Your relationship with him was the single ray of hope that kept me going during that time.

When I came through my time of darkness and we became a family of four once again, I felt such gratitude that Roy had not given up on me, our family, or the farm.

How conflicted I was when he betrayed the precious bond he forged with you. At that time, and confronted with those circumstances, I wasn't as strong a person as I wish I had been. From the distance of time, I realise I was frightfully lacking. Nevertheless, I thought I had at least made you safe at boarding school in Adelaide, well away from Rosenfeld.

I'm not proud to write that, when you ran away, one part of me was secretly pleased that you weren't dragged back home. I felt so inadequate that I didn't know how to protect you better. I was also unable to countenance any action that would destroy our family. I don't know if I ever would have become strong enough to overcome my helplessness, because things went to another level when Roy died.

I don't have any idea of how that managed to happen, but once your distressed phone call to me made sense, I knew there was a secret I needed to keep so that you remained free to live a life. After everything that happened, the last thing you deserved was to have that taken from you.

Keeping your secret was something I did unhesitatingly, even though it came with too much conscience and horror for me to face you at that time. I'm sad to admit that it remained a struggle within for which I attained barely acceptable peace simply by doing nothing. Early on, I used the grief of losing Roy (as flawed as he had become), and Ella's grief of losing her father, to distract myself from confronting the dilemma. To my shame, I allowed my reticence to last.

Despite all my failings, I hope that my letter provides you with resolution rather than sorrow. I hope also that you have found joy in your life and that you might find a small corner somewhere in your heart for me. My own heart has no such luxury, I'm afraid. It has always been filled to its absolute capacity by my two most precious daughters.

Your loving mother,
Always.

Lila's silent tears had begun mid-letter. She finished it and handed it to Ella without speaking. As Ella read, Lila turned to stare through the room's high single window at rooftops and a cloudless Wimmera sky. She didn't turn back until she heard Ella sniff away her own tears. Ella held the letter in her lap. Neither could speak out loud or even gesture. Their eyes locked in acknowledgement of each other's sadness. No words came until Dave gave a light rap on the door.

'Too soon?' he said to their teary faces.

'No,' Ella said and began wiping her cheeks with her fingers. She handed the letter to Lila to return to its envelope.

'It must be hard,' Dave told them. 'From beyond the grave.'

'Yes,' Lila whispered.

'Is there anything I can do?' he asked.

'I don't think so. Is there anything you need us to do?' Ella said.

'No. Not unless this has changed anything for either of you. Otherwise, I think I've covered everything. Is it still plan A? Fifty-fifty for everything? Or do you need time?'

Ella turned to Lila. They both nodded yes to each other.

'You mean fifty-fifty,' Dave asked.

They nodded again.

'So fifty-fifty it is. I'll need you to sign off on a few extra things of course, Lila, but let's not do that now. I think we've all had enough lawyering for one day. I'll be in touch and we can do what has to be done remotely.'

They reached the parking meter before they hugged, for a long time.

'Can we find a florist before we head back. I want to buy flowers and visit the Rainbow cemetery on our way home,' Lila said when they separated.

Ella nodded, suddenly too teary again to say yes. She found her voice once she was behind the wheel.

'You know, I didn't have any of your dread when we set out this morning. I thought we'd be celebrating our partnership. I even put a bottle of bubbly in the under-seat fridge of the combine harvester. I thought that's where we could celebrate.

In your new office.'

Lila laughed.

'God, we're so different aren't we,' Ella said and laughed too.

'Let's do that,' Lila said. 'But did you put a soft drink in the fridge too?'

'Come on, Lil. This is special. You can make an exception again.'

'I don't think I can, Elly. Not now.'

They had arrived at a red light. Ella's head swivelled to the passenger seat. Lila had a serious face.

'You're not?' Ella said in a loud, deep, and serious voice.

Lila gave a grinning nod.

'I'm booked in for a scan on Thursday.'

Ella's gaze at Lila froze — almost — her lips began to spread — gradually, and upward. The car behind tooted — then tooted again.

'The light has turned green, Aunty Ella.'

Acknowledgements

Thank you to Ben Gosling and Andy Gosling from The Lazy Farmers Sons duo for having no problem with me adopting the title Wire and Bone — the same evocative title as track 1 on their *Small Sky CD*. To Andy for allowing his lyric to be reproduced at the start of the book, and to Ben for sharing his broad local knowledge. You can catch them performing Wire and Bone on YouTube.

I am most grateful to Des Lowry and Belinda Smeal for their copy editing / proofreading. And thanks so much to Jennie de Jong, Graeme McKechnie, Gilda McKechnie and Rick Christie for their scrutiny of the manuscript, and to Tony Wright for his cracking back cover blurb. I am also indebted to Jaqui Lynch of Preloaded Design for her masterly cover design and for tirelessly producing the book layout in its many iterations. To Mary, my sage content editor, thank you always.

For sharing their knowledge, I thank Brian Lane, Dave Lane, Ashley Lane, Trent McGregor, Paul McLean, Damien Lehane, Charlie Bezzina, Brian Westley and Trevor Miles. Among the references I consulted, the following have been invaluable for portraying the Mallee and its history. *Wyperfeld: Australia's First Mallee National Park* by Geoff Durham 2001; *Mallee Country: Land, People, History* by Richard Broome, Charles Fahey, Andrea Gaynor and Katie Holmes 2019; *Manangatang* by Adam NcNicol 2011; Wyperfeld National Park *Visitors Book*.

NOTES: Lake Albacutya fills intermittently from Wimmera River flows during periods of high rainfall in its upper catchment. In Wire and Bone, the lake is depicted as being pretty much full some twenty years ago. In reality, the lake would have been shallow if not empty around that time.

The fictitious character of Senior Constable Chloe Lane at Rainbow police station is not based on any actual occupants of that role. The character is entirely the product of the author's imagination.